HARD
LIGHT

Also by Elizabeth Hand

Wylding Hall
Available Dark
Errantry
Radiant Days
Glimmering
Illyria
Generation Loss
Saffron and Brimstone
Chip Crockett's Christmas Carol
Mortal Love
Bibliomancy
Black Light
Last Summer at Mars Hill
Waking the Moon
Icarus Descending
Aestival Tide
Winterlong

HARD LIGHT

A CASS NEARY CRIME NOVEL

Elizabeth Hand

MINOTAUR BOOKS
A Thomas Dunne Book
New York

This is a work of fiction. All of the characters, organizations, and events portrayed in this novel are either products of the author's imagination or are used fictitiously.

A THOMAS DUNNE BOOK FOR MINOTAUR BOOKS.
An imprint of St. Martin's Publishing Group.

Printed in the United States of America. For information, address St. Martin's Press, 175 Fifth Avenue, New York, N.Y. 10010.

Epigraph page vii from *The Command to Look: A Master Photographer's Method for Controlling the Human Gaze* by William Mortensen and George Dunham. Feral House, 2014; Camera Craft Publishing Company, 1937. Used by permission.

Epigraph page 1 from *Flash in Modern Photography* by William Mortensen. Camera Craft Publishing Company, 1941. Used by permission.

Epigraph page 215 from *Pictorial Lighting* by William Mortensen. Camera Craft Publishing Company, 1935. Used by permission.

www.thomasdunnebooks.com
www.minotaurbooks.com

The Library of Congress Cataloging-in-Publication Data is available upon request.

ISBN 978-1-250-03038-2 (hardcover)
ISBN 978-1-250-03037-5 (e-book)

Our books may be purchased in bulk for promotional, educational, or business use. Please contact your local bookseller or the Macmillan Corporate and Premium Sales Department at 1-800-221-7945, extension 5442, or by e-mail at MacmillanSpecialMarkets@macmillan.com.

First Edition: April 2016

10 9 8 7 6 5 4 3 2 1

In loving memory of Bob Morales,
the best friend Cass Neary ever had.

To put it more simply, you look most quickly and instinctively at those pictures that suggest, in their mere black and white pattern, something that was *feared* by your ancestor that lived in a cave.

—William Mortensen, *The Command to Look*

PART ONE

LONDON

The coroner's photographer's job is gruesome, but it does not affect his appetite because when viewed objectively, his subject is little different from other still life, except it offers more complication.

—William Mortensen, *Flash in Modern Photography*

1

A stolen passport will only get you so far. In my case, that was through Customs and Immigration at Heathrow, where I stood in the line for EU travelers, praying I wouldn't have to fake a Swedish accent as an impassive official ran a check on my documentation.

"You're here for three weeks." She glanced at my landing card. "The purpose of your visit?"

"Vacation."

There are advantages to being a six-foot-tall blonde arriving on a flight from Reykjavík. The passport official nodded, slid the passport back across the counter, and turned her attention to the person behind me.

In a police lineup you could mistake me for the woman in the Swedish passport photo: we were both tall, with shoulder-length ragged blond hair and gray-blue eyes. The main difference was that Cassandra Neary, of New York, New York, could be charged as an accessory to more than one murder. Dagney

Ahlstrand of Uppsala, Sweden, was a junkie, but as far as I knew, she hadn't killed anyone. Yet.

I'd left Iceland under a cloud: Shortly after takeoff I looked out my window and saw a lurid red eye open then burst in the black wilderness far below. A volcanic eruption, an appropriate sendoff for a thirty-six-hour visit that had begun with me searching for my sometime lover and ex-con Quinn and ended with an escalating body count. The eruption delayed our landing, which gave me a chance to recover slightly from the lingering affects of hypothermia and a near-fatal amount of crank.

I was anxious to put as many miles as possible between me and Reykjavík, and even more anxious to meet up again with Quinn, who'd booked a later flight to Heathrow. We'd agreed to rendezvous at a bar owned by a friend of his in Brixton. I had my share of the blood money I'd earned in Iceland—a decent stash, but I had no idea how long I'd be in London, or how long until Quinn joined me. He'd said a few days. Given that thirty-odd years had passed before our most recent reunion, I could be in for a long wait.

I'd never been to London. Technically, I still wasn't here. Until recently, I'd spent my life thinking that downtown New York was the center of the known universe. The last few decades had eroded that belief system, as billionaires and chain stores moved in and NYU continued its land grab, converting the Lower East Side into dorms for kids whose dreams of beatnik glory didn't quite jibe with their eight-hundred-dollar Jimmy Choos and bespoke tablet cases.

The stolen passport belonged to an ex-girlfriend of Quinn's. Dagney resembled me in that we were both lanky women of a certain age with substance abuse issues. I could only assume I'd imprinted on Quinn back when we first got involved in high school—that would explain his predilection for rogue blondes who could throw a punch then hit the ground running.

I shoved the passport into the battered satchel that held my old thirteen-millimeter Konica, a couple of moth-eaten cashmere sweaters, socks, and an extra pair of stovepipe jeans, all black. That, my leather jacket and ancient Tony Lamas, and a few canisters of Tri-X B&W film were all she wrote. I don't own much, besides seven hundred vinyl LPs and 45s and an impressive collection of stolen coffee table books on photography, all back in my rent-stabilized apartment on Houston Street. No laptop, no smartphone, no presence on social media. I'm the ghost of punk, haunting the twenty-first century in disintegrating black-and-white; one of those living fossils you read about who usually show up, dead, in a place you've never heard of.

I unzipped my battered motorcycle jacket and headed for the exit, glancing back at the people who thronged the queue for non-EU and UK nationals. Three uniformed men were questioning a family group—a man in a rumpled suit, a burka-clad woman, and several small children. The man began gesturing angrily as a cop grasped his arm and dragged him toward a door. The woman began to cry.

I looked away, quickening my pace till I reached the door, where a beefeater on a brightly colored sign proclaimed WELCOME, WE HOPE YOU ENJOY YOUR STAY. I kept my head down and pushed my way through the crowd inside the terminal.

This, too, is what it means to be a ghost: You forever witness your own slow self-destruction, and that of those around you. But no one knows what you've seen until it's too late.

2

It was mid-afternoon when I trudged into a gray-lit tunnel beneath Terminal Three and made my way to the Heathrow Express platform to catch a packed train into London. I caught fragments of conversation among passengers who'd landed around the same time I had. A plume of volcanic ash from the Icelandic eruption had added to the disruptions caused by torrential rains and wind across the UK. Planes were being rerouted all across Europe. All flights from Reykjavík were canceled. Quinn's arrival no longer seemed a matter of *when* but *if.*

By the time I reached Paddington, the platforms were crammed with grim-faced people dragging suitcases. An overhead flatscreen TV displayed a glowing mountain that spewed magma and flaming contrails across a black sky. The scene switched to monstrous waves smashing into a lighthouse. I stopped to join a crowd reading the news crawler.

MILLIONS STRANDED BY ICELAND
VOLCANIC ERUPTION

FLOODING CONTINUES IN SOUTHWEST:
RECORD 90-FOOT WAVE DESTROYS HISTORIC
PERWITH LIGHT STATION
NO END IN SIGHT TO WORST RAINS IN 500
YEARS

I hoisted my bag and continued on to the Underground. After a few steps I halted, steadying myself against the wall.

The air around me shimmered. I felt dizzy, tasting copper in the back of my mouth. I coughed, touched a hand to my lips, withdrew it, and saw my fingertips flecked with blood. I struggled to remember where I was, stared numbly at an advertisement until Quinn's face filled my mind's eye, the shining arc of a metal wire slicing through a man's throat. I had a flash of the night terrors that had dogged me for months. When I looked up, I saw an armed policeman watching me from across the crowded concourse. I took a deep breath, and kept walking.

An hour later I emerged from the Brixton Underground station. The heavy rain had turned to sleet. My eyes watered as icy pellets stung my face. The cold felt good: Pain I could understand and fight, even if I lost. I hunched my shoulders, pulled up the collar of my leather jacket, and headed for the corner.

The clock inside the station had read 3:35, but outside it was already nearly dark. People rushed past me, half hidden beneath black umbrellas as they shouted into mobile phones. A ululating police siren wailed in concert with the sustained shriek of an ambulance. A guy wearing retro Ray-Bans and a knee-length black kidskin hoodie nearly shoved me off the sidewalk as he loped past.

I whirled, landed a kick just below the back of his knee with the steel toe of my cowboy boot, turned, and kept going. From the corner of my eye I saw him crumple as I turned the corner. I kept to the center of the crowd and after a few minutes ducked into an alcove, the entry to a boarded-up record shop.

A kid in a knitted cap and filthy hoodie leaned against a wall stained with piss. A scrawny dog crouched at his feet. The boy looked at me without interest.

"Wha' gwarn?" he said. The dog whined softly.

I dug in my pocket until I found the scrap of paper where Quinn had scrawled a name—Derek somebody—and the name of a pub. "I'm looking for a place called the Gambrel."

The kid blinked, his eyes so bloodshot they looked as though they'd been scooped from his skull. "Dinno."

"Rawlins Street," I said. "Know where that is?"

He gestured vaguely toward the corner. "Electric Avenue, ask 'im."

"I asked you." I tapped my foot, the tip of my boot ringing against concrete. The mongrel's head shot up, black lips taut against long yellow teeth, its rolling eyes the same raw crimson as the boy's. I held its gaze until it turned its head sideways, still watching me.

"He likes you." The kid grinned. "Or he'd'a tore your throat out. Rawlins off Electric Avenue."

I nodded thanks. "What's your dog's name?"

"Meat."

I tossed the boy a pound coin and headed back out into the freezing rain.

3

The London I'd always imagined was a mashup of *Blow-Up,* Thatcher's teenage wasteland, and the covers of a thousand LPs. Any details of place derived from rock and roll songs: Stepney, Muswell Hill, Knightsbridge, Waterloo Bridge, more soundtrack than landscape. Brixton meant a song by the Clash about the notorious 1981 riots.

Electric Avenue meant another song, and the soundtrack changed every few feet, fading from reggaeton to rap to techno to Abba to West African to Bombay pop. Awnings offered scant coverage from the sleet, but business didn't seem to be suffering much. I passed halal butchers and a stall selling nothing but pig snouts; open coolers where eels coiled and thrashed; carefully stacked pyramids of durians, melons, multicolored carrots and bundles of what looked like cattail rushes. One fishmonger had more exotic sea life on ice than I'd ever seen in the New York Aquarium. I peered into a basket filled with shark fins still seeping blood. Representatives of the World Wildlife Fund might net enough endangered species here to stock an ark.

I stopped to buy goat kebabs from a woman turning skewers on a hubcap grill, stood beneath a green tarpaulin and gulped down spicy meat hot enough to blister the roof of my mouth. I felt better when I'd finished. I left the shelter of the tarp and walked to a cart where a large umbrella advertised fresh jostaberry juice.

"What's jostaberry juice?" I asked.

A rosy-faced girl with facial piercings smiled at me from beneath the hood of her anorak. "It's a hybrid of gooseberry and black currant. You have to pick them every morning before sunrise."

I paid her and downed the contents of the paper cup she handed me. She pointed to a metal bowl filled with tiny black fruit. "Our farm's in Devon, if you'd like to come visit sometime. You can even help with the harvest if you like."

"I'd love that," I said. "Is there a bar called the Gambrel near here?"

"The gastropub? First right, that way. They do a brilliant ploughman's; we're one of their suppliers for nettle chevre. You might not be able to get a table if you haven't booked. I'll recycle that for you."

I gave her the empty cup, sloshed my way past more food stalls, and took a right onto a side street.

The sleet had subsided to freezing drizzle. In the sulfurous glare of sodium lamps, street and sky had the smeared look of a botched watercolor. Metal shutters hid storefronts covered with graffiti and an impasto of gig posters. I saw COMING SOON signs for an organic fromagerie, a Bangladeshi Wi-Fi cafe, and a Bruno Magli shoe store.

The Gambrel occupied a corner at the end of the block, across the street from a monolithic concrete structure I assumed was a public housing project. The pub, however, was well tended. Buttery yellow light streamed from windows hung with baskets of ivy, incongruously verdant in the wintry gloom. Strings of Christmas lights still shone above the door, where a painted wooden sign displayed the image of a metal instrument with the carcass of a pig suspended from it.

THE GAMBREL.

I thought of the nickname Quinn had been given by the folks he did business with in Oslo long ago: Varsler, butcher bird. I tightened my grip on my satchel and went inside.

A wave of warmth hit me, redolent of garlic, braised beef, and a sweetly earthy scent that might have been peat smoke. Candles glowed on trestle tables where well-heeled people sat drinking, eating, gazing enraptured at their mobile phones. A young woman in a beautifully tailored jumpsuit and knee-high boots approached me with a concerned look.

"Do you have a reservation?"

"I just want a drink."

"Of course." She gazed pointedly at my dripping leather jacket. "Can I take your coat?"

"No thanks."

A flicker of displeasure as she gestured toward the bar. "Herman will be happy to serve you."

I ignored the irritated glances of several diners as I crossed the room, leaving a trail of damp bootprints on the glossy hardwood floor. I knew I looked like shit, and I felt worse, shaky and sick from too much speed and booze. The only thing that would make me feel better was more of the same.

But for the first time in forty years, I was starting to get a bad premonition about that. The incident back in Paddington wasn't the first time I'd felt a sudden wave of dizziness, or worse.

Black flecks in my recent memory. Night terrors, and the even more terrible knowledge that I no longer dreamed when I slept.

Or maybe it was that I could no longer easily distinguish between wakefulness and nightmare. I'd taken a bad blow to the head in Iceland: This on top of a lifetime of more drunken falls than I could count made me wonder if there was some dark spider nesting in my skull, spinning a toxic web of neurochemicals and failed synapses.

I forced aside the thought. I needed to find Quinn.

There's a bar in Brixton run by someone I know; I'll give you his number.

I had no mobile and no way to get in touch with Quinn; nothing except the name of the pub and its owner, Derek. I'd found the Gambrel. Now, I'd make contact with Derek, then hole up for a few days, until Quinn got here.

Still, "here" didn't seem like a place Quinn would be caught dead in. His employment history for the last few decades included selling used vinyl and disposing of body parts for the Russian mob. The handsomely chiseled block of human granite behind the Gambrel's bar looked more likely to attempt a solo ascent of K2 barefoot than admit to knowing someone like Quinn O'Boyle.

"What can I get for you?"

"Shot of Jack Daniels. And a half pint of—" I squinted, reading the name of this month's craft beers. "Brambly Willy."

The bartender handed me a brimming shotglass, pulled my beer and slid it across the counter. I downed the Jack Daniels, asked for a second, then handed him a twenty-pound note. "Derek around?"

"Sorry?"

"Derek. The owner."

The bartender frowned. "You mean Derek Haverty?"

"Yeah, that's him."

"He's gone. Up in Camden, I think." He turned to a dark-haired girl slicing lemons at the other end of the bar. "Hey, where's Derek Haverty now? Was it the Hobgoblin?"

The girl set down her knife and wiped her forehead. "The Banshee, I think."

The bartender nodded. "That's it. The Banshee. Camden Town."

"Where's Camden Town?"

"Take the Underground to King's Cross, transfer to the Northern line northbound. Take you straight there."

I knocked back the second shot and chased it with the beer. A man stood at the bar with his back to me, a pack of Gitanes on the zinc countertop beside his mobile. I palmed the cigarettes and strode back out into the street.

Around the corner from the Brixton Underground station, the same grimy kid had nodded out on the steps. Ignoring his baleful mongrel, I dropped the pack of Gitanes into the boy's lap and hurried to catch the subway.

4

The quick infusion of alcohol had jolted me awake. But now my unease was tempered with dread. Had Quinn set me up? Given me Dagney's passport just to get me out of town?

The thought made me feel sick. Even after factoring in his CV as a former junkie, drug dealer, hired gun, and worse, I couldn't see him betraying me. I'd spent over thirty years mourning Quinn O'Boyle, certain he'd died in prison or OD'ed. We'd known each other since high school, when he'd been my first lover and my first muse, subject of hundreds of black and white photos I'd shot of him while he was awake or asleep, tying up or nodding out. There was a terrible light in his bruised eyes: Even in photographs it burned through me like acid, but I couldn't look away.

Those photos had been the portal to my career photographing the birth of punk on the Lower East Side, before I flamed out and hit the skids—one of the briefest artistic careers on record, though I had a lot of competition in those days.

Ever since, Quinn's wasted beauty had haunted me. I looked

for his face in every lover's, in every blasted landscape I wandered through, in every drink. Reykjavík was the first time I'd seen him since 1978: For the first time in decades, I felt something other than desperation, and craved something more than alcohol or speed. The fact that Quinn hadn't known the Gambrel was under new management didn't seem like a good portent for our reunion.

I found a seat in the back of the subway car and dug out the scrap of paper Quinn had given me, scrawled with four words.

The Gambrel Derek Haverty

Nothing about how Quinn knew this guy; nothing regarding how long it had been since they'd seen each other, or where, or under what circumstances. I was starting to get the feeling that maybe I didn't want to know.

I shoved the note back into my pocket and searched my satchel for the Focalin I'd bought from my connection back in New York, removed four caplets, and popped them dry. I could have done with something stronger, but I assumed London would be a good place for that. The entire 1970s punk scene had been fueled by speed and the same three guitar cords. I stared at the advertisements for cheap mobile phones and vacations in Ibiza, and waited for the buzz to kick in.

At King's Cross, I jammed myself into a Northern line train. I got off at Camden Town, following the crowd through the station. My nerves fizzed like a lit fuse. Freezing wind howled through the tunnels, strong enough to tear the Dr. Seuss hat off the head of the drunken kid stumbling beside me on the escalator.

Despite the icy drizzle, teenagers and twenty-somethings thronged Camden High Street. Nouveau hippies, teenybopper punks, dreadlocked stoners, rude boys, wiggers, black girls in do-rags and leather, Japanese Lolitas and a claque of French-speaking boys in soccer shirts. It was like a high-school prom where the theme was "Masque of the Red Death." A crap cover of "Creep" blasted from a stall selling Manchester United T-shirts and thongs emblazoned with the Union Jack. The French boys began to sing "Over the Rainbow" as a girl doubled over, puking. The only person close to my age was a rheumy-eyed guy in a gray mohawk who clutched a placard advertising Doc Martens.

Across the street were tattoo and piercing parlors, shuttered shops, a Super Drug pharmacy. I turned in the other direction and headed down the sidewalk, dodging touts who thrust cards advertising massages and cheap tapas at me. CCTV signs emblazoned with a yellow eye were everywhere: streetcorners, shop windows, above waste bins and newsstands. Halfway down the block, I spotted a second pensioner carrying a Doc Martens sign. A tattoo of a crown of thorns encircled his shaved head.

"I'm looking for the Banshee." I ran my tongue across my cracked lips. The Focalin had given me dry mouth. "This the right way?"

The grizzled punk took a cigarette from behind one ear and nodded. "Yeah. Toward Chalk Farm, past the canal."

He lit his cigarette, pulled a can of Foster's from the sagging pocket of a leather trench coat, adjusted his placard, and walked off.

I looked around for a place to grab a quick drink, but I didn't see much besides souvenir stalls and shops selling Chinese-made electronics. A line had formed outside a nondescript entryway with a neon sign. ELECTRIC BALLROOM. I wandered over, hoping it was a bar.

No such luck. Four bouncers stood behind a yellow rope, smoking as they ignored the queue that trailed down the block. Mostly girls shivering in the cold, many of them clad in polka-dot stockings that I assumed were an homage to whoever was the headline act.

I started back toward Chalk Farm. Near Camden Market, the crowds dispersed in a whirlwind of grit and discarded ad cards as people hurried toward the canal or ducked into tattoo parlors. The air reeked of cigarette smoke and weed, vomit and spilled beer. Sodium streetlights made everything look harshly lit and overexposed. It was a relief to reach a side street where the only illumination came from the sputtering gas lamp outside a steampunk clothing boutique.

I found the Banshee in a cul-de-sac formed by construction barricades and the skeletal outlines of a new high-rise. A mock-Tudor pub, walls encrusted with band posters and flyers protesting the ongoing construction. On the door was an Art Nouveau bronze shield boss of a woman's face surrounded by serpentine coils of hair, her eyes wide and her mouth open in a scream.

Inside, the pub was smaller than it appeared from the street. Scuffed floors and plain wooden tables; unadorned zinc bar counter. A trio of furry folk-music types occupied a table covered with empty pints. Otherwise the place was empty, except for a man polishing glasses at the bar as he stared at a TV replay of a football match.

But for once, my attention snagged on something other than the bar.

"Fucking A," I murmured.

In the near-darkness at the back of the room glowed a pristine 1952 Seeburg C jukebox. Ice-blue lights rippled up and down its Bakelite panels, and across the glass coping that protected the record selector and sunflower-yellow housing that held a hundred vinyl singles. The casing's mirrored interior reflected an infinity of forty-fives.

I walked toward it, entranced, then stopped and ran my hands across the fake wood paneling. Scores of hand-lettered labels identified the singles' A- and B-sides.

Roy Orbison, Hank Williams, early Stones and Electric Prunes. Tonto's Expanding Head Band and the Green Fuz; "Pretty Vacant" and "Time Has Come Today." An entire row of Chuck Berry. Big Star. Chris Bell's "I Am the Cosmos," a rarity even when it was first pressed. The Seeburg was the elephants' graveyard of rock and roll. I shook my head and laughed.

This was Quinn's work—not the immaculately restored jukebox, but the fortune in vinyl. I wondered if it was stuff he'd hoarded over the years, or tracked down for a serious collector—presumably, whoever owned the Banshee.

I checked the coin slot to see if it had been retrofitted for UK currency. It still had the original, with a yellowing note taped beside it.

SEE DEREK TO OPERATE.

I dug through my pockets until I found a handful of coins, picked through them for a quarter. I scanned the rows of 45s, finally slid the quarter into the slot, waiting for it to fall before I punched in three sets of numbers.

Familiar click and grind of the shuttle mechanism as the tonearm slid across the front of the machine, halting as a 45 locked into place. Hiss and pop as the needle dropped then skidded into a groove. Chuck Berry's Gibson roared into the opening chords of "Johnny B. Goode" as I turned and strode to the bar.

The bartender eyed me coolly. "Sign says to ask before using the jukebox."

"I'm all checked out on that." I dropped a twenty onto the counter. "Jack Daniels."

"Good choice." He was tall and ebony skinned, his head shaved, and wore a black donkey jacket over a flannel shirt. And he was close to my age, which meant he might be the guy I was looking for. He poured a shot and slid it toward me. "The song, I mean."

"Thanks."

Even with my brain sparking from the Focalin, I knew I should proceed cautiously. But then Berry's guitar rattled into the bridge, and I downed the whiskey.

"Another." The bartender refilled my glass as I glanced around the room and asked, "Derek here?"

"I'm Derek."

I raised my shotglass to him as he stared at me, unsmiling. "I'm Cassandra Neary. Cass." He remained silent. "Nice jukebox."

He grimaced. "It's wasted on the kids who come here. You don't keep a jukebox in a pub. Or gastropub," he added bitterly. I couldn't get a handle on his accent—something northern, maybe. "Cost me the Earth. Couldn't afford it now."

"No shit." I hesitated. "I'm a friend of Quinn O'Boyle's."

"No shit," he said, his voice expressionless, and walked to the end of the bar.

I'd lost him. I tried to think of a comeback that might buy me a second chance. Before I could say anything, he returned with a bottle of mineral water, opened it, and took a swig. "So how's Quinn?"

"Pretty good." True enough, considering he'd been pistol-whipped in the Icelandic highlands and now had a permanent grin carved into his face, along with the tribal tattoos he'd gotten in prison.

"You're American." I nodded. "At first I thought you were the other one. The Swedish chick."

"That junkie? Fuck no."

"Quinn here with you?"

"Not yet." I took a deep breath. "He's in Reykjavík. I'm supposed to meet him here in the next few days. Well, not here—your old pub in Brixton. The Gambrel."

"That was never my pub." Derek drank what remained of the mineral water in one long swallow. His hand tightened around the plastic bottle, crumpling it. "I think you need to find another place to meet up."

He dropped the crushed bottle onto the counter and held my gaze, his eyes the color of the kind of single malt I could never afford. Chuck Berry's guitar faded into near silence. There was an almost imperceptible click and whir as the Seeburg's Select-O-Matic once again slid back and forth, the tonearm replacing one 45 and withdrawing another.

Crackle of scratched vinyl as the needle hopped across a damaged groove and found its sweet spot. The hairs on my neck rose as an electric guitar soared into the sonic tsunami of Steve Hunter's intro to the live version of "Sweet Jane."

Derek's mouth parted. His eyes focused on something just above my head, something I knew wasn't there. We listened without speaking, until the guitar resolved into four familiar cords and the crowd's applause surrendered to Lou Reed's voice.

"Still gets me every time." Derek looked at me as though trying to remember where I'd come from. "What's your name again?"

"Cass."

"Cass." He got himself another mineral water, returned, and lifted the plastic bottle to me. "To Lou."

"To Lou."

Neither of us spoke until the song ended.

"That's how me and Quinn met," I said at last. "I went to the record store to buy *Rock 'n' Roll Animal* when it first came out. There was only one copy, and this skinny red-haired kid already has it in his hands. I couldn't talk him out of buying it, but he invited me back to his place and we listened to it for about three hours, nonstop, until his father threw me out." I downed my Jack Daniels. "I never knew there was a single of the live 'Sweet Jane.'"

"Only in the UK. 1974. Quinn found it—that's his copy." Derek inclined his head toward the Seeburg. "Everything on there came from him; he tricked it up for me when I bought it. Kept it at my flat till I found a proper place for it."

"You give him a playlist?"

"No. Quinn knows my taste. Always has."

Cold air blasted as the door opened and a group stumbled in, underdressed girls and a trio of boys with red-chapped faces.

"Excuse me." Derek turned to greet his customers. "What can I get for you gentlemen?"

Men was pushing it: Back home, none of them would've been legal. Not that I cared. As "Sweet Jane" segued into "Telstar," I looked down and saw a full pint in front of me. I nodded thanks to Derek, paid up, and found a table in the back.

The place was starting to fill up. Someone nabbed the empty chair across from me and dragged it to another table. I sipped my beer, eking it out as it grew warm as blood. Derek seemed to be the only one holding down the place. No one came to ask me if I wanted another drink. No one cleared my table. I stayed put.

After a while, a buzz-cut woman in her forties slid alongside Derek to work the bar. The jukebox had long since fallen silent, replaced by a rising din of conversation and the incessant, witless birdsong of mobile phones. The air smelled like sex and weed and drugstore perfume. Alcohol boosted the Focalin in my bloodstream: For a few minutes I zoned out.

When I looked up again, the buzz-cut woman was alone behind the bar. Derek stood feeding coins into the Seeburg. An old Dusty Springfield song came on. He crossed the room, extended one arm into a knot of drinkers, and, as if by magic, snagged an empty chair and pulled it toward me.

"Okay if I join you?"

I nodded. He sat and withdrew two bottles of mineral water from the pockets of his donkey jacket, slid one across the table to me, popped the other, and drank from it with his eyes closed. A raised scar traced his jaw like the outline of a hinge. I glanced down at the table, and noticed the ring finger of his right hand had been severed at the second joint.

After a minute, he opened his eyes. Dusty Springfield gave way to Amy Winehouse. Derek shook his head.

"These kids can't figure out how to work a fucking jukebox. I used to show them, but they'd just play the same goddamned song over and over. 'Rehab.' I had to take it off." He took a sip of water, gestured at my unopened bottle. "You should have some of that. Stay hydrated. You don't want them to find traces of blood in your alcohol stream."

"No danger of that," I said. But I opened the bottle and swallowed a mouthful.

Derek cocked his head. "How do you know Quinn again?"

"High school. I used to photograph him."

"You still a photographer? That's a dying breed." He laughed. "Make that 'dead.' You and that jukebox."

"How do you know Quinn?"

"We used to work together."

"At the Gambrel?"

"No." A muscle in his jaw twitched. "Quinn didn't do business there. He had more sense than I did. Back then, anyway." He stared at the Seeburg, its blue glare throwing the planes of his face into stark relief. "What were you doing in Reykjavík?"

"Just killing time."

"Nothing else?" An eyetooth flashed as he smiled, but his amber gaze remained cold. He pointed at the barely healed starburst beside my right eye. "That where you got that scar?"

"No."

"What about that?" He touched the fresh gash in my cheek, and I flinched.

"A bird attacked me in Iceland," I said. "A raven."

I thought he'd laugh. Instead he continued to stare at me. After a minute, he said, "You run with a rough crowd, Cass. But I guess you're aware of that. You know it's risky for Quinn to try to enter the UK?"

I nodded. I knew Quinn was afraid of being deported back to the U.S., but I'd avoided asking why. He had a laundry list that began with knocking off a pharmacy when we were kids. Somehow, I'd let desire for him and my own fear of remaining in Reykjavík override the obvious fact that if Quinn left Iceland, he was fucked. Quinn was a lot of things; stupid wasn't one of them.

I didn't want to think about the conclusion to this line of thought—that if Quinn didn't show up in London in the next few days, I was fucked, too.

I finished the dregs of my beer and stared into the empty glass. "Yeah. But I think he worked something out."

"That would be quite a feat. Where you staying?"

I shrugged. "Can you recommend someplace?"

"Around here? Holiday Inn, but it's expensive."

"How much?"

"Dunno. Three hundred quid?"

"For a fucking Holiday Inn?"

"This is London."

"Yeah, I get that part."

I looked away. At the bar, a pretty blond girl wearing polka-dot stockings and a fuzzy teddy bear hat leaned into a guy whose hair bore an unfortunate allegiance to LeBon-era Duran Duran. "Who's playing at the Electric Ballroom?"

Derek yawned. "Don't know. Hey, Kerry!"

"Hey, what?" the buzz-cut bartender shot back.

"Who's at the Electric Ballroom?"

Kerry inclined her head to the blond girl, mouthed a question then yelled, "Rapture of Lulu."

Derek turned to me. "There you are: Rapture of Lulu."

"Who the hell is Lulu?"

"No idea. I'm still trying to figure out which one is Baby Spice." He gulped down the rest of his water and stood. "Let me know if you hear from Quinn. He owes me money."

You and fifty other people, I thought, but said nothing.

5

I sat and brooded while the Seeburg pumped out a steady stream of rock and roll, Northern soul, and girl groups. Derek had pushed all the right buttons. The fact that Quinn had put those buttons there in the first place didn't make me feel any better. Eventually the jukebox fell silent. I saw Derek walk over to pull the plug, then return to the bar counter. I decided to get another drink. Someone grabbed my seat before I took a single step.

I ordered another shot. Derek pushed the whiskey across the counter to me, his face impassive. I paid for it and wandered to an empty patch of wall by the front door. The blond girl and her unfortunately coiffed boyfriend stood a few feet away from me, texting furiously. I never heard either one of them say a word to the other.

I sipped my whiskey and tried to come up with a game plan. I was unwilling to stay in a Holiday Inn on principle, especially if it cost five hundred bucks a night. I surveyed the room for someone I might hook up with. Derek was out, though the buzz-cut woman was a possibility. The three fuzzy folkies had left long ago. Everyone else looked half my age and nowhere near drunk enough to bring me home.

I focused on a nearby table, where a girl sat, texting, while the guys she was with stared at the game on the flatscreen TV. I edged close enough to read over the girl's shoulder.

worlds end?
k
cya

She set down her mobile and started to tug a voluminous scarf around her face. Beside her, a bearded guy gazed transfixed at the game, his phone beside a martini glass.

My fingers grazed the edge of the table: Neither the bearded guy nor the girl blinked as I slid his phone over several inches, then moved the girl's to where his had been. I quickly feigned interest in my bag as the girl tucked the end of her scarf into her jacket, grabbed the wrong mobile, and hurried outside. A minute later the man stood, pocketing the other phone, and pushed his way through the crowd to the bar.

I finished my Jack Daniels and dropped the empty shotglass into my pocket. At the bar, the man with the wrong mobile suddenly turned and raced back to the table.

"You see my phone?" His friends shook their heads. "Fuck!"

Cursing, he raced outside. As he did, a white girl in a vast buffalo plaid coat walked in, balancing precariously on red patent-leather platform boots. Slate-green eyes, bleached-out hair twisted into an elaborately teased bouffant that added six inches to her height. Subtract the blond wig and Arthur Kane footwear, and she'd barely scrape five feet.

The guy beside her wore a caramel-colored overcoat, a

brown fedora, and thick-soled brothel creepers: a look undercut by petulant, pretty-boy features starting to slacken with age and alcohol, as well as the fact that the collar of his expensive coat was spattered with vomit. He appeared about thirty, the girl a decade younger.

"Look." One of the guys at the table nudged his mate, who smiled and angled his mobile to take a picture. Several other people did the same; the rest regarded the girl with mild interest, trying to determine if she was someone they should recognize. The girl in the buffalo plaid coat grinned and tottered toward the bar, her scowling boyfriend hurrying to catch up.

I glanced down at the guy who'd taken the first picture. His mobile's screen displayed a blurred image that looked like a thumb with blond hair.

"So is that Lulu?" I asked him.

The guy shook his head. "That's Krishna Morgenthal—she sings at some of the clubs around here, does a bit of backup when she can."

"Is she famous?"

"Not really. In Camden, maybe. Brilliant voice."

He headed for the bar, where a small crowd had gathered to take photos or buy Krishna Morgenthal a drink. I ambled over to a newly vacated table covered with pint glasses, several bags of chips, and a glass of tawny liquid. I nabbed a bag of chips and the whiskey, and sloped off to the back of the room.

The whiskey turned out to be Jameson—on ice, which suggested it'd been ordered by someone who also didn't know how to operate a jukebox. I drank it anyway, and wolfed down the prawn and bacon–flavored crisps. They were as disgusting as they sound.

Behind the bar, Derek yelled at a kid to back the fuck off.

I settled in to watch the show, trying to psych myself up for a night at the Holiday Inn. I hadn't factored in that closing time came much earlier here than in New York. On a weeknight, anyway.

"Time!" bellowed Derek, to an answering chorus of curses and pleading.

"Give us a song, Krish!"

"Don't be a cunt, Derek!"

"Fuck off," Derek retorted.

I nursed my Jameson and stayed put. I've been thrown out of enough places to know last call doesn't really arrive until the cops do.

Despite their complaints, within ten minutes the Banshee's customers had all left without a fight. I drained what was left of the Jameson and started for the door, where the buzz-cut Kerry waited for me to leave so she could lock up. I shot a backward glance at the room.

I wasn't quite last: Krishna Morgenthal and her dour boyfriend stood talking to Derek behind the bar. When Derek saw me, he lifted his chin and called out, "Kerry. She can stay."

Kerry nodded, closed the front door and bolted it, then switched off the outside lights and most of the indoor ones. I watched her disappear through a door in back, and approached the bar.

"Can I get another drink?" I asked Derek.

Krishna's boyfriend swiveled to stare at me through bloodshot eyes. "Fuckeryou?" he slurred.

If Central Casting had sent over a bad drunk, they couldn't have done better than this guy. He'd lost the fedora, which would have been an improvement if it hadn't left a scalp tufted with greasy black stubble. His waxenly pretty features looked like they'd started to melt. He had an arm around Krishna, but as I approached she slipped away from him.

"Shut up, Lance." Krishna seized the bar rail to steady herself. She gave me a crooked smile, plucked at a blond tendril that had escaped from her bouffant, and pouted suggestively. The gesture was more childlike than seductive. "Derek—whatever she wants."

Derek poured a shot and handed it to me. "Compliments of Miss Morgenthal."

I sidled a safe distance from Lance and raised my glass to Krishna. She picked up her drink and teetered toward me, her platform boots echoing through the empty room.

"You American?"

"Yeah. Thanks for the drink."

"Noo Yawk Sit-Ay?" I nodded and she smiled in delight. "I always guess right!" Her own accent was so hyperbolically East End, I wondered if it was put on. She took a slug of her drink. A gimlet, light on the Rose's. I could smell the vodka seeping from her pores. "You at the show tonight?"

"Missed that one," I said.

She grinned. "Now that's your problem, innit?"

Up close she looked very young. Cleopatra kohl made her gray-green eyes appear huge. Cerise lipstick couldn't hide where her lips had been bitten raw. Beneath the ugly plaid coat she wore a sleeveless tank top and a red leatherette miniskirt. No stockings—inside those platform boots, her feet must have been rubbed as raw as her mouth.

I glanced down at her bare arms. There were bruises just above the elbow, the livid ghost of a handprint. When I looked up again, she was staring at me with those spooky green eyes.

I asked, "You got a band?"

"Nah. I do some open mics and pickup gigs, backup for people who come through London. Lulu, I sang with them tonight, they let me do a solo. Not everyone does."

She gulped her drink. I glanced to where Lance slumped against the bar, staring at us. Derek was nowhere in sight. "Your boyfriend a musician?"

"He's a fucking cunt." She raised her voice. "A fucking cunt!"

I stiffened. Lance only turned his back to us.

"Fucking cunt," Krishna murmured a final time.

She set her empty glass on the counter and made a wobbly beeline toward the jukebox. I knocked back the rest of my drink and followed, watching as she stooped to reach behind the Seeburg and plug it back in. The blue glow gave a leaden cast to her thin arms and sharp-featured face as she gazed at the rows of song titles, hand slapping repeatedly at her thigh. After a moment I realized she was searching for a pocket that wasn't there.

"Hey." I fumbled in my leather jacket for a quarter. "Here."

She grabbed the quarter and expertly flicked it into the coin slot, stood on tiptoe to run her fingers across the glass coping, and punched in a string of numbers. After a few seconds, six thunderous drumbeats echoed through the room: "Be My Baby." I closed my eyes.

Max Weinberg said that if Hal Blaine had only played drums on that one song, his name would still be uttered with reverence. It's the Big Bang of rock and roll—a rhapsody of tambourines, shakers, chimes, and guitars, abruptly snarled in static as the needle skipped across vinyl.

I turned to smack the jukebox. Before I could touch it, Ronnie Spector's voice once more filled the room.

Only it wasn't Ronnie Spector singing. It was Krishna

Morgenthal, silhouetted in the Seeburg's ice-blue halo, hands raised and body swaying as though she faced an audience. Her voice held none of the transcendent joy of Ronnie Spector's. Instead, the song became something far more ominous. A threat seethed beneath the girl-group lyrics, the words twisted into a pop aria of obsession and barely suppressed rage. For someone who'd loved the song for most of a lifetime, it was a profoundly unsettling command performance. I listened, stunned, until the final drumbeats faded into reverb, then silence.

"Holy shit." I stared at Krishna. "That's some set of pipes."

Krishna swiped a bead of sweat from her cheek, stepped over, and stood on tiptoe to kiss me on the mouth, her tongue darting between my lips.

"What's that for?" I asked when she drew away.

"That's for nothing." She gave me a sly half smile. "Now go do something." She spun on her platform heels and sashayed back to the bar.

I whistled softly. Where in that tiny body did she keep that enormous voice? I looked around the room. Kerry was gone. Derek was still MIA, and Lance appeared to have been texting for the last two minutes and forty-one seconds.

I licked my lips, tasting smoke and limes. Krishna had staked out a spot at the end of the bar. She gazed at me with that cockeyed smile, one hand splayed below the red leatherette miniskirt. I decided to count to ten before I crossed the room. I made it to five.

"So." I set my satchel on the floor beside her. "Krishna. Isn't that a guy's name? Or a god's?"

"Yah. My friends call me Krish. My mum was a fucking hippie in a caravan." She made a face.

"Where'd you learn to belt like that?"

"Singing in tube stations. Brilliant echo. I used to ride up and down the escalator and sing, but I couldn't make any dosh. Down in the station I could make fifty quid a night. When the cops chased me out I'd sing on the street."

"But you're doing clubs now, right? Backup."

"Make more money busking. DJ I know just uploaded a song of mine. No dosh in that, either, but maybe someday."

Her gaze slid sideways to take in Lance, still engrossed in his tiny blue screen. His head was tilted so that I could see teethmarks on the side of his throat. Either a love bite deep enough to draw blood, or proof that Krishna could hold her own with a violent boyfriend.

I scowled. "Tell me that asshole isn't your DJ friend. Because the whole Ronnie Spector thing is already weird enough."

She shook her head. "Nah. He's nobody. Just a guy."

"A guy as in a boyfriend and you can dump him? Like, now?"

I ran a finger along the back of her neck. Her skin felt hot. Channeling the Wall of Sound burned a lot of calories. Her leg brushed mine and she looked up at me. I touched her chin and bent to kiss her. Her tongue flicked against my mouth, but before I could pull her closer her head whipped back.

"Ow!"

"What the fuck?" Lance stared at me, his hand buried in Krishna's bouffant. "Fucking sket."

He yanked Krishna so hard I heard her jaw snap. Blood welled from her lip as she glared at him, shouting, "*You're* the fucking sket!"

He raised his arm to strike her and I lunged at him, the steel tip of my cowboy boot connecting with his kneecap. His legs buckled. With a muffled shriek, he fell.

I grabbed my camera bag. Krishna stared at Lance as he

clutched his leg, weeping in pain. I touched her shoulder. "You coming?"

She ran a hand across her head, pulled off the teased blond wig, and threw it Lance with a curse. "You—"

I pulled her toward the front door. "Save it."

"No." Krishna shook herself free. "This way."

She staggered to the back of the room on her platform heels. I followed, down a dim corridor into a storage area filled with crates of empty bottles. Krishna stopped, fumbling with the door latch until it opened, and we ran outside, startling Derek where he paced nervously, mobile pressed to one ear. His head jerked up as we darted past.

"Wait!" Derek shouted. "Don't—"

But we had already reached the High Street.

6

I ran with Krishna through a warren of alleys slick with icy rain. Sirens wailed in the distance, and a lone black SUV idled in front of a doorway. Stoned, bewildered kids stumbled along the sidewalks, looking like they'd missed the last boat from Pleasure Island. Without the wig, Krishna's own hair was a tangled mass of cinnamon-colored curls. A few kids recognized her—recognized her as someone they *should* recognize, anyway—but their gazes slid over me as though I were a reflection in a darkened window. The few times someone caught my eyes, they recoiled.

"They're scared of you." Krishna's tone was admiring. "I could do with some of that."

"Give it thirty years," I said.

We hurried down a flight of stone steps to a narrow path alongside the Regent's Canal. Trash floated on the sluggish water. Boats resembling anorexic barges were tied up beside the path. Krishna pointed at the opposite bank. "My place is just over there."

I saw only shadows cast by the thick curtains of ivy that covered the walls beside the path. The thrum of traffic had diminished to the faint buzz of a trapped fly. Something darted from the underbrush and disappeared into the night. I froze, looked over to see Krishna staring at me.

"You all right?" she asked.

I nodded and croaked, "Yeah. Sorry."

Years ago I'd been raped in a place like this—three AM shadows, an echo of drunken laughter as I stumbled home from CBGB, shitfaced and barefoot and alone. I still have the scars left by a zipknife above my crotch, tangled with the tattoo I got a few years later: TOO TOUGH TO DIE.

Ever since that night, I can sense damage, smell it like an acrid pheromone seeping from the pores of people around me. The wrong kind of street, the wrong kind of light, and the stink of my own terror floods my throat and nostrils. It's why I can read photos the way I do, like they're tarot cards or the I Ching. Because that's what photography is—or was, before the advent of digital—damage, the corrosive effect that sunlight has on chemicals and a prepared surface.

Krishna hooked her arm through mine, tottering on her platform shoes. "Come on," she urged.

We walked beneath an arched bridge that stank of piss, its security lights blurring Krishna into a blue-gray shadow at my side. When we emerged from the passage, I followed her up a set of stairs back to the street, where we crossed the bridge to the other side of the canal.

An ugly apartment block of council housing rose behind a gate, rows of identical windows looking onto minuscule balconies crammed with bicycles and flowerpots and gas grills, empty pet carriers and plastic chairs. Krishna punched a code into a security panel. We passed through the gate and entered the building.

"My flat looks like a tip," she said, as we walked down a corridor that stank of cigarette smoke and industrial cleaning fluid. "Lance left all his shit, I told him I'd toss it in the canal."

She stopped in front of a door and spent most of a minute searching through the pockets of her plaid coat. Frustrated, she thrust a key at me.

"Here. I can never get it to work."

I jimmied the lock, and the door opened. "That's why I keep him around," Krishna said absently. "He can always get the door open."

The flat was not much larger than a walk-in closet, and resembled Fresh Kills on a busy day. Clothes strewn everywhere, along with wigs, gig flyers, takeaway cartons, empty vodka bottles, and several plastic ukuleles. Two silvery, thigh-length boots protruded from a heap of clothing, giving the impression that a robot was buried there, or maybe Gene Simmons. It smelled of unwashed clothes and skunk weed and fenugreek, with that pervasive base note of vodka and lime.

Krishna swept a mound of clothes from a small couch. "You can sleep here."

I sank onto the couch, my satchel at my feet. If I lost sight of it, I'd never find it again. "That's okay. I can crash anywhere."

"I'm glad you crashed here," she murmured.

I pulled Krishna toward me and kissed her, pulling off the heavy coat until I found her nestled inside it. She was so slight I could slip a finger in the furrows between her ribs, her small breasts cool beneath my hands. She was surprisingly strong for a skinny girl: I remembered her loser boyfriend and the dark half moons on his throat.

Eventually we fell asleep, Krishna curled against me. I woke once and stared at her child's face, pale skin beaded with silver from the shadows of rain on the window behind us, her fingers pressed against her mouth, trying to keep a secret as she dreamed. Her eyelids twitched and her mouth twisted as though she were about to cry out. I kissed her cheek and her expression relaxed, fear fading back into some other dream. I fell asleep once more. Later, dimly aware that she was gone, I pulled my satchel close, my head pillowed on a crumpled camisole that smelled of smoke and limes.

7

I woke to gray light filtered through windows that overlooked a channel of greasy-looking water. I pushed aside a pile of clothes that weren't mine and sat up groggily.

"That doesn't look very comfortable," a voice intoned.

I turned. An extraordinarily tall man leaned against the wall and stared down at me, amused.

"Don't panic," he said. "I'm harmless unless provoked."

I wasn't sure whether to believe him. I pegged him at mid-forties, wearing a threadbare morning coat and pleated trousers over scuffed black winklepickers. The long-fingered hand he extended to me was so white it appeared bleached. His face was wearily handsome, deep-set dark eyes and strong chin, with a wry, thin-lipped mouth that gave him the air of an actor accustomed to making the best of a badly written, long-playing role. Both his height and appearance were enhanced by a top hat tall enough to hide a live chicken.

"Adrian Carlisle." The languid voice was coupled with a disconcertingly strong handshake. His fingernails were bitten to the quick. I caught the faint scent of damage in my nostrils, like spoiled apricots, a smell that was almost immediately gone. "I'm a friend of Krishna's. A friend to all humankind. I assume she's beneath the laundry somewhere?"

"I don't know. Yeah, I guess." I looked around. "Is there even a bedroom in this place?"

He gestured toward a cheap Chinese screen draped with scarves. "The seraglio lies yon. Coffin nail?"

He held out an alligator-leather cigarette case. I shook my head. He withdrew an e-cigarette, sucked at it, then exhaled an amethyst cloud of vapor. I grabbed my bag. "Bathroom?"

Adrian pointed at a door. "There's no hot water."

There was no tub, either, only a flimsy plastic shower stall veined with mildew. Also no medicine cabinet, though one wasn't necessary. I'd seen pill bottles everywhere in the flat—Fentanyl, mostly. On the floor, on windowsills, lined up on shelves beside empty vodka bottles. Here in the bathroom they jostled for space in the shower stall, alongside enough hair products to furnish a salon. Some of the pill bottles had Krishna's name on the label. Most did not.

And most of the bottles were empty, though I did find one half filled with something called Solpadol. I pocketed it, undressed, and took a flash shower. Afterward I dried myself on a cheap polyester kimono emblazoned with a red dragon—there were no towels, natch. I dressed quickly, pulling on a striped shirt and worn black sweater. When I returned to the living room, Adrian Carlisle was on the loveseat, his long legs stretched atop a pile of clothing.

"So which little friend are you?" He nudged a red lace bra with one winklepicker, flicking his foot so the bra sailed across the room.

"Cassandra. We just met last night at the Banshee."

"And such close friends already." Adrian removed his stovepipe hat, revealing thin, shoulder-length dark hair streaked with gray. "I try to check in on Krish every day. Make sure she has a pulse."

I perched on the opposite end of the loveseat, reaching to pick up an empty pill bottle. Haldol, 5 mg. "She has quite a habit."

Adrian raised a white hand that trembled slightly. "Let he who is without stain throw the first stone. May I see that?"

He took the pill bottle and inspected the label, sighing when he saw it was empty. "Years ago I spent an entire day going through this flat with a fine-toothed comb. I found exactly one Mandrax. Where do you think she hides them? I pulled up the floorboards, there's nothing there."

"What's Solpadol?" I asked.

"Codeine and paracetamol."

"What's paracetamol?"

"Acetaminophen. Did you find some Solpadol?"

"No. Just curious."

"You're lying." Adrian smiled. "I like that in a girl."

"You wouldn't have anything that might help me wake up?"

"Not today, darling."

"What do they call Ritalin here? Focalin, stuff like that."

"Ritalin. Methylphenidate hydrochloride, if you're a pharmacist. Which I somehow suspect you are not." Adrian peered at me. "You looking to sign on with the NHS?"

"No. Just tired."

"We'll all sleep when we're dead, won't we? Here." He withdrew a card case, scrawled something on a card, and handed it to me; collected his top hat and stood. "I came to remind Krish that there's a birthday party tonight for Morven Dunfries. I tried to ring but of course her mobile's dead. You're welcome to come along—you look like you could use a hot dinner."

"I'd rather find a drink."

"I'm sure Krish has something, somewhere. Or you could just squeeze her like a sponge." He tipped his hat. "Maybe I'll see you later."

"What time is it?"

He pulled out a mobile. "Half four."

"Jesus." I raked the damp hair from my forehead. "I was supposed to meet someone, only now I'm not sure where to find him."

Adrian nodded sympathetically. "I know just how you feel. Here in Camden?"

"Brixton. But I got the place wrong, or he did. Do you know Derek Haverty?"

"Derek? The barman at the Banshee? He's easy to find."

"Not Derek. Someone he knows." I hesitated, wondering if I could trust Adrian. Almost certainly not. "Is he an okay guy, Derek?"

"An okay guy? He did a bid in prison, if that's what you're after. I wouldn't sit on his Jimmy Shands."

He made his way through the midden of clothing to the door, waved without looking back, and left. I stared at the card he'd given me.

ADRIAN CARLISLE, ESQUIRE

On the back he'd written an address. It was meaningless to me, so I stuck the card in my pocket and went through the contents of my bag. I counted out some bills from a wad of twenty-pound notes and left them in my wallet with the stolen passport. Then I put my U.S. passport into a Ziplock bag, retrieved my Tony Lamas from under the loveseat, and stuck the Ziplock bag in the bottom of one cowboy boot, along with the remainder of my cash.

"Morning." I turned to see Krishna emerge from behind the Chinese screen. An oversized soccer jersey hung from her matchstick frame, falling well below her knees. Staring at her made me queasy: She looked about twelve. "Who was that?"

I held up Adrian's card. "This guy."

She walked over and took the card, yawning. "He's up early."

"He was here when I woke."

"Yah, Ado gets where he wants to be." She pronounced the nickname so it rhymed with Play-Doh. "He's like my fucking shadow, he is." She read what was written on the back of the card, scowled, and tossed it onto the floor.

"He said it was a birthday party."

"I know what it is."

She wandered to a corner that served as kitchenette, searched the fridge for a liter bottle of water. She drank a hefty amount, returned to the living room, and handed the bottle to me. I took a sip: vodka cut with what smelled like nail polish remover.

"It's got B vitamins in it." She flopped onto the couch and lit a cigarette. "What's your name again?"

"Cass. How old are you?"

"Age of consent's sixteen here. But I'm twenty-three."

"What's the deal with this party?"

Krishna yawned again, showing gappy teeth. "Ado knows all kinds of squiffy old people. No offense," she added. "Birthday Girl's on me like a cat every time I see her." She stood, stretching so that the jersey ran up along her skinny thighs. "Feel like treating me to breakfast?"

"Yeah, okay."

She padded off into the shower. I was relieved there'd been no discussion of last night. Daylight and what passed for sobriety on my part had burned off any residual desire. She wasn't my type—way too young, way too skinny, and the pharaonic eye makeup made me think of tombs. Still, that voice was one in a million.

And she knew her way around London. I hadn't had a proper meal in thirty-six hours. I still had no clue how I'd find Quinn, but I didn't want to do it on an empty stomach. I picked up Adrian Carlisle's card and stuck it in my pocket, waited impatiently until Krishna emerged from the bathroom, dripping like a wet ferret. Another half hour and she reemerged from behind the screen, dressed in black leggings and ankle boots, a knee-length orange sweater and freshly applied Cleopatra eye makeup, her cinnamon curls gelled into a pompadour.

"Ready?" she asked, pulling on her buffalo plaid coat.

Outside the light was already failing. Rain slashed down from a tarnished nickel sky. People hurried along the canal path, collars turned up against a wind acrid with the odors of diesel and dead fish. Krishna texted nonstop, mouthing the words to whatever she heard through her earbuds. Bicyclists rang their bells to warn us of their approach, shouting at me when they passed—I couldn't remember which side I should walk on. Krishna navigated like a bird in flight, never looking up from her mobile.

We ate at a sleek little bistro, not the kind of place I'd have pegged as Krishna's local. But then I was paying. Steak frites, a bottle of cheap Rhone. Every ten minutes Krishna would dash outside to have a cigarette, or turn sideways in her chair, whispering agitatedly into her phone.

"Lance?" I asked after about the seventeenth call.

Krishna nodded. "Yah. You know how it is."

I thought of the bruises I'd seen on her arm. "Not really. I thought you said he wasn't your boyfriend."

"Not your fucking business, is it?"

"Nope."

I ordered some coffee and popped a couple of Focalin. Krishna raised an eyebrow. "It's polite to share."

"Medicine for squiffy old people. You wouldn't like it." I paid the bill and we walked back into the street.

"You got a game plan for the night?" I asked, as Krishna scanned the rainswept sidewalk, stopped to swipe intently at her mobile. "What, is it that asshole Lance again?"

She shook her head without looking up. "Nightmapper. It's a free app that tells you what's on at all the clubs. Also which boozers have cheap drinks." She glanced at me and grinned. "You'd find that useful. Says there's half-price drinks at the Queen and Artichoke; I'm going to meet Lance in a bit."

I flashed Adrian's card. "Feel like going with me to this place first?"

"Not really."

"I don't know how to get there."

"134 bus, or you can take the tube to Finsbury Park then catch the W3."

"Yeah, but I don't know your friends."

"I told you, not my fucking friends."

"How about I pay you?" I pulled out two twenty-pound notes.

Krishna snorted. "I come cheap." She fixed me with those sarcophagus eyes and held out her hand. "Throw in some of those pills and I'll take you."

I gave her a Focalin. She swallowed it, then asked, "That it?"

"You're half my size. Come on, I'm freezing my ass off."

It was a long bus ride. I stared out the window while Krishna fidgeted and texted. After a while, I dug in my bag and pulled out my Konica. My father gave it to me on my seventeenth birthday; never a top-of-the-line rig but I'd done good work with it, back when I could no more think of going a day without shooting than without a drink.

Like Uncle Lou said, those were different times. Until a few months ago, I'd barely picked up my camera in twenty years. Now there was no film in it—I'd been relieved of the last two rolls I'd shot. Not necessarily a bad thing, considering the pictures I'd taken could have incriminated me in several countries. But I still had a few rolls of Tri-X.

I tapped Krishna's shoulder. "Give me your coat."

She shrugged it off, and I folded it into a makeshift dark tent in my lap. I didn't need to see the camera to load it: I could feel the sprocket's tiny teeth beneath my fingertips, smell the lactose odor of the raw emulsion as I wound it. When I was done, I closed the back of the camera, dropped the empty film canister into my satchel, and returned the coat to Krishna. She stuck her mobile in a pocket and flashed me a grin.

"Gonna take my picture?"

"Maybe."

The light was bad, but I was used to that. I'd made my name in underexposed black and white, shooting grainy photos of the downtown punk scene in its infancy. I loved that monochrome world, the way my viewfinder captured everything and held it in suspended animation until later, when I summoned lovers and musicians and corpses in the darkroom: gaunt faces under fluorescent bulbs; arms flailing at cheap guitars on a makeshift stage; a severed hand with strands of hair caught beneath a blackened fingernail. I'd published one book, an iconoclastic volume called *Dead Girls* that would have made my career, if I hadn't been dead-set on losing my reputation before I'd gained it.

But my eye hadn't changed. That and my sense of damage kept me alive, even if I spent more time staring into a shotglass than a lens.

I picked up the Konica and gazed through the viewfinder, playing with the focus while I waited for Krishna's grin to dissolve. One Cleopatra eye twitched: self-doubt or boredom or maybe just exhaustion. I pressed the shutter release, clicked to the next frame, and set the camera on my knee. I knew I'd gotten what I wanted.

"Can I see?" Krishna snatched the camera from me and turned it in her hands, frowning. "How do you turn it on?"

"You don't. Jesus, don't touch the lens!" I swore and grabbed it back. "That's a real camera. Not digital."

"How's it work?"

"Magic." I stuck the Konica into my bag. "We almost at this place?"

"Soon." She stared past me into the rainy night, at signs advertising chicken tikka and ESL classes and bargain dentistry, a pile of children's shoes in the window of a charity shop.

"So who's Morven?"

"The wife." Krishna pulled nervously at her oversized sweater. "Her husband, he's a gangster."

"Musician-gangster or gangster-gangster?"

"I'm not having you on. Mallory Dunfries, he chopped off some poor arse's fingers who owed him money."

"How do you know him?"

"I don't. Adrian does—he's a raver, puts on parties at empty houses round London. He and Mallo were partners—Mallo's blokes, they're the ones sold you anything you wanted. Acid, ketamine. Nothing serious, I dunno why they busted him."

"But they did?"

Krishna nodded. "Just a few months. Knuckle rapping, that's all. Morven's the scary one. She told me once she used to be a witch. I believe her—I don't know how Mallo sleeps nights. I told Ado I wouldn't be alone with her again for anything."

"Then how come you're going?"

" 'Cause you paid me. And it's a birthday party. I like cake." She licked her lips, but her expression suggested she was recalling something other than cake.

8

We finally got off at a busy intersection, hopping over ankle-deep water at the curb. Cars and double-decker buses whipped through a roundabout as we dashed across the street. I looked in the wrong direction for oncoming traffic and almost got creamed by a cab.

"Fucking hell!" Krishna yanked me to the sidewalk. "Watch it!"

It was pouring now. Krishna pulled her coat over her head. I tugged my collar high as it would go and followed her, jumping across puddles and ducking beneath awnings when we could.

"That's it," she announced, and pointed at a four-story Victorian edifice that occupied an entire corner. Its restored brickwork and ceramic tiles displayed classical Greek figures who appeared to be having much more fun than anyone else in the vicinity. The original windows on the top floor had been replaced with vast panels of sleek black glass. On the street level, a brass sign read BOUDICCA ANTIQUITIES & CURIOS.

"That's their shop now," said Krishna. "Now that Mallo's

gone straight. Gate's round back," she went on, fumbling for her mobile. "I don't know the code to get in—we'll have to wait for someone if I can't get hold of Ado."

At the end of an alley beside the building stood an impressive security fence, topped with shining razor wire and rows of stainless-steel spikes. A black SUV was parked in the courtyard beyond, rain streaming down the vehicle's black windows. It was impossible to see if there was anyone inside.

Krishna glanced at the SUV, texting in vain for Adrian. She shook her head, and a rope of wet hair fell across her cheek. "I told you, I don't like this place."

"They own the whole building?"

Krishna nodded. "Council was going to tear it down. Mallo bought it and fixed it up. They own that antique shop downstairs. Ado says they rent out the other floors, but I never see anyone else. Look, here's someone—"

A burly man in a dark overcoat emerged from the back door and raced through the courtyard in the rain. When he reached the security gate he halted, struggling with an umbrella as he punched a button. The gate buzzed: Krishna quickly pushed it open and we stepped into the courtyard, as the man with the umbrella ran past us into the street.

"I remember the code for this one." Krishna paused at the former stage door to tap at another keypad. "I watched Morven, last time I was here. 1993, year I was born."

"Christ," I muttered.

Inside, I wondered what the point was of buying a historic structure, then gutting it so it looked like every soulless office building on the planet: gray concrete tiles, gray walls, frosted glass. The entry was brightly lit and had the stale antiseptic smell of a hospital waiting room. A sign pointed the way to Boudicca

Antiquities & Curios. Except for a few damp footprints, the floors were spotless, as were the walls.

The sole exception to the modern renovation was an old-fashioned cage elevator. A seven-inch gap yawned between the car's kickplate and the tiled floor. I glanced down into a basement black as a pit.

"Mind the gap," said Krishna. She pulled aside the elevator's folding metal gate, and we stepped inside. There was no inner safety door.

"Seems weird they updated everything but this," I said as the cage slowly rose, gears clanking.

"Weird?" Krishna pressed her face against the grille and peered down the shaft. "I don't think so. Easy to arrange an accident."

"Yeah, but how many accidents before it doesn't look like an accident anymore?"

"Dunno. You want to find out?"

The elevator ground to a stop. Krishna yanked open the gate and bounced out into a windowless corridor. I followed, stepping gingerly over the gap. Behind us the elevator clanked softly, and I glanced back to see it rising to the next floor.

"There's a little room up top," said Krishna. "Morven's secret place."

Here too the walls, floor, and ceiling were all painted gray. Recessed low-light bulbs made the door at the end of the corridor seem to recede as we walked toward it. It was like gazing through the wrong end of a gigantic telescope. Krishna's wren-like figure didn't dispel the illusion.

"This is it," she said when we reached the door.

There was no number or name, no sounds from the other side. I knocked. Nothing.

I turned to Krishna. "You sure?"

She shrank into her vast coat, water dripping from its sleeves onto the floor. "Wasn't my idea," she said.

I knocked again, harder.

Abruptly the door opened, releasing a wave of laughter, jazz piano, and a rush of air ripe with competing perfumes and cigar smoke. A woman in a tight-fitting, plum-colored dress peeked out at us.

"Is that Krish?" she exclaimed, and grabbed Krishna in a sloppy embrace. "I'm so glad you came!"

Krishna extricated herself. "Happy birthday, Morven. Here, I brought a friend."

The woman looked past her at me. "I see. Who's this?"

"Cass," said Krishna.

Morven regarded me coolly, and I realized that sloppy embrace had been a proprietary one. I edged away from Krishna and said, "We just met. I'm new in town."

"Is Adrian here?" broke in Krishna.

Morven shook her head. "I haven't seen him, but that doesn't mean anything."

"I'll just have a peep," said Krishna, and slipped into the apartment.

I tried not to look pissed off: Now there'd be no reason for Morven to ask me to stay.

The same thought appeared to have struck Morven. "So. Cass. Have we met?" She had a mid-Atlantic accent, clipped and businesslike.

"Maybe in New York."

"Maybe."

Her eyes narrowed as she regarded me. She looked like a Morven—witchy. A mass of unruly hair had been dyed pale blond, auburn, and magenta before reverting to gray at the scalp, held back from her face with an antique tortoiseshell comb. Fair skin bore the marks of too much sun—seams around her eyes, freckles that had grown dark and blotchy, a map of broken capillaries across her cheeks.

Still, it was a striking face, more piquant than conventionally beautiful: large aquamarine eyes, pointed nose, small mouth, apple cheeks. Above her left breast was a small tattoo, a pair of interlocking, calligraphic letters in faded red ink—**FC.**

She wasn't quite tall enough to be a model, but she triggered a vague memory of a girl in a magazine. A long-ago ad for Herbal Essences shampoo, maybe, or Yardley English Lavender soap or Biba makeup—a slightly spooky hippie chick shilling dime-store perfume and lip gloss.

I expected her to close the door in my face. Instead she said, "Well, Cass. Come in."

I entered.

"Morven Dunfries." She extended her hand, a serpentine bracelet around her wrist. Not a Bulgari Serpenti: this looked much older, gold with emerald eyes, the stone rough-cut and the deep green of a bottle glinting from the bottom of a lake. "I'm sorry I missed Krish's show—she's marvelous, isn't she?"

Her hand dropped before I could touch it. "There's wine over there and all kinds of nibblies. Introduce yourself to Mallo if you see him; he's the one not wearing any shoes."

She turned to greet someone else, and I headed for the crowded living room. Hardwood floors and biscuit-colored walls; an eclectic mix of mid-century modern furniture and stuff that looked like it had been scavenged from the street. Paint-encrusted kitchen chairs, an end table decoupaged with pages from 1960s magazines and comic strips. Bill Evans on the sound system, "Detour Ahead."

I didn't see anyone who looked like a gangster. The guests appeared equal parts Young Bobo and Middle-Aged Money. Bespectacled guys in vintage band T-shirts or loose oxford-cloth shirts; women working the sexy anthropologist vibe with tribal tattoos and gaudy knitted headwear. I might have wandered into an Etsy conference, or a university faculty party.

I elbowed through the crowd, looking for the bar. Floor-to-ceiling windows provided an eye-popping panorama of Crouch End, a steep hill bristling with row houses and shops. The Gap, Starbucks, and American Apparel mingled with Finest Thai Fish House and Crown Prince of Falafel. Across the street, a down-at-the-heels pub put up a brave fight against gentrification, a clot of smokers clustered around its front door. The view made me slightly nauseous—vertigo, and also the sight of all those American corporate logos metastasizing along streets that had been around centuries before the U.S. War for Independence.

I found a table where a young woman in caterer's livery presided over ranks of wine bottles. "Red or white?" she asked.

"Any whiskey?" She shook her head. "Red, I guess."

It was good wine. I finished it, held my glass out for a refill, and helped myself to a third while the bartender tended to another customer.

I had enough of a buzz now to pretend to be sociable. Everyone seemed cheerful. I nodded but didn't introduce myself. I kept half an eye out for Krishna or Adrian but didn't see either of them. Birthday presents were piled on a table by the wall, a rainbow explosion of ribbons and shiny paper. I glanced at a hand-lettered card that had already been opened, and caught a whiff of Opium perfume.

Happy Sixtieth Dearest Creature!!!

I resisted the temptation to pocket one of the smaller packages and wandered to another table, covered with abandoned wineglasses and an incongruous object: a white stone statue, as long as my arm. Its face was as smooth and featureless as an egg. A straight line delineated its legs, with an inverted V to represent a vagina.

I put down my camera bag. After a glance around to see if anyone might object, I tentatively hefted the statue. It was heavy—marble, or maybe alabaster. I ran a finger across its strange eyeless face, smooth and cool to the touch, and set it back on the table, frowning.

It looked like an ancient Cycladic carving. But who leaves a four-thousand-year-old Greek artifact lying around on a battered piece of furniture?

My hosts, apparently. I'd seen things like this before, but never outside of a museum. It could be a fake, but then why go to the trouble of displaying it? More likely it was overflow from the business downstairs.

As I continued to prowl the room, I saw a few more oddities. Several stone figurines, crude representations of women; a quarter-sized fragment of gold foil, embossed with an eagle's wing; a tiny bronze statue of a mouse blowing some kind of curved horn.

I picked up the mouse, which was surprisingly heavy for such a small object. Its eyes were squeezed shut with the effort of blowing into the horn's mouthpiece, its tiny cheeks puffed out. Roman letters on the underside spelled out a name: CVRANVS. A two-thousand-year-old child's toy.

I was tempted to slip it into my pocket, but I set it back down and headed to the kitchen, hoping to find something stronger than red wine.

In front of an Aga stove, two men talked excitedly about a new restaurant that served nothing but marrow. I picked up a postcard announcing an auction of Rare and Important Comic Books. The music had grown livelier, burbling EDM. In the living room, several young women had kicked off their boots and were dancing close, surrounded by a group of guys more interested in their mobiles. Krishna and Morven stood in a corner, where Morven smoothed Krishna's damp pompadour, leaning close to murmur in her ear. She slid something into Krishna's hand, and the two of them began to kiss.

I wondered if Mallo Dunfries was okay with his wife making out with a twenty-three-year-old. It *was* her birthday.

I watched them, and felt a flicker of . . . something. Jealousy, maybe, or possessiveness. Not desire so much as some primal urge to protect. Morven could have made three of Krishna. She certainly seemed to be making a meal of her.

I did another lap around the living room and found a hallway, empty except for an older couple having an animated conversation about politics. I ambled past them, stopping to check out several framed vintage posters from the 1970s. Full-color advertisements for comic books: *The Creeper*; *The Tomb of Dracula*. There was a framed splash page for the latter—the count staring down into an open grave, the signatures of Marv Wolfman and Gene Colan floating above his head like thought balloons—along with pristine lobby cards for *Gorgo* and *Witchfinder General*. Some serious geek taste, matched to seriously deep pockets.

So it was odd to find two smaller frames hung at the end of the hall. One held a faded color photo of a stately home: ruddy ivy-covered brick, Tudor-era tower, a glimpse of well-tended gardens in the distance. The other showed a black-and-white reproduction of a nineteenth-century gothic painting. It looked like an etching or lithograph, probably a bookplate removed from the original volume then reframed. Flea-market kitsch.

The frame was askew. I automatically straightened it, then stepped back.

Was it a print? An image of a desolate moor, a circle of tall standing stones beneath a full moon chased by eerie white clouds. In the center of the stone circle stood a man in a long hooded robe, with tangled dark hair and a scraggly beard, his arms raised to the sky: face twisted and mouth open, imploring or invoking the elements. Art Deco block letters spelled out a title at the bottom of the frame: THE DRUID.

Despite the high cheese factor, there was something disquieting about the image. As I drew closer, I saw another face in the sky, gazing down from between the clouds. Pinpricks of light indicated eyes, a spectral gash of white that appeared to move whenever I tried to focus on it: a niveous gleam like a disembodied grin or the grimace of bared teeth.

"Fucking A," I said in disbelief.

9

"That's an interesting one, eh?"

I jumped, as a heavyset man in loose black trousers and a blue button-down shirt sidled up alongside me. He was barefoot, clean-shaven, with a quarter inch of impeccably trimmed, grizzled hair covering his skull, small bloodshot gray eyes, and a thick gold ring in one ear. He looked less like a rich geek than Mr. Clean on a bender, or the genie you should never have let out of the bottle.

But he had a seductive voice, soft, its slight burr coarsened with age and cigar smoke. "I'm Mallo Dunfries. And you are . . . ?"

"Cass." He stared at me pointedly, taking in the scar beside my eye and the gash below it, and I added, "Neary."

"Delighted to meet you, Cass." His strong hand tightened over mine. I tried not to wince. "You find a drink? Something to eat?"

"Yeah, thanks." I cocked a thumb at the picture of the druid. "Where'd you get this?"

"That?" He rubbed his chin. "An old friend gave me that painting, must be forty years now. Bit over the top, innit?"

"It's not a painting. It's a photo, by a guy named William Mortensen. I've never seen this one before—who'd you say gave it to you?"

"I didn't." Mallo smiled, but his gray eyes were cold. "Is it worth something?"

"If it's a one-off, yeah—might be worth a lot. Even if it's not, it's pretty rare." I pointed to a neat, controlled signature at the bottom of the photo. "See that? He even signed it. All this—" I held my finger a fraction of an inch above the matte print, traced the outline of the standing stones in the air. "He'd set up the shot with lights, models, sets—this would all have been done in a studio, probably early 1930s. His favorite models were his wife and a guy named George Dunham. Mortensen dressed him up like Cesare Borgia, Machiavelli, Paganini—"

"And a druid."

"Right: a druid. Mortensen loved the occult—he was working on a photographic encyclopedia of demonology, but no one's ever found it. He posed photos of the witches' sabbath, Black Mass, demons—all kinds of weird shit. He had a little bondage thing going on, too, sort of pre–Betty Page stuff. Women tied to the stake, Andromeda chained to the rocks. The gorier the better—there's a nice one illustrating 'The Pit and the Pendulum.' You know who Anton LaVey is?"

Mall scrunched up his face. "Name's familiar."

"Another brilliant wacko. Well, more like a really successful con man. He read one of Mortensen's books in the 1960s and founded the Church of Satan."

"You having me on?"

I shook my head. "Who could make this up? A first edition

of Mortensen's books go for big bucks. *The Command to Look*—that's the one LaVey read."

Mallo shot me an amused glance. "How the hell do you know all this?"

"I'm a photographer. Was, anyway."

"Yeah? More like a fortuneteller. " He laughed, crossed his arms, and stared appraisingly at the photo. "What else?"

I tapped a corner of the frame. "He would have spent hours of post-production work on this. Darkroom stuff, projecting images on top of this one—see that face in the sky?"

Mallo peered at the photo, looked at me in surprise. "There's a face there. I never noticed it."

"That's all post-production. He'd have to process the neg first then make a composite print. Wash the paper, dry and flatten it, print it—probably a lot of spot dodging—then mess with the emulsion. Paint over it with oils, scrape stuff off with a razor blade. He'd have to make a super-hard emulsion so the paper wouldn't tear.

"Then, you know, all kinds of retouching—carbon pencil, pumice stone, powder tone, gum eraser, ink, sable brush. I mean, look at this shit . . ."

I indicated the darkest part of the sky. "That's Chinese black—Sumi ink pigment. They'd burn black walnuts and mix the soot with animal glue. Mortensen would grind up the ink and make his own powder tone from crayons scraped across fine sandpaper."

Mallo snorted. "He sounds like a nutter."

"Definitely an obsessive. But he was a visionary, you know? You can do this kind of thing today with a fucking smartphone in ten seconds. He'd spend *days* on it. This is what Mortensen was famous for—manipulating images, almost proto-CGI. And he was vilified for it. Ansel Adams called him the Antichrist, but Mortensen's like the patron saint of Photoshop and Instagram."

"Very impressive. How much did you say this was worth?"

"If it's a monoprint, it could go for five, ten grand."

Mallo's mobile phone pinged. He glanced at it and made a face. "Well, thank you for the photography lesson. Morven will be pleased to know that picture's worth something—she's always hated it."

With a nod, he turned and walked back toward the living room.

I continued to peruse the druid photo. Mortensen's work had always made me slightly queasy: as though all the elements that comprised one of his images, ink and charcoal pencil, acetate and toner and silver salts, mutated into some kind of virus that attacked my optic nerve. After a few minutes, I shouldered my bag and hurried on, turning a corner into an empty hallway.

I rapidly opened doors—storage closets; a compact washer/dryer unit; a wall of circuitry that appeared to be a security system. I thought of the omnipresent CCTV signs in the streets, looked around for a camera. I didn't see one, but I bet Mallo could afford technology that would fit on the head of a pin. If anyone questioned me, I'd say I was looking for a bathroom. Which, of course, I was.

At the end of the corridor a door was cracked open. Inside was a large bedroom. More windows; polished floor covered by white Flokati rugs; king bed heaped with nubby silk pillows. A glass vase of red tulips on a nightstand, with a framed color photo on the wall above it: Morven Dunfries, maybe fourteen. Long blond hair veiled her face and blinding sunlight streamed through an open window behind her, so that her breasts could be clearly seen through a sheer white slipdress.

I leaned over the nightstand to examine the picture more closely. It had been taken in hard light, with a Big Shot camera—Andy Warhol's favorite, the one he used for all those close-up photos you used to see on the cover of *Interview Magazine.* Manufactured for only two years in the early seventies, the Big Shot was designed for indoor flash portraits, with a fixed-focus viewfinder set for thirty-nine inches from the subject. The photographer had to move around her subject until she got it in range, a bizarre little dance known as the Big Shot Shuffle. This photo had been shot indoors, but even with all that sun flooding though the window, the photographer had used a flash. Morven's pupils glowed eerily red, and I'd bet that the Big Shot's flash diffuser had been removed.

Hard light was a strange choice for a photo of a beautiful young girl. It gives a sharp edge to everything, throws it all into harsh relief, with no subtlety as it transitions from dark to light. It's what you get with a flash or other single light source, like the sun on a cloudless day. Ugly light.

And even if there was no sign of the ocean, I recognized the reflected glitter of sea and mica in the sun flooding that open window as Atlantic light. You get a more compressed light if you shoot by the Atlantic Ocean, in the Northern Hemisphere, anyway. The water's darker, and the composition of the sand's different—if you have sand, rather than rocky crags and gravel beach.

Pacific light is like you tossed handfuls of pearl dust into the air, milliseconds before you pressed the shutter release. The sand there is formed by eons of shells being ground into the shoreline and ocean floor, shells you don't find in the western Atlantic—abalone, tritons, Pandora clams. If you're a great photographer, or just a lucky one, you can catch a flicker of that lost iridescence in the light reflected from Pacific waves crashing on a beach.

Atlantic light is less forgiving. But whoever had taken this photo had captured it, to a degree that made it almost painful to look at, like squinting into the sun. I could see it in the girl's eyes, coruscating crimson within those turquoise irises, and in the nuclear-bomb glow of her bare arms and throat. Mostly I saw it in the dance of sun and skin and silk around her breasts, where her slip shimmered like a net filled with bioluminescence. You can't get that effect with digital—it's dependent on the granularity of film, the physical interaction of light with ferrous salts and gold chloride and glass or paper.

The image was disturbing. Morven seemed barely past puberty. It reminded me of the notorious original cover art for the *Blind Faith* album—a nude shot of a very young teenage girl, heavy-lidded and with Pre-Raphaelite curls, holding a model airplane against a backdrop of blue sky and unnaturally green grass. A totally in-your-face photo. Polydor pulled it from the LP's U.S. release in 1969. This Polaroid would have been taken just a few years later.

I looked around and saw another photo propped on a shelf above the bed. Same vintage, same camera, same harsh sunlight: three young teenage girls with their arms around each other. One was Morven, dressed as in the other photo. The second had dark curly hair that obscured her face, so all I could see was a full-lipped grin. The third was tall, auburn-haired, her head turned as though someone had called to her from just outside the frame. The nagging sense of some lost, long-ago memory tugged at me, but I pushed it aside.

I stepped away from the nightstand—Mallo's side of the bed, to judge from the reading glasses set atop a copy of the *Finan-*

cial Times—and crossed to where the wall held three recessed doors. The first two opened onto his-and-hers walk-in closets. Despite his predilection for going barefoot, Mallo had twice as many shoes as his wife, most of them riffs on biker boots.

Door number three opened on a bathroom that must have cost as much as a Tracey Emin nude. Heated terra-cotta tile floor. Gilt-framed mirrors on the wall. The twin sinks were Edwardian antiques retrofitted with nickel faucets. There were separate alcoves for toilet and bidet, and a celadon-tiled rain shower behind a glass wall. Bottles of Jo Malone bath scent, Orange Blossom and Pomegranate Noir.

None of this interested me. I was looking for a medicine cabinet.

There didn't seem to be one. Glass shelves held towels and apothecary jars of soaps and toiletries, but I saw no cabinets. Maybe they kept medication in the bedroom?

I wasn't above rifling a gangster's boudoir, but I wasn't that desperate. Yet.

I dumped my camera bag and returned to the wall beside one sink. I ran my hand across the wall, closing my eyes so I could focus on what was beneath my fingertips.

About four inches from the backsplash, a vertical seam extended from the ceiling to the sink counter. I opened my eyes, splayed my hand across the wall, and pushed.

A panel rotated outward, displaying an array of glass shelves, handily lit so I could see rows of prescription pill bottles and tubes of ointment. I picked up one bottle, turned to read the label, and in the mirror above the sink glimpsed a face. Not my own.

10

"What the fuck do you think you're doing?"

Mallo Dunfries's soft voice might almost have been amused, but his face was bright pink, his bloodshot eyes icy gray. He strode across the room, grabbing my satchel in one hand and my throat in the other. The pill bottle clattered to the floor as he shoved me against the wall, pinning me there as he dug into my bag. Terror flooded me as I thought of the U.S. passport hidden in my boot.

Mallo pulled the Swedish passport from my satchel, opened it, and stared at the photo. "Dagney Ahlstrand. You said you were Cass somebody."

"I am," I choked. "That's—"

"Shut up."

He rummaged in the bag until he found my wallet and driver's license. "Cassandra F. Neary, New York, New York." He looked at me. "I assume the *F* stands for *fucked*. Because you are."

His fingers dug into my windpipe, his frozen gaze never wavering from mine.

"How'd you get in?" His hand dropped from my throat. "Who sent you here? Gligor?"

"Adrian invited me," I gasped. "I only got here yesterday—check the passport. I was looking for speed."

I hate resorting to the truth, but sometimes it's the only way.

Mallo scowled. He checked the Swedish passport again, held it beside my driver's license, comparing the photos, and set the passport on the sink counter. He dropped the wallet back into the satchel and rifled through my few items of clothing until he found my camera. He examined it carefully, popping the lens cap and scrutinizing the shutter release, exposure settings, viewfinder.

"This a digital camera?"

"No. DSLR. I shoot on film. Black and white."

He opened the back of the camera, exposing the film, and I groaned.

"My Tri-X." I tried to keep my voice steady. "That's nearly all that's left."

"Yeah?" He yanked out the ribbon of film and tossed it on the floor. "Now there's none. Where's your mobile?"

I fought the urge to grab the camera and smash it in his face. "I don't have one."

Mallo looked at me in disbelief. "You don't have a smartphone? iPhone, anything like that?"

"No."

"You're telling me you're a photographer and you don't own a phone or digital camera?"

I nodded. His brow furrowed. After a few moments, he replaced the lens cap, closed the back of the camera, and tossed it into my bag on the floor. Then he pulled out a mobile, picked up the Swedish passport, and handed it to me.

"Hold that next to your face—open it, so I can see her photo. Dagney whoever the fuck she is."

I did as he ordered. Novae burst as the flash went off and bounced across the mirrors behind me. Mallo cursed and took another picture, this time without the flash. He eyeballed the photo on the mobile's screen, looked at me, and shook his head.

"You must be fucking out of your mind," he said. "Only a fucking idiot would come here and break into my things."

"I didn't break in. The cupboard was open. I told you, I was—"

"Looking for speed, right." He gave his mobile a cursory swipe. "Fucking drug addict. I should just call the cops. But it's Morven's birthday, and I don't really like cops. Care to tell me why you're here on a stolen passport?"

I stayed mum, and he shrugged. "No skin off my tits. May I have that?"

He held out his hand. I gave him Dagney's passport and stared at the floor, praying he wouldn't search me and find the U.S. passport in my boot.

"Where are you staying?" he demanded.

"With Krishna Morgenthal."

Mallo stabbed a finger at me. "Not now you aren't. Let's go."

He kicked my bag across the room, waited for me to retrieve it, and followed me out the door. "I won't mention this to Morven until later," he said as we walked back to the living room. "You'd be better off dead if she knew you'd been in her bedroom."

The flat was less crowded now, the air sweet with candle smoke and melted wax. People were holding plates with slivers of chocolate cake on them. In a corner Morven laughed as she drank champagne from a crystal flute, a bunch of red tulips cradled against her breast. Mallo smiled at her, and she blew him a kiss.

I looked away, afraid my face would betray me, and spotted Adrian Carlisle on a nearby couch, bookended by two women. One was Krishna, her eyes shut and Adrian's hat at a tipsy angle on her head. On his other side, a stocky redhead dug through a crocodile Birkin bag. I started toward the couch and Mallo grabbed my elbow.

"Don't leave," he said. "If you do, you'll never get back home."

He turned and headed toward his wife.

I hurried to join Adrian. He wore the same moth-eaten jacket he'd had on that morning, and his pointed leather shoes were stained with damp. His brow creased as he stared at me.

"You," he said.

"Ha!" The redhead beside him held up a screwdriver. "I told you I had one."

"That's lovely, Gretchen." Adrian gave her a perfunctory smile. "Go on now, love, see if you can find someone to stick it in."

She stumbled to her feet and lurched off. Adrian gently pushed Krishna aside so I could sit.

"Cassandra, is it?" he said. "Krish couldn't remember if you were here or not."

I stared at Krishna, leaned down to touch her cheek. Her skin felt slick and clammy. I knew if she opened her eyes, they'd be pinned. I recalled what I'd seen earlier—Morven slipping something into Krishna's hand.

"Doesn't look like she can remember her own name," I said. "She's nodded out."

"What's in a name? A nose by any other name would find blow as sweet. Here."

He slid a hand inside his jacket to produce a vial with a tiny spoon attached and passed it to me. I did a couple of spoonfuls and handed it back.

"Better?" he asked.

"Define *better.*"

I drank a glass of champagne someone had left on the side table, and thought of Mallo's photo of me holding Dagney's stolen passport. Quinn was going to kill me, assuming I lived to find him. I set down the empty glass and buried my head in my hands.

"There there. The cake's very nice." Adrian indicated a plate on the table. "Have a bite."

"I don't want any fucking cake."

"No need to be rude. Oh, look. Our host."

He rose to greet Mallo, who cut him off with a black look.

"My office," said Mallo. He pointed at me. "You too."

He stalked from the living room. Adrian glanced at me in dismay. "How do you know Mallo?"

"We bumped into each other in the bathroom."

Adrian said nothing, but his expression grew dire.

I followed him past the kitchen and down the hall to a small windowless office. Industrial shelving was filled with stacks of flattened cardboard cartons, FedEx envelopes, and packing materials. Rolls of candy-colored wrapping paper protruded from cubbyholes where loose coils of ribbon cascaded to the floor like a melted rainbow. Laptops and smartphones in charging stations covered another shelf. On a cheap Ikea desk, a framed photo of Mallo and Morven at the beach leaned against a glass paperweight shaped like a dachshund. It looked like a home office belonging to an eBay dealer, though with no indication as to what, exactly, was sold.

Mallo sat in a swivel chair by the desk. When he saw us, he turned to open a drawer, reached inside, and withdrew a silvery object. Light glinted off a wedge of steel blade as he spun his chair to face us. A cigar cutter. I heard the hiss of Adrian's breath.

"Cassandra." Mallo beckoned me toward him. "Please. Come on in."

11

I didn't move. Mallo watched me, then turned. He dropped the cigar cutter, opened another drawer, and removed something else. Without a word, he tossed it to me.

I caught it: a neatly wrapped box, roughly the size and weight of a brick. Foil wrapping paper imprinted with cobalt stars, a fizz of blue and silver ribbons.

"I'd like you to deliver that to a friend of mine," Mallo said. "In the Barbican. He won't be expecting you. Just tell him it's a birthday present."

I stared at the package. "What's the Barbican?"

"Adrian will show you; he's good at finding his way in the dark. Drop back by here when you're done. Shouldn't take more than, oh—"

He glanced at his mobile. "Let's say I'll see you at midnight. Adrian's evening will just be getting started. Right, Adrian?"

Adrian nodded. "Sounds about right."

As Mallo glanced away to shut the drawer, Adrian looked at

me with barely contained fury. I glared back, then turned to Mallo.

"What about my passport?"

"Your passport?" Mallo shrugged. "I wouldn't know about that. Swedish girl's probably reported hers missing by now. Not that much resemblance if you look closely."

He held up the mobile so I could see my own stunned face staring back at me, Dagney's passport alongside it. "Actually, it doesn't look much like you at all," he said. "Now, get the fuck out of here. Both of you."

He stood and watched as Adrian and I walked down the hall. I shoved the gift-wrapped box into my bag.

"Midnight, Cinderella," Mallo called after us. "I don't want to be carving any pumpkins."

Everyone else appeared to have left. Morven stood by the door, seeing the last few guests off. Adrian made a detour to get his hat from the couch, where Krishna was still passed out. He bent over her—he really *was* checking her pulse—then returned and grabbed my wrist.

"You wait here," he commanded.

He approached Morven Dunfries and kissed her cheek, retrieved his overcoat from a closet, and gestured for me to join him.

"Keep moving," he ordered, steering me toward the door.

I avoided Morven's eyes but knew she watched me closely. When we were in the hall with the door closed behind us, I turned to Adrian. "What about Krishna?"

"She'll wake up. Morven's given her some cheese so she can play with her later."

"Cheese?"

"Heroin and paracetamol. Starter junk."

Outside the rain had stopped, but the wind was raw and relentless, blowing sheets of water from rooftops and awnings. Not many people were braving the weather. A young couple huddled beneath an umbrella on the corner, seemingly oblivious to anything except each other. An elderly woman pushed a stroller wrapped in plastic, talking to herself. A younger woman—black, with cropped platinum hair nearly hidden inside the hood of a stained military parka, and eerily pale topaz eyes—stood inside a doorway, smoking. As I passed I could sense her gaze following me. I glanced back, and she turned away.

"Keep your head down," Adrian muttered.

The wind whipped his long coat around his scissor legs. With his top hat, black Chesterfield, and ferocious expression, he resembled a magician who'd pull a cobra out of that hat instead of a rabbit. When we reached an empty bus shelter, he darted beneath its metal awning and called a cab.

"Five minutes," he said, replacing his mobile. He removed his hat, snapped it closed, and slipped it inside his overcoat. Then he shoved me against the bus shelter wall. "What the fuck did you do?"

I shoved him back. "Nothing!"

"What kind of nothing?"

"I wandered into the wrong bathroom."

"I'd say so."

"What does he use the cigar cutter for?"

"What do you think?" Adrian's face was pale, his pupils huge and black. "Cigars. And fingers. He sells them to an artist he knows in Brick Lane who makes jewelry out of the bones."

"Who buys that kind of stuff?"

"Rich goths. Musicians. Can't keep up with the demand.

Back in the eighties, a mate of mine was arrested with some students from Cambridge. They were breaking into graves and making flutes out of the bones. He got off, I don't know how. The others did some prison time. Body snatchers."

I grimaced, and Adrian looked at me with contempt. "Oh, you're above that, are you? Never underestimate what folks will do to get by. The clock is moving backward—child slaves, plague, decapitations in the street. Soon they'll be burning women at the stake—wait, done that, too.

"You think London's like the books and movies? It is—only not the ones you'd want to live in. The golden city is dead."

We didn't speak again until the cab arrived. Once inside, I sat as far as possible from Adrian. The driver slid open the plexiglass window so Adrian could give him the address, then closed it again. Adrian slumped against his seat. I took out the gift-wrapped package and turned it over in my hands.

"Don't think of opening that," said Adrian. "Not unless it's addressed to you."

"It's not addressed to anyone." I held it to my ear and shook it. "What do you think it is?"

"How would I know?" His eyes said he was lying. "Not my business. Or yours."

"Drugs?"

"Did you hear what I just said?" he snarled. "Put it away, otherwise I'm off. I've spent my whole life getting along with Mallo. You've managed to fuck that up in an hour. You can get carved for a pumpkin on your own."

I put the package in my bag. My head felt scraped raw from fatigue. I wondered what the odds were of Adrian offering me more of his blow. Probably not good.

"It won't be drugs," he said after a minute.

"Then why does he need us to deliver this?"

"I'm not delivering it. You are. I'm just seeing you get there."

"And back."

"And back." His tone suggested he was considering a way to avoid this.

"Why didn't he just give it to you?"

"He wants me for a watchdog. That's my punishment for being idiot enough to bring you to the party. You're on a chain now, too. Stolen passport? No fixed address? Don't make any long-term plans."

"What's to keep me from just taking off?"

"Nothing, except that I won't let you. I *can't* let you. And you'd be dead by daybreak if you did, not that I give a fuck. But I don't fancy getting killed for someone stupid enough to go wandering around Mallo Dunfries's flat, doing whatever the fuck you were doing. What *were* you doing?"

"Trying to find the bathroom."

"Yeah, right."

Adrian had the cab stop a few blocks from our destination.

"You're paying," he said, opening the door to step out. I counted out the fare, handed it to the driver, and joined Adrian on the sidewalk. The cab drove off, leaving us on a nearly empty street.

"This is the City," Adrian said. "Bankers and day traders. Not much after dark."

I had to run to keep up with him, past forests of construction cranes, an ancient fragment of the original London Wall dwarfed by the skyscrapers surrounding it. Shadows drenched a narrow street lined with far older buildings, like a gaslight movie set. Adrian compulsively checked his mobile for the time.

My heart pounded from coke, exhaustion, blunt fear. I flashed back to something I'd seen when I was fourteen: a slowly rotating whirlpool of cloud with a huge implacable eye at its center, staring down to where I stood in a field.

"Watch it!" Adrian pulled me from a curb as a bus roared past. "You're looking the wrong fucking way."

We ran across the street and continued until we reached a vast complex of brutalist structures with pebbled concrete facades and rows of square windows.

"This is it," Adrian said, stopping at a concrete stairway. "Do you remember the address? Was it five-one-seven?"

"I think so."

Adrian started up the steps, two at a time. "I knew a bloke lived here twenty years, and he still gets lost."

We reached the next level, walked quickly down a passage, then raced up a second stairway. A passing couple glanced at us curiously. Adrian yanked me to his side.

"I told you to keep your head down," he warned.

An elevated walkway ran along the interior of the complex, overlooking a man-made lake. Security lights gave the water a sickly, irradiated glow. Another walkway ran parallel to ours, a long tube sheathed in plexiglass with barrel-vaulted crosswalks between its sections, like a human-sized gerbil habitat.

There were no people inside it. There were no people anywhere I could see. Plastic grocery bags blew along the concourse like tumbleweeds. The air smelled foul, like an abandoned swimming pool. Everything looked desolate in the way that once-trendy developments do, an aging club kid hanging on to a dead glowstick and cheap clothes that no longer fit.

"What is this place?" I asked. "They could shoot a zombie remake of *Logan's Run* here."

"1970s utopian experiment. Remember those? This was

Cripplegate, bombed out during the Blitz. The Barbican was supposed to be the future—one big complex with affordable flats, theaters, couple schools. Shops and cafes. All still here, except the affordable part. People bought into it forty years ago and never moved on. Supposed to be an artist's ideal, and I guess it was, if you had the tin. Costs a fortune now."

We halted in front of a security gate. Adrian gave it a push, and it creaked open.

"That's you." He gestured at a dank stairwell. "Five-one-seven's up there somewhere."

I shivered and jammed my hands into my pockets. "What about you?"

"I'll be waiting. Just drop it and run. *Go.*"

He pushed me, and I ran up the narrow stairwell, its landings strewn with flattened cardboard and empty bottles. Someone slept here. There were no windows, no doors; only water-stained walls, a flickering bulb at each landing above signs warning THIS IS PRIVATE PROPERTY. SECURITY WILL ESCORT ALL OTHERS TO THE STREET.

After six flights, the stairs ended. Another broken gate opened onto a slab of cracked concrete, where a metal fence surrounded a dollhouse garden of begonias. Their blossoms looked like chunks of uncooked liver. Behind the fence, almost close enough for me to touch, a curved glass wall enclosed a yurt-shaped room.

Whoever lived here got few visitors—the windows had no curtains. I could see a couch covered with kilim pillows, and the cozy yellow glow of table lamps. On the far side of the room, someone moved back and forth.

I took the wrapped package from my bag, pressed a buzzer on the fence. The shadowy figure stopped and looked around, then walked to the door and cracked it to peer out. A fortyish man with rumpled dark hair and bifocals jammed onto a beaky nose.

"Yes?"

I cleared my throat. "I have a birthday present for you."

I held up the beribboned box, and the man's eyes widened. A voice called from another room. "Who is it, Dad?"

"No one! I'll be right there."

"It's from your friend," I said. I doubt my smile was reassuring. "In Crouch End."

"Crouch End." The man opened the door, stuck his head out, and peered around. "Oh. Right . . ."

He thrust his hand at me, and I gave him the package. He turned it over, nodded. "Well, that was fast. Tell him thanks."

He ducked back inside, and I heard the snick of dead bolts being turned.

I raced down the six flights of steps, my satchel bouncing against my side. I listened for sirens, footsteps in the passage behind me. There was only silence. When I reached the bottom of the stairwell, Adrian flung open the security gate and held up his mobile so I could see the time: 11:38.

I paid for the cab back to Crouch End without argument. We stumbled out into the street and raced down the alley behind the old theater. Adrian identified himself at the intercom, and we were buzzed into the interior courtyard and then the building. Once inside the creaking elevator I turned to Adrian.

"What time is it?"

He flashed his mobile: 12:03.

12

Mallo opened the apartment door. I didn't dare look at Adrian. Mallo laughed.

"You made record time. I got a text saying the package was delivered half an hour ago."

He stepped out into the hall with us. A moment later Morven appeared behind him. She cocked her head at me. "Is this her?"

Her husband nodded. Without warning, Morven grabbed my hair and yanked me toward her. I kicked out, but before my boot could connect Mallo had me against the wall, his breath hot against my face.

"Don't you—"

"Let her go," Morven commanded. "I have a job for her. Get that package."

Glowering, Mallo released me and went back into the apartment. I met Morven's stare, her aquamarine eyes shining and cheeks flushed, snaky hair framing that sharp little face. She'd won a few catfights in her time. At the sound of footsteps, she glanced aside as her husband returned. "Thanks, love."

She reached to take a small package from Mallo. I tried to calculate whether there was any chance of making a run for it.

"Here," she said.

She waited for me to extend my hand, then set the package in my palm and folded my fingers over it. Her fingernails dug into my flesh. "Adrian, make sure she doesn't get lost."

Adrian gave a little hiss of displeasure but said nothing.

Mallo stepped alongside his wife. "Tomorrow's soon enough, right, love?" He winked at Adrian, then me. "He'll put you up."

I glanced down at the packet. Another gift box, this one wrapped in marbleized paper, gold thread twined around it instead of ribbon. Scarcely big enough to hold a ring, or earrings.

"Pretty," I said.

Mallo nodded. "I like wrapping them."

"And this." Morven handed me a Post-it note with an address scrawled on it. "That's where it goes."

I read the note. "Stepney?"

Adrian started. Mallo made a gun of his fingers and aimed it at him. "Once it's taken care of, let Adrian know. Don't come here again, and don't you ever fucking call me."

"I told you, I don't have a phone."

"You belong in a museum." Mallo looked at me with mingled disgust and admiration. "Only reason you're walking God's green earth is because of what you told me about your friend Mortensen's photo."

"What about the photo you took of me?"

"Hostage to misfortune. Or life insurance. Keep her in your sights," he warned Adrian, and stepped back into the flat.

Morven remained, eyes narrowing as she drew her face close to mine. I flinched as she touched the scar beside my eye. "What happened to you?"

I said nothing, and she pushed me away.

"Where's Krish?" asked Adrian.

"I've taken care of her," said Morven. She went back inside, closing the door in my face.

I wrapped the gift box in one of my extra sweaters and stuffed it into my satchel. I did the same with the Konica, and started to run down the hall.

Adrian caught up with me by the elevator. He grabbed my satchel and yanked it so that I spun around.

"You worthless cunt! For five quid I'd drop you down there—"

He pinned me against the elevator door, pushing aside the folding metal gate so that my foot dangled in the gap. I could see the metal roof of the elevator car, one floor below us.

"Mallo has a cleaning crew on call, twenty-four seven," Adrian whispered. "Do you understand what I'm saying?"

His arm snaked past me to punch a button on the wall. I heard the elevator car begin to inch upward. My hair tangled in the latticed gate as cold air streamed from the shaft, sharp with the chemical scent of disinfectant.

"Do you understand?" Adrian's eyes were aflame. "Say it."

"I understand," I gasped.

He moved away and I fell forward, catching myself before I hit the floor. Behind me the elevator jolted to a stop. Adrian pulled me with him into the car and pressed the down button.

"I hate this lift," he said.

Once outside, we trudged down the street in silence. The

freezing rain had started up again. Adrian took out his hat, snapped it open, and shoved it onto his head. I shivered miserably. My leather jacket and cowboy boots were soaked through, my feet wet and numb with cold. I wondered despairingly if my U.S. passport had been damaged.

I asked, "How far is it?"

"Bit of a ways, there's no direct route." He sounded resigned and as tired as I felt. "We could get a cab, but it's quicker to walk through Queen's Wood. What was all that Mallo was saying about some bloke's photo?"

"I'm a photographer." I opened my satchel just enough that he could glimpse the Konica and quickly shut it against the rain. "He yanked one of my last rolls of film. Fucking asshole."

"That looks like an antique."

"Almost."

"Do you actually use it?"

I flushed. Adrian laughed. "You've got to be joking. There's not a place left in London where you could get a roll of film processed. You ought to thank Mallo—he did you a favor."

I spat on the sidewalk and said nothing.

After about fifteen minutes, we turned from the High Street onto a road lined with semi-detached houses, and eventually reached a small park. We skirted this, stopping at an enclosed walkway that looked like part of an abandoned construction site. Beers cans and trash floated in filthy puddles beside a plywood wall. The other wall was a chain-link fence festooned with plastic bags. Beyond the fence stretched a forest of black trees.

"That's Queen's Wood." Adrian motioned for me to hurry. "Two people were killed here last year. They caught the guy who did it, but . . ."

I stooped to grab an empty wine bottle, smashed the bottom against the concrete, and straightened. Adrian raised an eyebrow. "You're not planning to use that on me, are you?"

"Not unless I need to."

I walked directly behind Adrian, pacing him until we reached the end of the walkway. I could see his shoulders relax as we stepped out onto an expanse of half-frozen mud, gouged with countless foot- and pawprints. Using his mobile as a flashlight, he swept it through the darkness so I could see.

"Some of these trees are a thousand years old," he said. "Queen's Wood, Hampstead Heath—this all used to be the Forest of Middlesex. Watch your step, it's rough going."

The trees were immense, far taller and older than any tree I'd ever seen. Their leafless, interlocking branches provided some protection from the rain, though the muddy trail was treacherously slick, its skim of ice giving way beneath each step I took. Tree trunks and blowdowns, rocks and half-rotted benches were all webbed with ivy that rippled as though unseen creatures moved beneath the green-black leaves.

I stopped and held my breath, listening to the steady drip of rain, branches creaking in the wind, a distant siren. I tossed the broken wine bottle and moved on.

Adrian walked unhesitatingly through the darkness, following the firefly glow of his mobile. He'd been this way before. We clambered up and down steep inclines, through mud that was ankle deep. I tried to keep my satchel dry. I didn't want to think about what Mallo would do if his precious packet got damaged. Once I tripped, and Adrian grabbed my arm before I impaled myself on a dead branch.

"This is insane," I gasped. "It's like fucking Mirkwood."

"Supposedly a coven met here at the full moon, but that was

before my time. Morven told me they were friends of hers. I think she actually joined in."

"Christ," I said. "Why doesn't that surprise me? Are you sure you know where you're going?"

"I live here. Be very careful—keep your foot on that log. And watch the steps, they're very slippery."

In front of us rose a set of mossy stone stairs. Adrian mounted them expertly, grabbing onto branches to keep his balance. I followed, gritting my teeth as the branches bit into my palms and stray vines whipped my cheeks.

When I reached the top, I found Adrian standing in front of a chain-link fence that was nearly invisible beneath a blanket of ivy, leaves black as though tarred. Motioning for me to keep quiet, he walked alongside the fence for perhaps twenty yards. I followed as silently as I could, until he stopped.

"I'll go first," he said in a low voice. "Hang on."

With great care, he pulled back a matted curtain of vegetation and slipped beneath it. I heard a scraping sound, then Adrian's muffled voice.

"All right, come through. Watch your step."

I pushed aside the ivy, revealing a hole in the chain-link fence large enough to step through. On the other side, Adrian held a plywood panel, painted black and covered with dead ivy. After I ducked through the gap, he slowly lowered the panel back into place. Once it was flush against the fence again, it was impossible to distinguish it from the overgrown wall.

Adrian turned and trudged across a rank lawn, almost as overgrown as the woods we'd just left. Cracked terra-cotta pots held thorny nests of dead roses. Something scrabbled in the ruins of a pergola. Broken glass surrounded the skeleton of a small greenhouse.

At the edge of the lawn stood a four-story Victorian brick home with boarded-up windows, slate roof shingles, and brick-and-clay chimney pots. Light leaked from the perimeter of several upstairs windows that appeared to be heavily curtained.

"Dulce domum," said Adrian, and headed for a back door.

13

At the door, I waited as Adrian pulled out an impressive bunch of keys. I counted four padlocks, all nearly new, in addition to the original copper doorplate, now green with verdigris.

"You're squatting here," I said.

"Me and a few others."

He opened the fourth and final lock, pushed the door, and stepped inside. I followed, peeling off my leather jacket to shake off the rain and knocking as much mud from my boots as I could. I checked my bag to determine that both Mallo's package and my camera were safe, and turned to Adrian.

"How long you been here?"

"Not that long." He removed his hat and ran a hand through his wet hair. "I came in July. It was more pleasant than it is now."

We were in what must have been a sun room or conservatory, dark save where Adrian's mobile cast its wan glow across a tile floor strewn with dead leaves. The window beside the door had been broken and repaired with a lattice of plywood and two-by-fours.

"It's owned by the Saudi royal family," Adrian went on. "Been vacant for years. There's places like this all over. The Arabs buy them up as tax dodges and never visit them. Or Russians. Billionaires Row in Hampstead. Highgate, Brixton. Used to be you could squat with impunity for months or even years. Pay for the electric and slide rent to the landlord if you felt noble. Then they passed laws to keep people out. Now it's a crime."

He pointed at the broken window. "That's where we got in. We put in all new locks. From outside you can't tell we're here, and so far no one's checked on us—this is probably the last house in North London with no CCTV. The water and electricity's turned off at the mains, but I was able to do something with the water. Just upstairs, and there's no hot. But it's better than nothing."

He bent to pick up a large flashlight, one of several beside the back door, switched it on, and swept its beam across the room. Bicycles leaned against the wall, along with stray tables and chairs, a collapsible baby stroller, and a carton of empty wine bottles. "Let's go."

We went upstairs, footsteps echoing. Silvery mold seemed inextricable from the peeling wallpaper's fleur-de-lis pattern. Everywhere were piles of damp plaster where the crown molding had collapsed, and glass sconces choked with dust. The dark stains left by seeping water looked as though innumerable hands had raked their fingernails down the walls.

When we reached the second floor landing, most of the doors were shut. But I heard voices and smelled cooking—cumin and fried onions, sesame oil, fish. Adrian stopped at a half-open door and poked his head inside.

"Knock knock," he said.

A young woman in a batik turban stood over a table with a

gas camp stove atop it. She turned, dreadlocks wriggling from beneath her turban like spiders' legs. "Hullo, Adrian. You're up early."

"You're up late."

"Just got off work." She poked a wooden spoon into a skillet, and my mouth watered. "I'd invite you in, but I've only got a bit of leftover nosh."

"Thanks, Mariah. We're not hungry, anyway."

"Speak for yourself," I said, as Adrian waved goodbye and we continued down the hall. "Why are you doing this?"

"Doing what?"

"Giving me a place to stay."

"You heard what Mallo said: Keep her in your sights. He wants you inside the tent pissing out. This is my doss."

He unlocked a padlocked door and went inside. I remained where I was.

"What?" he demanded. "You think I'm going to cut your throat? I could've done that back in Queen's Wood. No one would find you for a week. Sleep on the floor if you want."

He started to shut the door, and I quickly stepped inside.

The room was dark and cold and smelled strongly of kerosene. The flashlight's beam moved jerkily across bare walls as Adrian crossed to a table with a hurricane lantern. He lit the lamp, switched off the flashlight, and turned to where I stood, shivering.

"It'll get a bit warmer once I get the heater going. Petrol's so expensive, I mostly just throw on another jumper."

Besides the table, there was a mattress set atop box springs, an armchair upholstered in frayed red silk, and a folding wooden screen. A large kilim rug covered the floor beside the bed. There were no other furnishings, except for a rickety metal clothes rack, stacks of books, and a portable kerosene heater that Adrian was in the process of lighting. Against the wall were two tall metal tanks and a cardboard carton. The room's single window was covered with newspaper to keep light from getting out, or maybe in.

"That's a Tabriz rug." Adrian struck a match, and I heard a *whoosh* as the heater's pilot lit. "I don't ask for much, but what I have should be of enviable quality."

He took off his overcoat and hat and placed them on the floor near the heater, removed some dry clothes from the metal rack, and ducked behind the Chinese screen.

I crossed to check out the tanks: medical grade nitrous oxide, 99.9 percent pure. The cardboard box contained balloons.

"For raves," said Adrian as he re-emerged from behind the Chinese screen, wearing rumpled tweed trousers and a baggy Aran sweater patched at the elbows. I did a double take at his clothing, and he shrugged. "Protective coloration—this is my secret identity. Me and a few of my mates organize raves in abandoned housing."

"You can make a living at that?"

"If you call this living."

I cast a doubtful look around, and noticed a number of photocopied 1990s gig posters on the wall. Altern-8, Orbital, Chemical Brothers.

"I know." Adrian ran a hand across a psychedelic poster advertsing Paul Oakenfold's Spectrum acid club nights at Heaven in Charing Cross. "It used to be more fun. Ibiza, those Sunrise Mystery Trips in Buckinghamshire. Hands-on, balls out, all that. These days we have a Facebook page. At ten we post a number to call for the site of that night's gig. The DJ brings a laptop, someone else brings the sound equipment. Everything's outsourced. Bouncers, lightshow—"

"Drugs?"

He shrugged. "Mostly ecstasy and weed. Ketamine. That's how I got into business with Mallo. Supply and demand, I was the middleman. After he went down I devoted myself to organization. Only thing you need's a mobile and an abandoned site. London has both of those in plenitude. My own needs are modest . . ." He scanned the room. "As you can see. Used to be I stayed in art squats. Now it's just squats. Your turn," he added, gesturing at the wooden screen.

I got my bag, stepped behind the screen, and changed. Even after pulling on two pairs of socks and my two extra black sweaters, I couldn't stop shivering. I put my wet clothes and boots and satchel near the kerosene stove and squatted before it, trying to warm myself.

"Makes you appreciate all mod cons, doesn't it?"

Adrian took out his crocodile leather case and popped a nicotine cartridge into his e-cigarette. He began to wander the room, stooping to straighten books on the floor. After a minute I asked, "Why do you live here?"

"Because I can't afford anyplace else." He reached beneath the clothes rack and pulled out a rumpled sleeping bag that had seen heavy use. "Here."

I took the sleeping bag, nodding thanks. In the late 1970s and early '80s, I'd known plenty of people who squatted in Alphabet City. Most of them were like me, teenage refugees who jumpstarted the punk scene after hearing the Velvet Underground or New York Dolls on cheap stereos in our bedrooms in Wilmington or Jersey City or Trenton or Queens. They made their homes and art and music in abandoned factories by choice, just like they chose to fuck whomever they wanted, or pop heroin or speed, or drink until they blacked out. Within a few years, addiction and AIDS and the bullish NYC art market took all of that away from them, along with their refurbished lofts.

Adrian watched as I unrolled the sleeping bag. "Do you think I do this by choice?"

"I dunno," I said. "You just seemed kind of—"

"Old?" Adrian broke in. "White? Educated? All of the above?" He stared at me disdainfully. "Look at you, twitching because you haven't had a drink in an hour. Stolen passport and thick as a brick, thinking you could break into Dunfries's flat. You'll last fifteen minutes out there. They'll be finding what's left of you in the river or a ditch by the M25."

I scrambled to my feet and grabbed one of my boots. Adrian laughed and quickly sidestepped as I took a swing at him.

"That's the spirit!" His hand shot out and wrenched the boot from my hand. "Calm down. I just wanted to see if you were up to the task. Here: peace offering."

He handed the boot back to me, dipped into his trouser pocket and held up the vial of cocaine. I glared, then snatched it from him.

"Don't be greedy," he said. "There's no more where that came from. Not tonight, anyway."

A few bright bolts to the brain made me feel better. I returned the vial. Adrian finished off what remained, regarded the empty vial with a sigh, and set it on the windowsill.

I glanced around the room. No laptop, no sound system, no coffee maker. Not even a mirror. It was a strangely monastic place. With his top hat and languid air, Adrian had given the impression of being a dandy. Now he seemed like a dissolute college professor in an unraveling sweater and worn tweed trousers, doling out cocaine to a recalcitrant student.

I said, "That address. Where I'm supposed to make the drop. Who is it?"

"Stepney." He looked pained. "Poppy Teasel's."

I did a double take. "Poppy Teasel?"

"You know who she is?"

"The singer?"

"The one and only." Adrian regarded me with wary eyes. "Most people haven't thought of her in yonks."

Neither had I. Poppy had been a notorious California groupie in the early 1970s, only thirteen when she got her start. Her given name was Patricia Teasdale. Rock photographers loved her pansy eyes and tangled black curls, the tiny pentangle drawn on one cheek like a beauty mark. She was one of the two original Flaming Creatures, affecting the 1920s look popular with groupies of that era. Kohled eyes and bee-stung lips; satin negligees worn with lace-up Frye boots; enough long floaty scarves to choke a dozen Isadora Duncans.

Two years later—a century in groupie time—the fashion would shift to hot pants and platform shoes, halter tops over barely-pubescent boobs, floppy hats and long hair. The look that launched a thousand teenage prostitutes.

Poppy had always seemed smarter than that, the kind of kid who should've been cramming for her SATs, on the fast track to UCLA or Wesleyan. Instead she'd hooked up with the rock star A-list, guys who liked their meat rare and barely bleeding. These days, they'd be busted for pedophilia. Back then, no one batted a glittered eyelid at thirteen- and fourteen-year-olds giving blowjobs or doing threesomes in a suite at the Riot Hyatt.

Poppy ended up marrying a second stringer—Jonno Blitz, platinum-haired lead singer in Lavender Rage, a glitter band whose single ripple in glam's wine-dark sea was "Juice It Up (Ballad of a Silver Lover)," a three-minute amphetamine-and-sugar rush produced by Todd Rundgren. The song hit Number One in the UK charts and went Top Ten in the U.S., where it was picked up by an orange juice company. I bet Poppy still got residuals from that one.

Blitz quickly hit the skids and died in time to join the 27 Club. His nineteen-year-old widow had avoided hard drugs while Jonno was alive, but his death and the fact that he'd gone through two million dollars in two years sent Poppy into a tailspin. She started chipping heroin, and within a few months she was a full-blown junkie. A year later she was turning tricks in London.

The story might have ended there, with Poppy joining the same club as her husband. But Poppy had a few aces in the hole she hadn't shown while she was playing strip poker with her rivals in the GTO's and Plaster Casters. Poppy could write. Poppy could sing. And even after half a lifetime as a moving part of the rock-and-roll industrial complex, Poppy was still only twenty-six years old.

She kicked heroin. One night she renewed her acquaintance with Rundgren at London's Batcave. A week later she presented him with demos of half a dozen songs she'd written and recorded on a thirty-dollar cassette player in her basement apartment. Legend has it that Rundgren bought her a plane ticket on the spot and flew her back to the U.S., to record *Best Eaten Cold* in his Bearsville studio. It was the ultimate groupie's revenge: an album of tell-all songs that was a critical success, if not a commercial one. Poppy might have gotten five minutes of fame out of it. Still, that's more than most of us ever see.

I bent to remove Mallo's neatly gift-wrapped package from my bag and stared at it thoughtfully. "Is she still clean?"

Adrian nodded adamantly. He seemed rattled. "Has been for decades. I don't know what that little pressie is, but it's not drugs."

He was lying. Not necessarily about the drugs, but whatever Mallo was up to, Adrian was in it neck-deep. I dropped the packet back into my bag. "She did a gig at the Bottom Line when that record came out," I said. "Blew me away."

"You sound like a fan."

"I was. You know her stuff?"

"A bit. I'm more the 'high on hope' musical demographic." His expression was unreadable. "I'm going to retire for the night. Toilet's down the hall. Take the torch if you go."

He moved the wooden screen closer to his bed, tipped an invisible top hat, and disappeared behind the screen.

Exhausted as I was, that bump of coke made it impossible to sleep. The hurricane lamp guttered to an umber flame then went out. I crouched in front of the kerosene heater, and after half an hour of listening to Adrian's rhythmic breathing, I took the flashlight and ventured to the bathroom. Unfinished hardwood floors, expensive sink and toilet fixture, walls scraped in preparation for a paint treatment that had never materialized. No medicine cabinet, just a few copies of *The Big Issue* and *InStyle* magazine. As I crept back to Adrian's room, I heard a baby wailing from somewhere within the cavernous house, and the ghostly pings of text messages.

Adrian's room was pitch black save for the flutter of gas-blue flames within the kerosene heater, like a ring of tiny UFOs. I kept the flashlight with me and crawled into the sleeping bag, staying as near the heater as possible. My thoughts spun, a familiar amphetamine-induced Catherine wheel of panic, paranoia, and the teeth-grinding urge for another hit. But beneath all the neurochemical fireworks something nagged at me: the distant memory of a word associated with Poppy Teasel, the scents of musk and amber.

Happy sixtieth, dearest Creature . . .

It came to me so suddenly that I jolted upright, only to find myself constrained by the sleeping bag. I rolled onto my stomach, cursing under my breath, and gazed into the heater's ghostly light show.

Poppy had been one of the Flaming Creatures. Just like Morven Dunfries.

14

I pushed myself up onto my elbows and stared at the wooden screen that hid Adrian where he slept.

The Flaming Creatures: That was the source of my lost memory. The spooky hippie girl whose face I dimly recalled seeing in a magazine had been Morven. The magazine had been called *Tell Star!* It debuted in 1973, its subject teenage groupies, who were photographed and interviewed and written about as though they were on the shortlist for the Academy Awards, rather than fourteen-year-old girls whose sole claim to fame was fucking rock stars and roadies.

I'd scanned *Tell Star!* a few times on the newsstand, where it stood alongside *Creem* and *Circus* and *Tiger Beat*, but it was boring and far more banal than any of those. Someone figured out pretty quickly that *Tell Star!*'s most devoted readers were probably not teenage girls in the heartland who dreamed of groupie glory, and pulled the plug on the magazine after three issues. Needless to say, these days copies are scarce and worth a mint.

I thought of the photo of a young Morven in the Dunfrieses'

bedroom. I wondered again who took it; also, who the third girl had been. She too seemed vaguely familiar, but the connection between Morven and Poppy was of little interest to anyone, even me. Adding Mallo Dunfries and Adrian Carlisle and illegal drugs to the daisy chain made it marginally more interesting, if only to a member of law enforcement.

Yet I had the nagging sense that there was something else going on, some hidden pattern I wouldn't be able to discern unless I broke my memory's skin and watched it bleed. Just as Morven's face had lit up some long-buried sector of my brain, so did Poppy Teasel's name.

And Adrian Carlisle's. A song echoed through my mind: no title, just the melody and a few words.

The wind, the wind, the wind blows high . . .

One of Poppy Teasel's—I could hear her hoarse alto prolonging the word *high* like it was the last drag on a cigarette. I closed my eyes and tried to summon the title from my memory.

It was hopeless. If Quinn's musical memory palace was a meticulously restored 1952 Seeburg C, mine was a demolished Sears Lift 'n'Play. I ground my fists against my eyes, pulled the sleeping bag over my head, and tried to sleep.

At some point I woke. It was still dark, save for the blue glow of the gas heater. Behind the wooden screen, something moved, very slowly. Not something: Adrian. I stiffened and watched through slitted eyes, fearful he'd shine a light on me.

But he didn't emerge from behind the screen. It was too dark to see any silhouette or sign of movement, but I could hear him step stealthily from the mattress to the floor. After a moment, I heard another noise, so faint as to be nearly imperceptible—the sound of a carpet being pulled back—and then the faint but distinct scratching of fingernails on a wood surface.

I held my breath and very carefully extended my hand from the sleeping bag until it rested flat against the worn floorboard. I heard a soft *thump,* and beneath my palm felt the floor vibrate slightly.

Where do you think she hides them? I pulled up the floorboards, there's nothing there.

It takes one to know one. I withdrew my hand into the sleeping bag and listened as Adrian picked up something. After a few minutes, he set it back into the floor. I heard a furtive kiss of wood as he replaced the board, drew the carpet across it, and returned to his bed.

I lay awake, trying to judge from his breathing whether he was awake, asleep, or just pretending to be asleep. What was hidden beneath the floorboard? Drugs, probably, or whatever it was that Adrian was helping Mallo smuggle.

But it could also be something that would pose a more immediate threat to me: namely, a gun. I huddled in my sleeping bag and watched light gradually trace the outlines of the room's sole window, until it shone brightly through a rip in the newspaper covering it.

At last Adrian stirred beneath his blankets. I kept my eyes slitted, feigning sleep, and watched until he at last sat up and stepped out from behind the wooden screen. Like me, he'd slept fully dressed. He rubbed his forehead, blinking; then stood and crossed to the kerosene heater and adjusted its setting. A low *whoosh,* and he held his hands over the gas mantel to warm them. I squeezed my eyes shut, willing him to leave. After a few minutes he yawned, then padded from the room, pulling the door shut behind him.

I scrambled from the sleeping bag, darted to the door, and locked it. If Adrian returned I'd say I wanted to get dressed and was worried someone would walk in on me. I hurried to his bedside, dropped to my knees, and slid my hand beneath the kilim rug, running my palm back and forth across the worn wood boards until I felt a small gap. Quickly I yanked back the carpet.

The wooden planks were wide and four or five feet long—the original oak flooring, sanded but unfinished. Old square-head nails pierced the fine grain, but they had been removed from one board and replaced with newer, round-head nails. When I prised my fingernails beneath the edge of this board, it lifted easily. Beneath was the subfloor, its ancient, pitted wood black with age. There was a rectangular gap between two of the boards. I glanced over my shoulder and thrust my hand into the hole.

It was surprisingly deep, and even colder than the room around me. For a moment I was afraid I wouldn't be able to reach whatever was hidden there.

Then my fingers brushed something soft. I grabbed it and pulled it out—a small gray canvas bag, like an old-fashioned mail-bag. I opened it and reached inside. My fingers closed around an object, one of several, none larger than my hand. I turned toward the window to get a better look.

It was an arrowhead. Flint, I guessed; the length of my middle finger and not much wider. Beautifully worked, its edges serrated. The stone was so thin it seemed impossible that someone could have created it without the flint splitting.

I withdrew one of the other objects: a bone, not much larger than a matchstick. I held it up to the light, then tipped the contents of the bag into my palm. Another arrowhead, so tiny I wondered what it might have been meant for—fish? Mice?—and a number of small bones.

I arrayed these on the floor and stared at them. To my unpracticed eye they appeared human. I moved them around as though they were the pieces of a puzzle, arranging them into the shape of a skeletal hand.

Can't keep up with the demand, Adrian had said. For a long moment I stared at the gruesome little tableau, then swept bones and flints back into the canvas bag, folded it, and replaced it where I'd found it. I dropped the floorboard in place, covered it with the rug, and hastily unlocked the door.

I didn't need to hurry. Several more minutes passed, and still no Adrian. I checked to see if my boots had dried, making sure the ziplock bag with my money and passport was still safe, and did a circuit of the room to see if there was anything useful I might have missed last night.

If there was, Adrian had hidden it even better than the artifacts. Other than a few framed pictures propped on the windowsill, I saw nothing new.

I picked up a photo of a younger Adrian with Vivienne Westwood, and another photo of a tall, strong-jawed woman who stood with arms outstretched atop a cliff overlooking the ocean. Judging from her bobbed blond hair and makeup—frosted pink lipstick, blue eyeshadow—the photo dated to the late 1960s.

The only other picture looked as if it had been clipped from a magazine. It showed a stately home of rosy brick, with wood-framed casement windows, turrets, and a neatly raked, circular gravel drive in front. I recognized it as the same Tudor-era building that Mallo had a photo of on the wall beside the

Mortensen print. The highly saturated color suggested it had been taken in the late 1950s. A caption ran beneath the image.

Kethelwite Manor, ancestral home of

The rest of the caption had been cut out of the frame.

Behind me the door opened. I set the photo back onto the sill and turned to see Adrian toss a towel at the clothing rack.

"Bathroom's free." His lugubrious voice filled the room. "I'd take advantage of that before someone else does."

I scooped up my bag and headed down the hall, musing on that magazine photo. The name Kethelwite Manor was unfamiliar, but the place had the look of one of those abandoned country homes taken over by rock stars who'd hole up with snowdrifts of blow and a dozen teenage hangers-on. Fairport Convention at Farley Chamberlayne, Led Zeppelin carousing in Aleister Crowley's Boleskine House. These days they're owned by Russian oligarchs and the same members of the Saudi royal family who'd invested in Adrian's squat.

Why would Adrian and Mallo both have pinups of the same stately home?

There weren't any hints in the hallway here. In daylight, the house was even more depressing. I saw no signs of the anarchic glee I associated with squatting on the Lower East Side half a lifetime ago. No posters or graffiti, no attempts at painting walls or repairing broken windows, beyond covering them with newspaper or cardboard. A baby's thin wail echoed from upstairs, and a black plastic bag tossed in a corner smelled unmistakably of shit.

The bathroom was occupied, so I waited until the young woman I'd seen the night before emerged. Her dreadlocks were now covered by a blue scarf, and she wore faded hospital scrubs patterned with flowers.

"All yours," she said, and gave me a tired smile.

I cleaned up best I could. I ducked my head beneath the cold water tap, then toweled my hair with a newspaper I found on the windowsill. The gash on my cheek was still fresh enough to seep blood if I touched it, so I left it alone and hoped it wouldn't get infected. The star-shaped scar beside my eye shone stubbornly through, no matter how much concealer I used.

In the last three months, two people had said I carried the dead with me. I was starting to look it.

Back in Adrian's room I beelined back to the heater. Adrian had changed into black pants, black Doc Martens and a black Alexander McQueen sweater with a tiny grinning skull on the collar.

"There someplace around here I can get coffee?" I asked.

Adrian stared intently at his mobile, shaking his head. "Caffè Nero down the street. There's some strange shit coming down."

"Meaning what?"

He held up the mobile so I could see a jittery soundless video of running figures silhouetted against a wall of flames, a building engulfed by smoke. Dark starbursts blotched the screen, falling snow or maybe ash from the fire.

"What the hell is that?"

"Police car responding to a call went off the road and smashed into a pump at a petrol station by Sainsbury's. Went up in a fireball. A lot of people were doing their shopping because of the storm; they don't know yet if anyone was killed."

More images flashed across the screen: a woman's mouth open in a silent scream, overturned cars. People crowded outside the entrance to a big-box supermarket, staring in horror at something just out of my range of vision. It was hard to imagine anyone *hadn't* been killed.

"Jesus. Is that nearby?"

Adrian shook his head. "Alperton. They're saying he was going after some kids throwing snowballs at cars. They ran for the petrol station and he plowed right into them. Fucking filth. This is how it starts. Soon they'll be kettling all those folks, right?"

He swiped at the screen. "Yeah, look. *Looters by Canal at Alperton*. Narrowboat in flames, someone says they saw people throwing someone or something from a rooftop. Shit. Now there's a flashmob by Wembley Stadium. Let's go."

He stood and headed for the clothes rack. I stared after him. "What the hell? You're going *out*?"

"We have a job to do. *You* have a job to do. Alperton's an hour and a half away. You hear anything out there?"

He gestured at the window. I walked over and pressed my ear against the glass. "No."

"London is a very big place. But if transport gets fucked up, you'll be on foot. Come on."

I remained where I was. Adrian yanked his overcoat from the rack, glancing over his shoulder. "Did you hear me? Get your stuff, we're leaving."

He pulled on his coat and wrapped a scarf around his neck, stared at his top hat before heading to the door without it.

I got my bag and followed him downstairs, out the back door, and across the rank lawn. Frozen grass splintered beneath my feet, shining in the morning light. A car alarm whooped in the street, setting off a volley of barks from the house next door. High overhead a jet droned. No sirens, nothing but the ordinary sounds of a waking city, somewhat muffled by the snow.

I ducked behind the ivy-covered panel, trailing Adrian. He walked quickly, following the chain-link fence until it ended at the edge of a small parking lot. We crossed the lot without speaking and trudged on to the Highgate Underground Station.

An hour later, fine snow swirled through the streets as we exited at Stepney Green. Despite the bad weather, people still rushed to work, cursing as they slid on the icy street. Snow shovels and calcium chloride appeared to be unknown here. I saw a few shop owners sweeping ineffectually at the sidewalks outside their doors, but no plow trucks or sanders. I stopped at a stall and bought a cheap black watch cap and gloves to replace the ones I'd lost in Iceland, along with a knockoff McQueen scarf covered with tiny grinning skulls.

"Four quid?" Adrian looked offended. "Some Chinese kid got paid ten pence for that."

"Right, and you're the conscience of the nation." I reached to flick the collar of the McQueen sweater peeking from his overcoat. "What did that cost?"

"More than four quid."

"Explain how that's a better thing?"

He remained silent and stony faced as we trudged through the snow. On the train, he'd scrawled a map on the back of one of his cards, along with a phone number. When we reached a busy intersection a short distance from the station, he stopped.

"You're on your own. Ring me when you've done the drop."

"How am I going to do that without a phone?"

He held up a TracFone. "That number goes to this mobile. After I hear from you, it's gone."

He handed me the TracFone, and I pulled the watch cap down over my ears. "That's it? I deliver this and I'm free to go?"

Adrian shrugged. "If Mallo wants you, he'll find a way to be in touch."

With a flick of his long black coat and scissor legs, Adrian disappeared back down the snow-driven sidewalk. I hunched into my jacket and tried to make sense of the map he'd drawn for me, shoved the card into my pocket, and crossed the street.

This part of Stepney was an expanse of aging tower blocks and council housing, pound stores and kebab shops, puncuated by a few terraces that hadn't been bombed to rubble during the Blitz. Blowing snow imparted the grainy texture of damaged film stock: backward glimpses into the ruins of wartime or a keyhole image of a grim near-future. The cold did nothing to cut the stinks of diesel and scorched grease and cigarette smoke. I ducked into a Caffe Nero for some coffee and popped a Focalin from what was left of my stash. I'd have to find another source, or steel myself for the scratched-eyeball panic of withdrawal.

Back outside, I stopped to pull on the cheap gloves I'd just bought, my head down against the snow. When I looked up, I glimpsed a young woman racing past me on the sidewalk. I sucked my breath in and edged back into the doorway.

I'd only seen her for a fraction of a second, but that was enough time to recognize the worn military parka with its dirty fur hood, her cropped platinum hair and topaz eyes. It was the same woman who'd passed me and Adrian on the street last night in Crouch End, minutes after we'd left Mallo Dunfries's flat.

15

They say there's no such thing as photographic memory. But years of seeing the world through a viewfinder left me with the ability to reconstruct an image in my head, as precisely as if I were staring through a loupe. I waited in the doorway until a trio of customers left the cafe, then strode alongside them until I reached the corner, where I sprinted across the street the instant the light changed. I glanced back but saw no sign of the woman in the parka. It might not have been the same person. But I wasn't betting on that.

Poppy Teasel lived in Arbour Square, on a block that had survived both the Blitz and reconstruction. Snow sifted across a terrace of neat three-story brick-and-stucco structures, nearly identical save for one that sported a door painted turquoise. I double checked the address: This was Poppy's place. I glanced down a sidewalk empty except for a man walking a pitbull, hurried up the steps, and rang the bell.

No one answered. I pressed it again, this time kept my finger on the buzzer. I was sweating despite the cold, and the sound of the doorbell lanced me like a fever. I needed a drink. After a minute I heard someone moving inside the house. A shadow passed across curtained windows covered by a metal grille.

"Who is it?" a voice rasped.

"I'm a friend of Morven's."

"What?"

"Morven Dunfries. I have, uh, a present."

Long silence, followed by the click of bolts being drawn. The door suddenly swung toward me and something small and white darted out.

"Who are you?" a slight, white-haired woman demanded. "God damn it."

She lunged down the steps to grab something, then raced back up and tossed a cat through the open doorway before glancing at me in irritation. "For Christ's sake, get inside."

I stepped in, and the door shut with a muffled boom. She turned the dead bolts and straightened, gazing up at me.

As a young teenager, Poppy's intelligence and humor provided ballast to her luscious face and wolf-whistle figure. By the time I saw her at the Bottom Line, junk and cigarettes and general hard living had eroded her beauty while perversely enhancing it, like one of those ancient statues whose iconicity is associated with their deterioration, and even unimaginable without it. Smoking had coarsened her voice: If you closed your eyes in the club that night, you wouldn't have guessed the woman singing was still in her twenties. Betty Boop had morphed into Lotte Lenya.

Now, like Morven, Poppy Teasel looked like one of the Weird Sisters, if she shopped at OxFam. Offstage, she was much smaller than I remembered—almost a foot shorter than me—and much thinner. Her pale skin appeared chalky, almost friable, as if it would crumble if you touched it. Behind a pair of cheap reading glasses, the famous pansy eyes were sunken, the irises so deep a brown they appeared violet. Her once-wild dark hair was straight, bright silver and cut in a severe chin-length bob. She wore loose black yoga pants, beaten-up leather clogs, and gold hoop earrings. A baggy lavender sweater revealed a glimpse of the cleavage that had made her irresistable to every male singer who'd graced the cover of *Circus* magazine. Above her left breast was a calligraphic tattoo identical to Morven's: **FC**. Flaming Creatures.

"Who are you?" She whipped the reading glasses from her face and peered at me, frowning as she took in the scar beside my eye. She smelled of Opium perfume, with an underlying chemical tang.

"Mor—"

"I heard: Morven sent you. Who are *you*?"

I stared at the snow melting around my feet. "Cass. Here."

I reached into my bag for the package and handed it to her. Poppy stared at it, bemused, then smiled wistfully.

"Right. It's her birthday. I'm the one should be sending a present. I've not been well. Were you there?" I nodded. "It must have been a good time."

"It was."

I assumed she'd turn me back out into the snow. Instead she said, "Would you like coffee? Tea? Unless you're in a hurry. I'd like to hear about it."

I hesitated. "Yeah, sure. Coffee would be great."

"You're American," she said, beckoning me down the hall. "I'm from Laguna Beach originally. New York?"

"That's right."

The flat was large but in rough shape. It reeked of cat. Scuffed hardwood floors, cracked plaster walls, a framed poster for the *Best Eaten Cold* album, Poppy resembling a black-haired Stevie Nicks after a long night. In the kitchen: chipped flame-orange Le Creuset pots and a formica-topped table. An old yellow raincoat hung beside the back door. Leggy geraniums in pots lined the windowsill, their blossoms a defiant fuchsia.

Poppy set Mallo's package on the table and began to fill an electric kettle. "Sit. So, how do you know Morven and Mallo?"

I said, "I'm a friend of a friend."

"Which friend?"

I decided to risk the truth. "Adrian Carlisle."

"Adrian?" Poppy started, quickly recovered, and removed a bag of coffee from the freezer. "Is he still in London?"

"As far as I know."

"He was such a beautiful kid." Her voice sounded strained; anguished, even. "So smart, we used to talk about Lawrence Durrell. I always wished we could have stayed close."

I tried to hide my own surprise as I unzipped my jacket, shoved my hat and gloves into a pocket, and dropped my scarf on the table. I looked for any sign of a bottle. Nada, except for some Pellegrino on a counter by the fridge.

"Want some fizzy water?" asked Poppy.

"No thanks."

"I don't have anything else. I quit drinking a long time ago. Quit everything. That was fun." She made a face. "So do you live here?"

"Just visiting."

"Have you been to London before?"

I fought the impulse to snap at her questions. I recognized the defensive maneuver, deployed by people who've spent too much time at the receiving end of a microphone. I wondered how long it had been since she'd had a visitor. The flat had a melancholy air, enhanced by its sweetish, sickroom scent.

"I've been here a couple of times," I said. "Not in a while."

"I miss New York. California, never. But I loved the city."

She leaned against the sink and looked at the floor. Her bright cap of silvery hair had shifted so that I could see dark lesions on her bare scalp. A wig. Poppy raised her head to stare at me, violet eyes burning in her haggard face. She nodded, as though I'd asked a question.

"I have cancer," she said. "Milk or sugar?"

"Black's fine."

She poured boiling water into a cafetière, watched the grounds swirl then settle. "I lost touch with Adrian a long time ago. He stayed away from smack but got pretty badly into coke, didn't he?"

"I wouldn't know."

"Bad for the heart." She laughed hoarsely, pressing one hand against her chest. "That and lead guitarists. He would have been better off getting heroin through the NHS."

Her mouth twisted as she reached to pick up my scarf and traced the outline of one of its patterned skulls. "Now this never goes out of style, does it?"

She let the scarf's folds slide through her knobbed fingers, turned away to pour coffee. "Here, we can take these into the living room." She handed me a mug and picked up her package. "Pretend it's my birthday; you can watch me open my present."

Again, I recognized the old-style groupie manner—ingratiate yourself with strangers, confide in journalists, plead with drug dealers; then seduce all of them. In another era, she would have been an aging survivor of the Parisian Beau Monde. Now she was a relic of another lost demimonde. Beautiful People who die young become immortal. The rest just die.

The living room faced the street. Yards of dusty orange silk were draped across the windows. A once-white sofa took up most of the space, its cushions now a fungal gray. A white cat slept on one end, curled like a smaller, cleaner cushion.

"Sit wherever you like," said Poppy.

She settled onto a Moroccan leather hassock, the package in her lap. I sat on the sofa opposite the cat. The room was overheated. I sipped my coffee and waited for the throbbing in my head to subside. I was in no hurry to rush back out into the snow, but the craving for alcohol was starting to gnaw at me. Rats in the brain, Quinn called it.

"I bought this place when the album came out," Poppy said, as though picking up the thread of an interview. "The neighborhood was sketchy—it still is—but it was cheap. I thought I could fix it up when I had money. Only I never did have money." She gave that raspy laugh. "I could have bought a flat in Mayfair for what I spent on smack before I moved here."

She had a beautiful, smoky voice. Honey on sandpaper, Lester Bangs once described it. In the half light, her gaunt features made her resemble one of the Dunfrieses' carved figures as she stared past me at the window. Her skin glistened with sweat and gave off a scent like spoiled peaches. My neck prickled: Whatever damage Poppy had sustained over the decades, it was now indistinguishable from her disease.

"Shall we open this?" she said at last.

She set her mug on the floor, picked up the little box, and shook it. She smiled, not at me but at some recalled memory, and began to unwrap the package. Slowly, unraveling the long ribbons and running a thumbnail beneath each bit of tape, unfolding the bright paper with painstaking care, then smoothing it across her knees. It was like watching someone create an origami in reverse. At last she held up a plain brown cardboard box.

"What do you think it is?" she whispered, her bruised eyes huge.

I said nothing, and she tossed the wrapping paper onto the floor. The cat stirred, then coiled back into slumber. Poppy bent avidly over the little box and withdrew something wrapped in layers of white tissue that fell like a bandage unrolling at her feet. The lines in her face faded, her sunken eyes blanked into shadow.

"Oh," she murmured. "Oh, my goodness."

She picked up a small object and cradled it in her palm, put on her reading glasses then moved to scrutinize it under a lamp. She seemed to have forgotten I was in the room with her.

I started to sweat. What was the protocol for delivering contraband? Did you express polite interest in the product? Ask if there was a return message for the sender?

Or split as silently and quickly as possible? I had just started to my feet when Poppy glanced up at me.

"Look at this."

She extended her hand so that I could see a small disc, about the size of a silver dollar and bone-pale. I stared at it without comprehension. I'd been expecting a ziplock bag of white powder or pills, a wad of cash.

"Go ahead," she urged. "You can pick it up."

I did, careful not to drop it. I thought at first the disc was plastic or maybe Bakelite. But when I leaned into the circle of lamplight I saw that it was irregularly shaped, its surface striated with fine lines easier to feel beneath my fingertips than to see. There was a small hole drilled through the center.

I looked at Poppy. "Is it bone?"

"Mammoth ivory."

"Mammoth ivory?" I held the disc closer to the lamp, turning it back and forth to catch the light. Very faint lines were incised in the center, a pattern that was oddly familiar. "I recognize this," I said, and frowned.

Gingerly, Poppy took the disc from my hand and turned it over. Almost the same image was engraved on the other side, only slightly larger and more rounded: a crude figure, with tiny gashes for eyes. Twin inverted triangles symbolized breasts above a pair of diagonal lines that indicated arms. The figure seemed misshapen until I realized it depicted a pregnant woman, crude arms angled protectively above her distended abdomen. The hole had been positioned where her naval would have been. I looked at Poppy.

"A goddess figure?"

"Maybe," she said. She turned it over, so that I could again see the first image, noticeably thinner than the other, its triangular breasts narrower and its eyes larger. "Here, come with me."

I followed her into an adjoining room that seemed to be an office. A small desk with a laptop and scattered papers, an armchair beside a chrome standing lamp, shelves filled with books. On the wall, a framed poster for a show of Ice Age art at the British Museum.

Against the wall stood an antique curio cabinet. Poppy opened one of its drawers and removed a slender length of rawhide about eighteen inches long. Carefully she threaded the rawhide through the bone disc, stepped to a standing lamp, and beckoned me over. She switched on the light, and I shaded my eyes from a halogen bulb.

"Now watch," she commanded.

She took one end of the rawhide in each of her hands, holding it slack with the disc suspended in the middle. In one smooth quick motion she pulled the string taut. The disc spun, flipping from side to side. I stared at it, confused. "I don't get it."

"I'll do it again," said Poppy. "Move closer."

I did, near enough to feel the halogen bulb's heat on my face. Once more I heard the *twang* of the rawhide string when she tightened it. Inches in front of me, the disc spun in a whitish blur. In a flicker so fleeting it happened in an eyeblink, the carved figure's abdomen swelled. I felt goosebumps rise along my arms.

"Do it again," I said.

Without a word, Poppy repeated the gesture, not once but over and over. Each time the spindly image of the woman's belly expanded then deflated, like a tiny, humanoid balloon.

"That's fucking incredible," I whispered.

As a kid, I'd drawn a stick figure on the bottom corner of every page of a history textbook, each image in a slightly different position than the previous one. A crude flipbook—a trick every kid learns, or used to, and probably the simplest form of animation there is. My teacher confiscated the book and made me stay for detention. There she showed me a book of Eadweard Muybridge's sequential black-and-white photos of running horses, the stop-motion effects that predated motion pictures.

That was when I became obsessed with photography: the moment I realized that a camera could stop time, and even allow you to see back *through* time. It was a kind of magic, especially the revelation that a series of static images could fool the brain into perceiving motion.

Old-fashioned motion pictures run at twenty-four frames per second—much slower than that and you detect a noticeable flicker. But the brain perceives motion in as few as ten frames per second, like a flipbook. And like this spinning disc—proof, if it was genuine, that prehistoric humans had understood the persistence of vision.

I stared at Poppy, stunned. "It's a thaumatrope."

She nodded. "That's right. A paleolithic thaumatrope."

"How old?"

"About thirteen thousand years. They found the first one in a cave in France in 1868. They thought it was a button—it was only a few years ago that they've speculated as to what they really are. I've known for longer than that. I figured it out by mistake, fooling around with that one. Probably there'd be more scientific discoveries made, if people played with the things they found, rather than locking them away in storage cabinets."

She laughed. "But there's only two or three of these in museums. One shows a hunter being attacked by a cave bear, but the disc's not intact. The others are of animals. No humans."

"Two or three." I turned toward the curio cabinet. "And how many are in there?"

"Two more." Her eyes shone feverishly bright. "They both have images of people carved on them. One's a woman. I think women made them."

"Really?"

She pointed at the cabinet. "See for yourself."

I looked at the bone disc hanging limply from the rawhide in Poppy's hand. "You're showing these to a total stranger?"

"You're Morven's friend—I thought she might have mentioned them. And you know what a thaumatrope is. Are you an archaeologist?"

"I'm a photographer. It's one of those things you learn about."

She smiled, and I glimpsed the girl trapped within the cage

of bone and decaying flesh. "I knew it. I can always tell a photographer—their eyes are always clocking the light."

"I know who you are," I said. "I saw you at the Bottom Line in 1979, when you did that stand for *Best Eaten Cold*. You were fucking brilliant. That song about the wind—when you sang that it made me cry."

She shut her eyes. After a moment her fingers grazed my wrist, her touch so hot that for a second I thought I'd burned myself on the halogen bulb. "Thank you. That was such a long time ago. You're kind to remember."

"I never forgot." I gestured at the cabinet. "But I don't know anything about this kind of thing. All this stuff—you should take it to a museum. Or an antique dealer. Mallo and Morven, they own that shop in their building, right?"

"Mallo has no interest in these, other than financial. I don't know anything about his other customers, or his supplier. I don't want to."

So Adrian was right: Mallo wasn't dealing in drugs any longer, but illegal antiquities. I watched as Poppy folded the thaumatrope into a scrap of chamois cloth and set it aside. She crossed to the curio cabinet, opened the bottom drawer, and ran her fingers across the glass lids of numerous small boxes. Each contained some kind of artifact: flint arrowheads, stone ax heads, beads made of shell or bone. With her aureole of silver hair and heavy gold earrings, she looked as though she were deliberating over a card for a tarot reading. At last she selected a box, removed another bone disc, and held it out to me.

"In July 1980 I was in Paris, that same tour. I'd just finished my first stint in rehab. This was before my relapse—I had nine good years, then . . ."

She closed her eyes and drew a hand to her forehead. I

thought she wouldn't continue, but her hand dropped to her lap, fingers trembling, and she went on.

"After one of the shows, this girl came backstage and gave me something wrapped in a bandanna. I thought it was going to be a crystal or pentangle or some kind of little amulet. People were always giving me things like that.

" 'Something to keep you strong,' the girl said, and she left. I never knew who she was. I unwrapped the bandanna and this was inside, on a bit of ribbon. I wore it around my neck for years. I knew it was old, but I didn't know *how* old. Then one day I was playing with it, like cat's cradle."

She mimed pulling a piece of string back and forth between her hands.

"And suddenly I saw it—the same way you did, all at once I saw that the figure was moving. That you were *meant* to see it move. But I had no idea what it was. This was before the Internet, so I talked to someone at the British Museum. I didn't bring it to him, just described it as something I'd seen in a museum in France. I told him I thought the image would change as you spun the disc. He said it was an interesting idea but completely ridiculous. Like I said, there were only one or two of these discs in museums, and everyone thought they were buttons. So I tried searching for one on my own. It took years."

"On the black market," I said.

She nodded. "Morven found it for me, actually. She's like my sister. Was, until I did something terrible. Unforgiveable." She drew a hand across her eyes as though the light pained her. "And of course Mallo and Leith were like brothers. Mallo was doing other things back then, and he . . . knew people. He—"

She stopped. "Oh, none of that shit matters. The future

wasn't meant to be like this, that's all." She smiled ruefully. "I alway thought that *Best Eaten Cold* would be the beginning of my career. Instead, it *was* my career."

"You seem to do okay."

"I still get residuals from 'Juice It Up.' But I had to cut most of my ties from back then. Morven and I stay in touch, but not really. These things—" She gestured at the disc in my palm. "These are my real daughters."

I examined the disc. Like the first, it was made of bone, and had a crude face scratched into it: eyes downcast, mouth down-turned, twin gashes to indicate age. An old woman. On the other side, a similar face had been carved. But its eyes were up-tilted, the mouth upturned with a second curved line beneath it, to make the lips appear full. A crosshatch above the eyes indicated hair, or perhaps a knitted cap.

"When you spin it, you see her age," said Poppy. "From a girl to an old woman and back again."

I shivered. I felt the same unease as when I stared too long at a face in a daguerreotype—the uncanny sensation that the subject of the image stared back.

But now I had the even more disturbing sense that whoever carved the thaumatrope had been aware that she was gazing forward through the millennia: For an instant, our eyes had met. I looked at Poppy. "I still don't understand why you're showing me these."

She shrugged. "You seem interested."

"Yeah, but what if I went to the police? How do you know you can trust me?"

"I don't. That's why they call it trust."

She took the disc and handed me a third object: a flattened

oval with a circle etched in its center and a hole drilled in the middle of the circle. An eye—the hole formed the pupil.

On the back of the disc was another eye, this one closed. When the disc was spun on a cord, the eye would seem to wink. It was perhaps the simplest thaumatrope. And, maybe, the oldest.

I recalled the vision I'd had as a teenager: an immense, remorseless eye within a vortex of cloud above an empty field, gazing down at me. I stared at the thaumatrope, finally returned it to Poppy. She wrapped it in a piece of chamois cloth, did the same with the other two; slowly walked to her desk and put the three wrapped objects into an orange plastic Sainsbury's bag.

"There," she said. "Now you've seen the eye of god. Or goddess. Let's get more coffee."

She left the room. I lingered, feeling the way I did after watching a movie I didn't quite understand. My gaze drifted across the shelves, clocking books on archeaology and prehistoric art, rock and roll, experimental film. A framed photo of the members of Lavender Rage after a gig, Poppy draped across Jonno's sequined torso like a lamia in tie-dye and fringed leather.

And a picture of Poppy, Morven, and the same woman with auburn hair. I could see her face more clearly in this one: high cheekbones, high forehead, russet hair held back with a Liberty print scarf. She looked a few years older than the other two, though that might just have been her expression, haughty and somewhat hostile, as though she disliked whomever was behind the camera. Beside this was another photo, curled with age. The charred ruins of a mansion, its towers blackened, broken glass glinting from heaps of rubble.

I picked it up. On the back, someone had written *Kethelwite September '73*. Both Adrian and Mallo had pictures of the same place.

I frowned, slipped the photo into my pocket, and perused the next shelf. Shelved between a couple of early collections of Helmut Newton and David Hamilton photography was a large book, spiral bound.

I pulled it from the shelf and whistled softly. The stiff board cover showed a photo of a nude woman's torso, cropped so that her face was barely visible. Her skin was paper-white, so flawlessly smooth that the photo might have been of an alabaster statue.

But the woman's skin was flesh, not stone, and I'd seen her image enough times to recognize it immediately, even before I read the book's title.

MONSTERS AND MADONNAS
A BOOK OF METHODS
WILLIAM MORTENSEN

I checked the copyright page: 1936, the proper first edition. It was Mortensen's best-known work; as a collectible, more desirable to most folks than *The Command to Look* because of its full-page reproductions of Mortensen's work.

I'd never held a copy. I drew the volume to my face and breathed in deeply.

"Do you always go around sniffing books?"

Poppy stood in the doorway, steadying herself with one knobby hand. She looked decades older than she had only minutes earlier, the end product of a time-lapse film.

"Just the ones that are worth a few hundred bucks," I said.

She glanced at the book with disinterest. "What is it?"

I held it up.

Poppy wrinkled her nose. "Oh, right. Someone gave me that a hundred years ago. I could never get into it. You can have it if you want."

"You sure?" I asked, already sliding it into my bag. "It's a valuable book."

"Not to me. It's yours."

I followed her back into the kitchen. She pulled out a chair and sat, picked up my skull-patterned scarf and stared at it for a long time before dropping it onto the table beside the orange Sainsbury's bag.

"I'm deaccessioning," she said at last. "It's late-stage brain cancer. Inoperable. I don't take painkillers because I'm an addict. I have about two good hours a day, if I'm lucky. This is one of them, but I think it's just about over."

She sighed, and added, "Everything's over. Most people, if they remember me at all, it's because of Jonno. A few people know my album, but mostly I had nice tits and fucked rock stars. So . . ."

She pointed at the orange plastic bag. "I'm donating them to the British Museum. Everything else as well. There's a curator there I've spoken to; she's the first person who hasn't dismissed my ideas outright—that the artifacts might have been made by women. I could sell it all to the museum, but then I'd have to get a solicitor involved, and there'd be questions about their provenance that I'm not interested in answering.

"So I'll just make the donation while I'm still alive and relatively *compos mentis*. They should be able to establish provenance by carbon dating or paleomagnetism or whatever. If they're as smart as they say they are, someone will figure it out.

My things will be in a nice glass vitrine in the British Museum, and it will say *Gift of Patricia Teasdale.* No one will know who that is, but maybe they'll figure that out, too."

She gave that spectral laugh and struggled to her feet. "I'll get the door for you."

"There a place around here I can grab a bite?"

"The Blackbird used to be a decent pub. If you're just looking for a sandwich, there's a Pret a Manger by the tube station."

I zipped my leather jacket and stood. Poppy picked up the Sainsbury's bag and stuck it on the windowsill between the bright geraniums. She rubbed one of the green leaves between her fingers, brought her hand to her face and inhaled, smiling. Then she walked me to the door.

I stepped outside, pulling on my watch cap. Frozen BBs beat against my neck: the snow had turned to sleet. Poppy remained in the doorway, scooping up the white cat before it could dart after me.

"Thanks for what you said about my show that night," she said. "I was a different person then. Not a good person."

"But you were an amazing singer."

"It's funny, I never really think about any of that anymore. It was all such a long time ago. The twentieth century's dying away."

"The twentieth century's dead," I said. "We're the ones who're dying."

"And look at you. Last punk standing." She stroked the cat in her arms, and in a raspy voice began to sing.

"The wind, the wind, the wind blows high
Ash comes falling from the sky

And all the children say they'll die
For want of the Golden City."

Her words vanished into a motorcycle's roar and the rumble of buses as she slipped back into her flat and closed the door. I felt a twinge of grief and regret, a strange despair that lingered like the last notes of Poppy's song; then I checked to make sure the Mortensen book was safe in my bag and hurried off to find a drink.

16

I walked quickly down the block, looking over my shoulder for the platinum-haired woman I'd seen earlier. Near the bus stop, I elbowed my way through a small crowd, pulled out the TracFone Adrian had given me, and hit redial. He answered, his voice terse.

"Yeah?"

"Done."

I disconnected and walked on. When I saw an empty alleyway, I stepped aside, my back to the street, dropped the TracFone, and ground it beneath the heel of my cowboy boot. I gathered up the pieces and headed on toward the pub, dropping bits of shattered circuitry and plastic into drains and waste bins along the way.

No tidy window boxes or faux-antique signs marked the Blackbird, just the pub's name above the door and a warning that CCTVs were in use. The room was dark and cold, with that lost-bar smell of spilled beer and Windex. I didn't see any CCTVs, or any other post-1960s technology except a computerized cash register.

The male bartender was young and disinclined to smile or make eye contact. I got a tumbler of Scotch and a bag of salted peanuts, and retired to a stool at a small table. At a neighboring table, a young woman wearing boots and a too-tight pencil skirt stared at a pack of Camel Lights, her bare legs goosebumped with cold. Two tiny, wizened men, identical twins in identical tweed caps and Costa del Sol sweatshirts, sat side by side and gazed at the wall, occasionally taking a sip from their pints. Behind the bar, an old regulator clock ticked softly as the young barkeep polished glasses with a white cloth. There was no radio or piped-in music; no ringtones. No one spoke. Except for the clock's pendulum, and the bartender's hands flicking his white cloth, nothing stirred.

I drank and ate my peanuts and thought about Poppy Teasel. Collecting priceless prehistoric artifacts was an odd hobby for a groupie, but I've heard of worse. The memory of her voice rasping "Golden City" was like something half-remembered from a drunken sleep; that and the word *thaumatrope*. When my glass was empty, I went to the bar and ordered another by pointing at the tumbler, paid without speaking, and returned to my table.

I'd never been in a public space that was so quiet. I felt I'd become a figure in a diorama, motionless, my fingers melded with my glass. Maybe this was what junkies like Quinn or Poppy Teasel had experienced, back when they were using.

I took out the Mortensen book and turned a few pages, then glanced up.

There were no photos in the room around me, no paintings or portraits on the wall, no mirrors. It felt strange. Still, for most of human history, and prehistory, people lived without images of themselves. Portrait paintings and sculptures had belonged only to the wealthy.

Ditto cameos and miniatures and mirrors. Daguerreotypes were mementos mori, sacred to the memory of the dead. The Mayans believed that mirrors operated as portals between the worlds. In the nineteenth century, some Native Americans thought that a photograph could steal an individual's soul. In the 1970s, photo critic A. D. Coleman would ask his students if they had photographs of loved ones in their wallets. He told them that they could show them to others in the classroom, but only if they were willing to then incinerate the photos immediately. No one did.

I thought of the single photo of Quinn in my wallet, all that remained of the hundreds I'd taken of him as a teenager. I didn't remove it.

The pub's door opened and a young woman entered, talking loudly on her mobile.

". . . can't fecking meet you, I tol you I already fecking left!"

Cold air trailed her as she hurried to the bar. I exhaled, the spell broken; pulled on my hat and gloves and stood to leave.

Where was my scarf?

I peered under the table, searched my camera bag, retraced my steps to the bar. It wasn't there. I had a flash of Poppy Teasel's kitchen, of Poppy playing with the skull-patterned scarf on the table in front of her.

"Shit," I muttered.

The twin gnomes in tweed caps turned to glare at me. So did the girl yattering into her mobile, and the bartender. It was like the dark side of Ealing Comedy. I glared back, grabbed my bag, and left.

It was raining now, hard. The sidewalks were a slurry of melting snow. A man running to catch the bus slid across the greasy pavement, past four teenage boys and a woman who wore a chador beneath a transparent pink rain poncho. The boys whooped as the man fell. The woman's kohl-lined eyes met mine then quickly looked away.

I thought of the platinum-haired black girl I'd seen that morning, the girl in the military parka. I put my head down, strode on toward Poppy's building and up the steps. I pressed the buzzer.

Nothing. I held the buzzer down, its tone echoing loudly inside.

Still nothing. I craned my neck to see if there was any motion behind the front curtains. The scarf had only cost a few quid; I could get another at any of the million stalls that sold tourist crap. I don't think I've hung onto a scarf for more than a week in my entire life.

Still, the fact that Poppy had seemed to admire it made me suddenly want it back.

And I had a furtive, almost guilty desire to see her again, to once more hear her hoarse voice singing a song I had forgotten decades ago and watch that bone disc flicker in the air between us like a conjurer's trick or a magical, tiny moon. I rattled the doorknob. Beneath my gloved hand, the knob turned.

"Hey, Poppy? It's me, I forgot my scarf." I stepped inside, holding the door ajar behind me. "Poppy?"

I left the door cracked and entered the hall. Something white caught my eye—Poppy's cat, crouched in the middle of the living room. Rose petals were strewn across the floor and on the sofa where Poppy dozed. The cat bent over one tiny crimson blossom. When I stepped into the room, it froze and stared up at me with beryl eyes.

A red starburst bloomed around the cat's mouth: It hissed, ears flat against its skull, and went back to lapping at the floor.

"Poppy," I said, staring at the couch.

The wig had slid to one side so that a fringe of silver hair fell across one eye, giving her a coquettish look. A spike dangled just above the crook of her elbow. A red tendril trailed down her wrist to blossom on the floor below.

I did an about-face and raced back to the front door. Stopped.

I held my breath.

I could hear nothing. From where I stood, nothing seemed out of place. After a minute I turned the dead bolt. I pulled off my boots, set them by the door with my camera bag, and walked silently into the kitchen.

Here too everything seemed exactly as it had when I'd left. Coffee grounds in the cafetière; two empty coffee mugs on the counter. My scarf on the table, its rows of bright skulls grinning at me. I looped the scarf around my neck and stepped to the sink. I washed the mug I'd used, dried it and set it back on a shelf; squeezed detergent onto a sponge and scrubbed the table and chair where I'd sat. Grabbing some paper towels, I wiped up the damp spots left by my boots on the floor by the front door, wiped off my fingerprints from the door doorknob and dead bolt, stuffed the wet paper towels into my pocket, and returned to the living room.

They say that certain butterflies are drawn to the scent of carrion. I used to feel like that, in the Bowery in another century. Doubling back to see if the motionless heap in an alley or doorway was a dead wino, or just a mound of rotting clothes that hadn't been claimed yet by a crazy person pushing a shopping cart.

There was no decaying flesh here, but the corrosive smell of damage was enough to make my neck go cold. I knew I should get the fuck out of there. But I didn't.

I stared down at Poppy. Her eyes were shut, her mouth slack. I stooped to peer at her fingertips. They already had the bruised blue sheen that comes with an overdose. I straightened and gazed at her face.

All the lines were gone. Except for the lesions on her scalp, she appeared much as she had as a seventeen-year-old, clinging to Jonno outside the Filmore. That strange simulation of youthfulness sometimes happens in death, but usually not so quickly. Poppy's tranquil expression was courtesy of whatever she'd injected.

Why would a recovering junkie who'd been clean for more than three decades decide to shoot up again? Terminal cancer would be one really good reason, but she hadn't struck me as someone who was on the verge of using the minute I walked out the door.

Yet something—pain, fear, the knowledge that the man in the bright nightgown was waiting in the wings—must have become too much.

So she relapsed.

But mainlining after thirty years of abstinence is a pretty dramatic way to go off the wagon. Recovering heroin addicts are especially susceptible to overdosing, regardless of the product's purity. I'd have been less surprised if she'd been chipping or popping—snorting or injecting subcutaneously. Mainlining takes a certain amount of skill, and Poppy had been out of practice. To judge by the mess on the couch, really out of practice.

She might have injected an air bubble, which would also have killed her. But it looked more like she'd hit an artery. My old roommate Jeannie, the one who used to yell "Scary Neary!"

whenever she saw me coming, checked out like that. So did a kid I'd photographed in an alley, a shot that made it into *Dead Girls*. That was back when you'd see junkies lined up around the block on the Lower East Side, waiting to get inside a shooting gallery to buy packets stamped with the brand of heroin they contained—Black Cat, China Blade. That neighborhood might have cleaned up over the decades. But last time I was in the city, business had been brisk again.

I leaned down to get a better look at Poppy's arm. Ropy scar tissue snarled around the crook of her elbow, long-healed abscesses. The needle was on the inside of her arm, about three inches above the elbow. It had been plunged so deeply that the needle bulb—the entire tip—had jammed in her flesh. Around it, a small constellation of pinpricks shone red against her white skin. She'd tried to hit a vein several times before succeeding.

Not a vein. The brachial artery. Once when he was shooting up as a teenager, Quinn had pointed out his.

"This is what you don't ever, ever want to hit," he'd said, tapping the inside of his upper arm with the barrel of the needle. "Unless you don't want to ever wake up."

Now I drew back and scanned the floor for other needles. Not even a needle cap, nothing but a purple bandanna she might have used to tie off. I crouched to examine the spike again.

It was a disposable, a Monoject or the UK equivalent. The inside of the barrel looked clean. None of the sludgy residue you get from slamming tar, the cheap Mexican heroin you find in the States. Poppy had mentioned getting her heroin through the NHS before she cleaned up. She could have had a stash somewhere, or pills that she'd ground up and cooked, or maybe some loaded spikes.

But this looked like a modern hypodermic needle, not one that had been hygienically shrinkwrapped since 1980.

I stepped away from the sofa, careful to avoid the blood spattered underfoot, and retreated back into the hall.

Poppy hadn't OD'd. Somebody had killed her.

17

It was a clever idea: off a onetime junkie turned cancer patient using what had been her drug of choice. To any casual observer, Occam's razor would suggest that Poppy had overdosed, intentionally or not. From what I knew, she had no next of kin. Considering her late-stage cancer, it seemed doubtful that the police would bother to mount an investigation. Unless they found signs of sexual trauma, or employed a forensic scientist who took a real interest in the case, they'd just see another dead junkie.

The fact that she was middle-aged and a woman probably wouldn't help. No one would look for a killer, because the killer was sticking out of her arm.

The real killer was an amateur. I was sure of that. She or he hadn't tied off Poppy's arm with that bandanna—there'd been no bruising. It had to have been someone Poppy knew, or she wouldn't have let them in. Morven Dunfries? Mallo? Adrian?

Whoever it was, Poppy had opened the front door; when the killer split through the same door, they'd left it unlocked because the dead bolt couldn't be turned without a key. The attacker might have been armed. I tried to imagine Morven Dunfries standing in her old friend's living room, forcing her at gunpoint to shoot herself up. The image was too bizarre even for me.

Poppy didn't seem to have put up a fight. There was no overturned furniture, and I hadn't noticed skin or hair under her fingernails.

But she hadn't been the one to slam the plunger in. And her killer had done a lousy job of doing it for her. I'd seen enough Tarrantino movies to know that in certain circumstances, an amateur can be just as effective as a pro, and far more dangerous.

I stepped into Poppy's office. The bottom drawer of the curio cabinet was ajar. I knelt and opened it, staring at the rows of small glass-topped boxes. None seemed to have been touched. I yanked open the other drawers: more of the same.

I stood and scanned the room. Poppy's purple reading glasses were on top of her desk, but the mess of papers had been moved to one side. And the top drawer of the desk was open. Letters and envelopes were scattered on the floor beneath it, along with pens and paperclips. Poppy might have done that, if she'd been in a hurry, or if she'd been interrupted.

So might have an intruder, looking for something they hadn't found in the desk or cabinet: the thaumatropes.

I raced to the kitchen. On the windowsill between the geraniums was the orange plastic Sainsbury's bag. I grabbed it, reached inside, and felt three soft bundles of chamois cloth. Folded inside each was a thaumatrope. There was also a business card for a curator of European Archaeology at the British Museum, presumably the woman Poppy had mentioned.

I stuffed the business card into my pocket. Then, clutching

the plastic bag, I returned to Poppy's office and searched through drawers until I found several coiled lengths of rawhide. My hands shook as I peeled off my gloves and threaded a length of rawhide through each thaumatrope. I knotted the cords, slid each over my neck and beneath my black turtleneck, the bone discs cool against my bare skin. I put on my gloves and turned to go.

A chime sounded—the incongruously sweet tone of a Tibetan temple bell. Panicked, I looked around and saw something glowing on the desk. Poppy's mobile. I grabbed it and hurried to the front door to retrieve my bag and cowboy boots. Peering outside, I saw it was pissing down rain again. A small crowd of kids swarmed around a bus shelter halfway down the block, and a police siren wailed. I closed the door, turned the dead bolt, and headed back to the kitchen, my bag in one hand and my boots in the other.

As I passed the living room I paused. The doorway neatly framed the dim space: Poppy seemingly asleep on the couch with her silvery wig askew, a scattering of dark petals and that tiny bright dart glinting in one arm. It looked like one of Cindy Sherman's early Untitled Film Stills.

I shifted my bag and cursed under my breath. Like Weegee used to say, a camera's like a gun—useless if it's not loaded. I hadn't yet loaded another roll of Tri-X in my Konica. I had Poppy's smartphone but no clue how it worked.

Probably this was for the best. I stared at Poppy, fixing the image in my mind, and turned away.

In the kitchen, a back door led to a fenced-in area that had once been a garden. There was no dead bolt, just a cheap metal knob with a button you could depress so it would lock. I wondered why the killer hadn't left this way. Too much of a hurry, maybe, or maybe they'd had a last-minute change of heart and hoped someone might find Poppy before she died. I stared out at a dreary dripping jungle of dead nettles, piles of moldering leaves, a sickly plane tree. I grabbed Poppy's old yellow mackintosh from its hook beside the door and pulled it on, tugged the hood over my head, and shoved my feet into my boots.

I let out a stifled shout as something nudged my ankle. The white cat. I opened the door and tossed it outside. I didn't like thinking about what it might get up to, locked in a house with a corpse.

I slung my bag over my shoulder and stepped out into the rain. I made sure the door was locked, then walked slowly down the steps. It was now dark enough that anyone who saw me might think I was Poppy.

At the back of the garden was a derelict wooden fence. A stone Buddha guarded its sagging door, the statue's face leprous with lichen. I raised the door latch and stepped into an alley. When I glanced back, I saw a ghostly white shape creeping through the darkness, its beryl eyes flaring as they caught the light.

I walked as quickly as I could for several blocks, dodging crowds until I eventually managed to push my way onto a bus. I tried to catch my breath, staring fixedly at my soaked Tony Lamas while a young couple talked about the apocalyptic weather.

". . . six inches in Reading. Stanstead's shut down."

"Gatwick, too."

"Cop killed some kid in Alperton, see that?"

"Fuck."

I staked out a place near the bus's rear door and pulled out

Poppy's mobile. I might have been looking at a cartouche from Third Dynasty Egypt. Back in the city, my old connection Phil Cohen had given me shit for refusing to get a cell phone or digital camera.

"Yeah yeah, I get it—you're *old school.*" He'd twitch even more than usual as he pronounced the last two words. "Graduation day, Cassandra Android. Stop being a fucking Luddite."

Truth was, a few months ago I couldn't have afforded a cell phone or new laptop. Now, with a few thousand quid stashed in my boot, I could.

Still, Phil was right—I *was* a Luddite. But I'd watched enough people with cell phones to have a vague idea of how to use one. I ran a finger across the screen of Poppy's mobile. It lit up, and I stared at the rows of candy-colored icons. If they'd been pills, I would've popped a few. Instead I dropped the phone back into my bag and stared out at the rain.

I got off at the first stop where the announcement was for an Underground station and made my way into the street. In an alcove beside a shuttered Ladbrokes, a teenage girl wrapped in a garbage bag had passed out. Her dark hair was matted, and the soles had peeled from her zebra-striped Converse hightops. At her feet, a filthy baseball cap held a few coins.

I walked past her, then doubled back and ducked into the alcove. I stuffed a few ten-pound notes in a pocket of Poppy's mackintosh along with my wet gloves, pulled off the raincoat, and draped it across the girl. Then, reaching beneath my layers of clothing, I touched the three bone discs.

These are my daughters.

I chose one at random, tugged the rawhide cord over my head, and held up the disc to see the faintly etched outline of a woman's pregnant form. I bent and carefully looped the cord over the girl's head, poking it beneath the plastic trash bag and the grimy sweatshirt she wore. She sighed but didn't move. I headed for the Underground.

18

Inside the station I perused a map for the best route back to Camden Town. When the train arrived, it was so jammed I could barely edge my way onboard. I hate crowds, but for the first time since leaving the Blackbird I relaxed. I closed my eyes and let the surrounding throng hold me upright.

Half the subway car cleared out when we reached Camden Town, mostly kids tricked out in some variation of Doc Martens and black leather. Camden Town was definitely where punk had gone to die its slow death. Everyone crowded onto the escalators, exhilarated from the cold and all but spitting out sparks at the buzz of bad news—rumors of looting, flashmobs, a riot in Birmingham.

"Another eruption."

"Plane went down in Indonesia."

"No, Indiana."

At the station exit, a dozen or so cops in fluorescent vests stood chatting, eying the crowd as we shuffled through the gates. There were more cops outside the station, some in riot gear, but they seemed less interested in hassling people than in observing them. Two mounted police guided their horses at a slow gait along the sidewalk, lords surveying their domain, and pairs of cops strolled among the throng on the other side of the High Street, like uniformed window shoppers. Double-decker buses and cabs inched along the High Street. A few brave cyclists zipped between stopped vehicles.

I pulled up the collar of my leather jacket. Adrenaline and nerves had kept me from feeling the cold; now it washed over me as though I'd fallen into an icy sea. Drumbeats echoed from somewhere close by, and amplified voices chanting words to a song I didn't recognize. The wind carried the smells of cannabis and frying garlic. On the corner, a bubble machine sent iridescent clouds whirling overhead as a girl handed out flyers for a vegan takeaway.

The rain gave everything the sheen of a midnight carnival. But there was a malignant undercurrent to all the revelry—not just the presence of so many cops, but the sense that everyone was waiting impatiently for some prearranged signal. I'm all for chaos, but only if I have a good view of the exit.

I thought of what Adrian had said about kettling, and pushed my way through the throng until I reached a less crowded side street. I was wary of returning to the Banshee. Adrian knew I'd met Krishna there; if Poppy's death had leaked and anyone was looking for me—Mallo, the police, Adrian—the Banshee would be the first place they'd check.

Still, "anyone" included Quinn, and I had no idea where else I might find him. I decided to hold off on the Banshee, but I was freezing and needed a drink. I saw a pub on the next corner, a few smokers huddled out front in the rain. I went inside and ordered a double shot, then found my way to a nearly empty side room where two men sat arguing drunkenly.

I headed for a wood-paneled booth with half doors that reminded me of a confessional. It had worn maroon velvet banquettes with a narrow trestle table between them. I went inside and pulled the half doors closed, dumped my bag on the bench, and had just started in on my whiskey when one of the doors creaked open and a young woman slid onto the bench across from me.

"I'm surprised you didn't want to sit with them," she said very loudly, and pointed at the drunk couple. "Make some new friends—oh, too late," she said, as the two men slid from their table and left. "Guess they had to be somewhere."

It was the platinum-haired woman I'd seen on the street outside Mallo's place that first night, and again in Stepney. The same topaz eyes and frayed military parka; the same pointed face, now split by a grin that displayed white, slightly protruding teeth. I grabbed my bag, but she'd already shut the booth door and tripped the latch.

"No rush," she said. "Sit and finish your drink."

The crossbar beneath the table made it difficult for me to land a kick. I stared at her, and she flashed an ID badge.

ELLEN CONNORS
EUROPOL: ICOTIA

My stomach clenched. "You're a cop?"

"I'm conducting a criminal investigation."

"I want to know if you're a cop." I hoped she'd mistake my fear for righteous fury. "You've been following me. I'm an American citizen—"

"I'm with ICOTIA. International Commission on Traffic in Illicit Antiquities."

"Antiquities." I picked up my drink and took a sip. Beneath my turtleneck, the two bone thaumatropes burned against my skin. "That what you call antiques over here?"

"Don't be obtuse. I have a few questions, and I suggest you cooperate in answering them."

"You got a warrant? I'm not saying anything without an attorney."

"I'm investigating your companion, Adrian Carlisle. He's under suspicion for being part of a black market in illegal artifacts."

"He's not my companion. I only got here two days ago."

"I saw you leave Mallory Dunfries's home with Carlisle and accompany him to the Barbican."

"It was a birthday party for his wife. There a law against that?"

"Mallo Dunfries is a career criminal who's been linked to several unsolved murders. He ran an organized crime ring trafficking in narcotics. Twenty years ago he got his knuckles rapped and spent a few months in prison. When he got out, he changed horses and began dealing in looted artifacts. Do you know who benefits from that?"

"No clue."

"Terrorists. In Iraq they've looted so many archaeological sites that there's nothing left. Nineveh is gone. The museums are gone. A Sumerian stone seal this big—" She measured out an inch between thumb and forefinger. "Twenty thousand pounds—that's more than thirty thousand dollars. Right into al-Qaeda's pockets."

I had no idea if this was true, although Poppy's artifacts

seemed older than ancient Sumeria by a factor of at least seven, and none had appeared to be from the Middle East. The word *terrorist* freaked me out, though. I drank my whiskey and shrugged. "I told you, I barely know Adrian, and I met Dunfries for about three seconds."

"That's three seconds too long. You were with Carlisle this morning. He accompanied you to Stepney Green to make some sort of a delivery. I'd like you to tell me what you delivered and to whom. If you cooperate I can ensure you'll be treated fairly."

I laughed. "Don't you have skulls to split over in Alperton? Or here?" I gestured at a barred window. "It's like the dress rehearsal for the apocalypse out there. Leave me the fuck alone."

Whoever this chick was, she wasn't a cop: She'd flashed me a badge and was questioning me in a pub, rather than a station house. If anything, her demeanor suggested she was a former cop—in my experience, a lot more of an immediate threat.

Could she be Poppy's killer? Had she followed me to Stepney, waited for me to leave the flat, then somehow gained entry? Had Poppy known her?

That's why they call it trust.

Ellen Connors leaned back, and her uniform jacket flopped open. Beneath it she wore a heavy cable-knit sweater whose bulk suggested it covered a cross-body holster, maybe a Kevlar vest. I wondered what else she had hidden in there. Poppy's artifacts? Another set of heroin works?

Connors cleared her throat. As though following a script, she announced, "Trafficking in antiquities is a crime."

"So's harassing tourists." I slung my bag over my shoulder, and before she could stop me I kicked the door open and hopped from the booth. "Fuck off."

"Wait!" She grabbed my arm—she was fast; also strong. If not an ex-cop, she spent a lot of time at the gym. "Here—"

She thrust a card into my hand. "Call me next time you hear from Mallo Dunfries—"

I pushed her away and took the steps two at a time as I ran upstairs.

19

I walked as quickly as I could past Camden Market to the canal path, looking over my shoulder for any sign of Ellen Connors. The card she'd shoved at me was printed with her name, along with a little medallion and the words *International Commission on Traffic in Illicit Antiquities*. The medallion was blurred, as if it had been scanned. It looked like the kind of card you order online, five hundred copies for twenty bucks. I started to toss it, thought better of it, and stuck it in my wallet.

By now I was soaked to the skin. The precipitation shifted from rain to freezing rain to sleet to snow squalls, but with two constants: It was always cold and it was always wet. The whiskey's false warmth had long since worn off. I decided to chance running into Connors and headed back to the High Street.

The crowds that had jammed Camden Town earlier were gone. Maybe there'd been a viral signal of more excitement elsewhere. Or maybe they'd just gotten cold and gone home. The cops were still around, though, and I could hear a helicopter droning overhead.

I fought growing panic. I was being tracked by people I didn't know, for reasons I couldn't get a handle on. What I knew of archaeology came from watching Indiana Jones movies while stoned. I kept flashing on Poppy's beautiful, ravaged face as she gazed at a bone disc beneath a halogen bulb, and the flickering image of an eye that stared at me from some unfathomable distance.

I felt beneath my jacket for the loops of rawhide around my neck. I couldn't bring myself to ditch the remaining two thaumatropes, but I wasn't going to give them to the British Museum, either. Quinn might know of someone who'd buy them.

I reached the Super Drug, stopped short. It was still open. Inside I found black hair dye (semi-permanent, the kind that washes out after a few weeks), hair scissors, a pair of overpriced sunglasses, mascara, and kohl. I paid for these, stuffed them into my satchel, and hurried on to the Banshee.

The pub wasn't crowded. A dozen or so customers, Amy Winehouse on the jukebox, Derek behind the bar. I would have preferred a crowd to get lost in. I ordered another double and dropped a twenty on the counter. Derek picked it up without a word. He looked bad: red-eyed, and there was a blue smudge on his jaw, like someone had taken a swing at him. As he handed me a glass, he inclined his head toward the jukebox. I nodded and stepped away.

A rangy figure leaned over the Seeburg. He wore a motorcycle jacket even more weathered than my own, heavy work boots, and black jeans. His head was shaven, and as he leaned into the jukebox its eerie blue light picked out the cross that had been branded into his scalp.

My heart tightened. I knew better than to creep up on him,

so I let my boots fall heavily on the wooden floor as I approached. He didn't turn, but I could see his body tense, then relax when I drew alongside him.

"Cassie." He pulled me to him, holding me so tightly my chest ached.

"Quinn," I whispered.

The Seeburg's icy glow made a gaunt mask of his face, the Inuit tattoos he'd gotten in Barrow Prison stark against his skin: three vertical red lines between his eyes and a set of black horizontal lines on each side of his mouth. A fresh scar slashed through one of these, giving him a grotesque half-smile. His bruised eyes were so deep-set their color was lost in the carnival light, but I knew they were the color of a frozen lake, the pupils black cracks in the ice. Morning sun might reveal a few green flecks, all that remained of the boy I'd photographed in 1975.

He cupped my chin in his hand, ran his thumb along the starburst scar beside my eye, the gash in my cheek.

"Christ, we're a pair," he murmured. "The gruesome twosome. Come on."

He grabbed a backpack from the floor and steered me past the bar, nabbing a brimming pint glass on the way. Derek gave Quinn a brisk nod as we entered the back hall. We passed the toilets, stepping over empty liquor cartons, and Quinn halted in front of a door with a sign that read FUNCTION ROOM.

"In here," he said.

Inside were more tables and chairs, a dusty billiards table, and an empty microphone stand. A limp green banner drooped from an overhead light: GOOD LUCK SEAMUS.

"That'd be a good name for a band," said Quinn, and locked the door behind us. He set his drink and backpack on a table, walked to a narrow casement window and cranked it open, then lit a cigarette and blew a thin stream of smoke outside.

I put down my camera bag and sat. I'd thought I'd feel relieved when I found Quinn. Instead, I felt the way I always did around him, off-balance from a toxic cocktail of impossible yearning, lust, and apprehension. I watched him, nursing my Jack Daniels; finally I stood and walked over. His arm snaked out to grab my wrist and he tossed the cigarette out the window, pushing me against the wall as we kissed. I tasted blood—his, mine—smelled the bitter tang of his sweat and that faint, sweet green-apple scent I recognized from when we were young, a million years ago in a different world.

At last Quinn drew away from me. Gingerly he touched the gash on his cheek and withdrew a red-tipped finger. He turned and touched my forehead, leaned down to kiss the bloody fingerprint.

"Did you find a place to stay?" he asked.

"Not really."

We sat, and I told him everything that had happened since I arrived in London. When I got to the part about Morven's party, Quinn looked taken aback.

"Morven? You mean Morven Dunfries?" he asked. "Was her husband there?"

I nodded. Quinn downed the rest of his beer. "Son of a bitch. Fucking Adrian, what the hell's he thinking?"

"Adrian? What does Adrian have to do with anything?"

Quinn shook his head. "Go on, what happened?"

I told him about Mallo discovering me in the bathroom. Quinn stared at me, any flicker of green burned from his ash-colored eyes. "That was fucking stupid, Cass."

"You know Mallo?"

"Yeah, I know him." He lit another cigarette and took a quick nervous drag. "Knew him, anyway. He's a small-time drug dealer who got in the way of people who actually know what they're doing. So he changed his business model. His wife's a crazy bitch."

I waited for him to say more, but he only began to pace, smoking as he stared at the floor. After a minute I continued with my account. I steeled myself for his reaction to the news that Dagney's passport was gone, but he remained silent until I recounted Poppy's death.

"Jesus fucking Christ." He covered his eyes with one hand. "Dagney is gonna kill me."

I glowered. "Why should you care if Dagney kills you?"

"Because she's a psycho. And you're Hurricane fucking Cass."

"I didn't kill Poppy."

"Do you think that matters?" He slammed his fist on the table, then snatched my wrist. "I'm trying to get us out of here, Cassie—trying to get us someplace where you're not going to be a person of interest to the police. Which right now is nowhere on this fucking planet."

He let go of my hand and stared at the wall. "You know there's CCTV cameras all over this city, right?" he said after a minute. "She could have one in her place."

"I didn't see one."

"The whole goddamned point is you don't see it. What were you wearing?"

"This." I pointed at my leather jacket. "When I left, I put on a raincoat of hers and left by the back door."

"Great. So if they did get you on CCTV, they'd see you went in but didn't come out." He mused on this. "You're tall enough;

maybe they'd think you were a guy. Ditch the hat and scarf. The jacket, too."

"Jesus Christ, Quinn, I'm not a goddamn terrorist. There's not going to be an APB out for someone connected with a dead groupie. They're gonna think she OD'd, and that's all she wrote."

"Maybe. You better pray it's a slow news day whenever this story breaks. You still have your own passport, right?" I nodded. "Well, that's one disaster averted. What about the money I gave you?"

I tapped my boot on the floor. "Good place for it," said Quinn. "Keep it there. What else?"

I told him about Ellen Connors. He glanced at the card she'd given me, handed it back. "That's a fake. ICOTIA—bad acronym. Sounds like coitus interruptus. Did you take anything from Poppy's flat?"

I nodded. Quinn grimaced and held up a hand. "I don't want to know. I shouldn't even have asked. Whatever it is, dump it before we get to Greece."

"Greece? Are we going to Greece?"

He snorted. "Not if you have anything to do with it."

For a few minutes neither of us spoke. I drank my whiskey. Quinn paced to the window and lit another cigarette. Faint sounds came from the pub—a bassline from the jukebox, droning voices. Once someone tried the doorknob before continuing on down the hall.

"Poppy what's-her-name—she had that one great album," Quinn said. "I didn't hear it till I got out of Barrow. I remember when she was with that guy in Lavender Rage. She was hot. Great tits. Who do you think killed her?"

"I don't know. Ellen Connors? Morven? Or maybe Adrian."

"Adrian?" He shook his head. "Never."

I looked at him, puzzled. "You know Adrian?"

Quinn said nothing. At last he shook his head. "Mainlining after you've been straight for thirty years . . . that's a quick way to check out."

"I told you, I don't think it was her idea."

"Maybe." He tossed his cigarette outside, then closed the window. "But it can happen to anyone, falling off the wagon. Ten, twenty, thirty years—" He snapped his fingers. "Like that."

From my bag came a muffled chime. Quinn shot me a quizzical look as I took out Poppy's mobile and set it on the table between us.

"You have a mobile phone?"

"It's Poppy's."

"You took her *mobile*?" Quinn closed his eyes in dismay. "God, I don't fucking believe it. You haven't used it to call anyone, right? 'Cause they can track these things if they're stolen."

"I didn't steal it. She was dead."

"Good point." Quinn picked up the mobile. "I got a guy can wipe that. Worth a few hundred quid. I'll get it cleaned up and sell it. Probably live for a month on Anafi for what we get."

"Anafi?"

"It's an island, good place to disappear. Greece is like flu right now; no one wants to get near it. I just have to figure out a few things. Once we're there, we ain't going anywhere for a while. You okay with that? Anyone gonna wonder what happened to Cassandra Neary?"

"They did that a long time ago."

"What about your old man?"

"I'll tell him I'm on vacation."

Quinn laughed. "Endless vacation, wasn't that a Ramones song?"

I pointed at the mobile. "Can I use the camera without someone tracking me?"

"Yeah, sure. Just don't open the other apps or make a call." He cocked his head. "You want to use it for a camera?"

"I thought I might try it out."

"Isn't that against your code of honor?"

I felt myself flush. "I'm just curious."

"Curiosity killed the Cass."

"Listen, I'm not going to use the goddamned phone, okay? Who would I even call?"

"I dunno. Your defense attorney." Quinn looked at me. "God, Cassie, you and those big gray eyes. Okay, whatever—you just have to be *sure* not to touch anything else. You'll have to upload your photos into a computer—you don't have a laptop, right? So when we get somewhere safe, you can use mine. It's the icon that looks like a camera."

"Just point and shoot?"

"Yeah, point and shoot." He shook his head. "You always used to hate that shit."

"I just want to see what it's like."

"If you lose it and it makes its way to the cops, they'll find your prints on it. Any photos you take, they could trace to you."

"I'm not going to fucking lose it!"

"This is a bad idea, Cass." Quinn sighed. "Go for it."

I dropped the mobile into my bag. Quinn chewed his thumb, an anxious gesture I recognized from when he was seventeen. When he saw me looking at him he stood, throwing his backpack over one shoulder. "All right. Time to blow this pop stand."

We left the pub through the back door without saying goodbye to Derek.

"What he doesn't know can't hurt us," Quinn said, and steered me toward the tube station.

"Where are we going?"

"Isle of Dogs. Canary Wharf. I need to think."

I zoned out in the Underground. Being in London was like falling into some vast interactive computer game where I didn't know the rules, didn't know the landscape, didn't know which characters could kill me.

I barely even knew the language—most of the people on the train seemed to be from somewhere else. If I heard an English accent, half the time it belonged to a tourist. Most of the conversations I overheard were about the weather: more eruptions, floods along Britain's southwest coast, near-blizzard conditions in the Scottish Highlands, wildfires in California.

Here, the freezing rain had turned to snow again. When our train rose out of the tunnel onto the overground tracks, the panorama outside grew dreamlike, slashes of white against sleek dark towers, an immense high-rise silver-blue against a graphite sky dappled crimson with aircraft landing lights. No trees or green space. I couldn't even see any roads.

When we reached Canary Wharf, Quinn took my hand, and we disembarked in silence.

We were on an opened-ended train platform not far from the base of the towering high-rise. The platform's curved roof acted as a wind tunnel; within seconds I was numb from the cold. Quinn zipped his leather jacket and pulled on a black Mao cap. Shivering, I hugged my satchel to my chest.

Quinn didn't speak until we were outside the station. He leaned against a wall to get out of the blowing snow, lit a cigarette, then motioned me to follow him down the sidewalk, past a trio of beautiful young blond women in short skirts and heels, smoking and texting beneath a metal awning.

"Essex girls," said Quinn. "They come in to hang out at the clubs and restaurants after work, hoping to meet a rich young banker."

"Doesn't seem like your normal stomping ground."

"That's why we're here."

He ran to catch a light and I hurried to keep up with him, dodging patches of snow and a Humvee limo. On the other side of the street he halted.

"See that?" Quinn pointed up at a towering obelisk. "Prince Charles said he'd go insane if he had to work in there."

I grimaced. "I would, too."

"This place is nothing but banks. Terrorists ever take it out, the world economy melts down like Greenland."

We walked on, hunched against the cold. The whirling snow smelled of gasoline. A few people hurried past us, businessmen and women ill-prepared for the storm. Belstaff overcoats stained with slush, spines poking through broken umbrellas like the vestigial fingers of bats. Overhead, helicopters droned as distant sirens echoed through the financial canyons. From the corner of my eye I glimpsed flashing blue and red lights that never materialized into a police car. It was like Fritz Lang's *Metropolis* filtered through a Lexus commercial.

After several blocks Quinn turned and headed toward a shimmering skyscraper, its roofline fan-shaped. Rows of phenylblue LEDs cascaded down its facade like rain.

"I have a bolt hole here," he said as we approached the

entrance. Behind its glass walls stretched a lobby that might have been a screenshot from a computer game, with floors, walls, and ceiling all the same shade of azure. Quinn withdrew a key card and slid it into a glowing blue slot. He withdrew the card, touched the glass door, and we entered.

20

Inside, the illusion of being inside a gigantic video game gave way to one of freefall. A young security guard sat behind a stainless steel desk that reflected the enveloping blue. He glanced up from a monitor as we headed toward the elevators. I thought he'd stop us, but he only nodded.

"Evening, Ron," called Quinn.

"Good evening, Mr. Bogart."

The guard turned back to his screen. Once inside the elevator, I looked at Quinn and laughed. "Mr. Bogart?"

"Trust me, he's never heard of him."

We got out of the elevator on the twenty-fifth floor. Quinn hurried down the empty corridor, stopped at a door, and fumbled with a keycard. A green light flashed: He quickly punched numbers into a keypad, opened the door, and pulled me inside.

For an instant the room around us was dark. Then hidden lights slowly brightened, revealing chrome-and-glass furniture, a black leather modular couch, a glossy black marble floor, and cement-colored walls. Windows overlooked Canary Wharf, that silver tower looming above it all like a rocket poised for launch. The flat's gray walls were empty, except for a single small drawing that looked like it might be a Mike Kelley. I stepped toward the windows and heard the almost subliminal hum of an air purification system. Otherwise it was deathly quiet.

"Who lives here?"

"My son," Quinn said, and walked behind a stainless steel kitchen island.

"Your *son*?"

"He works for Clearstream. That's in One Canada Square, so he really *is* insane. He spends most of his time in Italy. This is his crash pad when he's in London."

I continued to stare at him. "You have a son?"

Quinn removed two glasses from a cabinet, opened a bottle of Scotch, and filled each of them, then returned to the living room and handed one to me. "Cheers."

He swallowed most of his Scotch and gazed out at the fractured skyline. Helicopters buzzed between neon towers and steel canyons, searchlights igniting the falling snow so it looked like embers.

"This always reminds me of *Blade Runner*, you know? I keep looking for the blimps advertising the Offworld Colonies." He turned to me and sighed. "Christ, Cass. Yeah, I have a son."

"How old is he?"

"Thirty-two. No, wait—thirty-three."

"Why didn't you tell me?"

"What, during one of those heart-to-hearts we had over the last thirty years?" He stared at me, his pale eyes gin-clear. "You dropped off the map when I did time, Cass. It never crossed my mind to tell you anything."

I wrenched my gaze from his and stared out the window. "I never stopped thinking of you."

I heard him walk back to the kitchen and refill his glass. When he returned he stood beside me, his gaze fixed on the snow-filled sky.

"I was only with her for a summer. In Berlin, before I went to Oslo to work with Anton. She didn't tell me till after he was born." He took a swig of his drink. "Europeans."

"Did you care?"

"That she didn't tell me? No. That I had a kid?" He shrugged. "I saw him a few times when he was growing up. Tossed some money to them when I could. It's not like I was a role model, you know? I've spent more time with him now that he's grown. He's good with money. He bought this place a couple years ago and gave me a key when he visited me in Reykjavík."

I said nothing. After a long silence he downed his Scotch. "I'll see if I can rustle up some grub."

I drank while he rummaged through the kitchen. The place was small but probably cost a thousand pounds a square foot to build and furnish. Big flatscreen TV, expensive speakers hooked up to an iPod dock. A silver-framed photograph of a young man and an attractive Asian woman standing on the Millennium Bridge. The young man looked shorter than Quinn and more compact, but he had his father's pale eyes and the same grim set to his mouth. The spartan bedroom had a vertiginous view of the financial canyon; also a painting of *Star Trek*'s Sulu by Mr. Brainwash.

I didn't see a single book anywhere, not even a magazine. The flat looked like a carefully appointed residence designed for the dead: a twenty-first-century tomb in a glass-and-steel pyramid. Millennia from now, an excavation would suggest that the Isle of Dogs had been a necropolis.

Back in the kitchen, Quinn had cobbled together a meal from spaghetti, some olives, and a tin of anchovies. He'd also found a good bottle of 2005 Medoc.

"Bruno got a deal on a case," Quinn said as he refilled my glass.

"Your son's name is Bruno?"

"Nothing to do with me."

We ate without talking much. The truth was, we'd never talked much. Quinn had never been what you'd call a conversationalist. I'd always sensed him as something subcutaneous, a tremor just beneath my skin; less a real person than the distillation of an emotion I couldn't put a name to. Photographing him obsessively was almost like having sex with him: It replaced the need for words, or maybe it just was another way for us both to avoid them.

After we ate, I cleaned up while he opened his laptop on the couch and scrolled through local news.

"No mention of Poppy showing up dead." He closed the computer and stood. "Which doesn't necessarily mean anything."

"Maybe no one'll report her missing till Sunday."

"Maybe." He took out his mobile and headed into the bedroom. "I have to make a few calls."

I briefly debated whether I should try to eavesdrop on his conversation. Whatever Quinn was up to, I probably didn't want to know. After a few minutes, he came back into the living room.

"C'mon," he said, and put his arm around me.

We went to bed. With the lamp off, ghostly bluish spiders

seemed to crawl across our skin, the wash of searchlights from helicopters that droned above Canary Wharf.

"What's this?" Quinn touched one of the bone discs that nestled between my breasts. "Bad luck charm?"

He pulled me to him, the map of scars across his chest cool beneath my fingertips. I pressed my palm against the raised imprint left by a brand, three interlocking skeletal hands with a death's head between them: the Gripping Beast. When he came, it tasted like bitter almond.

"Cassie," he whispered, and drew me to him till our foreheads touched. "I love you."

"Quinn," I whispered back, and held him so tightly my arms ached.

I watched him sleep, arms crossed upon his chest and head half turned, listening for some dreaded sound even while dreaming. In the snow-splintered light, his scars and tattoos and scarifications rendered him into something not quite human, a white clay effigy or a mummy, beautiful and unearthly. I slipped from bed and got my Konica and reloaded it, removed the lens cap and adjusted the settings without looking down. My fingers knew the camera as well as they knew the topography of Quinn's flesh.

I crouched beside the bed and shot the entire roll of film. My last two rolls had been lost to misadventure. I still had a small stash of Tri-X in the freezer back in New York, but that was it. Black-and-white film is as antiquated as daguerreotype now. You can buy it online, but it's difficult to process unless you have your own darkroom or mail it off somewhere. I didn't know how these photos would come out under such low light, using a long exposure. But I was spooked at the thought of losing all my film, and even more spooked at the thought of losing a chance to shoot Quinn.

I had just settled onto the floor when the window erupted into a milky blue flash as another searchlight strobed past. Quinn's mouth parted; his eyes fluttered open then closed. I hit the shutter release.

The room plunged back into near-darkness. I heard the helicopter's engine, barely louder than the hum of the air exchange system. Quinn sighed and turned onto his side, fists pressed against his chest. I set my camera on the nightstand, stood and watched him sleep, the pulse of blood beneath his temple and the fleeting play of light across his face.

A flicker of the same despair I'd felt outside Poppy's flat overcame me. The world I knew was dying, and nothing I could do with a battered camera and some grains of silver nitrate would keep it from crumbling into ash and bone. No photograph of Quinn, no matter how perfectly timed to capture light and shadow, the intake of a silent breath, would ever bring back the damaged boy I'd known before prison—and whatever came after—had devoured him.

Tears stung my eyes. I raked my nails across my thigh, let the pain flood my thoughts until nothing else remained. I pulled on Quinn's worn flannel shirt, walked into the kitchen, and poured myself a glass of Scotch. I got my bag and settled on the couch, took out the copy of *Monsters and Madonnas* and opened it to the frontispiece. Someone had written an inscription in faded blue fountain-pen ink.

For my dearest Papaver, something to haunt your dreams.
Lovingly, Leith

I took a swallow of Scotch, read the inscription again.

Lovingly, Leith

A hail of fragmented memories across my mind's eye: the image of a teenage Morven, the brutal light scraping youth from her face. She might have been carved from sandstone. Adrian Carlisle. Poppy's husky voice, singing.

"The wind, the wind, the wind blows high
Ash comes falling from the sky
And all the children say they'll die
For want of the Golden City.

I pulled out the photograph I'd found in Poppy's office and stared at the wreckage of Kethelwite Manor.

Of course Mallo and Leith were like brothers.

I grabbed Quinn's laptop, typed in *kethelwite leith thaumatrope,* and stared at what popped onto the screen.

Leith Carlisle, British cinematographer best known for his sole directorial effort, experimental film Thanatrope *[1974], and the disastrous fire that claimed the lives of several of the movie's cast and crew members.*

"Gotcha," I said.

21

I leaned back and sipped my Scotch. I remembered *Thanatrope*. It had tanked on its initial UK release, and played in the U.S. for about fifteen minutes before it was yanked from theaters. Even art houses refused to show it, after viewers vomited during the film and demanded their money back.

I first saw it at the Thalia in 1978. *Thanatrope* owed a lot to Kenneth Anger's wacked-out occult flicks, also to Jack Smith's *Flaming Creatures*, the movie that gave Poppy and her groupie friends their nickname.

Most of all, *Thanatrope* owed a lot to LSD. The movie was shot at that confluence of counterculture, cinema, and hallucinogenics when a lot of really bad ideas looked like harbingers of a new age in human consciousness. For every *El Topo*, you'd get *Manos: The Hands of Fate*, or *Invasion of the Blood Farmers*, a flick that cost twenty-five grand to make and has yet to earn back its advance.

Leith Carlisle's bad idea had been to re-create, on film, what he imagined the ebbing consciousness of a dying person would look and sound like. He'd read a *Scientific American* article stating that human brain cells continued to fire for forty-five minutes after death and decided to replicate the experience on film. You can see how this might have been difficult to pitch to a major studio, though perhaps not to a roomful of tripping film school grads.

But Carlisle had worked as a cinematographer with guys like Carol Reed and Nicolas Roeg. He was friends with Donald Cammell, who got funding for *Performance,* a movie famously pitched to Warner Bros. as a Swinging London comedy like *A Hard Day's Night.* Carlisle couldn't get backing for his own movie, but he'd filmed some of Pink Floyd's early shows at the Marquee and hung out with a lot of rock stars, including the members of Lavender Rage. He was good-looking, confident in the rakish way of someone who has a safety net.

That would be his wife: the eccentric aristo Tamsin Gregollan, who claimed she'd been deflowered by Salvador Dali and carried a stuffed badger in a fire-engine-red Kelly bag. Leith and Tamsin met at a party at Cotchford Farm, just weeks before Brian Jones drowned in the swimming pool there. She was the only daughter of minor gentry who'd made their fortune in tin, thirty-four years old to Leith's twenty-eight. They married just a few weeks later, and after a long honeymoon in Tangiers, split their time between Tamsin's digs in Kensington and Kethelwite Manor, an Elizabethan manor house in Cornwall.

A statuesque redhead who once punched out Eric Clapton for being mean to Pattie Boyd, Tamsin was an early 1970s figure who had an even shorter shelf life than the Flaming Creatures. I scrolled through Leith Carlisle's Wiki and found only a brief mention of her. Same when I trolled the 'net. There were interviews and photos of Leith, a handsome, tanned white man who showed a lot of teeth when he smiled.

But other than a few token pictures that showed the Carlisles as a happy bohemian couple, Tamsin had been edited out of the movie's history. Only Grindarcana.com had a lengthy essay by film historian Nicholas Rombes, who not only credited Tamsin with providing the setting for *Thanatrope,* but also speculated that she might have edited the movie after her husband's breakdown, and even shot new footage that she incorporated into the original.

Back before VHS or the Internet, there were only two ways you could see *Thanatrope*: You could own a print, or you could wait for it to be trotted out every few years at some avant garde film festival. The movie consisted of forty-seven minutes of disturbing images, mostly shot on deteriorating film stock. A time-lapse sequence of human corpses rotting in a field; pigs being slaughtered by a grinning figure who wore a PEACE NOW! T-shirt beneath a blood-spattered butcher's apron; naked teenage girls cavorting in a garden, having sex with each other and a series of boys and older men.

Yeah, those were different times.

The deteriorating film stock had been a deliberate choice on Carlisle's part. His old pal Cammell came across a hoard of unused thirty-five-millimeter film canisters, stored in a warehouse not far from Ealing, and tipped off Leith. Rumor had it the film had been set aside by Michael Powell in the 1960s for *The Living Room,* Powell's unproduced movie based on a Graham Greene play. Heat and time had damaged the raw stock, but Carlisle insisted it was the only way he could afford to shoot on thirty-five millimeter, prohibitively expensive for an independent project in the early 1970s. He also thought the damaged film would be the ideal medium on which to represent images of a disintegrating consciousness.

He was right.

When the footage was processed, it looked as though it had been shot through a series of unfocused lenses smeared with blood, the camera pointed at the sun. Carlisle made no effort to create the conditions preferred by the famous directors he'd worked with over the years. This, as much as his transgressive subject matter, is what destroyed his career when the movie was released. David Lean famously excoriated him during an interview broadcast from a BFI event, accusing Carlisle of betraying the ideals of the British Film Academy.

Even Michael Powell, who you'd think might have stood up for him, considering Powell's experience with *Peeping Tom,* chided Carlisle when they were on a panel together at the same BFI event.

"It's an ugly movie, Leith. Not *what* you're showing us, but *how.* Why make such an ugly movie?"

There's no magic hour in *Thanatrope,* no diffuse sunlight or lens correction. Like his decision to use ruined film, this was all deliberate on Carlisle's part. Even the film's poster was ugly: a rusted pylon, like an electrical tower, silhouetted against a blood-red sky. The pylon's tip skewered a single dark cloud; it was only if you looked closely that you saw the cloud was in fact the photograph of a human eye imposed upon the background. Some of the movie was so underlit it was like watching a movie filmed beneath the surface of the Gowanus Canal.

But most was shot under hard light so glaring that you couldn't actually see what was being depicted, only the stark interplay of shadow and sun, figures irradiated in a flare of crimson or blinding white.

You'd think this might be a good thing, when what you were staring at was maggots and blowflies crawling through a man's skeletal ribcage. Of course it had the opposite effect: You'd imagine what you couldn't quite see there on the screen, and that was invariably worse.

I assumed it was worse, anyway—god knows what actually went on with those bodies in the field. In a *Sight and Sound* interview, Carlisle claimed that Scotland Yard brought him in for questioning. He calmly told them the corpses were all special effects.

"Like Roger Corman, you understand? *Night of the Living Dead*—those aren't real zombies."

Whatever Carlisle was up to, no bodies were ever found. Not in the field, anyway.

The fire was a different thing. The cause was never determined, but the likely suspect was a stack of film canisters stored in the pantry at Kethelwite Manor, some of which contained cellulose nitrate film dating to the early 1900s. Cellulose nitrate film is notoriously volatile, made from the same material used in nineteenth-century explosives. The buildup of gases inside the canisters can cause them to detonate like a bomb. It's one reason so few films from the early twentieth century have survived. Those that did were eventually transferred to cellulose triacetate, and then onto videotape or digital formats.

Carlisle claimed he had no idea there was cellulose nitrate on the premises, but there's no doubt he was the one responsible for bringing the canisters onsite. Late one August night when the cast and crew and hangers-on associated with *Thanatrope* were passed out in Kethelwite Manor, one of the canisters of nitrate film exploded. The resulting fire swept through the house as though it were a haystack. A young film student working as

Carlisle's cameraman was killed, along with three of the teenage actors, and Leith and Tamsin's infant son. Kethelwite Manor was destroyed.

Miraculously, however, the movie itself survived. All of Carlisle's equipment—film, cameras, tape recorders, editing deck—had been stored half a mile away, in the barn at one of the manor's old farmsteads.

After that, everyone associated with *Thanatrope* dispersed. Carlisle and Tamsin decamped to London, where Leith had a nervous breakdown. Yet less than a year later, he and Tamsin returned to Cornwall and settled at the old farmstead, along with a few of the crew members who'd worked on *Thanatrope*. Within a few months, a dozen people were living in the shadow of the ruins of Kethelwite Manor, including two of the girls who'd been filmed frolicking on the open moor: Poppy Teasel and Morven Tempest.

22

I spent about forty-five minutes on Quinn's laptop, reading everything I could about Leith Carlisle and *Thanatrope*. There's not a huge amount of information, but you can watch the movie in its entirety on the avant garde site Ubuweb, and read commentary by Derek Jarman, Nicholas Rombes, and Sally Mann. Elsewhere, you can find a few conspiracy theorists who believe there's an arcane message encoded into the film, or a curse activated every time the movie's shown.

"Hey. What're you doing?" I slid over on the couch so Quinn could sit beside me, a bathrobe hanging loosely from his lanky frame. He lit a cigarette, peering at the laptop. "Come back to bed."

"I want to see this first."

"What the hell is it?"

"It's a movie, shut up."

The sound quality wasn't good, but that didn't matter. Carlisle had shot it without sound, later dubbing in buzzing flies, random laughter and conversations, snatches of music. Rundgren's opening guitar riff from "Juice It Up."

"Right!" I turned up the sound. Quinn looked at me curiously. "Poppy Teasel would've cleared that song for him. And she knew Rundgren. And—wait."

The screen showed a field, high grass bleached out to a lunar white, red-streaked clouds. Blobs and shimmers of violet appeared and disappeared like birds shot out of the sky, or silent explosions in the grass. Three long-haired teenage boys walked in a line, followed by three young girls, all of them naked. Occasionally one of them would turn to face the camera, smiling beatifically. In the background shone the sunlit towers of what I now recognized as Kethelwite Manor, the castle in an acid-fueled waking dream.

If you factored out the visual effects caused by lens flare and damaged film stock, it was an idyllic scene. That wholesome adolescent frolicking in the nude, proto–Ryan McGinley stuff. Yet the overdubbed soundtrack, that aural mosaic of random sounds, was unnerving—birdsong, the drone of bees, snatches of conversation, none of it miked at the same level.

And while I could remember that whole Free Love vibe from when I was a teenager, right now I felt complicit in Leith Carlisle's brand of seedy voyeurism, and not my own.

There was something else going on, too; something that made me wonder if those conspiracy theorists, with their chatter about subliminal images, might not be so crazy.

The double-exposed scenes of people were disquieting, as if I stared at a cave wall and only gradually became aware of the human figures painted there. I felt a strange queasiness, like seasickness and also what I can only describe as a kind of moral nausea. It was a sensation I'd experienced once before, when I'd taken THC that turned out to be PCP—angel dust—and felt my consciousness reduced to a spark in a yawning abyss, the closest I've ever come to believing in hell.

"You okay?" Quinn touched the back of my neck. "Your skin is clammy."

"Yeah." I tore my gaze from the screen. "It's giving me vertigo or something."

"Probably the aspect ratio's wrong. Gives me a headache."

I looked back at the laptop. As the kids walked out of the frame, Poppy Teasel's unaccompanied voice echoed eerily from the soundtrack—the sixteen-year-old Poppy, not the ravaged woman I'd seen a few hours ago, her words so high and sweet and charged with yearning that tears filled my eyes.

"The wind, the wind, the wind blows high
Ash comes falling from the sky
And all the children say they'll die
For want of the Golden City."

As her voice died away, a smaller figure came running up behind the teenagers. A child, three or four years old, with a dandelion puff of dark hair. A little girl, I thought at first, T-shirt flapping to her knees like a tunic. One of the girls turned and swept the child up into her arms.

"Hey!" I leaned forward to pause the film. "That's Poppy."

It was definitely her, very young—she couldn't have been older than seventeen—and heartbreakingly beautiful. It was almost impossible to reconcile her with the woman I'd seen in Stepney. I thought of the words of the doomed girl in *The Picture of Dorian Gray*: "I knew nothing but shadows, and I thought them real."

"Yeah, that's her," said Quinn. "Great tits."

I hit play and pause, running the same few seconds back and forth. Between the original film quality and the laptop's poor resolution, I couldn't get a good look at the little kid's face.

"Is that Adrian Carlisle?" I asked. "I think it is."

"Adrian?" Quinn seemed alarmed.

"Why not? They have the same last name. Him and Leith Carlisle. They all seem to have known each other—Leith and Poppy and Morven and Mallo."

Quinn took a nervous drag at his cigarette. "So this guy, he's Adrian's old man?"

"I don't know. Maybe. Probably." I looked at Quinn. "What's the deal with Adrian? I don't know a fucking soul in London. He turns up, and now it turns out you know him."

Quinn stared at the laptop. At last he said, "Yeah, okay, I know Adrian. We used to do business. When it looked like my flight was gonna be delayed I called him and asked him to track down Derek and look out for you. He's owed me for a while. Now I owe him," he added ruefully.

"You asshole." I punched Quinn's arm. "I can look out for my own goddamn self."

"I think we have proven beyond a reasonable doubt that is not the case," said Quinn, rubbing his arm. "I should have known better. Hurricane Cass."

"Fuck you."

I turned back to the frozen image of the child on Quinn's laptop. Was it Adrian? I did the math and yes, he would have been about the right age. I tried to remember what Poppy had said.

He was such a beautiful kid. I always wished we could have stayed close.

"Look, I'm sorry." Quinn ran a hand along my thigh. "I thought he'd put you up till I got here."

"He's living in a squat," I said without looking up. "I slept on his goddamn floor."

"Yeah, okay, I get it. Next time I'll put you in touch with Ronnie Wood."

"You know Ronnie Wood?"

"Nope. Can this wait? I don't see you for thirty years and you're gonna spend the night on YouTube?"

"It's not YouTube," I said, but he'd already closed the laptop.

"Come back to bed." He finished what was left of my Scotch and stubbed his cigarette out in the empty glass, kissing me as he pulled me to my feet. "Now."

Afterward, I again watched him sleep, his skin a ruined canvas on which the history of the last thirty years had been carved and inked and burned. What had happened to him back in New York, in Barrow and Oslo, before he ended up in Reykjavík and tracked me down?

I knew better than to ask. Instead I breathed him in, nicotine and alcohol and whatever other chemicals kept him alive. Finally I slept. When I woke, Quinn was seated on the edge of the bed, holding a mug of coffee.

"Here," he said, and handed it to me. "I've got to go out for a few hours. I'll be back before eleven."

"What time is it?"

"Almost eight."

The coffee was way too sweet. Every junkie I've known loves sugary coffee and coffee ice cream. I set down the mug and started to my feet. "Give me a couple minutes and I'll be ready."

Quinn shook his head. "I have some last-minute stuff to

finish up. Just be packed and ready to go when I get back, okay?"

I frowned. "Yeah, I guess. Can't I just meet you?"

"No. You need to lay low. You got your passport?"

"I told you—"

"Let me see it."

I fetched my wallet and showed him the passport. He stared at it, then at my face. "You do look like Dagney in this. I think she's taller, though."

"Like I give a shit."

I snatched back the passport. Quinn gave me a crooked grin. "You jealous?"

"Fuck you. Do I need to be?"

I stared at him until he looked away. "No," he said.

He went into the living room, slid his laptop and a few other things into his backpack, then sat for a few minutes speaking softly on his mobile before sticking it into his pocket.

"Okay, I'm outta here," he said, pulling on his leather jacket. He'd shaved earlier, nicking the new scar alongside his mouth. Blood seeped to his jaw; I stepped over and wiped it away with a finger. Quinn took me gently by the shoulders.

"Cassie, listen. Do not let anyone in. Do not answer the phone. And do not under any circumstances use that fucking mobile. I'm going to get us both some TracFones while I'm out."

"What if I need to call you?"

"You won't. I'll be back in a couple hours. If someone knocks at the door, ignore it. If by some insane chance Bruno shows up, just tell him you're my girlfriend. I'll see you in a bit; we can grab lunch then split."

"Where you going?"

"Rotherhithe; I know a guy there with a barge. Trying to finalize our plans."

"We're taking a barge to Greece?"

"That's the first leg. You didn't enter the UK on your own passport. Neither did I. We need to make other travel arrangements—that's what I'm going to do now. We'll leave tonight if I can swing it. Sooner the better."

He held me close and kissed me, and I could feel his heart beating hard against my breast. "See you in a bit, Cassie. Lock the door after me."

I did, then went to make more coffee and scrounge for breakfast. The kitchen was like a Williams-Sonoma showroom: Bunn coffee maker, La Cornue stove, Misono knives in a block of bird's-eye maple, a miniature washer/dryer. Everything but food. The fridge held nothing but liters of bottled water and cans of Irn-Bru and, in the freezer, a half-full bottle of Sapphire gin and a miniature bottle of Polish vodka with a stalk of buffalo grass inside.

I settled for tuna from a can, washing it down with Scotch, then popped a Focalin and threw my clothes into the washing machine. I spent a few desultory hours doing laundry and watching TV, compulsively flipping back to Sky News. Poppy's death still seemed to be unreported; that or it had been bounced to the bottom of the newsfeed by the most recent round of explosions, machete attacks, volcanic eruptions, tornadoes, child abductions, and celebrity deaths. Most coverage focused on the apocalyptic storms in the southwest UK: gales and whiteout conditions, monster waves pounding Penzance and Falmouth. The coast guard had suspended efforts to search for onlookers swept out to sea in Trevena. A section of the Great Western railway line had been destroyed by flooding.

At last I switched off the TV, pulled a chair in front of the floor-to-ceiling window, stared out at the stark canyons of Canary Wharf shining through a curtain of fine snow, and waited for Quinn to return. He never did.

23

By one o'clock I was pissed off. By two, I was still pissed but also starting to panic. After that I cycled between anger and escalating anxiety, spiked with rage whenever I thought of Dagney Ahlstrand. Had Quinn ditched me and returned to Reykjavík to be with her? Had she come to London in search of him, me, or her stolen passport? Was all that shit about going to Greece just a lie to keep me in line?

But in line for what? It didn't make sense that Quinn would track me down in London just to fuck me—or fuck me over—then take off. He was in too much danger himself if he got nabbed by Interpol or the TSA or the Metropolitan Police. Which raised the possibility that he had, indeed, gotten caught.

The thought made me sick.

I finished the Scotch and started in on the Sapphire gin, pacing the apartment as my brain raced through every disaster I could imagine. The fact that Quinn knew Mallo Dunfries meant I could come up with an endless stream of scenarios, each one worse than the one before.

Quinn set up in some kind of sting; Quinn busted on the street right outside this building; Quinn in a bar fight where the cops were called in; Quinn breaking his decades-old resolve to score smack and ODing like Poppy Teasel. When I ran through those, I started in on scenes where Quinn met Dagney at Heathrow and they took off together for the South of France, or simply checked into some local hotel where they were even now fucking their brains out. Then I'd start back on visions of Quinn strung up or strung out or lying somewhere with his throat cut.

I was so wasted I eventually slumped on the couch and stared out at the vertical lines of sleet, a flickering test pattern. From my clenched fist dangled a length of rawhide with its carven eye. As I gazed at it, the eye winked at me.

I staggered to my feet, raced to the bathroom, and vomited. I hung my head over the sink, my face raw from crying. At last I undressed and stepped into the shower. I stood there until my skin puckered, stumbled out, and leaned against the bathroom counter.

My eyes ached as though I'd been staring into the sun. Everything I touched, including my own skin, felt coated with a layer of finely ground glass. Blood-red specks floated across my vision: The room looked like a frame from Leith Carlisle's film. I felt the numb dread that follows a blackout drunk: I'd lost the ability to map the line between nightmare and everyday life, or even recognize that a boundary existed between them.

I took a deep breath, wrapped myself in a towel, got my satchel, and removed the scissors and hair dye I'd bought at Super Drug. Beneath the kitchen sink, I found a plastic bag and a container of bleach. I returned to the bathroom, stood in front of the mirror, and began to cut my hair.

In my twenties, I'd wear my hair in a ragged Johnny Lydon

crop, dye it black or orange or red or platinum blond, then after a few months or a year, grow it out again.

But that had been years ago, before I retreated to the stockroom of the Strand and the decades-long, speed- and alcohol-fueled aftermath of my brief life as a working artist. After a few minutes I put down the scissors and ran my fingers through the few inches of hair that remained on my scalp, carefully swept what I'd cut into the plastic bag. I wiped the floor and counter with a washcloth soaked in bleach, dumped that into the bag as well. Then I opened the box I'd bought at the Super Drug and squeezed the dye through my hair.

After half an hour I stepped back into the shower, watching the dye swirl and disappear down the drain like blood in a black-and-white film. When the water ran clear I got out and toweled myself off. Only after I dressed did I look in the mirror.

A ghost's face had been superimposed upon my own. Or, maybe for the last thirty-odd years, I'd been the ghost. The halo of ragged black hair made me appear younger and even more gaunt, my gray eyes no longer bloodshot but wolf-pale and piercingly alert. Close inspection might prove me to be the same woman in my passport or the photo that Mallo had taken. But if you passed me on the street, you wouldn't recognize me; not unless you'd known me thirty years earlier.

The leather jacket and cowboy boots might be more of a giveaway. I rifled Bruno's bedroom, opening drawers and rummaging through his closet. Dries van Noten, Raf Simons, The Elder Statesman. I grabbed a black sweater and a black henley and several pairs of socks, all cashmere, then spent a few minutes examining overcoats before choosing a long, drapey black cashmere coat with a leather hood, big enough to wear loosely over my leather jacket.

His shoes were too small, which was a moot point. There was no way I'd be giving up my Tony Lamas.

I went to the kitchen and drank a liter of Pellegrino from the fridge, filled the empty bottle with tap water and drank that as well. Then I found my camera bag and returned to the bathroom.

I did one more sweep through the bathroom cabinets. No medications except for a bottle of ibuprofen. I popped four capsules and kept the rest, wiped everything down again with the bleach, and made a final circuit of the kitchen.

I'd drunk everything except the mini of Polish vodka, which I pocketed. I ate the last can of tuna, then inspected Bruno's cutlery and selected a paring knife as a shiv. I returned to the living room and switched on the TV to check the time.

Wednesday, 7:37 P.M. Quinn had been gone for almost thirty-six hours. I'd lost an entire day. I flipped through channels, searching for mention of Poppy's death, anything that might relate to Quinn or myself. There was nothing but the now-familiar litany of bad weather, airport and road and train closures, automobile pileups, flooded roads, and reports of scattered looting.

Maybe Quinn had just gotten stuck somewhere. Maybe, maybe I could find him.

I switched off the TV. In the kitchen I found a pen and some scrap paper, wrote down the time and date and set the note on the counter. Then I stuffed the bag filled with my hair clippings and bleach-soaked rags into my satchel. I dropped the paring knife into the pocket of Bruno's cashmere overcoat, along with a cigarette lighter that Quinn had left on the counter, then slid my hand into the pocket of my leather jacket and withdrew Poppy's mobile phone.

Do not under any circumstances use that fucking mobile.

There was no landline in the flat. I'd memorized Quinn's mobile number but had never used it. I stared at the mobile, and turned it on.

Cartoon-colored icons fizzed across the screen, the Disney version of the blobs in *Thanatrope*. I tapped in Quinn's number, after a few seconds heard an electronic bleat, followed by silence and then Quinn's voice.

You've reached Eskimo Vinyl in Reykjavík. Leave a message, I'll get back to you.

I disconnected and slipped the phone back into my pocket, picked up my bag and walked out of the flat. As the door shut behind me I had the dreamlike apprehension that my skin had dissolved, leaving no barrier between me and the cool recycled air.

Both hall and elevator were empty and silent. I saw no one until I reached the lobby, where the same security guard sat behind the desk. He looked up as I approached, betraying no recognition whatsoever.

"Mr. Bogart," I said. "Have you seen him?"

"Not today." He glanced at his laptop. "Would you like to leave a message?"

I shook my head and left.

24

Outside, I pulled up the hood of Bruno's overcoat and shaded my eyes, dazzled by the infernal grid of towering highrises and the headlamps of approaching cars. The sidewalk hadn't been swept or cleared; footprints shone eerily in the ice. I picked my way toward the Underground station, past another cluster of blond women smoking near the entrance. Inside I paused to check a transport map, locating Highgate. I shut my eyes and tried to visualize the path from Adrian's squat to the tube station. I decided I would wing it.

It took a long time. Trains were running but delayed. By the time I got out at Highgate, the sleet had turned to rain again. I took several wrong turns, but at last saw the stretch of chain-link fence where we'd emerged from the woods. After a few minutes I found the sheet of ivy-covered plywood, slipped through the gap, and walked cautiously across the ice-brittle lawn.

Light seeped from the perimeter of Adrian's window. Otherwise the place appeared desolate and empty. The back door was padlocked; I knocked but got no response. I was reluctant to break a window, so I grabbed handfuls of gravel and pitched them at Adrian's window.

I kept it up until a good-sized stone thunked loudly against the sill. I looked up, shielding my eyes from the rain. Someone peeled back the newspaper curtain and I waved frantically, pointing to the door, then ran to take cover on the stoop. A minute later the door cracked open and Adrian glared out. He wore his Aran sweater over black trousers, his feet bare on the wet tiled floor.

"Who is it?" he demanded.

"It's me," I said, dropping the hood of Bruno's coat. Adrian's eyes widened, and I shoved past him into the hall. "Is Quinn here?"

"Quinn? No. Why?"

"Because he's gone. He left early yesterday morning; he was supposed to be back by eleven but he never showed up."

"So?"

"So something happened to him. He told me he asked you to look out for me—"

"Sounds like he's the one needs looking after," broke in Adrian. He peered at me and reached to touch my hair. "It's rather good—takes about ten years off. I hardly recognize you. Good work with that drop."

"Poppy's dead."

Adrian laughed. "What on earth are you talking about?"

"I delivered the package to her and left. But I forgot my scarf. When I went back to get it, the door to her flat was open. I went inside and found her on the couch with a spike in her arm. OD."

"That's impossible. She's been straight for years. She would never do that."

"She didn't. Someone else did. I thought it was you."

"Me?" He let the door slam shut and grabbed my arm. "What the fuck are you talking about?"

"Someone stuck a needle in her brachial artery, and she bled out. Whatever they gave her was pure enough that she didn't feel any pain. There was no sign of forced entry—whoever it was, she let them in."

I hesitated. Adrian's shock seemed genuine.

"She told me she had brain cancer," I said, prising his fingers from my arm. "Maybe it was a suicide pact—maybe she asked someone to help her."

"She would never do that," Adrian repeated. "Heroin? Never."

" 'Once the needle goes in it never comes out.' "

"Do you fucking understand what I'm saying?" His voice rose threateningly, and I took a step away from him. "She *would not touch it*. If she wanted to die, she'd find another way. She used to say it was like being dead—if she just thought about shooting up, she felt like she was dying, over and over again. She could have gotten it from the NHS but she refused. It was the most terrible thing she could imagine—the worst way she could think of dying."

"Listen—you can think whatever the fuck you want, but she's dead with a spike in her arm."

His face twisted; I thought he might cry. Instead he said, "Come upstairs."

The house was silent save for the drumming of rain. Water trickled down the steps and pooled on the second-floor landing. When we reached his room, Adrian immediately locked the door behind us. It was dark, except for the glow of the propane heater and the blue lozenge of a computer tablet on the bed.

I remained by the door, and reached in my pocket for the paring knife I'd nicked from Bruno's flat. Adrian lit the hurricane lamp, perched on the edge of his mattress, and gazed up at me, stricken. "I hope you're lying."

"Why the hell would I lie? You didn't know?" He nodded, eyes brimming. "What about Morven and Mallo? Would they have heard something?"

"I don't know, I don't know." Adrian's voice cracked. "Probably not—they would have rung me."

"What about Krishna?"

"Krishna?" His eyes widened. "Christ, no. They never met. I'd be surprised if she even knew who Poppy is."

He pulled out his mobile. I stepped over and knocked it from his hand. "Don't call them. Don't call anyone. Her place was ransacked. Not ransacked—someone knew exactly what they were looking for. They went through her drawers and looked at things."

"What things?"

"Artifacts. Prehistoric stuff."

Adrian drew a sharp breath. "How do you know?"

"She showed them to me. She asked me in, we had coffee. She talked about the cancer. Dying. I gave her Morven's present, and she showed me other stuff she had. She said she was leaving everything to the British Museum; she'd been in touch with a curator and she was donating her collection."

Adrian covered his face with his hands. "Oh, fuck."

I settled on the opposite corner of the bed and watched him cry. "I'm sorry," I said. Adrian's shoulders heaved, but he said nothing. "I—she seemed like she needed to talk to someone. Like I said, I loved her music."

With a groan Adrian lashed out, striking my hand so the

paring knife clattered to the floor. "Fuck her music! You know nothing about her, *nothing*!"

He clutched a pillow to his face. I recovered the knife and stared at the hurricane lantern, listening to rain beat against the window. At last Adrian turned to me, his face raw and pale.

"What was it? Morven's gift? Did you see?"

I made a circle of my thumb and forefinger. "It was a bone disc, carved on both sides."

He shut his eyes, as though hearing news he'd long feared. "A thaumatrope."

"Right." I looked at him in surprise. "You know what that is."

"Yes. Do you?"

I slipped my hand beneath my collar and touched one of the amulets, cool against my skin. Slowly I withdrew it, holding it up so that it candled in the lantern's glow. Adrian's expression turned to astonishment, then fury.

"You stole it!"

"No! I saw where she put it—this and two others, they weren't in the cabinet with the rest. She stuck them in a grocery bag on a shelf in the kitchen, like she was planning to take them with her somewhere. When I saw the place had been ransacked, I grabbed them and split."

I twisted the disc between my fingers, then slid it back beneath my sweater.

Without a word Adrian jumped to his feet and began to race around the room, grabbing things. A backpack and a dark green anorak, hiking boots, another cable-knit sweater. He ducked behind the wooden screen, returning moments later with an armful of socks and underwear that he stuffed into the backpack, then he hurried to a bookshelf and pulled out an oversized black volume that looked like a journal, thick with newspaper clippings and loose pages. He jammed that into the backpack then glanced up at me.

He said, "You have to leave."

"Is this about Quinn? Did something happen? If you—"

"I don't give a fuck about Quinn. I'm leaving, and if you're smart you'll do the same."

He hurried to his bed and knelt, then rolled back the rug and pulled up the loose floorboard. His arm disappeared into the hole, reemerging first with the gray canvas bag I'd discovered earlier, then a smaller bag from which he removed a set of keys. He stuffed everything into the backpack, replaced the floorboard and rug, and stepped over to turn off the space heater.

"What are you doing?" I asked.

He ignored me, whipped out his mobile, swiped, and waited for the call to go through. He listened, his face grim, tried again, then a third time. He tapped out a text, stared at the screen, and cursed.

"They're not answering."

"Who?"

"Mallo and Morven. And Poppy. None of them are picking up." He glanced at my bag. "That's getting to be heavy—can you get rid of anything?" I shook my head. "What about the camera?"

"I'm not getting rid of my camera."

"Dragging around that antique," he sneered. "Why don't you just hang it around your neck for a millstone?"

He bent over the hurricane lantern and blew out the flame, held up his mobile so that cold blue light showed the way to the door.

I followed him downstairs and outside into the freezing rain. This time he walked around to the front of the house, picking his way carefully along an uneven concrete path, to where a crumbling brick wall with a broad wooden door hid the house's entrance from the street. A padlocked chain was looped through the door's wrought-iron fixtures; Adrian took out his set of keys and opened the padlock, holding the chain so I could slide out onto the sidewalk. He followed, taking care to pull the door tightly shut behind us.

"I'll text Mariah that I've left the lock off," he said, pulling out his mobile as he started down the street. He glanced at me, and I recognized the same bleak gaze that had met me in the mirror at Bruno's flat when I realized Quinn was gone. "Did you call 999? Emergency services? When you saw she was dead," he added impatiently.

"No."

His expression flickered into fury, then despair. "No. Of course not."

"Where are you going?"

"Mallo's."

He began to walk quickly down the street. I stood and watched his tall, lean figure disappear into the city's fractal light and shadow.

"Wait!" I yelled.

I caught up with him at the corner. "I'll go with you," I said.

Adrian scowled but otherwise ignored me. A black cab approached, and he swore under his breath when he saw its OFF DUTY light.

"I found her." I grabbed his arm. "Any CCTV footage, it'll show whoever it was killed her."

Adrian made a face. "Are you telling me Poppy Teasel had a CCTV in her flat?"

"No," I admitted. "I still didn't kill her."

"Who said you did? You protest too much." He yanked his

arm free. "Maybe it's a good idea. You tell Mallo, and I'll go back home."

"That's not what I meant. I want to know if he's seen Quinn."

Adrian stared at me in disgust. "Of course. You and O'Boyle—you deserve each other. Suit yourself. Morven's the one I'd worry about. Not Mallo. Here's a cab."

There wasn't much traffic, but the roads were slick. The driver spoke softly into a Bluetooth device as we crept along, a soothing litany of Arabic. Adrian sat with his backpack between his legs and gazed at the icy streets. I made a point of looking for a photo-processing shop sandwiched between joints that sold SIM cards and cheap mobiles. I never saw one.

"Who do you think killed her?" I asked at last.

Adrian rubbed his eyes. "I don't know. It doesn't make any sense."

"Murders never make sense, unless you're the one with the gun. Or needle. How did you meet Quinn?"

"One of the DJs I know did a gig in Reykjavík. Quinn got him some rare LPs. Year or so later my mate and I were in Reykjavík for the Airwaves Festival and he introduced us." Adrian glanced at me. "I thought he couldn't leave Iceland for legal reasons. Has that changed?"

"I doubt it. He takes his chances." I took a breath. "Your father—he's Leith Carlisle? The director?"

"Jesus Christ." Adrian sank deeper into his seat and stared at the roof of the cab. "Poppy and now my father—how do you even know about these people? Everyone else has forgotten them."

"I saw his movie. It was fucked up, in a good way."

Adrian gave a barking laugh. "Leith couldn't tell a story to save his life. Not a story you'd want to hear when you were a kid. Not if you wanted to fall asleep afterward. When I finally read Conrad, the penny dropped—every one of Leith's bedtime stories was *Heart of Darkness*. He's been gone since 1980. Took off for Tangiers to hang out with Paul Bowles. *Finis*."

"Do you remember when he made it? *Thanatrope*?"

Adrian's mouth tightened. "I remember everything."

"I watched it again the other night, online. I dunno what it is, but it gets you. It got me, anyway. It's like a subliminal message or something. A recovered memory. Ever since then, I keep thinking I'm seeing stuff from *Thanatrope*."

"That says more about you than the movie, doesn't it?" Adrian cracked his window, letting in a stream of cold air. "Don't romanticize him. Leith was a decent cinematographer who hung out with a lot of groovy people and got ideas above his station. He dropped acid with Brian Jones and Dennis Hopper, and it went to his head—it destroyed his head. He fancied himself the paterfamilias of this marvelous movable feast, only the feast never went anywhere. Him and his wife and his girlfriends and his kids and all the arsehole hippies who wanted to work with him. Three of us were born the same year. All Leith's kids. All different mothers."

"Jesus."

"Tamsin, Poppy, Morven," he said. "Morven was so caught up with Mallo and Leith, she had no time for anyone else. And Tamsin—Tamsin was just evil. Poppy was the one who took care of us—she loved all the kids. I mean, she was still a kid herself. All those girls, none of them was more than eighteen. They'd breastfeed us in turn, the three of them. It was like a bad Thomas Hardy novel. I never knew who my real mother was until I was sixteen."

"You're kidding."

"I should clarify," said Adrian. "I thought Poppy was my mother. I *wanted* her to be my mother. I didn't understand about the drugs—everyone was always stoned, but I just thought that was what grownups were like.

"She would sing me asleep at night, that song about the Golden City—that's where we were all going to live someday. The dream of a golden city. Sometimes she was a little scary, but not as scary as Morven. Or my father, who was sectionable. Eventually everything imploded. Poppy got involved with that guy from Lavender Rage. Morven and Mallo stayed around a little longer but eventually they split, too."

"So you were left with Tamsin. Process of elimination: She's your mom?"

Adrian winced. "Tamsin is not strong on what you might call maternal instinct. And she's batshit crazy, just like Leith. No, she's worse than that," he said, musing. "Leith truly was mad. Bipolar, schizophrenic . . . maybe it was just all the drugs. I don't know what was wrong, but he was obviously extremely disturbed.

"Whereas Tamsin was quite brilliant, but cold-blooded. Wicked. She used to have a dog, a pure-blooded greyhound bitch that got pregnant by some farmer's collie. Tamsin was enraged. She shot the collie, and when the puppies were born she wrung their necks, one by one. Last of all she killed the mother. Bullet in the head, just like the collie. She buried them on the moor. The soil's so acid that it eats away the bones. I looked for them a few years later, and all I found were the metal links from her dog's collar."

"That's gruesome." I stared out at the black rain. "Why would anyone stay with her?"

"Don't ask me. I was a kid, what did I know? I guess because they could all live rent-free, squatting in Cornwall. She made the best of a very bad situation, I'll credit her that—her parents never trusted Leith, and they cut her off once it became clear she'd turned Kethelwite Manor into a commune for a bunch of drug addicts. But the ink had dried on the deed. Tamsin owned it free and clear, that and the abandoned farm.

"After their baby died in the fire, that was the end of it. Her and Leith moved back to his flat in Islington. Me and the other kids stayed with Morven and Mallo and their friends, traveling around in a caravan from one commune or festival to the next."

"Sounds romantic."

"It wasn't romantic," he snapped. "It was fucking sordid. People fucking a few feet away when we were trying to sleep in the caravan, people trying to mess with us. I learned how to bite." He bared his teeth. "They'd give us booze and drugs, cough syrup to knock us out. After a while I wouldn't eat or drink anything unless I knew where it came from. *Who* it came from. Poppy would catch up with us when Jonno was off on tour. That was the only time I felt safe.

"Then Leith had his first big crackup and was in hospital for six months. After he got out, Tamsin had the bright idea of moving everyone back to the farm. They were going to raise sheep like the McCartneys. So we all trundled back to Kethelwite, only instead of living in the manor we were squatting in a derelict farmhouse. My place in Highgate is a considerable improvement. The kids at the village school tormented us, so we stopped going to school. There were six of us by then. Morven taught us to read. Most of us, anyway."

"When did you find out Poppy wasn't your mother?"

"When she seduced me."

Adrian turned to me with a steady gaze, daring me to look away. "I was sixteen. We were at the farm, just the two of us. Everyone else had gone to Glastonbury, even the littlies. I got really sick—we kids were always sick. It was a few years after the mad cow outbreak and I was scared I had that. Turned out to be the flu. Poppy stayed to take care of me. I loved to read, and she'd bring me books. Henry Miller, Anaïs Nin. Just what a mum should give her young teenage son."

He laughed. "Lawrence Durrell was a big one. I lived in those books. One night we smoked a joint together and Poppy put the moves on me. I was right freaked, but then she said, 'You know I'm not your real mum, don't you?' I guess at some level I must have always suspected, because I didn't waste time feeling bad about what happened next. That came later—the feeling bad part, I mean."

I ran through the numbers. "So you were sixteen and she was, what—thirty?"

"Thirty-three."

"Holy shit." I whistled softly.

"It gets worse. She got pregnant—not that first time, we were involved for a few months. Sneaking about, because even at Kethelwite Farm this would not have been on. This was 1989—the seventies were long over. Poppy didn't tell me she was pregnant. She just disappeared. I completely flipped out. I never saw her again."

"Never?" I looked at him skeptically. "But Mallo and Morven . . . you still know all the same people."

"I know. I—I just couldn't. When I was a kid, it was just too much. It's still too much."

I thought of the cancer-ravaged woman in a bad wig, making coffee in her kitchen, and tried to square that with a wasted thirty-something groupie seducing her teenage stepson. "What happened to the baby?"

"I only found out years later that there *was* a baby. Some horrible friends of Poppy's took it right after it was born, raised it in a caravan in Wales. I tracked them down and contacted them, but they didn't want to hear from me. I don't think they believed me—they wanted to imagine the baby's father was Mick Jagger or something. I think that's what Poppy led them to believe."

"Does the baby know you're the father?"

"No."

"Then—"

He held up his hand. "Stop."

We didn't speak again till we reached Crouch End.

25

Adrian had the driver stop a few blocks away from the Dunfrieses' building. The streets and sidewalks remained nearly deserted, the curbs clogged with trash and clumps of slush. I looked around uneasily for Ellen Connors, but saw only a handful of drivers standing in the rain outside the minicab office.

The Dunfrieses' security gate was ajar. So was the building entrance. Adrian and I exchanged a look, shivering from nerves as much as the cold, then hurried into the foyer as the door hissed shut behind us. Adrian bent to shake rain from his anorak. I yanked back my hood and looked around.

Overhead, the tiny red light of a smoke alarm blinked intermittently. A WAY OUT sign above the main door gave off a faint blue glow. Otherwise, the entry hall was dark.

"There's no power," I said.

Adrian straightened and looked up sharply. "Shit. What's going on?"

We approached the elevator. Adrian rattled the metal grille as though it were the door to a prison cell. I looked up into the empty shaft to where the unseen elevator car waited, then down into the yawning pit beneath us. A brisk draft poured from the shaft, smelling strongly of disinfectant. I stepped away with a shudder as Adrian swiped at his phone. He stared at the blue screen, his expression grim.

"They're still not answering," he said. "We'll have to take the stairs."

He made no move to leave. I waited, glancing longingly at the door behind us, until Adrian headed for the stairwell. As he pulled the door open, he looked over his shoulder at me.

"You don't have to come, you know. I wouldn't."

I recalled my last sight of Quinn, his lanky, leather-clad frame growing smaller and smaller as he hurried down the corridor in Canary Wharf; of Poppy, seemingly asleep on her sofa with a thread of blood stitched across her arm. I nodded for Adrian to keep going and followed him.

Adrian took the steps two at a time. I went more slowly, wary of falling. It was even darker and colder than in the foyer. On each landing, the glow of a WAY OUT sign bathed the stairwell in blue. I felt as though I climbed an ancient tomb passage or grave shaft. With every step I fought the urge run back downstairs. Best case scenario was that Mallo would be so enraged by the news of Poppy's death that he'd kill both of us outright. I didn't want to think about what a worst case scenario would look like.

But neither could I picture myself holed up in some squalid London hotel room or bedsit, measuring hours and days and months by the bottle as I obsessed over what had happened to Quinn. I'd had enough of that back in New York. I hurried to catch up with Adrian.

On the top floor I stepped gingerly out into the corridor, one hand on the wall. The air smelled fetid and dank—the filtration system had shut down when the power failed. The folding gate to the elevator was half open. A few yards away, Adrian stood in front of the door to the Dunfrieses' flat, spectral in the mobile's ghastly blue light. As he reached for the doorknob, I ran to knock his hand away.

"No," I whispered.

I held up my own gloved hand, and Adrian nodded as I grasped the knob. It turned with ease. We looked at each other, and even in the dim light I could see Adrian's pupils dilate in fear.

We stepped inside, neither of us speaking. The flat was dark, save for the carnival splash of light from the high windows overlooking the shops and streetlamps in Crouch End, and two votive candles flickering on a coffee table beside two nearly empty wineglasses. On the kitchen counter sat a third, half full glass of red wine.

"Morven?" Adrian called softly. "Mallo? Anyone in?"

There was no answer.

I followed Adrian into the living room. Everything looked much as it had several nights ago, minus partygoers and the accompanying mess of glasses and plates and scattered clothing. Adrian crossed to the window and gazed out. I stepped soundlessly to the side tables where the Cycladic statuette remained, undisturbed, along with the bit of gold foil.

But the tiny bronze figurine of a mouse blowing a horn was gone. Adrian turned from the window, and I motioned for him to join me.

"Something's missing," I whispered, pointing at the small table. "There, a little statue of a mouse—"

He looked at the table, alarmed, then held up his mobile to light the way to Mallo's office.

The office door was ajar. Adrian stopped, and I could smell the acrid chemical tang of his fear and hear his ragged breathing.

Mallo was in the swivel chair, his back to us and his head dangling so that he stared at us upside down. His eyes bulged and his tongue lolled from a gaping mouth. What I could see of his face was plum-colored, the swollen lips almost black. A rainbow swirl of ribbons circled his neck like a farthingale, and a leather belt was wound so tightly around his throat that it had cut into his flesh.

I looked at Adrian. His face had gone dead white. I grabbed his arm, but he only stared at me as though hypnotized until I dragged him back into the hall.

"What the fuck?" he gasped. "What the fuck was that?"

"Lock the front door," I whispered as we hurried to the kitchen. "Cover your hand so there's no prints."

Swiftly I checked the kitchen for any sign of intrusion. As with the living room—as with the entire flat so far—nothing seemed out of place except for Mallo's corpse and the missing figurine. I picked up the half-full glass of red wine and sniffed. I removed my glove, dabbed a finger in the liquid, and drew it to my tongue. As far as I could tell, it was red wine. I replaced my glove and held the glass to the light from the windows, looking for the telltale impression of lipstick on the rim. There was none.

I found an open bottle on the floor beside the candlelit table with the two other wineglasses. Napa Cabernet. I sniffed at the bottle, removed my glove again, and dabbed a finger in each glass. I tasted nothing unusual.

But that didn't prove anything. Date rape drugs are notorious for being impossible to detect if they're dropped into a drink.

Mallo Dunfries would have been a hard man to take by surprise, and a harder man to kill, especially in his own home—

unless someone had slipped him a Mickey Finn. I tilted the first glass, and saw the faint crescent left by a woman's lipstick on the rim. The other glass held a blurred imprint where someone had drunk from it.

I stared at the scene in front of me—candlelight and wine, very romantic—and glanced back into the kitchen at the half-full glass of wine on the counter. Behind me, Adrian called out softly.

"Look at this."

Silently we tiptoed toward the bedroom and stepped inside. "Shit," I said.

The bed was covered with broken glass and the torn remains of the photo of a young Morven. I looked under the bed and peered into closets, then went into the bathroom.

I was worried that whomever had killed Mallo might have gotten to the medicine cabinet before I did. But when I pressed the wall, the hidden panel opened, revealing glass shelves filled with pill bottles and packets of prescription drugs. Downers, mostly—Ambien, Alprazolam, Atenolol. Krishna was wrong: Mallo didn't seem to sleep nights. I hit pay dirt with a bottle of Vyvanse, a stimulant used to treat binge eaters.

"What the fuck are you doing?"

Adrian stood in the doorway, staring at me in disbelief. I scooped the bottles into my bag and closed the cabinet. "This is where I walked in. Let's get out of here."

"Are you crazy? The police will see that's been stolen!"

"Yeah, and they'll think whoever killed Mallo was here for drugs."

I strode back to Mallo's darkened office and edged past his slumped corpse, its bloated face like a rotting pumpkin. I yanked open the top drawer and immediately saw what I wanted, nestled beside the cigar cutter—Dagney's passport.

I grabbed it, then searched his desk, pushing aside drifts of paper. Finally I got on my knees and peered under the desk. There was Mallo's mobile phone, a spiderweb of cracks across its face. I shoved it into my bag and ran with Adrian into the outer corridor.

26

We raced down the stairwell to the second-floor landing, where Adrian halted so suddenly that I ran into him. He grabbed me and pointed at the ceiling.

"Look," he said.

Above us, a fluorescent light fixture flickered on, humming ominously. We stared at each other, and I turned and cautiously opened the door to the second floor so we could peer in. A sickly green glow indicated the power had returned here, too, and presumably to the entire building. I looked at Adrian.

"Isn't it weird for the power to go out during a snowstorm? Aren't the cables buried?"

Before he could reply, a low grinding noise made us both jump: The elevator had begun its slow descent from Morven's studio on the top floor.

"Let's go," Adrian said, and headed back down the steps.

But as though its cables had looped around my ankles, I found myself irresistibly drawn into the second-floor corridor, and toward the elevator. Its folding gate was shut. The same seven-inch gap yawned between the car and the tiled floor.

"What the hell are you doing?" Adrian called from the stairwell.

"Just hang on."

I stepped toward the gate, grabbed its metal struts, and gazed up into the shaft.

Above me, in the shadows, the elevator glided downward along its cables, as slowly and inexorably as in a dream. Its brass fittings gleamed where the light touched them. There was a large blotch on the underside of the car, like an oil stain. I tightened my hold on the folding gate, braced both feet against the floor, and leaned forward to look down.

Two stories below, dim light illuminated the bottom of the shaft. The floor had a glossy liquid sheen beneath a sprawled figure, its arms and legs tangled like those of a floppy discarded doll. There was no head, only a wad of multicolored hair. I thought of the open gate to the elevator upstairs. Three glasses of wine, one seemingly untouched.

Adrian hissed at me from the stairwell. "For Christ's sake, Cass!"

Silently I ran back. We raced downstairs, slowing only when we reached the door that led outside. Adrian pulled the hood of his anorak over his face. I did the same with mine. We strode through the courtyard, out the security gate, and onto the rainy street.

"Keep going," he ordered. "Keep your head down. What did you see?"

"Morven," I gasped. "At the bottom of the shaft. The elevator door was open upstairs."

Adrian shuddered. "That fucking lift—like 'The Pit and the Pendulum.' "

He glanced over his shoulder. "Come on, let's catch this bus."

We sprinted toward the stop and clambered onto the crowded bus. The time on the schedule display read 23:42. We found seats near the back and sat, me clutching my camera bag, Adrian hugging his backpack.

"We're fucked, you know," he said in a low voice. "CCTV, Mallo's got security cameras all over that place."

"Maybe there'll be some kind of delay because of the power. But is that normal, to lose electricity during a storm?"

"No. Yes. How the fuck would I know?" He dug out his e-cigarette and twisted it between his fingers. "It should be connected to the mains, but maybe there's a panel in the flat. Maybe it was an accident."

I stared at him in disbelief. "Really? Mallo strangled himself by mistake?"

"Autoeroticism, people do that all the time."

"Christ, don't be an idiot. Someone doped them, someone they know. One of those wineglasses wasn't touched. Whoever it was, they just happened to drop by after the power went out, poured the nice Cab they'd brought, and gave Mallo and Morven a roofie. Mallo managed to stagger to his office while Morven zoned out on the couch. He got the belt and party ribbons, and Morven got escorted to the elevator shaft. The guest left; we arrived just in time for the power to come back on."

"You think it was set up on purpose? So we'd find them?"

"Probably not. Probably just our bad luck. Whoever it was, Mallo and Morven knew him. And he took that little statue—the one of the mouse blowing a horn."

"That's from the Roman occupation—Londinium. I always loved it, it . . ."

I waited for him to go on, but he got out his mobile, and spent the next few minutes agitatedly texting before placing a call.

"Yo, Leon," he mumured. "Adrian. I'll be there in about thirty minutes with a friend. When you see Krish, tell her to wait for us. Cheers."

He slid the phone into his pocket and turned to me.

"Tamsin," he said. "It has to be. Her and Morven fell out years ago. They never fell back in. She's the one person knows Poppy and Morven and Mallo; none of them would be surprised if she showed up at the door. Or, they might be surprised, but I doubt they would have slammed the door in her face. Leith used heroin; he was never properly a junkie, but Tamsin knew her away around getting it, either from the NHS or someone else."

"What about Mallo? Wasn't he a dealer?"

Adrian shook his head. "Only for the raves we did together. It was like a franchise—I'd arrange for the DJ and the venue. We had no overhead—we always worked out of abandoned buildings, so we only had to charge five quid at the door. Mallo would supply the drugs; him or one of his mates would be up on the second floor of wherever we were. That's how we made money. But not heroin or freebase. Ecstasy and ketamine and acid. Speed. Cocaine sometimes, but mostly X and acid. No hard drugs."

I shifted in my seat, wishing I'd thought to nab a bottle from the Dunfrieses' liquor cabinet. The aisle grew more crowded as people filed onto the bus. A woman who wore a fast food uniform beneath her parka; an off-duty bus driver; several teenage girls dressed improbably for a late night on the town, their pink puffy coats soaking wet and bare legs goosebumped with cold.

In the seat in front of me slumped a middle-aged woman with a child on her lap.

Everyone except for the girls appeared as exhausted as I felt. I rubbed my eyes and looked at Adrian. "Why would Tamsin suddenly freak out like this? How could she think she'd get away with it?"

"She *has* gotten away with it," Adrian retorted. "I still can't find anything about Poppy online. She'll just sit in that flat until . . ."

His voice trailed off. He seemed decades older than when I'd first met him just a few days earlier, his skin gray and dark eyes sunken, his louche expression hardened into a despair that appeared close to fury. I thought of Quinn, the beautiful boy I'd first known decades ago, and how smack and booze and blood had transformed him into something almost unrecognizable, except to another creature like himself.

I asked, "Does Quinn know Tamsin?"

Adrian gazed at me with loathing. "How would I know? I never saw them together, if that's what you're hoping for. Or maybe you're hoping he murdered them? Would that make your sick little romance complete?"

I clenched my camera bag to keep from hitting him. "Fuck you," I said. The woman in front of me turned to shoot me a disapproving look. "If you're so worried, call the fucking cops."

"Keep your goddamn voice down," Adrian warned. "If the police get dragged in, we're both fucked. Quinn, too, if they can finger him."

"So we find another squat and crash there until they *do* find us? Screw that."

"No. We're going to get Krish and get out of here."

"Krish? Why the hell do we need Krish?"

"Because whoever killed Poppy and Morven and Mallo probably knows Krish, too."

"And you."

"And me. And maybe you, too. Krish says she's at a squat party not too far from here. I know the guy who's running it. Can you drive a standard?"

"You mean a car? Yeah, sure."

"Good." He cocked his head toward the bus exit. "Get off here."

We grabbed our bags and pushed our way down the aisle. When I glanced back, I saw the woman with the child glaring after me. I mouthed the words *fuck off* and loped down the sidewalk after Adrian.

27

The rave was in a large free-standing structure that had been a hotel early in the last century. Now its piss-colored brick was covered with graffiti, the windows boarded up and the doors repaired with plywood. A small crowd had gathered in the street, smoking and talking. A girl bent to scoop up a snowball and tossed it, laughing, at someone on the curb. Near the far end of the block, two policemen stood and observed it all with bored expressions.

At the front of the building, a brick arch bore the name CUDLINTON HOTEL, the first word effaced so it read CUNT. Beneath this was the building's once-grand entrance, now reduced to a bashed-in metal door guarded by several men in black anoraks and Happy Face–yellow T-shirts bearing the name REGICIDE PROJECT.

"Hullo, Adrian," one of them said, bumping fists with him. "Lovely weather."

I'd become so inured to the sleet and cold that I hadn't registered it was snowing again. Adrian shook a flurry of white from his anorak's hood. "Yeah. Happy Christmas, Usman. Tolly said Krish is here?"

Usman nodded. "Was earlier. I saw her go in—can't say if she left by a back door. I haven't seen her since then."

"Thanks." Adrian held out his hand, and Usman stamped it with the image of a broken crown. "Can you do her, too? She's with me."

Usman nodded and stamped my hand, and we went inside. A few of the anorak-clad guys called greetings to Adrian as we walked down a dingy corridor, but within moments it was impossible to hear anything over the pulsing din of electronic music. Dubstep, basstep, Schranz—it all boils down to the throb of blood in the skull and a migraine nightmare of flashing lights and smoke machines.

Back in the day, I'd spent plenty of time at Xenon and Hurrah, where you could dance ecstatically, inhale enough amyl nitrate and blow to induce a heart attack, and get laid more than once without leaving the premises.

The scene here looked—and smelled—pretty similar. Sweat and the eye-watering tang of poppers, skunk weed, and beer hung over a cavernous dark room irradiated by blinding flashes of colored light and dazzling pops of crimson and emerald from LED-enhanced clothing. Less public sex than forty years ago but more beats per minute, bass heavy enough to reduce my bones to sludge if I stuck around too long.

The crowd was young, clots of dancers with eyes closed, arms raised or held stiffly at the side, and faces intent with concentration as though deciphering some crucial message from the cacophony of clicks and pops, sampled strings and voices, snatches of long-forgotten songs and ethereal synthesizers. Against one wall, a DJ had set up on a makeshift platform. Banks of speakers and cables snaked around a spidery figure, backlit by lasers as it hopped back and forth between a pair of laptops and a turntable.

I shaded my eyes against the light and pushed my way through the crowd. I had grown accustomed to feeling like a ghost. Here I saw I was only one in a room thronged with phantoms who stared at their mobiles while they twitched restlessly, life-size avatars of whatever stared back at them from their glowing blue screens.

I kept Adrian within my line of sight, not as difficult as I'd feared. There only seemed to be a few hundred people in the vast space. Maybe the weather had kept the crowd down, or maybe this was par for the course. If so, I now understood why Adrian had to live in a squat—at five quid a head, the take would only be a thousand pounds, and the DJ and sound crew would take a substantial share of that.

Adrian wove in and out of the crowd, occasionally waving at someone or stopping to ask a question. As we neared the DJ's setup, Adrian suddenly arrowed toward the wall, where a tattooed giant in a REGICIDE PROJECT T-shirt guarded an open doorway.

Adrian greeted him and the guard let us pass, into a small dark hallway with a narrow set of stairs. A few people leaned against the wall, eyes shut, catching their breath or perhaps nodding out. The only light came from a large battery-powered flashlight propped above the door.

I followed Adrian upstairs. It was even darker here, the corridor crowded with shadowy figures who filed from a black doorway to head back down to the dance floor. A man leaned against the wall, holding a flashlight beneath his chin so that his head appeared to float, disembodied, in the darkness.

"Is that Tolly?" called Adrian.

"It is." The disembodied head grinned and shook back a sheaf of red hair. "Looking for Krishna?"

Tolly pointed into the shadowy room beyond, and we entered. The floor vibrated from the steady bass thud downstairs. Around us, an unseen crowd moved slowly, talking in hushed voices or laughing shrilly as in mockery of the party below. The air had a faint smell of rotten wood and excrement. I heard someone gag as a reassuring voice murmured, "That always happens."

In the center of the room a woman and a man sat on folding chairs. Adrian made his way to the woman, her head lowered as she counted pound notes and folded them into a nylon pouch.

"Tatiana," he said.

She looked up sharply, then nodded. "Oh, Adrian, hello. You on a busman's holiday?"

"I'm looking for Krishna Morgenthal. Tolly said she was here earlier?"

"Still is," said the man beside Tatiana. He turned on a flashlight and swept its beam across the room. Cadaverous figures appeared to jerk and leap in the sudden flare, until it settled on a girl who sat on the floor, legs stretched out before her. "Feeling no pain. Did you want anything?" He fanned out a handful of small white envelopes, like a deck of cards.

"Not tonight. Can you point that torch over there for a moment?"

The man nodded. The flashlight's beam fixed on Krishna, and she held a hand in front of her face as though warding off a photographer's flash. Adrian stared at her, then glanced back at the man. "I hope that's not what it looks like."

"I told her not to do it all at once. She's such a wee thing."

"Been a couple hours," said Tatiana. "She'll have danced it off by now."

I walked over to Krishna and crouched beside her. She didn't look like she was up to much dancing. I thought at first that someone had beaten her. The sarcophagus makeup was smeared across her face, and her pupils had shrunk almost to invisibility. I touched her cheek, the skin hot and moist, like a feverish child's. Her hair stuck in wormy tendrils to her forehead. I pushed a strand behind her ears.

"Wakey wakey," I said.

Krishna blearily looked up.

"Ado." Her voice was thick, and I couldn't tell if she actually saw Adrian—it seemed more like she was still in the grips of whatever drug she'd taken. She ran her tongue along her cracked lips, set one hand on the floor, tried to push herself up, then flopped back. "I know," she whispered, staring at me with pinned eyes.

I pulled her up, pinching her chin between my thumb and forefinger until she squealed in protest and slapped at me.

"That's better," I said, and turned to Adrian. "Can you get her other side?"

We got Krishna to her feet, slung one of her arms around each of us and carried her downstairs. She cursed at Adrian, kicking at him ineffectually until abruptly she went limp and became a hundred pounds of dead weight. I couldn't tell if this was out of spite—she was still breathing—or if she'd passed out once more. I began to wish she'd remained unconscious, or that Adrian had just called an ambulance.

At last we got outside. I'd feared the cold and snow might conspire to wake Krishna from her stupor. Instead she moaned and sank to the ground, talking incomprehensibly to herself. It was impossible to move her—when we tried, she gave a garbled shriek and attempted to claw at Adrian's face.

"Fucking *bastard*."

Frowning, I glanced at Adrian. What the hell had he done to piss her off? He looked around in despair. People were watching us; pretty soon we'd draw a crowd. I saw the two cops at the end of the block gaze in our direction, and turned back to Krishna.

"Come on, Krish," I urged. "You're gonna fucking freeze to death."

I peeled off Bruno's heavy overcoat and draped it across her shoulders so the leather hood shielded her face. There was nothing to be done about the rest of her attire—a man's pinstriped suit jacket draped over a floppy red sweater and a short plaid skirt, and chunky Doc Martens with no socks. Her bare white legs were goosepimpled with cold. I hugged her tight, hoping that any onlookers would mistake our clinch for passion and not desperation.

"Remember me? 'Be My Baby'?"

Krishna's eyelids fluttered. "Yah, maybe. Who're you?"

I zipped up my leather jacket and ran a hand across my cropped black hair. "Cass. We met at the Banshee a few nights ago. I got a haircut."

"Cass." She screwed up her eyes, staring at my cropped head. "I like it."

"That's great." I gave Adrian a nod, indicating he should move fast, then said, "Listen, Krish—I'm getting a cab, why don't you come with me?"

"Where we going?"

"I have no fucking clue," I said, and she laughed.

"Yah, sure." She staggered to her feet, and I caught her before she could fall. "Less go."

We managed to get her around the block and out of sight of the cops. "C'mon, Krish, straighten up," I said impatiently, but it was hopeless. She was surprisingly strong for such a tiny person. Her head lolled onto her chest and she dragged both feet. When I glanced over my shoulder, I saw two ragged lines drawn in the snow, as though a tiny, drunken skier accompanied us.

"Hang on to her while I find a cab," Adrian said at last, defeated. "Try to make her not look like a drug casualty."

"Yeah, right," I said.

Adrian stood beneath a streetlight and spoke into his mobile. He held up his hand and mouthed *Five minutes*. It took a little longer than that, but when a taxi at last pulled over, Adrian quickly opened the door. I slid inside, dragging Krishna after me, and Adrian hopped in last.

The driver looked at Krishna, then Adrian. "Hospital?"

"No, no. " Adrian shook his head and recited an address before leaning back, eyes closed. "God, I haven't spent this much time in cabs in my entire life."

Krishna put her head in my lap. Her drug-fueled rage toward Adrian appeared to have run its course: She stared at him, glassy-eyed, before her lids fluttered and she zoned out. I turned to Adrian.

"Now what? Back to your squat?"

"No. I need to get out of London. Krish, too."

"Fine. Just drop me off wherever. Someplace I can find a hotel."

He took a breath, then said, "Look, I know it's a huge favor to ask, but I'd appreciate if you came with me and Krish."

"Go with you?"

He nodded. My mental portfolio of bad scenarios expanded to include my own corpse, and maybe Krishna's, laid out on the floor of an abandoned building, or floating in the Thames. Krishna might not have been the best judge of character—her dalliances with me and Lance proved that. But her sudden animus toward Adrian unnerved me slightly.

"Forget it." I tapped at the plexiglass window that separated us from the driver. "Hey, stop here. I'm getting out."

The driver ignored me.

"I'm not a murderer," Adrian insisted. "I don't have the discipline. Or the imagination."

"Doesn't take much imagination to push someone down an elevator shaft or put a roofie in their drink."

"I was home—Mariah and several others can testify to that. And I detest red wine—it gives me migraines. Listen—

"This is not a good place for you to be right now, Cass." His tone became more urgent. "Poppy's death might have gone unnoticed, but that's over. People will connect the dots between her and Morven and Mallo. If there's any CCTV footage, you and I will show up. We're neither of us easy to miss. But I have an alibi. You don't."

"So why help me out? Why not just leave me here for the wolves? It's what Mallo would do."

"If Mallo was going to throw you to the wolves, he'd have done it when he caught you fondling the medicine cabinet. I have my own reasons for not wanting a conversation with the local constabulary. And I'm not particularly fond of wolves. Nasty hairy things."

I remained silent and refused to meet his gaze. After a few minutes, the cab pulled over. Adrian thrust several five-pound notes through a slot for the fare, opened his door, and hoisted Krishna to a sitting position.

"Could you please offer some assistance?" he asked with a glare.

I swore and I grabbed my bag, took Krishna's other arm, and helped him maneuver her onto the sidewalk. She might have weighed only only a hundred pounds soaking wet, but she was well on her way to *being* soaking wet, by the time Adrian and I managed to get her down a snow-covered alley that ended in a cul-de-sac.

"Hold on to her," commanded Adrian, and slogged toward the door of a garage bay.

With Krishna propped alongside me, I watched Adrian fiddle with his keys until he found one that worked. He opened the garage door and I hurried over, half carrying, half dragging Krishna. Adrian flipped a switch, and a fluorescent light flickered on.

In the middle of the garage stood a small vintage Land Rover, pale green and remarkably free of rust. One back window was cracked. Peeling decals formed an intaglio on the other, along with a membership chevron for a single-marque car club. I looked at Adrian.

"What the fuck is this?"

He withdrew his alligator cigarette case, removed an e-cigarette, tapped it against the case, and looked at me with eyebrows raised.

"Fancy a road trip?" he asked.

PART TWO

KETHELWITE FARM

Carry on in this systematic manner until half of your film is gone. At this point change your approach: abandon system, abandon logic, abandon sanity. Keep moving . . .

—William Mortensen, *Pictorial Lighting*

28

I ran through my options. I could foray solo through London, in hopes of finding Quinn and avoiding arrest. Or I could turn myself over to the Metropolitan Police and the mercy of the British legal system. The best outcome there might be deportation back to the U.S., where I'd face questioning about a suspicious death in Maine, and also about several murders in Iceland.

Of the people I knew in London, three were dead. One was MIA. One was tending bar and could ID me in a police lineup, cropped black hair or not. One was unconscious.

And one was now offering me a way out of town.

I let Krishna slide to the floor. The cold might counter the effects of whatever she was stoned on, as long as she didn't develop hypothermia. I walked over to the Rover. Adrian sat on the driver's side, the door open beside him, and stared intently at the dashboard. I watched as he turned the key then pressed an ignition button.

There was a click but nothing else. He repeated this process a few times before he opened the glove box and pulled out a wrench. He hopped from the cab and opened the hood, peering at the battery.

"Now for brute strength." He glanced at me. "Will you please get in the driver's seat?"

"Yeah, okay."

"When I tell you, press the ignition button."

He smacked something under the hood, and at his command I hit the ignition. With a wheeze the engine turned over, releasing a plume of diesel exhaust. Adrian gave me a thumbs up and hurried to Krishna on the floor.

"Now give me a hand with her," he yelled.

Two jump seats faced each other in the back of the vehicle. We manhandled Krishna into one of these. She cursed and thrashed around, but it wasn't much of a fight against two of us. Adrian buckled her in, retrieved his backpack, and hopped back behind the wheel. I got my camera bag and slid onto the bench seat, then took the wrench from him before he could replace it in the glove box.

"I'm keeping this. Last time I got in a car with a strange guy he cold-cocked me."

Adrian scowled, but his face relaxed as he gazed at the gash on my cheek and the starburst scar beside my eye.

"Okay, I get it," he said. "No sudden moves. However, I thought we established that I am unlikely to kill you, seeing as I've had several opportunities to date. You said you can drive a standard?"

"Yeah, of course. Can you?"

"Being a flâneur doesn't preclude a driver's license. What about snow?"

"I grew up in New York State."

"Excellent. This was my father's car; I haven't driven it in a while. It's got four-wheel drive—go straight up a cliff if it needs to—but the drum brakes were shite even when this was new. So use the hand brake if you have to. I'll do the first leg."

As the engine warmed up, Adrian glanced at his mobile.

"Parts of the M4 are shut down," he said. "Jackknifed lorry—there's a twenty-mile backup. After Exeter we might do better."

He put the Land Rover into gear and eased it from the garage bay, let it idle as he jumped out to close and lock the door, then slid back behind the wheel.

He began to drive. The wipers scraped noisily at layers of grime and cobwebs. After a few minutes, snow was added to the mix. There was little traffic, which was a good thing. I couldn't believe Adrian had ever driven a car before, let alone an ancient four-wheel-drive Land Rover.

"Stop riding the goddamned clutch!"

Adrian ignored me and stared grimly out the window. The shocks were shot, and the bench seat had as much padding as a box spring. "It'll be better on the A303," Adrian assured me.

"I doubt it. Where we going?"

"Cornwall."

"Cornwall's west?"

"Southwest. If Britain's a shoe, Cornwall's the tip. If you want a vision of the past, imagine a winklepicker kicking into Mount's Bay, forever."

"How far?"

"Three hundred miles. Five hours under optimal conditions. Which these are not. We're going to my father's house."

"Your father? I thought he was in Tangiers."

"Well, he didn't take the bloody house with him. Home is where you hang your head, right? Or where they hang you. I don't have much of a choice, do I? And you . . ."

He shrugged. "You don't really have any fucking choice whatsoever."

I turned to stare out at a bleak sprawl of buildings: coal black, gray, rust colored, all streaked white with snow. New construction gave way to older residential towers and blocks of council flats. Ice-sheathed chain-link fences were topped by coils of razorwire and metal spikes. A group of hooded figures loped silently along the sidewalk, faces glowing blue in the darkness, and veered suddenly down an alley like a shoal of luminous fish.

A police car raced past us, sirens wailing. Adrian steered the Rover onto a side street. A short while later, we merged onto the ramp for an elevated highway, where a seemingly endless line of vehicles crept between emergency flares ablaze like roman candles. I looked back and saw a burst of marigold light bloom and immediately fade above the skyline.

Adrian glanced into the rearview mirror. "Shit."

"What?"

"Nothing. Everything."

I got the mini of Polish vodka from my bag and gulped down a mouthful. Adrian held out his hand and I passed the bottle to him, then rolled down the window to let the snow pelt my face. The thought of Quinn coiled inside me, an adder poised to strike. I closed my eyes and rested my forehead against the cool glass.

"Here." I jumped as Adrian prodded me with the bottle. "Any more?"

I shook my head and got a Focalin from my bag, chasing it with the last mouthful of vodka.

"Is that to keep you asleep or awake?" asked Adrian.

"Awake." He held out his hand and I gave him a capsule.

It was more than an hour before the city loosened its grasp. The snow never did. Red and blue lights strobed in the corner of my eyes. Once we were stopped at a roadblock. Adrian rolled down his window, and a policewoman swept a flashlight's beam inside the car. She was heavily padded in cold-weather gear, her cheeks and nose bright red and eyelashes dusted with snow.

"Where are you headed?"

"Staines."

The cop peered at us, then at Krishna in the back.

"Sleeping it off." Adrian flashed the cop a grin. He stuck out a hand and watched snowflakes melt into his palm. "D'you think it's ever going to stop?"

The cop shook her head. "By morning, they say." She drew a gloved hand across her eyes and stepped back to take in the Land Rover. "Well, you've got the right vehicle for it. Drive carefully."

The snow changed to rain, then sleet, then snow again. The motorway looked like the aftermath of a disaster movie, cars and eighteen-wheelers everywhere on the shoulder, some with passengers huddled inside, others abandoned. I saw as many emergency vehicles spun off the road as on it. Every other exit was closed or marked DIVERGENCE. Adrian appeared to handle the Land Rover by force of will alone, yanking then releasing the hand brake, his hands so tight on the wheel I wondered if I'd have to cut them off if he ever stopped.

After two hours we pulled onto the A303. It continued to snow steadily, fine flakes like sand, but there was much less traffic, and I could see Adrian's shoulders relax.

"Hand me one of those fake fags, will you?" he asked. I got one from his backpack and he sucked at it greedily, then sighed. "Not really the same, is it? But then nothing is."

He glanced into the back seat at Krishna, still out like a light, and asked me quietly, "What did you talk about? You and Poppy?"

"Not much." I tried to gauge if he was suspicious or just wanted to assuage his grief. The latter, I thought. I could see how Poppy would cast a spell on you for life, especially if you were just a kid at the time. "Like I said, she told me she had cancer. I don't know why."

"She's always more inclined to talk to strangers than whoever she should have been sucking up to, Nick Kent or Paul Rambali. She hates music critics."

"Everyone hates music critics."

Adrian fell silent. His face was haggard, his louche good looks replaced by exhaustion and heartache. His hands clutched the wheel as though it were a life preserver.

After a minute, I said, "It can fuck you up, if you meet the most important person in your life when you're sixteen, seventeen. You imprint on them, and you never escape from it. That's what happened to me."

"Quinn?"

I nodded. Adrian winced. "Can't picture Quinn as a kid. All those tattoos and scars."

"Those were years away." I stared out the window at the blowing snow. "He was beautiful. Just the most beautiful thing I'd ever seen."

"Her, too," Adrian said softly, and began to weep.

29

Sometime in the middle of the night we stopped at a service area. The parking lot was crowded, with the usual cadre of smokers huddled by the entrance. Adrian filled the tank while I went inside to get us some coffee and food, along with a couple of bottles of cheap red wine and a can of Foster's. When I returned, Krishna was still snoring softly.

"Christ." I shook my head and handed Adrian a bacon sandwich wrapped in cellophane. "I want whatever she had."

"I was thinking of waking her."

"That's a terrible idea."

Adrian mused on this, then nodded. "I suspect you're right."

He cranked the Rover's heater, pulled away from the gas pump, and found a parking spot near the motorway ramp. "Do you think you could drive in a bit? I need to rest, or I'll drive into a truck myself. "

"Yeah, sure. Want to switch now?"

Adrian took a bite of his sandwich, grimacing. "I'll get us past the next few miles, where it's narrow. We can switch after that.

It's a fairly easy stretch after that for a short while. Just remember to wake me before Exeter."

There was hardly any traffic now. The snow had stopped, though a steady wind continued to blow gouts of white across the roadway. The landscape was mostly flat: I could see a far-off wind farm, lines of towering electrical pylons, a scatter of village lights. The clouds had pulled away, revealing an obsidian sky and a few stars.

"Look," said Adrian. He slowed the Rover, rolling down his window to point something out.

Above the horizon hung a three-quarter moon that cast a radioactive brilliance across the blue-white plain. In the near distance, several distinct shadows appeared to hover above the ground—a trick of the lunar light. Adrian pulled the car onto the shoulder, turned off the ignition, and stepped outside.

I remained where I was while Adrian stood with his back to the vehicle, anorak flapping in the wind. After a minute he turned and beckoned to me. I retrieved the wrench and warily joined him, my boots crunching on brittle, snow-covered grass.

"What is it?" I asked.

Adrian said nothing. I stared across the plain, to where the hovering shadows resolved into blocks, dead black against the snow. Even from here I could see how huge they must be.

I turned to Adrian in amazement. "Is that Stonehenge?"

He nodded, the skin beneath his eyes glistening. "It is."

"Have you ever been there?"

Adrian wiped his eyes. "Many times. It was easier twenty years ago. Poppy said they used to camp out under the Heel Stone. But it's better like this, from a distance. I think so, anyway."

He turned and walked back to the car, calling out to me, "Ready to take over?"

I stood for another minute in the cold night, staring at the eerily moonlit panorama, and then returned to the Land Rover.

I hadn't been behind the wheel in months. It felt good, even as I tried to remember to drive on the opposite side of the road. Beside me Adrian slept, his head pillowed against his backpack. Krishna continued to snore in the jumpseat. I popped the can of Foster's and took a sip, balanced it on the seat beside me.

Adrian was right: The brakes were shit. Fortunately I didn't have much cause to use them. Outside, the moonlit plain stretched like the landscape of a dream. Adrian slept with his head thrown back and his mouth open, lank gray-streaked hair falling across his eyes. His breath came in quick shallow bursts, as though he were racing across the snowy fields that surrounded us, the last of the Focalin sparking in his brain.

I thought of Poppy lying on the couch with a spike in her arm, her preternaturally peaceful expression, no evidence of a struggle. Despite what Adrian had insisted about her relationship to heroin, maybe she had, in the end, welcomed the chance to go out on a wave of oblivion. I might make the same choice.

I looked at Adrian and tried to imagine him as a sixteen-year-old, seduced by a beautiful woman twice his age, someone he'd known and trusted since infancy. He looked younger, with his mocking smile gone and that sardonic laugh silenced. His sleeping face tugged at my memory, the same way that Morven's had when I first met her. Some long-ago photo of his father, Leith Carlisle, as a young man, or maybe a photo of the young Adrian I'd glimpsed somewhere—the Dunfrieses' flat, Krishna's—without registering who it was.

In the road ahead of us, several inches of snow had drifted. I downshifted to ease the Rover through the patch, glancing into the rearview mirror.

Krishna stared back at me, her teeth bared. Her dark eyes had sunken into a Medusa's face and black tendrils wormed across her naked scalp. I gasped and slammed on the brakes, remembered too late to yank on the handbrake. The Rover skidded several feet before coming to a halt just inches from a ditch. I whirled around to see Krishna reaching to grab Adrian's hair.

"What the hell?" I snatched her wrist and yanked her away from him. "What the fuck are you doing?"

For an instant I thought she'd spit at me. She seemed to think better of it. She looked quickly out the window, then slouched into the jumpseat. "Where are we?"

Adrian muttered and turned in his seat, pulling his coat over his head. I waited until his breathing slowed, spoke his name softly several times.

"Adrian? You awake?"

He seemed to be back down for the count. I let the Rover idle and turned back to Krishna.

"What the hell's going on with you and Adrian?"

She stared at me obdurately and said nothing. After a minute I grabbed my bag and began to dig through its contents, holding pill bottles up to the dashboard light until I found the Solpadol. I held up the bottle so Krishna could read the label.

"These'll help you sleep."

"I don't want to fucking sleep."

"Really? You feel like walking back to London?"

I cocked a thumb at the car door. Krishna ground her teeth, then leaned forward to look at the bottle. I poured three pills into my palm and held them out to her. Her eyes narrowed.

"How do I know that's not a roofie?"

"You just saw the bottle."

"Yah, but you could have put something else in there. *You* take one."

"I'm driving. Last chance . . ."

I started to withdraw my hand. Krishna grabbed it. "Anything to drink?"

"No."

She gave me a half nod and swallowed the pills.

I waited a few minutes, debating whether I should try to find out if she knew anything about the Dunfrieses. I decided against it. Krishna was too much of a loose cannon; given her constitution, I hoped three downers was enough to put her out. If this was some sick lovers' quarrel, I didn't want to hear about it. If it had something to do with the three corpses back in London, the Solpadol might buy me a few hours until I could figure a way out of this mess.

When Krishna's eyes reached half-mast, I put the Rover back into gear and began to drive once more. It wasn't much later that Adrian stirred, yawning, and turned to me.

"Everything all right?"

"You missed the excitement. Krishna woke up and tried to throttle you."

"Really?" He didn't sound surprised.

"Yeah. Is there something going on with you two?"

"No. She's a high-strung lass, that's all."

I could hear the lie in Adrian's affected drawl, and felt a pang of unease as I caught the faintest trace of the spoiled-fruit scent that had signaled damage when I first met him in Krishna's flat.

"I gave her a few Solpadol to knock her out."

"You're a human pharmacy. Her, too. Actually, I'm surprised you didn't have to use a tranquilizer gun."

He peered over his seat at Krishna, sleeping with her fingers pressed against her mouth. Tenderness mingled with desolation in his expression. I quickly looked away as he turned to me and shot me a smile as false as his tone had been.

"Shall I drive? You should rest for a bit. You look knackered."

"Yeah, sure."

We traded places. I wedged myself against the door with my bag in my lap, so that I was facing him. I had no intention of sleeping: I trusted Adrian about as far as I could throw him. But the soft rumble of wheels on the snow-covered road and the monochrome world outside conspired to do me in. I zoned out. If any dreams broke through the wall of exhaustion that surrounded me, I never knew.

30

I woke some time later and sat up like a shot to see Adrian still behind the wheel. He appeared both wakeful and apprehensive, but also strangely composed, his gaze fixed unwaveringly on the road ahead. Wherever we were, it was not unknown to him. I looked outside.

The moon had set. On the eastern edge of the horizon, the night sky had taken on a violet tinge that gradually paled to green. Smooth hills and ragged stony outcroppings rose stark against the sky, as sharply defined as though they'd been cut from black paper. It all looked beautiful and unearthly, like a world under glass, or one of those intangible landscapes glimpsed inside a spun-sugar Easter egg.

There was no shoulder—the desolate road seemed only wide enough for a single vehicle. I rolled down my window. The cold air had a mineral scent, snow and raw earth, and the coppery tang of the sea.

I stared across the moor, overcome by a sudden yearning. Not for booze or Quinn or my own lost life; not even for the camera in my lap, the meticulously calibrated way it allowed me to experience the world at a safe distance.

Instead I was overwhelmed with longing for the world itself: the cold sting of air against my cheeks, the smell of diesel and the gradual play of shadow across the moorland, as the eastern sky brightened from beryl to gold. No camera could ever capture any of that.

I swiped a hand across my eyes and nudged Adrian. "Hey. Do you know where we are?"

"Padwithiel."

"Are we near the ocean?"

Adrian nodded, yawning. "Yes—West Penwith. You're never more than a few miles from the sea here. Land's End is that way." He pointed. "From there it's only three thousand miles and you're home. But you don't want to wander off. The moor is dangerous. I need to stop and lock the hubs to put this into four-wheel drive. The way gets a bit iffy up ahead."

Krishna was still asleep. The rats in my head were starting to claw. Adrian drove a few more miles before stopping to lock the hubs. I got out to stretch and see if I could get a mental map of where we were. It was tough.

One side of the narrow road was bounded by dense hedges, too high to see over. On the other, a low tumbledown wall gave way to barren moor and gray-green fields studded with a few stone farmhouses that looked like they'd stood for a thousand years. A seemingly random jigsaw of stone walls and hedgerows crisscrossed the fields, as though a drunken giant had attempted to draw a map across it. In the near distance I glimpsed a standing stone, man-high, surrounded by gorse still studded with a few yellow blossoms. The sun hovered just below the horizon, and patches of snow shimmered like phosphorescence.

In a place like this, a film like *Thanatrope* made perfect sense.

"That's done," said Adrian, straightening. The wind lashed his hair across his face as he turned to face the direction of Land's End. I was startled by how much at home he looked here. A sort of fierce joy overtook his features and he turned to me again, his anorak hanging loosely from his lanky frame.

"You know how they say the past is another country? Well, this is it."

I hesitated, then slipped a hand beneath my layers of clothing and withdrew one of the thaumatropes on its rawhide cord. "You freaked out when I showed you this back at your place. Did Poppy steal it?"

Adrian's thin mouth tightened. "No."

I dug Ellen Connor's card from my pocket and handed it to him. "A cop cornered me at a pub in Camden Town. Europol or something."

"'International Commission on Traffic in Illicit Antiquities,'" Adrian read aloud. "Did she try to shake you down?"

"Yeah. I blew her off and got out. Is she for real?"

"Define 'real.' She's former law enforcement, if that's what you mean. But ICOTIA was disbanded several years ago. I'm not sure what Ellen's doing these days. We're out of touch," he added delicately.

I scowled. "Well, she was pretty intent on giving me a hard time."

"I suspect she's working for a private collector." Adrian inclined his head toward the bone disc. "Even if she was still with ICOTIA, you would have been safe. Any British artifact made of bone, or clay, or stone—as long as it doesn't contain more than thirty percent gold or silver, you don't need to turn it in to the authorities."

"Authorities meaning the British Museum? Inspector Wexford?"

"Under the Portable Antiquities Scheme, if you discover something you're supposed to report it. But the law's almost impossible to enforce. That's why you see nighthawks out with metal detectors at three A.M. They're looking for treasure. Saxon hoards, Roman coins—something like that can set you up for life, if you sell it on the black market. Or go through the legal channels and sell to a museum. Usually nighthawks will strike a deal with the landowner and agree to share it with him. Sometimes they go it alone. But they're looking for metal, not bone."

I looped the cord over my head and held up the thaumatrope. "So something like this, you wouldn't be required to report it."

"That's right."

"But this isn't from the UK, is it?" I ran a finger across the disc's implacable graven eye. "I assumed it was from, I dunno. France or Spain, someplace like that. You know, with cave paintings. Ice Age stuff."

"We had an Ice Age, too. Several of them."

"Yeah, but were people here making things like this?" I wound the thaumatrope on the string and spun it. The ancient eye opened and shut, opened and shut. "Because that would backdate the British film industry about ten or twenty thousand years. That would be kind of a major scientific breakthrough, right?"

Adrian's eyes cut at me sharply. I glanced into the Rover to make sure Krishna was still asleep. In a low voice I asked, "Where the hell did this come from?"

Adrian extended his hand to let his fingers brush the bone disc. "The fogou at Kethelwite."

"What the hell's a fogou?"

"An underground passage. Like a barrow. Fogous are a bit different—no one knows what they were actually used for. Some sort of Iron Age ritual, maybe. The one at Kethelwite has a long central passage with chambers branching off of it. I only went in there once—it scared me to death. There are ruins everywhere at Kethelwite; we played in them when we were kids. We were always digging up ax heads and flints."

"Bones?"

"No. The soil's too acidic—anything buried a few thousand years ago is peat now. But there were all kinds of other artifacts. We'd pretend we were knights in Middle Earth. When Morven and Mallo bought the place in Crouch End, they took a good many with them. I think Morven only wanted them as souvenirs, at first. The gallery and black market, that came later."

I looked at him dubiously. "Kind of bizarre souvenirs. Is that what they sell in their shop?"

"The Boudicca shop's mostly British antiquities—legal ones. They have suppliers out in the field; everything's registered before they take it on to sell. But the grave goods from Kethelwite, that's what they used to open the shop after Mallo got out of prison. Up until then it had all just been lying around their flat. Like I said, souvenirs. Tamsin was furious—she said the artifacts belonged to her, she thought of them as family heirlooms. She went into a red rage when she found out they'd been sold."

"That's when they all fell out?"

He nodded, and his fingers closed around the bone disc. I didn't stop him from gently sliding it from my grasp.

"This," he said, and held it up. "This was mine. I found it when I was ten, that time in the fogou, and I gave it to Poppy as a present. I wrapped it and everything."

As he spoke, he turned the disc, tracing the eye on each side.

"I just thought it was so amazing—an eye! The bizarre thing is that the few thaumatropes they've discovered in Europe predate our barrows by thousands of years. So how did it get here? Trade routes? Or did someone independently come up with the idea in West Penwith five thousand years ago?"

"You know an awful lot about some pretty obscure shit."

"I grew up surrounded by it."

"All those ruins—no one ever studied them? No excavations? Archaeologists, nothing like that?"

Adrian shrugged. "The barrows go back thousands of years. So yes, at some point someone must have explored them, a farmer or maybe one of Tamsin's ancestors. Gentleman antiquarian. But archaeologists or treasure hunters? Absolutely not. That land was in Tamsin's family for centuries, and they did not look kindly upon trespassers. So, no Victorian antiquarians raiding the tombs. No crazy hippie witches, except for Tamsin's friends. Every cairn and field system in the UK is on the ordnance survey map, or in Julian Cope's book—he begged Tamsin to let him look at the fogou. Every *rock* in this country is mapped—except the ones at Kethelwite."

"What about Google Earth?"

"From the air, all you can see is moor—gorse, blackthorn, maybe some rocks. Everything's hidden in plain sight."

He handed the thaumatrope back to me. I looked at him in surprise. "You don't want it?"

"If I'd wanted it, I wouldn't have given it to Poppy." After a long moment, he nodded. "No, you keep it. I think she would have wanted you to have it."

I stared at him, then at the bone disc. Finally I slipped the rawhide over my head again. "She told me a fan gave her one of these after a show one night in Paris. This would've been before you and her . . . got involved. Did she ever tell you about that?"

He pondered before answering. "I'm pretty sure not—it's something I would have remembered."

"You're kidding me." My disbelief flared into outright suspicion. "Two different people gave her the exact same thing? The same *prehistoric* thing?"

Adrian smiled. "You know, it doesn't surprise me one bit."

He turned to gaze out at the moor. "Poppy didn't believe in coincidence. She thought the world had a plot, even if we didn't understand what it was. That there might be consequences to our actions that we'd never understand or even know about, but that would all make sense, if you could stand back far enough to see the pattern."

He turned to me. "Haven't you ever felt that way?"

"Never," I said. But I was no longer sure that was true.

31

We got back into the Land Rover. "Who lives here?" I asked Adrian as he pressed the ignition button.

"People who can't afford to move. And a lot of people who can—every other farm's a second home now. There was a tinning industry here for thousands of years, one of the oldest industrial sites in Europe. But the last mine closed in the 1990s. The fishery's pretty much been destroyed. You have gastropubs and holiday camps—caravans, surfers at St. Ives. But the farmers barely get by."

We rounded a blind curve. Ahead of us, the moor sheared off into cliffs, hundreds of feet high. Beyond was the sea—deep indigo churned white along the rocky shore. I saw no sign of human habitation. It didn't look like land's end but world's end.

Without warning, the Land Rover halted beside a block of granite painted with faded white letters. KETHELWITE FARM. Beyond, a dirt track arrowed into the moor. Knee-high ruts were gouged into the soil, where the snow was already starting to melt. Adrian pulled out his e-cigarette and drew at it, exhaling blue vapor into the chilly air. Finally he gunned the motor and pulled the Rover onto the dirt track.

The road to the farm was almost a mile long, across rock-strewn fields that had long since reverted to moor. Gorse, desiccated heather and bracken, lethal-looking coils of black-thorn. The ocean might have been a thousand miles away. Adrian drove one-handed, deftly steering past a few contorted trees and countless piles of stones, easing the Rover up vertiginously steep, teeth-jarring tracks, up one hillside then down the other.

We reached a fast-moving stream, with a ramshackle bridge of buckled boards balanced on stone piers. I clutched the door handle as the Rover jounced across, but Adrian seemed utterly at ease. His urban skin had peeled away; the lines in his face smoothed out as Poppy's had when she first showed me the thaumatrope.

"I remember making that one." He pointed to a heap of gray rocks. "Poppy would bring us down here and watch while we stacked cairns. That's what we did for fun. And you can see just how much fun we had."

There must have been hundreds of cairns, some only three or four stones laid neatly atop each other, others four or five feet tall. I pointed to a massive stone fortress that loomed atop a distant promontory. "Did you make that?"

"That's Carn Scrija—Castle Scream. Natural outcropping."

I squinted at the huge structure. "I can see a window."

"Natural phenomenon. When the wind comes howling through that hole, you'd swear it was a person screaming. Hang on—"

The Land Rover crept down one last hill, slowing to a halt

when we reached the bottom. Adrian let the shifter slip from his hand. The engine died.

"Home again, home again, jiggety jig," he said.

Before us stretched a compound of stone buildings separated by bare earth churned into icy muck. A grim, two-story granite farmhouse, with a few deep-set windows and a low-pitched roof; long low barns of the same charcoal-gray stone; a number of makeshift sheds. It all looked untidy but not neglected.

Some outbuildings were of the same vintage as the house and barn—1700s, I guessed. Others were constructed of rusting corrugated metal and plywood, two-by-fours and cannibalized car bodies. A hut made of flat gray stones stood alongside a child's plastic sandbox shaped like a turtle, filled with rocks not sand. A doll clung to the metal chain of a sagging swing set. I saw an Alfa Romeo convertible, its cloth roof in shreds, and an antique tractor buried up to its axles in mud. Farm implements that belonged in an agricultural museum: scythes, wooden ox yokes, rusted axes.

Behind a metal fence near the stone barn, a shaggy brown cow bent over a pile of hay. It raised its head to regard us, its horns twin crescents above long-lashed black eyes. A timeworn sign perched above the barn's open door, and I recognized the logo for *Thanatrope,* with its rusted pylon and ghostly eye.

"What the *fuck*?"

Behind us, Krishna sat bolt upright and stared out the window. "Where the fuck are we? What are you *doing*?"

She tried to open the back passenger door, kicking at it frantically, but I knew her fury barely masked raw fear.

"Hey, chill," I said.

"Krish, please—" Adrian began.

"Don't you fucking chill me!" She punched my arm, hard, then Adrian's. He flinched as she screamed, "Where's Tolly? *Where's Tolly?*"

I jumped from the car and yanked the back door open, grabbing her by one leg. Krishna fell out, Bruno's overcoat flopping around her like a blanket. "Shut the fuck up, okay? We're in—someplace."

I looked accusingly at Adrian, who was trying to help Krishna up.

"Penwith," he gasped. West Pen—*ow!* Goddamn it, Krish—"

"You're a fucking pervo!" She stumbled to her feet, shoved him away, and stared at me venomously. "And you! You drugged me up!"

"You did that all by yourself," I snapped. "Do you even remember who I am? I'm Cass—we met at the Banshee in Camden Town."

"Camden?" She blinked, pushed her matted hair from her face, and looked around. "What is this place?"

I looked at Adrian. "I'm gonna let you field that one."

"Krishna, I need you to listen to me." Adrian's deep voice seemed to drop another octave. "Something bad happened. Very bad."

Krishna paled. "What?"

He gave her a quick account of Morven's and Mallo's deaths, but with no mention of Poppy. Krishna began to cry.

"No, no, no . . ."

"I know, it's horrible." Adrian laid a tentative hand on her shoulder. "I'm sorry I had to tell you."

"Did you go the police?" Krishna's voice faltered.

"No. I thought it was more prudent to leave."

"With her?" Krishna whipped around to fix me again with

that Medusa glare. "Me, now Adrian—are you having it off wth him too?"

Adrian said, "Don't be stupid, Krish."

"Stupid? You did everyone else, right? You and . . ."

She began to cry again, smacking her palms against the car. Adrian ran a hand through his hair. He turned to get his backpack from the Rover and hoisted it over his shoulder.

"Stay here," he said. "In the car. Keep your heads down. The keys are in there. Krish, if you see anyone coming, text me."

"Where are you going?" I demanded.

"I need to talk to Tamsin."

He walked off, his Doc Martens ringing against the frozen ground. Krishna clutched the too-big coat around her spindly frame. Her eyes widened.

"Tamsin's," she repeated, her teeth chattering. "That's where we are?"

"I think so."

"Fuck me."

"Do you know her?"

"Morven's told me about her. She—"

She turned to scan the outbuildings and muddy drive, frowning. "I been here, I think. When I was a kid. With the caravan. My mum and dad knew someone here."

"Tamsin?" I asked. Krishna shrugged. "What about a girl named Poppy Teasel? A singer."

"I've heard that song," she said softly. " 'The wind, the wind . . .' My mum used to play that in the caravan. You know her? Poppy?"

"I've met her. Amazing voice."

Krishna's face twisted. Her eyes narrowed: She looked at me

as though I'd struck her. She drew a long hissing breath, and began to sing.

"The wind, the wind, the wind blows high
All the children say they'll die
For want of the Golden City . . ."

I felt as though I might jump out of my skin. As uncannily as she'd channeled Ronnie Spector singing "Be My Maby" at the Banshee, she now channeled Poppy Teasel, head thrown back as she gazed into the sky. Moisture glistened beneath her eyes as she repeated the last line, her voice rising to a shout that became a hoarse scream.

"For want of the Golden City
For want of the Golden City
For want of the Golden City . . ."

She fell silent and began to tremble uncontrollably inside the heavy overcoat, hugging her arms to her chest. My flesh crawled: The song's final notes rang in my head like the impact of a blow. After a long moment, I forced myself to speak.

"Back there in London, when we found you—heroin?"

"Not your fucking business," she said dully. "I drank too much, is all. And it wasn't heroin, it was K."

"What's going on with Adrian? Are you and he involved?"

Krishna gave me a look that combined repulsion and disbelief. "You having me on? Not if he were the last man in London."

She stared at the house, then broke into a run, her feet sliding across the icy ground. When she reached the door, she flung it open and stormed inside. Seconds later I heard her excoriating someone in an enraged shriek.

". . . never fucking told me!"

I dug my hands into the pockets of my leather jacket, shivering. I waited to see if anyone would emerge from the house, but the argument continued unabated, Adrian's deep voice vying with Krishna's.

The frigid wind whipped at me so relentlessly, I might not have been wearing a jacket at all. I pulled up my collar. Across the muddy yard, the Highland cow looked up to regard me with eyes dark and liquid as Krishna's. It stepped to the barbed-wire fence, shook its head, and snorted, nostrils flaring, before turning to race across its paddock, hooves churning the frozen mud.

I got my bag from the Land Rover, found the bottle of Vyvanse, and took four. I opened one of the screwtop wine bottles from the service area and drank until I felt the familiar burn in my chest.

I capped the bottle and stuck it back in my bag. A few yards away, the stone barn loomed dark against the early morning sky. I trudged over and stopped in front of the open doorway.

Above me, the sign painted with the *Thanatrope* logo knocked rhythmically against the wall in the wind. The eye made sense, now that I knew its origin in the bone amulet around my neck.

But the pylon remained inexplicable, though not out of place within this barren landscape of stone and ancient ruins. I shut my eyes and saw molten whorls of crimson where the sun struck my eyelid, the skeletal outline of the pylon.

A bird flapped noisily overhead. I blinked and looked up to see a large crow or raven settle onto the top of the sign. It clacked its long red beak and tipped its head to regard me with one inky eye. The feathers on its throat fanned out, making it appear as large as a good-sized cat.

I expected it to fly away. But the bird remained where it was, opening and closing its beak. The sound made me think of someone whetting a blade. I shoved my hands into my pockets and stepped into the barn.

Slats of light slanted down from the ceiling where broken roof tiles had dropped to the floor. The place was filled with junk. Old wooden trunks, translucent plastic storage bins stuffed with newspapers and magazines, wooden crates of tools. It smelled musty, though not unpleasant—of dried grass, linseed oil, moldering paper, and some sweet herb I didn't recognize. An enormous hay rake was suspended between the rafters, its tines laced with cobwebs and dust.

I picked my way to the back wall, where a dozen painted canvas flats leaned. Childlike renderings of green mountains and blue skies, a sun with rays like spider's legs. Peace signs and astrological sigils; figures from a tarot deck. The sets from *Thanatrope.* I ran a finger across the picture of the High Priestess, her imperious face pleached with mildew. The paint flaked away like blue and yellow snow.

I walked to the far end of the barn, where a ramshackle structure rose above a canyon of cardboard boxes. Nowhere as tall as it appeared on film, its rusted struts buckled with age: the pylon. Behind it was a door.

I pushed it open and stepped into a dark storeroom filled with film equipment. Cameras, rigs, microphones—all state of the art, circa 1973. Stacks of film canisters. A vintage editing table with a swivel chair—a Steenbeck flatbed deck, with its distinctive blue and brushed nickel hardware. I recognized this bit of archaic technology from my brief stint at NYU, when I'd occasionally hang out with a friend who was in the film studies program.

I sank onto the swivel chair and ran my hand across the Steenbeck's surface. It was free of dust. A reel of thirty-five-millimeter film sat on one of the aluminum plates. The acetate threaded between myriad spindles, then through the picture gate where the projection lamp would shine on it, frame by frame, and onto the take-up spindles and take-up plate. Beside the guillotine splicer was a white chargraph grease pencil, wth a single frame of thirty-five millimeter beside it. Someone had drawn a vertical white line through the frame, indicating it needed to be cut.

I picked up the piece of film. It was too dark to see inside the storeroom, so I stepped into the doorway and held the frame to the light.

Squinting, I could just make out a figure lying in a patch of grass. A corona of sunlight bloomed in the upper corner of the frame, burnishing the figure's blond hair, limbs, and naked torso. Magic hour. Lens flare had ruined the effect, presumably why the frame had been cut. The tiny figure was turned so I could only see bright hair, an arm cocked at an unnatural angle beside its head. It was impossible to tell if it was a doll or a child.

"Dad?"

I turned to see a boy standing in the barn. Twelve or thirteen years old, rope thin and big boned, dressed in filthy jeans, muck boots, and a black hoodie so big it came to his knees. His eyes widened when he saw my face. "The fuck are you?"

"A friend of Adrian's. Who are you?"

"Samsung." He took a step away from me.

"Samsung?"

He blushed. "Sam. I'm not the cunt what named me."

"That's good." I cocked a thumb at the contents of the room. "What's all this?"

"What do you think it is? Crap."

The boy dug in a pocket of his hoodie and produced a crumpled, hand-rolled cigarette and a lighter. He had a sharp pale face, good-looking in a ferrety way. Tangled black hair to his shoulders; Adrian's deep-set black eyes; thin lips, chapped and bitten. He only came to my shoulders but looked like he'd get much taller: he had big bones and large, long-fingered hands, their nails blackened and knuckles seamed with dirt. He lit the cigarette—tobacco—took a few quick drags, and walked away.

"You live here?" I called, following him.

The boy looked back at me disdainfully. His eyes narrowed. He quickened his steps then broke into a run, heading for the farmhouse.

The door opened before he got there. Adrian stepped aside as the boy ran up to him.

"I thought he was you," Sam said, gesturing.

"She," said Adrian. He waved me toward him. "I see you've met the family."

Inside it was dim. Flagstone floors, whitewashed stone walls, wooden beams overhead. The cramped hallway led into a pantry filled with baskets of apples and large burlap sacks. This opened onto a large kitchen outfitted with scuffed furniture, gas range, and noisily humming 1950s refrigerator, and another dim room with an enamel-topped dining table and mismatched chairs.

All the windows were small and deeply recessed, with lead-muntined panes. Where panes were missing or broken, rags and cardboard had been stuffed into the gaps. Like the barn, every inch of available space was crammed with stuff—empty food tins, flattened boxes, soiled clothing, fishy-smelling cans of cat food fuzzed with mold. A few chairs and inexpertly handmade tables. Writing covered the walls: grocery lists, lists of names, bad poetry, a rant against the Sunshine Free School.

Here and there something hinted at an earlier, more affluent life for both the house and its inhabitants. Peeling ribbons of vintage Art Nouveau wallpaper; an umbrella stand made of an elephant's foot; a crystal chandelier, gray with dust and draped with tarnished Christmas tinsel. In the kitchen, an antique oaken daybed was shoved against a wall, its rumpled bedclothes trailing onto the floor. Sam kicked at these and darted off. I followed Adrian into a living room.

"Have a seat," he said.

"Where's Krishna?"

"She took off," he said dully. "I'll make some tea, if I can find any."

He left, and I surveyed the room. Sisal carpeting had disintegrated to a web of filthy straw. A brown, deflated soccer ball sat abandoned in the corner opposite a fireplace. The only furniture was a pair of threadbare red velvet armchairs.

I collapsed into one of these. The room had a pervasive fetid odor that I could taste as much as smell—sweat and smoke and mold, rotting vegetables, beer and urine. The reek of rural poverty. People had lived here for centuries. I burrowed into the chair, hugging my bag to my chest, and closed my eyes.

"Hey—"

I sat up blearily. The black-haired boy, Sam, squatted in front of me. "My dad said to give you this."

He held out a steaming mug and I took it. "Thanks."

It was strong black tea, bitter and very hot. I cradled the mug and let the steam warm my face. The boy remained where he was, barely a foot away, staring at me. He reminded me disconcertingly of the raven I'd seen by the barn.

After a minute I said, "You mind giving me some space?"

The boy frowned but scooted back an inch. "Who're you?"

"Like I said: friend of your dad's. Adrian. He's your dad, right?"

"You'd know that if he was your friend."

"Good point."

I drank my tea and ignored him, in hopes that he'd go away. That usually works with dogs, except when it backfires and they attack you.

But the boy didn't seem overtly hostile—not toward me, anyway. His forehead was creased, and there was a pronounced *V* at the bridge of his nose, suggesting a glare was his customary way of observing the world. After a few minutes he asked, "You got a fag?"

"I don't smoke."

"You drink. I can smell it on you. You stink."

"Nice manners." I glanced around the room. "You live here?" The boy shrugged, then nodded. "Know where Adrian went?"

"To find Tamsin. I told him, she's not here, she—"

"Never mind. Where's the bathroom?"

He pointed at a door but didn't move. I had to step over him to leave.

The bathroom held a cracked porcelain toilet with a corroded metal tank above it, the chain reduced to a single link and frayed twine. No medicine cabinet, no towels. A string of red LED lights dangled from the ceiling, reflected in an old mirror with most of its silver rubbed off. I looked at the mirror and ran a hand through my hair.

I bet I stank. I looked like shit. The black hair dye made my face look cadaverously pale, save for the livid star-shaped scar beside my eye. The cut on my cheek appeared inflamed. I wondered if it had gotten infected.

I splashed my face with cold water and then returned to the living room, tossing my jacket on the chair. Sam was gone. Adrian stood by the window, smoking a real cigarette.

"You scared Sam," he said. "She thought you were me, and then she thought you were a ghost. I can see why."

"She?"

"Yes," Adrian said curtly. "I'm going to have a lie-down—I'm knackered. You should do the same. Come on."

I got my bag and we climbed a flight of narrow steps beneath a ceiling so low we had to duck. On the second floor were three bedrooms, each one smaller than the last, like a grim variant of the Three Bears' house.

"That's Sam's room," said Adrian, pointing.

I glanced inside and saw a narrow bed with a brightly checked afghan thrown across it, some books on a small student's desk by the door. *The Serpent and the Rainbow, Harry Potter and the Goblet of Fire,* J. G. Ballard's *High Rise.* "She has catholic reading taste," I said.

"Does she? I haven't kept up. This is Tamsin's room, and this was mine—Krish can have that one when she gets back. I'll doss in the kitchen, and you can have the garret."

"Is Tamsin here?"

"Sam says she went to Penzance on Tuesday and texted that she'd gotten stranded there by the storm. Road closure, she's supposedly staying with friends. I tried calling and texting her, but she's not picking up."

"Do you think she's still in London?"

"I don't know." His deep voice rasped with fatigue. "I hope so. I hope she's in hell."

"What if she comes back here?"

"That's why I'm staying downstairs."

At the end of the hall was a wooden ladder. We climbed to a whitewashed attic beneath the eaves, with blackened wooden beams, bare stone walls, two windows. It was cold enough that I could see my breath. A tattered rag rug covered the floor. On the windowsill, cigarette butts overflowed from a McCann's Oatmeal tin. There was a little door at the far end of the room and the pervasive, vinegary scent of apples.

Adrian opened a window, propping it up with a stick. He knelt and opened the little door, rooted around inside, and pulled out an armful of quilts.

"Here." He tossed the quilts at me. "I'll see you later."

The quilts were slightly damp. I made a lumpy pallet of them, then zipped up my leather jacket and removed the Konica and bottle of wine from my bag. I put the camera on the floor beside me and stretched out, using my bag as a pillow. Immediately I passed out.

32

I must have been asleep for several hours when I heard a soft sound. I opened my eyes and shouted in alarm.

A figure sat on the floor a few feet from me, his—her—knees drawn in front of her. I threw one of the quilts at her. "What the fuck are you doing?"

"Just looking."

"That's a good way to get cold-cocked." I stumbled to my feet and glared at her. "You're lucky I didn't put your lights out."

Sam brushed a sweep of black hair from her eyes. "Is that what happened to your eye?"

"No."

I crossed to a window and peered down into the yard. It looked to be late morning. Bedraggled chickens picked their way between the tractors. The shaggy cow stared over its barbed-wire fence. Most of the snow had melted, but the distant crags of Carn Scrija were dappled white. Watery sunlight streamed between lichen-gray clouds, brightening to gold as a burst of rain fell.

I grabbed my camera. I'd used up my last roll shooting Quinn, so I'd have to reload. But if I moved fast I might catch the light.

Sam stared, fascinated, as I dug into my satchel and pulled a plastic canister of Tri-X from a ziplock bag. "What are you doing?"

I strode to the little door. "Loading my camera."

"Can I watch?"

"There's nothing to watch. You have to do it in total darkness, otherwise the film's ruined."

"I'm not afraid of the dark."

I opened the door and peered inside. The apple smell was stronger here. Threads of light spun from holes in the roof, igniting dust motes. I turned to Sam. "Hand me one of those blankets."

"Can I—"

"Yeah, whatever! Just give me that blanket and get inside. Quick. Shut the door."

She grabbed a blanket and scrambled after me into the storeroom, pulling the door tight behind her. I angled myself as far from the door as I could—it was close quarters—then draped the blanket over my head and settled onto the floor. I could feel Sam bump up alongside me.

"What are you doing?" She sounded excited.

"Putting film in my camera. Here, hang on to this."

I stuck my hand out from under the blanket and gave her the empty film canister. I opened the Konica, removed the roll I'd shot of Quinn back at Canary Wharf, pocketed it, and slipped the virgin Tri-X into the camera. I drew the camera to my face, inhaling the lactose-sweet scent of the emulsion, and threaded the film onto the sprockets of the take-up spool, then closed the camera back and hit the shutter a few times to advance the film, making sure it had loaded correctly.

"Okay," I said at last, and tossed the blanket aside. Sepia light and slowly moving dust turned the storeroom into a frame of grainy film, with Sam's stark white face, black hair, and inky eyes superimposed on it. She hugged the blanket to her thin chest and stared at my camera.

"I don't get why you have to do it in here," she said.

I made my way back into the garret. "I told you, because it's dark."

"That's where they used to keep the apples." She dogged my heels to the window. "A hundred years ago. Why does it have to be dark?"

"Shit." I stared outside. "I lost the light." I turned to her. "Do you even know what film is? Do you even fucking care?"

She stared at me with those hard black eyes. "My grandfather was a famous director."

"He was a famous cinematographer. Did you know him?"

"No. He died a long time ago. Before I was born."

I wondered if mastery of light was an inherited trait. I held up my Konica. "This is an SLR camera—single lens reflex. Not digital. There's film inside it—do you know how that works?"

Sam started to nod, stopped. "No."

"It's a very thin piece of plastic with special chemicals on it. Different kinds of chemicals interact differently when they're exposed to light, especially silver salts, which is what you use in black-and-white film. I only use black and white, so no matter what I shoot, it comes out in black and white. You could scan it into a computer and Photoshop it or something like that, but the original product is good old monochrome."

"That's weird." Sam stepped beside me, transfixed, and gazed at the camera.

"Here." I popped the lens cap and indicated the viewfinder. "You look through that. This is the shutter release, but don't touch it—I don't have much film left."

I handed her the camera. She squinted through the viewfinder. "How do you make it bigger?"

"You don't."

"It's all blurry."

"There's no autofocus. There's no auto anything. You have to know how it works."

"Can you teach me?"

I took the camera from her. "No."

She appeared crushed. "Look, it's hard," I said. "It takes a long time to learn how to use it, focus and depth of field and correct exposure time, what F-stop to use—that kind of shit. Then on top of that you have to know how to develop the film, how long to leave it in the processor and adjust for any imperfections in the contrast or . . ."

I looked at her: I might have been speaking in tongues. I sighed. "Don't you have a smartphone or something? A digital camera? They're supposed to be really easy to learn."

"Then why don't you have one?"

"Because I have to do everything the hard way." I slung the camera over my neck and picked up my bag. "I'm going to see if I can rustle up some grub."

The doors to the other bedrooms were shut. Sam followed me downstairs, where the cottage was silent and very cold. The brown soccer ball now sat in front of the fireplace. I saw no sign of Adrian, but when I entered the kitchen, Krishna stood in front of the sink, washing her face. She straightened and eyed me suspiciously.

"Where you been off to, then?"

"Sleeping," I said.

"Surprised you could," retorted Krishna.

Sam glared at her. Krishna glared back, but her gaze softened as she took in Sam's frayed cargo pants and ragged hair. "Don't they take you out ever?" she asked.

"Fuck off," Sam said, and opened the fridge.

I went outside to retrieve the other bottle of wine from the Land Rover, skirting chicken shit and puddles in the brick-colored mud. The cold made the scar beside my eye ache, but it was exhilarating, too—the wind bore the smell of the sea, the calls of birds skirling high overhead and a low, moaning cry from the broken towers of Carn Scrija.

Back in the kitchen, Krishna was gone. I raised an eyebrow at Sam. "You scare her off?"

"Take more than that," she said. "She looks like a vampire."

I took the bottle of wine from my bag, filled a chipped white mug, and drank. Adrian's backpack sat on the wooden daybed, where the blankets had been neatly folded. A brace of dead rabbits hung beside the stove.

"I was supposed to skin those for dinner," Sam said. "Till I forgot."

She set bread and Nutella on the table, along with a carton of milk, then dragged an old electric heater alongside her chair. Its cord was dangerously frayed. She switched it on: The grill glowed orange, and I held my hands in front of it.

Sam made herself a sandwich, took a bite, and looked at me. "You want one?"

"Yeah, sure."

We sat across from each other at the battered kitchen table and ate. After a few minutes I asked, "Where'd Krishna go?"

"Krishna?" Sam looked puzzled, then scowled. "You mean that crazy sket screaming at my dad?"

"That would be her."

"Dunno. Ran off. She'll be in a bog out there. Dead," she added with relish.

I refilled my mug with wine. Sam opened the milk, sniffed it, and poured it down the sink. She got a jelly glass and picked up the wine bottle.

"Hey," I said, "how about asking?"

"Can I have some?"

"Aren't you kinda young to be hitting that?"

"No."

"What about your dad?"

"He doesn't care."

I shrugged. "Knock yourself out."

She filled her glass to the brim, and I grabbed the bottle back from her. "Christ, you really *are* gonna knock yourself out. Pacing, kid."

We finished our sandwiches in silence. Sam drank most of her wine, pushed her empty plate away, and walked, a little unsteadily, toward the bathroom. I drank what remained in her jelly glass and stuck the bottle into my camera bag. Adrian was right. The bag was starting to get heavy.

After a few minutes Sam returned and sat. When she saw her empty glass, she shot me an accusing look. "Did you throw out my wine?"

"No. I drank it. I don't want you puking. How old are you, anyway?"

"You can drink here when you're sixteen."

"That's not what I asked."

"I'm twelve. I'll be thirteen in January."

"Wow, only two years and eleven months till you're legal. What's the deal with your grandmother?"

"She went to Penzance a few days ago. She got caught in the storm."

"How far's Penzance?"

"About ten miles. But it takes a long time because of the roads."

"You've been alone here all this time?"

Sam dabbled a finger in some spilled wine on the table, drew a circle. "I like to be alone."

"Don't you have school?"

"I don't go to school. I used to, when I was with my dad in Islington. He was living with a bunch of anarchists from Occupy. Some of them got arrested. My dad wouldn't let me go." As she spoke, she kicked the table leg distractedly. "My school, everyone there was a cunt. They beat me up and said I was a freak."

"Why?"

"Cause I look like a bloke."

"So? Who gives a fuck?"

"My dad went in and got in a fight with my teacher. They called the police, they were going to take me away, so we came back here so I could stay with Tamsin."

I grabbed her foot. "Stop kicking, it's driving me nuts. How can you live here?"

"Same way I lived in London."

"I mean, how do you pay the bills? Buy food, stuff like that."

"Tamsin sells stuff. She knows a dealer in Penzance—she brings him things and he sells them online."

I looked around. Nothing even remotely resembled an antique that might be worth more than a few pounds. "What kind of stuff?"

"Things that get plowed up in the fields. Flints. Beads. Broken pots."

"You can survive on that?"

"It's getting harder to find things." Sam kicked the table again, then stopped. "The ground's been so worked over for so long. You can still find things on the moor, but you have to be lucky. I had a metal detector, but it broke. We never found any metal, anyhow, except once a bronze ring. Tamsin says it used to be you couldn't kick a rock but you'd find an ax head or a little statue."

I feigned surprise. "Really? What happened to them?"

"People stole them from her."

I looked around. "You'd have to be a pretty hard-up thief to break in here."

"It was people she knew. I don't know how they stole them, but they did. It was a long time ago."

I nodded and stared out the window. The clouds had lifted. Beyond the dour granite compound, the open moor stretched green and gold beneath an azure sky. On the western horizon, slanting rain fell from massed charcoal clouds onto the ruins of a building atop a towering hill.

"Is that the manor that burned down?" I pointed, glancing back to see Sam's nod. "Can I go there?"

"I'll take you." She jumped to her feet. "Wait while I get my coat."

I didn't want a kid tagging along, but I was afraid that if I left, she'd wake Adrian and I'd have someone else dogging me. I stepped outside and took a shot of the hillside while I waited for Sam. She came running out, wearing a black anorak way too big for her skinny frame, and knee-high Wellingtons.

"This way," she said.

33

We walked past the barn, along a rudimentary path that climbed a steep hillside covered with stones and rubble. The snow was gone, save for a few white pockets between the rocks. A broken plow blade thrust out from the underbrush, along with a pitchfork, its wooden handle rotted to a black nub. A tire swing hung from a dead tree near a trampoline folded in half like a giant taco.

"So is it just you and your grandmother?" I asked.

"Tamsin." Sam shot me a quick look. "She doesn't like being called anything else. Yeah, just us."

"Don't you get lonely?"

"Not really."

"Even when she goes off and leaves you alone?"

"We have a shotgun; she taught me how to use it. Tamsin collects guns."

"I thought you English were gun-shy."

"We hunt rabbits with them. And this is Cornwall—we're

not really part of England. More Celtic. We used to have our own language."

"Yeah? Can you speak it?"

"No."

She stopped in front of a barbed-wire fence surrounding a small garden plot. A few corn stalks rustled in the wind. Everything else had surrendered to weeds. Several ratty bundles hung from the barbed wire, spaced a few yards apart. I stepped closer and saw they were dead crows, skulls picked clean, wings dangling like empty black gloves.

"Sends a message," said Sam. She reached between the barbed wire to pluck a sprig of something, lavender-gray with dry, teethlike leaves, and handed it to me. "Heather. For luck."

"Thanks. I could use it."

We continued on. After ten minutes we neared the top of the hill. Shreds of high white cloud raced across the sky like gulls. Gorse rattled ceaselessly in the wind. I stopped to catch my breath and looked back.

I didn't think we'd climbed that far. Yet from here the farm compound appeared impossibly distant, its buildings toy sized. Something moved outside the stone cottage, but I couldn't discern whether it was a person or animal, or just a shadow thrown by the clouds.

Sam stood beside me. With her anorak's hood pulled up she resembled a young monk. "Looks like you could just jump down onto it," she said.

"We must've walked fast."

She shook her head. "Everything here always looks closer or farther away than it really is. That's how people get lost. That and the mist and wind."

She lifted her face to the sky so that the hood fell back. "The wind, the wind," she sang.

"The wind, the wind, the wind blows high
Ash comes falling from the sky
And all the children say they'll die
For want of the Golden City."

Her voice was high and sweet, slightly out of key and weirdly bloodless; more like a bird's song than a girl's. I shivered. "Where did you learn that?"

"Don't remember."

"A woman named Poppy Teasel sang it. Do you know her? She was friends with Tamsin a long time ago. And your father."

"No." She began to walk across the moor, head down against the wind. "I wasn't here a long time ago."

I hurried to keep up with her, the camera bouncing against my chest. She walked fast for such a skinny kid. We passed a midden composed of old tires, a chest freezer, and snarls of barbed wire. A raven picked at something in the shadows. It lifted its head to stare at us impassively before it opened its wings and took off, a black ribbon trailing from its beak.

"That song—it was in Leith's movie," I said. "Your grandfather. *Thanatrope*. Have you ever seen it?"

"Only about seventy times. Yeah, that's where I heard it—I forgot. But that's Tamsin's movie, not his."

"What do you mean?"

"He filmed some of it, but she was the one did all the real work. He had to be sectioned, so she finished it. All the editing. He didn't shoot enough film to make a proper movie."

"Who told you that?"

"She did. Tamsin."

"Not exactly an unbiased source." I kicked at a stone and sent it tumbling downhill behind us. "But you're not the only one who thinks that. A film critic named Nicholas Rombes wrote about it online a few years ago. You should read it."

"I don't need to read some online shite. It's true 'cause I know it's true." She picked up a rock and threw it after mine. "We don't have Internet anyway."

"Then how'd you watch *Thanatrope*?"

Sam looked at me with pitying disdain. "On a proper screen. There's a projector in the barn."

I mulled this over as we approached the top of the hill. The revelation that a woman—a socialite, at that—had been the creative force behind an obscure underground movie might not be groundbreaking news. Still, it was interesting enough that some feminist film historian might get an article out of it.

But wouldn't Tamsin have taken credit for *Thanatrope*? She didn't sound like someone who'd hide behind her husband's reputation, especially after he ditched her to smoke kef in Tangiers.

"She's crazy, too," Sam said, as though I'd spoken my thought. "Crazy like a fox."

Up here the wind roared like a jet turbine endlessly revving for a takeoff that never came. With only a fringe of cropped hair to protect them, my ears ached so badly that I walked with my hands pressed against the sides of my head. Sam did the same. We looked like refugees from *The Scream*.

She gestured to where the broken walls of Kethelwite Manor reared against the sky, perhaps a quarter mile distant. "There's a windbreak over there."

We crossed an ancient field stitched together by stone walls. It reminded me of the webs woven by spiders given LSD in research experiments, a lunatic crosshatch of rock walls and hedges and the occasional sagging metal fence. Sam clambered over these like a squirrel, but the pointed tips of my Tony Lamas caught treacherously between the rocks.

Overhead, tiny white specks bloomed and disappeared in the blue sky, like flaws on an old film strip: gulls, their cries drowned out by the wind. A ridge topped by tall standing stones aligned with the wreckage of the manor house. Beyond the ruins sloped the highlands, ending abruptly in those cliffs above the north Atlantic.

"People don't know how to watch that movie." Sam said. "You have to know what to look for, otherwise you won't even know what you're seeing."

I wondered if this was some rote speech of Tamsin's that she'd memorized. "So what do you see?"

"This." She kicked through knee-high bracken, jumped onto a broad flat rock, and turned with her arms out, pretending to fly. "The movie's a map of all this, only a map through time. A guy's dying. It's what he remembers of this place over thousands and thousand of years. Tamsin says it helps if you're tripping."

"I was tripping first time I saw it. Didn't help me."

"Me, too."

"Your grandmother gave you acid?"

"Mushrooms. It made me puke. There's these shamans in Siberia, they drink reindeer piss. The reindeer eat poisonous mushrooms and the psychoactive ingredient comes out in their urine and the shamans drink it. Otherwise if they ate the mushrooms they'd die, 'cause they're deadly poison. Fatal," she added somberly.

I shot her a skeptical look.

"Tamsin's training me to be a shaman." Sam's tone implied this was as commonplace as soccer practice. "She studied it in Barcelona from Salvador Dalí—that's how she met my grandfather. People like me, we're chosen to be shamans."

"I wasn't aware that was still a career track."

Sam glared at me. "It's true."

I was starting to see why this kid had a hard time in the school cafeteria. She pushed away the anorak's hood, gathered her lank hair in one hand, and pulled it away from her face. The hard light made the angles of her cheekbones and pointed chin appear even more pronounced, her deepset eyes dead black against skin white as bone. She didn't look like a girl or a boy but some unearthly amalgam of both, an eerie rendering of what a human face might be, reduced to its simplest planes.

She let go of her hair and it whipped across her face. "They call it the Man-Woman. At the Furry Dance at Helston. Other places, too. In the movie, there's a scene where they do it. My grandfather played the Man-Woman."

"I don't remember that scene."

"That's 'cause you don't know how to watch the movie."

I was too tired to argue. We continued on, past a tall cairn. Someone had drawn an eye on one of the stones in red paint, so faint I could almost imagine it as a natural feature, except for the skeletal pylon drawn beneath it.

We reached a stone wall. Sam held open a rough-hewn gate. We stepped out onto what looked like an extension of the moor, more thorny vegetation and spiny grass.

Only the ground wasn't earth, but shattered brick and pulverized stone. I picked up a scorched chunk of concrete and dug my fingernail into the surface, drew my finger to my face and sniffed the black residue. Even after forty years, it stank of burning.

"There was a castle here," said Sam. "Tamsin says it was the real Castle Scream."

She held out her arms and ran toward a wall of crumbling brick, with the ruins of a clerestory window in the second storey. Without pausing, she clambered up the wall, her black anorak billowing around her. When she reached the top, she let out a piercing shriek, swung herself onto a ledge, then stepped onto the sill of the empty window, bracing herself with a hand on either side.

The wind tore at her hair as she stared down at me and screamed again. Her face contorted and her black eyes fixed on mine as her voice deepened into a howl. Her skinny body shook with the effort.

"Get down!" I yelled, breaking into a run. At the foot of the ruined wall I looked up.

Above me, Sam looked terrifying and beautiful, like one of those figures painted on an ancient Greek vase, half girl and half bird. I grabbed at the Konica around my neck, popping the lens cap and adjusting the focus even before I looked through the viewfinder.

I shot three pictures and lowered the camera. Sam remained within the shattered window, silent, her mouth gaping. She leaned forward, stared down at me, and grinned.

"You better look out below!"

She let go and fell backward.

With a shout, I ran alongside the ruined wall till I found a way through, into a courtyard thick with blackthorn. At the base of the ruined wall, Sam lay on her back atop a sagging trampoline.

"Ow." She rolled over and got to her feet. The trampoline's fabric slumped beneath her as she hobbled to the edge and hopped down. She tugged at a frayed nylon rope dangling from the bent aluminum frame. "I really need to tighten this."

"You really need to *not be an asshole*." I grabbed her hair and shook her. "You want to kill yourself?"

She yelped in pain, swinging at me. "Why the fuck should you care?"

"I don't," I snapped. "But I don't want to be the one to tell your goddamned father his idiot daughter just jumped off the roof."

I stormed off across the courtyard. Broken arches rose above the devastation. A dagger of glass pierced a charred wooden beam gone soft with rot. I kicked it, and the wood exploded into a foul-smelling brown cloud. Some ruins are beautiful. Kethelwite Manor was just grim.

I walked to a large, battered dome, its verdigris pocked with lichen—a small fortune in salvageable copper. Given the local economy, I'd have thought someone would have poached the metal long ago. Maybe they really were afraid to tussle with Tamsin.

I picked up a rock and threw it at the dome. It made a hollow boom, answered by a deep, sustained hooting I could feel in my bones, like an oncoming train. I looked back to see Sam atop a pile of broken roof slates, staring at the black crags of Carn Scrija.

"It doesn't like that we're here," she yelled.

I wanted to tell her to fuck off, but I had a feeling she was right. I shouted back. "Let's go."

Sam climbed down from her perch and ambled toward me, hands jammed into her pockets. For the first time I saw that her deep-set eyes weren't black or brown but indigo, a color picked up by the delicate capillaries across her pale face. Whatever issues she had with her sexual identity, she was a striking-looking kid and might be a beautiful adult, if she made up her mind to live for a few more years. I replaced the lens cap on my camera, clicked the film transport lever.

"I saw what you did." Sam looked at me defiantly. "Taking pictures. You don't give a fuck about me."

I laughed. "I don't give a fuck about anything."

Her mouth hardened to a slit. But I could see her watching me from the corner of her eyes, as we retraced our steps across a landscape frozen between Leith Carlisle's vision of late-twentieth-century apocalypse and some mystery that seemed to flicker just out of sight.

The sun hung low on the horizon, beginning its plunge into the ocean. The wind had died, so I could hear the sea, mindlessly gnawing at stones and shingle. I started as something flew past my face, a bird or a large insect.

Sam touched my arm, pointing. "That was a chough!"

"What's a chuff?"

"C-H-O-U-G-H." She spelled it out. "Like a crow, but with a red beak. They're very rare. Extinct, almost." Her white cheeks were pinked from the cold. "It's bad luck to kill one—they say King Arthur's soul went into a chough when he died at Avalon."

I looked around, but the bird was gone. I turned to Sam. "Zip up your coat. You're making me colder just looking at you."

I gazed across the hillside. There was no sign of Kethelwite Farm, nothing that resembled a path among the gray boulders and gorse.

"You know the way back, right?"

" 'Course." She hadn't zipped the anorak, but she pulled it

tight around her and drew up the hood. She pointed at a small promontory to the east, where two upright stones rose from what looked like another pile of broken masonry. "Do you want to see the dead babies?"

I blinked. "What?"

"Just over there." She indicated two standing stones. "But we need to hurry; it'll be dark soon."

We scrambled down a steep incline and followed a path slick with moss and yellow fronds that fed on a rivulet of black water. A line of knee-high rocks marched up the hillside. Not a wall, but some kind of boundary or marker. At one time they might have stood sharply against the sky, but over the centuries the moor had grown up around them. They looked like all that remained of a city submerged beneath the turf.

Then, as though the earth had swallowed her, too, Sam disappeared.

34

"Sam!" The wind threw her name back at me. "Sam, wait—"

I ran until I reached the top of the hill. On the northern horizon the sea glimmered. Directly in front of me was a broad concave space, about twenty feet in diameter and three feet deep, thatched with wiry grass and dead ferns. It looked like the impact crater of a tiny asteroid, but it had been made by human labor. Two lines of small stones formed a path that led to the upper edge of the hollow. Sam stood there like another standing stone, black against the twilight sky. Her hood had dropped, and her hair lashed about her head like a dark flame.

I started to reach for my camera. Instead I let my hand slip beneath layers of clothing until I felt the two bone discs against my skin.

"This way," Sam called.

I walked to where she crouched beside a doorway set directly into the hillside, its sides formed of stone slabs and capped by a massive rock lintel. The stones were rough and unadorned, the same leaden hue as the surrounding landscape and tufted with dead grass. If Sam hadn't been there, I might have walked right past it.

I stooped to peer into the dark tunnel. A dank, earthy scent wafted from inside, undercut by a very faint smell of something foul—stagnant water or maybe a dead animal. I grimaced. "What is it?"

"A passage grave." Sam's pale face was taut with excitement. "It's not on any of the ordnance survey maps."

I nodded. "Your dad said something about that."

"Our family owns all this land—Tamsin says they never let anyone come here for, like, a thousand years."

"What about all those people in the movie?"

Her face fell. "Well, except for them." She brightened. "But they're all dead now, right? I found this myself but I never told anyone. Tamsin doesn't even know."

I found this hard to believe. The farm was out of sight, but it couldn't be more than a mile from where we were. "Yeah, well, that's very interesting. How about we head back now?"

"You said you wanted to see the dead babies."

"In *there*?"

"Of course, what'd you think?" She dropped onto her hands and knees. "Once you're inside, you can stand up. Just do it slow so you don't mash your head."

"It's pitch black—I can't see a fucking thing."

"I know! I keep a torch here." She reached into the darkness and a moment later triumphantly held up a flashlight. "It's really brilliant, you'll see."

Before I could protest, she crawled into the passage. I hesitated, then got onto my knees and crept after her.

The interior of the passage made the twilight outside behind seem bright as midday. I saw nothing but the soles of Sam's

Wellingtons a few inches in front of me. Sharp stones bit into my palms as we inched along. After a minute, Sam halted.

"We can stand here," she said, and scrambled to her feet.

I stood more cautiously, wary of bashing my head against the ceiling, and waited for my eyes to adjust.

The passage was a claustrophobe's nightmare. I could only extend my arms halfway before my palms pressed against cold stone. When I raised a hand, it grazed the ceiling mere inches above my head.

Sam's white face bobbed in front of mine. "You're not claustrophobic, are you?"

I gritted my teeth. "No."

"That's good."

She continued on through the tunnel. I stared resolutely at the steel tips of my boots until I realized that Sam was out of sight.

"Slow down!" I yelled.

"Hurry up, then!"

I kept one hand on the wall as I walked, feeling the warmth drain from my fingertips into the rock. The flashlight's beam picked out where the immense slabs had been fitted together. I couldn't imagine the effort it had taken to get them there, or what now kept them from crashing down on top of me. After several yards, the passage widened, and I saw Sam standing in an alcove to one side.

"How the hell did you find this place?" I asked, drawing up alongside her. I wrinkled my nose: The foul smell was stronger here. "Ugh. Is it safe to breathe?"

"I think so."

I jumped as something crunched beneath my foot. "What the hell?"

"It's just winkles." Sam pointed her flashlight. "Dog whelks. See? They'd bring them up from the beach and eat them here."

I took a step back, looked down to see several bushels' worth of small shells heaped across the packed earth. Each shell was no more than an inch long. Their colors shaded from indigo to gray, with here and there a swath of pale violet that glistened in the faint light.

Most of the shells had been crushed. I prodded at the pile with my boot, then bent to fill my hand with dark fragments.

"That's a lot of work for not much food." I sniffed, caught a whiff of the sea. "How long ago was this?"

"Thousands of years. There were no farms then, they had to eat whatever they could find."

"Yeah, but gathering all these tiny shells, then carrying them all the way up here from the shore? There had to be an easier way to get dinner. Aren't there any fish?"

"Sure. Gurnards and pilchards, lots of those. But they might not have had boats. There's even more of them in the fogou—great heaps that come up to here." She held a hand to her waist. "Maybe they just liked winkles. Like cockles—people still eat cockles."

I let the shells fall between my fingers. "Maybe."

"Come over here." Sam turned to shine her flashlight into an alcove. She sounded somber. "There they are. Poor babies."

The wan light fell across several white stones. I stepped closer and saw that they weren't stones but skulls—three of them—so small I could have cupped one in my hand, and arranged so that their crowns touched. Carefully placed beside each was what appeared to be an intact, tiny skeleton.

I looked at Sam. "Jesus. What the hell is that?"

"It's an Iron Age burial. Maybe Bronze Age. But I think

probably Iron Age. They used to think everything in Penwith was Neolithic, but now they think they're maybe not so old." Her tone grew slightly smug.

I knelt beside the remains. "Who thinks that?"

"Archaeologists. I read a book about it. And online, I read a lot when I go into Penzance. Julian Cope has this whole website about ancient ruins, it's brilliant. They're everywhere—not intact graves like this one, but longbarrows and burials. If anyone found out about the babies, they'd take it all away and sell it to a museum."

The words echoed in the passage as she tilted her head to stare at me. Her eyes seemed to have been gouged from her face: When the flashlight caught her pupils they blazed green, like a feral dog's in the night, then receded into shadow.

"They don't belong in a museum," she said. "They could be my ancestors. They belong here."

Gingerly I reached to touch one of the skulls. It felt so fragile I was afraid my fingers might pierce it, like a sheet of paper.

But when I picked it up, it had a surprising weight. As I turned to the light, something fell from the skull, jingling as it struck the floor.

"Don't drop it!" cried Sam.

I set the skull back down and scanned the shadows until I saw a glitter beside my boot. I stooped to pick up a delicate, badly tarnished chain of beads. When I held it up, the chain broke. The beads scattered. Sam hurriedly knelt beside me.

"Be careful," I warned.

I set down the broken chain and swept the gritty floor with one hand. Sam did the same, moving the flashlight back and forth as we searched.

"Here's one," she said after a moment. "And another . . ."

I found one of the beads, no larger than a peppercorn, and in a few minutes found three more. Sam searched for several minutes before she gave up and looked at me. "How many do you have?"

"Three."

"I found four."

The beads were grimy, black with dirt. I licked my fingertip and rubbed one between thumb and forefinger.

"Bring the flashlight close," I said.

I held the bead to the light, tightening my fist around the other six, and squinted. "I can't make it out," I said at last. "Can you see anything?"

Sam bent over my hand. "It's an *A*," she said. "The letter *A*."

We looked at each other. Quickly I set the beads on the ground between us and we began to clean the rest.

"This is an *S*!" She held up a second one.

"This is *E*."

"And *D*."

Sam set her beads on the ground and trained the flashlight on them. I lined up my beads with the other four. Sam began to read off each letter.

"*S, I, R, E*." Her voice grew excited. "*Sire*—it says *sire!* Like a king."

"Jesus," I whispered. I took a bead and rolled it between my fingers. Like a white peppercorn, or a pearl embossed with the letter *D*. I brought it to my mouth and gently bit down on it.

"What the hell are you doing?" Sam snatched at my hand. "Stop!"

"Calm down." I pushed her away and set the bead back on the ground. "They're plastic."

"What?"

"They're plastic. It's a name bracelet. A baby's name bracelet."

I rearranged the letters, and sat back.

"*RESSIDA*?" Sam read the word aloud with a scowl. "That's not even a name."

"*Cressida*. The *C* is missing."

I picked up the broken silver chain. It barely circled my thumb, but the letters would have made it long enough to fit around a very tiny wrist. The baby must have been a newborn.

"The links are there somewhere." I gestured at the surrounding shadows. "And the *C*. The links are so small, they'd be hard to find."

Sam gazed at the beads, as though waiting for the letters to move into another configuration. Finally she said, "What are they doing here?"

"You tell me."

I stood, walked over to the three skeletons, and stared down at them for a long time. Whoever had put them there had done so with care: The bones formed a disturbingly beautiful pattern, moon-white against the black floor. The image reminded me of the triskele I'd seen in Iceland, the ancient pagan symbol known as the Gripping Beast.

I removed the lens cap from my camera and glanced back at Sam. "Shine that flashlight on them. Get as close as you can."

She did. I shot half a dozen pictures before reaching the end of the roll.

"Shit." I shook my head wearily and wound the film back onto the reel. "I'll tell you one thing: This is not a Neolithic burial."

"Someone killed them?"

"Unless they crawled in here and fell asleep like that. Yeah, somebody killed them. They might have died of natural causes, but then why bury them in a hidden grave?"

"Poor little babies." Sam blinked. For an instant I thought she might cry. "How could somebody kill a baby?"

"It happens. Infanticide—some poor girl gets knocked up, she doesn't know what to do, so she keeps the pregnancy secret then kills the baby once it's born. How long has abortion been legal here?"

"I don't know. When do you think it happened?"

"No clue." I bent to scoop up the beads, put them and the bit of silver chain into my jeans pocket. "My guess would be back when they were making *Thanatrope.* So, forty-something years ago. There were a bunch of teenagers living here, not much older than you are now. I know some of them had kids. One of those kids was your father. He told me that Tamsin and your grandfather had a baby who died in the fire." I nodded at the skeletal triskele. "Maybe he's one of those."

Sam crouched to run a hand over a doll-size skull. "Wouldn't it have burned up?"

"Not if it died of smoke inhalation. But I dunno."

I stepped beside her and felt the two thaumatropes brush against my skin. Almost without thinking I drew one out, pulled the rawhide string over my head, and let it dangle from my hand. The disc turned slowly, displaying first the sparely etched features of an old woman, and then a young girl.

"Have you ever seen something like this?"

Sam stepped to me, her eyes widening. "Sweet! Did you find that?"

"In a manner of speaking. Do you know what it is?" She shook her head. "Okay, I'll show you. It's called a thaumatrope. Watch."

I wound the disc tightly as Sam held the flashlight a few inches away, snapped it taut so that the disc became a bright blur, the face morphing from old to young. Sam stared, mesmerized.

"I saw it! A face." She waited for the disc to grow still, then reached for it. "That's fucking brilliant. Can I do it?"

I smiled wryly. "It was probably made in a place like this. Yeah, okay, but be careful."

She handed me the flashlight, and I observed as she imitated what I'd done, repeatedly winding the string then yanking at each end so that the thaumatrope worked its magic.

"It changes!" she exclaimed. "That's so brilliant."

Seeing the play of wonder and delight on her face, I felt the hairs on my neck rise: Thousands of years ago, someone had done exactly the same thing, with exactly the same reaction. I thought of Quinn and me in an earlier century on the first day we met, lying on his bed and listening to "Sweet Jane," the way we'd laughed for pure joy at the opening guitar cords, and how nothing since then had ever recaptured that exultation.

Yet I felt a flicker of it now, watching Sam: mingled joy and anguish at what I'd lost irrevocably. Quinn was gone, and with him whatever scant chance I might have had for a different life.

I looked at the three tiny skeletons on the floor of the barrow. That was all that survived the millennia. Nameless bones and darkness.

"Stop," I said.

I grasped Sam's arm and held it until she relaxed her hold on the string. I expected her to protest as I took it from her hand and looped it back over my head. She just stared at me with the same obdurate hostility as when I'd first met her in the barn.

I pointed to the central passage. "We need to get back. And I don't think you should bring these dead babies up to anyone, okay? Not unless you want cops crawling over this place like flies on shit."

"Like I fucking would."

"Good. Now go—I'll follow you."

She turned and left the chamber.

35

It was full dark when we reached to the house. We hadn't spoken the whole way. If Sam had been a normal teenager, she would have had a mobile clamped to her face, which might have dispersed some of the bad vibes she emanated like static electricity. But if she'd been a normal teenager, she wouldn't have led me across the moor to view three infant skeletons in a Neolithic grave mound. She made a detour by the Highland cow's pen, loping into the shadows.

I had no intention of following her, but I was reluctant to go back into the house alone. I slowed my pace and looked around the yard.

The Land Rover was gone. Besides the dead Alfa, there were no other cars. I walked over to the house and stood in front of the kitchen window, waiting to see if Adrian would appear, or Krishna. After several minutes I went inside.

"Hey," I called in a low voice, then louder. "Hey, anyone here? Adrian?"

There was no reply. I stomped my boots on the mat, trying

to dislodge clumps of mud, and stepped cautiously into the kitchen. "Krishna? Adrian? Anybody home?"

My voice echoed through the cold room.

I dumped my bag on the table and turned on the space heater, opened the ancient fridge, and immediately slammed it shut—it smelled like something had died in there. I glanced around, looking for food or booze, and saw a bottle of Scotch—Talisker—on a high shelf above the fridge. I couldn't reach it, so I started to climb onto the daybed, and noticed Adrian's backpack sitting on the neatly folded blankets.

I glanced outside to make sure the Land Rover hadn't returned, settled quickly onto the daybed, drew the backpack toward me, and opened it. I thrust my hand through socks, underwear, and T-shirts, until I found the oversized book Adrian had shoved in there. I drew it out and set it carefully on the mattress.

As I'd thought, it was a journal, its covers starting to detach because so much stuff had been crammed between them. The pages at the front of the book were dated to the early nineties. I couldn't make much of the sloppy handwriting—some adolescent shorthand that seemed mostly to record the names of DJs and gigs, a few longer notations that involved girls and sex.

At the back of the volume it was much the same, minus the girls and sex, though here the DJs and gigs were ones that Adrian had arranged for various venues throughout London. Scores of newsclippings, postcards, and gig flyers had been crammed between the pages.

Most had to do with music and music festivals. A great many had to do with Poppy Teasel.

Newspaper articles dating to the late 1980s; interviews and reviews and ads clipped from *NME, The Face, SFX;* zines with titles like *Noskirts* and *All Fall Down.* All of these were associated with the release of Poppy's single album, *Best Eaten Cold,* and the tours she did to promote it over the next two years. After that there was the occasional review of a comeback tour. After that, nothing except for a handful of brief "Whatever Happened To?" features, one from the *Telegraph* and another from *Filament*. There were also a lot of grainy pictures of Poppy, cut from newspapers and magazines.

More surprisingly, there was a small clipping from an issue of *Tell Star!* magazine, part of a feature called "Lovestruck." I remembered the feature—brief, breathless interviews with girls who'd stepped onto the first rung of the rickety ladder of groupiedom—but not this image of Poppy. She couldn't have been older than fourteen, wearing smudged blue eyeshadow, a glittery scarf tied pirate-style over her dark curls, and a deep-cut negligee with purple platform boots.

> *California Girl Poppy Teasel has stars in her eyes—one star, anyway! She's joined Lavender Rage as lead singer Jonno Blitz's wardrobe girl/friend—and the best thing is, she can wear his clothes! (And vice versa!) "I believe in breaking the rules," she confided to Tell Star! "If I want something, I take it! Guys have been doing that forever, now it's our turn." The Rage will be all the rage back in Olde England this summer when the band goes on tour, with Poppy in charge of boots, belts, and bell-bottoms. Just don't lose the key to the costume trunk, Poppy!*

I winced. If the adult Poppy had lived by her adolescent credo, one of the things she'd taken might have been Mallo. That would explain her falling out with the Dunfrieses. The thaumatrope might have been a Trojan horse, disguised as a peace offering sent by Morven. When Morven appeared shortly after my departure, Poppy would have welcomed her with open arms—one of which soon had a spike in it.

I glanced again at the *Tell Star!* image of Poppy, and felt a pang for the young Adrian. He'd been an infant when this photo of Poppy ran, but he might have been the same age as the teenybopper Poppy when he first saw it. She must have given it to him. Or maybe it was lying around the farmhouse when he was growing up, a tawdry memento of her own childhood. Either way, it had been handled so often over the years that the fragile paper left yellowing fragments on my fingertips. I slipped it carefully back where I'd found it, then flipped to the end of the journal.

Most of the pages here were empty. A few had dates or phone numbers scribbled on them. Stuck between two pages were several folded clippings from the *Camden New Journal,* with photos and club listings.

Newcomer Krishna Morgenthal left a lingering impression at last night's open mic at World's End, doing covers of classic girl group pop as well as Adore's current hit, "Hitting the Brake." Well worth checking out.

Fans looking for the next Adele or Laura Burhenn can cool their heels at the Banshee near Kentish Town, where a nineteen-year-old with the unlikely moniker of Krishna Morgenthal (her real name) has been drawing comparisons to those two, not to mention Dusty Springfield and Amy Winehouse . . .

Adrian's musical taste might run to electronica, but he definitely seemed to have his own groupie thing going on. I stared at the picture of a doe-eyed Krishna glammed up in a slinky halter dress, replaced the clippings, and slid the journal back where I'd found it. I looked out the window. Still no Land Rover.

I swiftly went through the rest of the backpack. Other than a rumpled sweater and a mobile phone charger, there was nothing. But when I unzipped the front pocket and stuck my hand in, my fingers closed around a small cardboard box. I pulled out a blister packet of prescription tablets. The scrip on the label was for someone named Lazslo Chesna. I read what was printed on the back—*Dormicum [Midazolam] 15 mg.*

Midazolam is a very powerful, fast-acting sedative and muscle relaxant. It doesn't stay in your system long: There's a quick recovery time, which is why the IV form is used for short-term surgical procedures. Combined with other drugs, it's used in lethal injections for prisoners undergoing execution. In lower doses in oral form, like these tablets, it's prescribed as a sleep aid—it knocks you out, but only for a few hours. The sedative effect is exacerbated by alcohol, and one of the side effects is amnesia, which is why it's used as a date rape drug. In high doses it can be fatal, as when it was administered to Michael Jackson to counter his insomnia, along with Ativan, Valium, and propofol.

The blister pack in my hand had contained twenty pills. Now it was empty.

I peeled away the foil covering and ran my finger along the surface where the tablets had been. An almost invisible blue residue adhered to my fingertip. Ground into a powder, the drug would have dissolved quickly. In a glass of red wine, it would have been undetectable. Mallo and Morven would have welcomed Adrian into their flat. He'd opened the bottle of Cabernet, dosed their wine with Midazolam, and waited the thirty minutes or so until it kicked in.

He'd probably done in Mallo first—the ribbons had been a

nice touch. If Morven had been chipping heroin that evening, she would have done most of Adrian's groundwork for him. The drug's anti-anxiety effects would have taken care of any suspicions the Dunfrieses might have had, ex post facto, which would have made it easy for him to strangle Mallo in his office, and even easier for Adrian to assist Morven into a nonexistent elevator going way, way down. But why?

It was easy to imagine bad blood seeping between the three of them over the years. Maybe Adrian wasn't crazy about being cut from Mallo's new business plan. And if Adrian and Krishna had some sort of history, past or present, Krishna's dalliance with Morven might have pushed him over the edge.

It was harder for me to square Adrian as Poppy's killer. If he'd faked his reaction to news of her death, he was primed for a career in politics. That, or he was more of a headcase than I was. I recalled the image of Poppy as I'd found her, any trace of pain or regret effaced. The same expression of vacant calm I'd seen in the teenage Quinn when he'd nodded off. Perhaps she'd chosen her own exit via a familiar door, despite Adrian's insistence otherwise. If so, it had been messier than she'd intended. But the result was the same.

From outside came a faint roar that gradually grew louder. The Land Rover. I dropped the empty drug packet into the pocket and zipped it, then hurriedly went through the other pockets but found nothing except some nicotine cartridges. I shoved the backpack onto the mattress and hopped up from the daybed, peering out the window to see the Rover's headlights as it veered closer to the farmyard. I stuck my camera bag under the table and sat, angling my chair toward the space heater.

Five minutes later, the front door opened. I heard Adrian

stamping in the entryway as I'd done earlier, followed by muttered curses as he trudged into the kitchen.

"What're you doing?" He removed his anorak and tossed it onto the daybed, shot me a stony look then yelled, "Sam!"

"She was out by the barn," I said.

"She feed the cow?"

"No clue."

Adrian lumbered into the living room, shouting. "Sam!"

As he passed me I caught a strong reek of Scotch and tobacco smoke. He soon returned, his stony gaze now outright hostile.

"I'm just keeping warm," I said, lowering my face toward the heater so I could avoid his eyes. "Trying to, anyway."

"You been here all day?"

"I took a walk with Sam. Did you go to find Tamsin?"

He shook his head. "You missed her. She's been here—been and gone. Got back from Penzance then went down to the garage to get a tire repaired. No worries, you'll have your chance later." He grimaced.

"Where's Krishna?"

"Out wandering the moors, trying to get a mobile signal."

Adrian reached up to pull the bottle of Talisker from the shelf, along with two glasses. He blew into each glass, raising a puff of dust. The bottle of Talisker had seen more recent active duty. Sam must have inherited her father's taste for Scotch. Adrian poured two inches of whiskey into a glass and pushed it across the table to me.

I picked it up and sniffed. The scent reminded me of the night I'd seen someone pitch a propane tank into a bonfire. I didn't taste it, keeping an eye on Adrian as he filled his own glass.

"Cheers," he said, unsmiling, and knocked back the whiskey.

I took a sip. It tasted better than it smelled. I watched, warily, as Adrian finished his glass, then did the same to my own and helped myself to another shot, finishing the bottle.

"Thank you," said Adrian.

"You're welcome." I cupped the glass in my hands. "Is this the only heat you've got? Other than that—" I nudged the electric heater with my boot.

Adrian staggered from his chair. "I'll start a fire in the other room. I've got another bottle there."

When he was gone, I peered out into the yard. I could just make out Sam's gangly figure moving between the outbuildings, the thin beam of her flashlight dancing before her. I watched her for a few minutes, then went to join Adrian.

He was crouched in front of the fireplace, whiskey bottle beside him. A small stack of what looked like charcoal briquets perched atop the fire dog. Gray smoke filled the air with a pungent, grassy smell: peat.

"Be aware this is only psychological warmth."

Adrian stepped away from the fireplace, pushing aside the deflated soccer ball with his foot. He took the other chair, pulling it so close to the fire that the tips of his Doc Martens touched the smoldering peat. He was unshaven, his handsome features blue-shadowed and eyes bloodshot. A scratch on one cheek oozed a watery red. He wiped it absently with the back of his hand, leaving a crimson smear beside his mouth.

"Christ, I'm tired." He shut his eyes, and remained silent for such a long time I thought he'd fallen asleep.

Without warning he kicked at the fireplace. A brick of smoldering peat skittered across the floor. He scooped it up and tossed it back. I picked up the bottle, took a long swallow of Scotch, and glanced at the window. It only threw back the pale blur of my own face.

I edged my chair closer to the fire, trying to put some distance between Adrian and myself. "How long has Sam been here?"

"Two years. She was bullied at school in London. I decided she'd be better off with Tamsin."

"She told me she's training to be a shaman."

"Did she?" Adrian snorted. "God, that's all we need. Tamsin is relentless. I remember her trying that on with me when I was the same age. It didn't stick."

"Samsung—what the hell kind of name is that?"

"It was a festival thing. Her mom and me. It was her idea—Justina's. You know, embracing the power of technology. When Sam was three, Justina went to Burning Man and never came back. We'd been living with a group of anarchists in Islington; they moved on but I stayed in the squat with Sam. I was able to make ends meet. Barely."

"Yeah, well, she's living like a wild animal here. She'd be better off back with you in the squat."

Adrian turned to me, his eyes brighter than the embers. "You saying I abandoned my kid? Fuck you. You and Poppy and all that hippie punk anarchist rhetoric. You think we're animals? That's because we bought into your fairy tales. There is no Golden City. I was a kid, how was I to know better? Now we're living in the ruins like dogs."

"What's your problem?" I gulped my whiskey. It wasn't Talisker. "I'm not the one who screwed you up. Give your kid a decent home. Get a fucking job. And I'm not a fucking hippie."

Adrian laughed. "Listen to you. You and your mate Quinn. You know what he is? A contract killer. He scarpered off to Reykjavík when it got too dangerous in Oslo, but he didn't change his spots. Do you want to know why?"

He leaned toward me, and his deep voice dropped to a whisper. "Because he fucking loves it. Twenty years ago I watched him strangle a bloke outside a club in Brixton. The guy had taken Mallo Dunfries for a thousand quid, and Mallo asked Quinn to deal with it. He did, and he took his own sweet time. I saw it with my own eyes. Strangled him with a piano wire, sliced right through his windpipe and his spinal column. Put the head in a bag and dropped it in the river, dumped his body somewhere in the Isle of Dogs. You could see from his face that he got off on it."

"You're lying."

Adrian's gaze pierced mine. "I'm not. And you know I'm not. Do you know why he asked me to watch you? Because he's gone. Someone offered him a job back in Oslo, Sweden, someplace like that. He gave me three hundred quid to make sure you were safe, I'll give him that."

He sank deeper into his chair. The breath left my body. I stared at him, trying to force myself to speak. He avoided my gaze.

"Here." He thrust a hand into his pocket and pulled out a wad of notes. "Count it. I spent some on petrol, but the rest is there. Three hundred quid—that's what you're worth to Quinn O'Boyle."

He shoved the notes at me. I struck at him. "Get away from me."

"You know it's the truth."

He looked at the empty glass on the floor beside him, as though wondering how it got there. His expression grew pained.

"Look, I'm sorry," he said. "I am. I should've left you in the city to find your own way. I should have done that. But Poppy and the others . . . It was too much. I was worried about Sam and Krishna. I couldn't do it alone. I wasn't thinking."

He slid the money back into his pocket. "All I wanted was to get Krish away from London and make sure Sam was safe. I thought you'd be better off here than there."

I looked at his face. The cut by his mouth had started to scab over. "Where's Krishna?"

"I told you—outside, trying to get a mobile signal. Good luck with that." He noticed my stare, and touched his cheek. "She gave me that. Like a mad cat. Every woman I know is mad. Why is that, you think?"

He picked up his empty glass and stared into it, musing.

I gazed numbly into the fire. I saw Quinn in Iceland, garroting a man with a guitar string, blood like crimson sparks. I thought of a girl in Finland, now dead, who had told me about the bouncer at an Oslo nightclub.

This guy took the bodies and cut them up and buried the pieces. Someone I know saw him, he was with his girlfriend one night; she was carrying a bag, and there was a head in it.

I said, "He was going to see some guy so we could go to Greece. A guy with a boat."

"He's gone. I don't know the details. There was a job he had to take; he couldn't turn it down, he said. But he wanted you safe."

"Safe?" I stumbled to my feet. "This is safe?"

I grabbed the bottle of whiskey. "Don't you fucking touch me," I said. "You or anyone else. Don't you say a fucking word to me."

I found my way back to the attic and flung myself onto the pile of blankets. I finished the bottle then buried my face in my arms, until I could no longer hear the sound of my own voice repeating Quinn's name, over and over and over again.

36

Light blistered my eyelids. I turned and retched onto the floor. Someone wiped my face with a wet cloth. I pushed away a hand, groaning.

"Hello," said Sam. "You're alive."

She sat back on her heels, head cocked. Beside her was a plastic basin and some wadded towels. I tried to sit up, but my head felt as though an ax were embedded in it. "What time is it?" I whispered.

"Drink this." Sam held out a liter soda bottle filled with water.

I started to reach for the bottle, stopped. "You first."

Sam looked affronted. "It's only water." But she took a swallow, then handed it to me.

My stomach lurched as I drank, but after a moment the nausea passed. It took all my effort to murmur thanks.

Sam edged closer to me. "I thought you were dead. You puked over everything, it was disgusting. Lucky you were on your stomach, or you'd've choked. I had to throw the blanket in the bin outside."

"I just said thanks."

"No—I mean, I thought you were *dead*. I shone the torch in your eyes and the pupils were like this—" She screwed up her face, pinched her fingers together. "Invisible."

I made another, more successful attempt to sit up. "Is there more of that water?"

"I'll get some." I listened to her footsteps recede downstairs, then return a few minutes later. "Here. I got two."

"What time is it?"

"Just noon."

I drank the water slowly and tried to avoid looking at the windows. Sam sat crosslegged on the floor, watching me intently. I frowned.

"Why are you wearing my leather jacket?"

"I had to clean it off. I peeled it right off you, and you didn't even move. I'm saying, you weren't breathing. Dead as dead, I thought." She tugged the jacket's sleeves until they covered her bony wrists. "Into the grave with the babies."

"Well, thanks for waiting before you buried me," I said. "Hand me my bag, will you?"

I groped around till I found the bottle of ibuprofen and took four. My head throbbed as I struggled to recall the previous night.

Three hundred quid—that's what you're worth to Quinn O'Boyle.

I took a deep breath and waited for the black wave to pass before looking up at Sam once more.

"What did you say about my eyes?" I asked. "When you shone the flashlight in them."

"You couldn't see the pupils. It was like they disappeared. It was freaky."

"No fucking lie." I finished the water. "That doesn't happen when you're drunk."

Sam shook her head. "You were definitely drunk."

"That's not what I mean. I've spent more years drunk than you've been alive—your eyes don't get pinned, even if you're completely wasted. Alcohol makes your pupils dilate. Opiates constrict them."

I glanced around for the whiskey bottle and found it rolled alongside my pallet. I picked it up and sniffed it. No tell-tale scent, of course—that was the whole point.

"Shit," I said.

"Shit what?"

"Shit someone tried to poison me, is what."

Her eyes widened. "Who?"

"That's the million-dollar question." I pushed myself to my feet, grimacing, and leaned against the wall. "Or maybe the three-hundred-pound question, minus petrol money. Unless it was you?"

"Me?" Sam looked appalled. "No!"

"Well then. That leaves everybody else."

"Fuck! How'd they do it?"

"They put something in the bottle, I drank it. End of story. It wouldn't be much of a challenge," I admitted.

"Why aren't you dead?"

"Because me and Keith Richards were separated at birth. Wait—"

I jammed my hand into my jeans pocket, pulled out the plastic beads and silver chain. "You didn't tell anyone about these, did you? Your father or Tamsin?"

"You think I'm an idiot? No."

"What about Krishna?"

"Her? I don't even know her."

"Well, that's one good thing. Don't say anything about those babies to anyone. Don't even mention it to me again—I want to forget I ever fucking saw that place. There a shower here? Bathtub, anything like that?"

"Downstairs. I'll show you."

I stepped woozily to the head of the stairs, and let her take my arm to steady me. "There a lock on the bathroom door?"

Sam nodded.

"What about a window?"

"A small one. But it's high up the wall."

I reached to touch my leather jacket, hanging loosely on her skinny frame. "Listen. I want you to stay outside that bathroom door—if anyone comes, you let me know. Quietly, though. Then you take off, okay? Don't let them see you."

"Sure."

She didn't even blink. I shook my head. "You're a piece of work. Let's go."

This bathroom was tacked on to the far end of the farmhouse, a few steps down a dark hallway that also held a washing machine and piles of clothing. Sam closed the hall door, pulling a wooden latch to secure it, then sank to the floor beside the bathroom door.

"I'll wait here." She took out a hand-rolled cigarette and a lighter. "I always smoke in the bath. They'll think it's me."

I locked the door behind me. There was a large claw-foot tub, its enamel streaked with rust. Two well-worn towels hung from nails in the wall. There was a spindly wooden chair and a collection of nearly-empty shampoo bottles on the floor beside the tub. A porcelain dish held slivers of soap. The shampoo had come from D. R. Harris. The soap still gave forth a faint fragrance of eglantine. I wondered how many other aging English aristocrats were holed up in similarly impoverished circumstances, freezing their bony asses off as they ate tinned beans and drank the dregs of their forebears' wine cellars.

The hot water came from an on-demand gas water heater, which meant there was an unlimited supply. I undressed and carefully looped the two thaumatropes over the back of the chair. Then I filled the tub and sank into it. I washed my cropped hair and did my best not to fall back into unconsciousness, lulled by hot water and the remnants of whatever drug still remained in my system.

I opened my eyes with a start: I'd nodded off.

I hastily sat up and splashed water on my face. I'd been living so long on speed and alcohol that the bones in my hands stood up like the tines of a rake. I needed a good night's sleep and a decent meal. Neither seemed likely. I could hightail it across the open moor, but I had no idea where I was, and I suspected the locals here didn't take kindly to strangers. I could hijack Adrian's Land Rover, but that would mean getting the keys. I wondered if Sam's skill set included jumpstarting a car.

More than anything, though, I wondered who wanted me dead, and why.

Morven's own relationship with heroin would have made it possible for her to kill Poppy, if her onetime friend and fellow Flaming Creature had betrayed her with Mallo. And that empty packet of Midazolam pointed to Adrian as the Dunfrieses' killer. He might have kept a hidden stockpile of Midazolam.

But why go to all the trouble of dragging me here? As he'd pointed out, he'd had ample opportunity to off me back in London. Krishna seemingly had access to enough opiates to kill me several times over, but she seemed barely able to walk upright. And while I wouldn't quite put it past Sam to slide someone a roofie, I had a hard time imagining she'd do it to me. Not on her own.

That left Tamsin. Or maybe the fake ICOTIA agent, Ellen Connors. Like Adrian, she could have done the job far more easily in London: Why chase me across the West Country in a blizzard?

So, Tamsin. Adrian had described her as batshit crazy. Based on what I'd heard, she was certainly unstable, and guilty of child neglect, if not actual abuse.

A few days ago, I'd never heard of any of these people. Since then, I'd slept with one of them and found the corpses of three others, but nothing else connected me to their daisy chain of sexual dalliances, stemming from Leith Carlisle and god knows how many teenage girls.

Except for two things.

I leaned over the tub and removed a thaumatrope from the chair. The disc with the eye, the disc that Adrian had found in a barrow here at Kethelwite. It twisted slowly, its malicious gaze fixed on me from a vantage of thousands of years.

"Cass!" I looked up sharply at Sam's urgent whisper. "Adrian's looking for me. If I don't go he'll come down here."

I looped both thaumatropes over my neck and stood, grabbing a towel, then went to the door and cracked it. "Go!"

Sam averted her eyes from me. "What will—"

"I don't know—just *go.*"

I closed the door and dressed, tucking the thaumatropes beneath my black sweater, henley, and T-shirt. Too late I remembered that Sam still had my leather jacket.

Silently I stepped into the hallway. Before I could reach the door that led out of the annex, it opened.

A woman in mud-covered Wellingtons and a faded red barn jacket stood in the doorway. She seemed spindly as a scarecrow as she approached me, leaning on a walking stick. Then she straightened, and I saw that she was taller than she'd first appeared—strong jawed, her angular face slightly mannish, with thick ash-gray hair cut in a messy bob. Her eyes were pale blue, slightly opalescent: cataracts, probably. She didn't much resemble her son, except in the grim set of her mouth, streaked with incongruously bright pink lipstick.

"Ah. That girl was telling the truth." Her voice was an imperious rasp. "We do have another unwanted guest."

"What girl?" I retorted, but she ignored my question.

"Out!" she commanded, gesturing at the door as though I were a wet dog. "Now!"

I walked past her quickly, hoping to get enough momentum to break into a run. She grabbed my arm, pulling me up short—she was strong for a living scarecrow. Whip-fast, she struck the back of my knees with the walking stick.

I cried out as my legs buckled, and she prodded me with her cane. The handle was gold—a gryphon's head with ruby eyes. *"Go."*

I limped down the hall into the living room. Adrian sprawled, his face impassive, in one of the old armchairs. Krishna sat in the other chair. Her face was scrubbed clean of makeup, skin milk-white and lips cracked. Without the Cleopatra eyeliner, it was easier to focus on her bloodshot eyes, their dark irises flecked with amethyst. She gazed in dazed fascination at Sam, who knelt in the middle of the floor, speaking softly to the brown soccer ball.

"Come on, Tithonus. Say hello." As we entered, Sam looked up at the gray-haired woman. "He won't come out."

"He doesn't like strangers."

The woman leaned forward to bang her cane on the floor three times. The soccer ball shifted ever so slightly. Very slowly, an etiolated neck extended from it, ending in a small, bulbous head.

"I expect he's hungry." The old woman nudged Sam gently with the cane. "Go see if there's some lettuce in the icebox."

Sam stood. She made a point of not glancing my way as she headed into the kitchen.

"That's a turtle," I said.

"Tortoise," the woman corrected me. "His name is Tithonus. He belonged to my great-grandmother Calantha when she was a girl. He's a spider tortoise, brought to this country by an obscure relative who had business in the southern desert of Madagascar. We never thought to ask what the nature of his business was. Something sinister, I would suspect. I believe the species is now extinct, which would make him the last of his kind, as I am of mine. Tithonus is one hundred and forty-seven years old. Nearly as old as I am," she added as Sam returned.

"Spinach," said Sam. She dropped to her knees beside the tortoise and held out a green wad. The tortoise raced toward her, surprisingly fast, its claws clittering against the wooden floor.

Krishna grimaced. "Ugh."

The gray-haired woman regarded Krishna, then me. "I am Tamsin Carlisle. I gather you also arrived with Adrian yesterday."

I glanced at Adrian. He gave a slight nod, and I looked back at Tamsin. "Yeah."

"Did Morven send you?"

"Who?"

"Don't try to lie to me. I can smell her on you." Swift as a striking hawk, her face jabbed against mine, forcing me backward. Her breath reeked of carious teeth and gin. "You thought you'd wash away her stink, but I can smell her."

She spat at me. I raised my fist.

"Don't!" cried Sam.

"Stop it." Adrian grabbed my elbow. "Calm down."

"Right," pronounced Krishna. "Calm down. *Calm down*. Because this is all so *fucking normal,* right?"

Tamsin fixed her with a cold stare. "Get up," she said, indicating the armchair.

Krishna rose with preposterous slowness. "Your Highness Lady Muck," she said, and sidled to the wooden stool.

I waited for Tamsin to retaliate, but she only sat. "Thank you," she murmured. She reached for a teacup on the floor beside her, lifted it, and took a sip. "This has already been a long day."

All this time, I'd been thinking of her as a contemporary of Morven and Poppy, only a few years older than me. But she'd been six years Leith Carlisle's senior. Living alone on this hardscabble farm might have contributed to her formidable manner and unnerving agility, but she'd still have to be in her late seventies.

Which meant she'd have been within shouting distance of forty when Adrian was born: twice as old as Poppy and Morven and all the other teenagers running around Kethelwite Manor, all those girls whom Leith screwed. Tamsin's first child died in the fire: If what Adrian had said was true, and Leith's teenage lovers had borne him children, that could explain the two other infant skeletons in the barrow.

Tamsin's eyes closed. Within moments, her facial muscles

slackened. Her mouth opened, exposing several missing teeth. She began to snore.

I glanced up at the others to see what they made of this macabre interlude. They regarded Tamsin so intently she might have been a cat video, their faces lined up in profile: Adrian, then Krishna, then Sam, all of them backlit by the window. The trio of silhouettes made for a strikingly odd affect—human faces fanned out like three-card monte. I reached for my camera bag, then froze.

It wasn't just the angle, or a trick of the light. Their features were strangely, disconcertingly similar. The same strong chin and deep-set onyx eyes, the same thin mouth and black hair, even the same expression as they stared at Tamsin—a sort of expectant apprehension, as though waiting for the curtain to rise on a show they knew would be a disappointment. Sam shared the same lanky, big-boned frame as Adrian.

But Krishna had inherited her mother's spare figure, along with her voice, and the violet flicker in her dark eyes.

I dropped my gaze, praying Adrian wouldn't notice my face flush in anger and fear. Did Krishna know her parents were Poppy Teasel and Adrian Carlisle? Adrian had lied to me about it, which stacked the deck in favor of him lying to Krishna, too.

Had he told Sam?

Because even now, sitting side by side, neither Krishna nor Sam seemed to show much interest in the other. Given Sam's isolation and over-eager response to the slightest bit of adult attention from me, I found it hard to believe she wouldn't have latched onto Krishna like a tick, once she learned they were half-sisters.

If they *were* half-siblings. I totted up the years: Poppy would have been in her mid-forties when Krishna was born—like Tamsin, an older mother. Though if Tamsin had any children, none of them were in the room with us at the moment.

I picked up my bag and got slowly to my feet. I half expected Adrian to stop me, but his gaze just flicked over me before returning to Tamsin. Krishna appeared preternaturally still, her amethyst-flecked eyes fixed on Adrian. Only Sam briefly looked up, before she returned to crooning at the tortoise.

I walked into the kitchen. Bruno's heavy coat hung beside the door; I grabbed it and pulled it on and hurried outside, toward the barn. The sun had already begun its slide into the west. Ice skimmed a large puddle beside the Land Rover. An older Range Rover was parked beside it—Tamsin's car.

The living room windows overlooked the moor, not the yard. As far as I could tell, no one watched me as I entered the barn, and I recalled a fairy tale where goblins were hypnotized by a campfire and never moved again.

Bruno's overcoat was warm, but I wished I'd remembered to get my leather jacket from Sam. I'd wait till nightfall, then hightail it down to the main road, and walk or thumb a ride to Penzance. Nothing I'd seen so far suggested an active constabulary, and at this point I'd risk an encounter with the locals. They couldn't be much crazier than the Kethelwite clan.

At the back of the barn, the storeroom door was ajar. I slipped inside, closing the door behind me.

I flipped the lightswitch. A bare overhead bulb came on. I jammed a lighting rig under the doorknob to keep anyone from entering easily, then checked out the canisters stacked along the wall.

The ink on the labels was faded and, in some places, unreadable. Those I could read seemed to be reels from *Thanatrope,* the dates out of order and written in blue ink.

Than. May 72
Than. August 73
Spot Reel June 72

I counted seventeen cans—a lot of thirty-five-mm footage for a flick without any studio funding, even if the film stock had been damaged to begin with. Something poked from between two canisters. I carefully pulled it free. A photograph, torn on one side. It showed the teenage Morven and Tamsin with their arms flung over each other's shoulders. A ghostly extra arm on Morven's shoulder indicated where a third girl had stood beside her. Someone had ripped Poppy out of the frame.

I set aside the photo and turned. Curling lengths of acetate were draped over the back of the Steenbeck, like old nylon stockings left out to dry. Another photo was propped on top of the editing deck—Sam and Tamsin crouched beside the tortoise Tithonus, both of them laughing. A strip of footage was still in the Steenbeck's guillotine splicer, ten or so frames of color stock, with a container of splicing tape alongside it.

It appeared that someone was continuing to edit *Thanatrope.* Tamsin, if she had indeed been the guiding force behind the film. Maybe some outlet specializing in obscure or transgressive movies was interested in a director's cut, or maybe Tamsin needed a hobby to occupy her golden years.

Editing with a Steenbeck would certainly take up a lot of time. It's a slow, painstaking process, almost entirely superseded by digital software like Final Cut. A Steenbeck flatbed cost thirty or forty grand when they were first introduced over a half century ago, to compete with and ultimately replace the Moviola. The rig looked like a scale model of some intricate futuristic city, but the big table was an analogue morgue for what had once been state-of-the-art German technology: brushed nickel fittings, rollers and spools, take-up reels and relays, spindles, mirror optics and lenses, a projection lamp and viewing screen, along with two sets of aluminum plates for both sixteen- and thirty-five-millimeter film.

You mounted the film reel on the aluminum plate to the left, then threaded the film through a dizzying number of spindles and rollers and spools and relays, so it could pass through the picture gate and be rewound on the take-up reel on the right-hand side of the table. It seemed impossibly complicated.

Yet the setup was low-tech. You turned a dial to adjust how fast or slow the film would move, which enabled you to view the film at the customary thirty-five frames a second—the speed at which a film was projected in a movie theater. You could move the film forward or in reverse.

Or you could slow it down, so you could watch it frame-by-frame on the screen in front of you. You could pause the mechanism to view a single frame, though you couldn't leave it in the picture gate too long, or the heat from the projector bulb would melt the acetate.

All editing used to be linear editing, and it was almost inconceivably intensive, detail-oriented work. With a computer, you're not restricted to a linear approach: You can move digital images around however you want.

But back then, you had to scroll through it all reel by reel—tens of thousands of individual frames—looking for flaws in the film stock, lens flare, a clapper or boom mike in the frame—any one of the countless things that can go wrong during a shoot. After deciding which frames to remove, you had to cut the acetate using the guillotine, then splice it all back together with tape. Then look at it again to see if your edit had improved the film or not.

Film editors are the silent sharers of cinema: They form a sort of cinematic binary star system with the director. Robert Wise and Orson Welles; Thelma Shoonmaker and Martin Scorsese; Susan E. Morse and Woody Allen.

And, it seemed, Tamsin and Leith Carlisle.

I made sure the door was still guarded by the lighting rig and settled into the swivel chair. Something clanked as the chair moved—a metal trash can.

I picked it up. The bottom was coated with black sludge and peppered with dozens of spent matches. The perforated edge of a piece of acetate adhered to its side. Gingerly I peeled this off. The charred acetate was shriveled into a wormy black string where it had melted. Whoever used the Steenbeck wasn't taking any chances with edited clips left on the cutting-room floor. They were burning them.

37

It didn't take long to figure out the basics of running the Steenbeck. I located the main switch and turned it on. The motor whirred to life, and after a brief warmup settled into a steady drone. The screen went from black to stark white as the projector's bulb shone through the gate. I began turning the black dial: the film moved quickly through the gate, way too fast for me to get a clear sense of what I was seeing. I played with the dial for a few minutes, running the same loops of film back and forth until I got the hang of it. The apparatus made a low whirring as the turntables spun.

Images flickered across the small screen, out of focus and harshly lit. I adjusted the focus and dialed down the contrast, reversed the film and ran it through the projector again. Now the picture was clear enough for me to discern six or eight people lying on the floor of a large room, with high clerestory windows set into the stone wall behind them. I recognized the setting, and this scene, from *Thanatrope*—one moment the room was empty, the next it was filled with revelers. A flash cut, amateurish but also spookily effective.

When I watched it again, the people on the floor writhed with a strange languor, moving so slowly that I checked the Steenbeck's speed to be sure I wasn't watching something that had been shot in slow motion. Just out of frame, someone held a fill light closer to the action, but he or she wasn't doing a very good job. Both the lamp and the hand that clutched it juttered in and out of sight.

And the fill light was way too bright. It washed out the actors it was supposed to illuminate, even as it threw an etiolated shadow across the wall behind them—a grotesquely thin form, one long spidery arm gesticulating violently, its elongated head topped with a ragged crown of hair, so monstrously distorted I thought it must be cast by an immense puppet.

But then the camera, too, went crazily awry. For a second it threw a blinding flash onto a tall figure with wild red hair, wearing a long white apron and pants tucked into Wellington boots. The camera swung back to the bodies on the floor. They continued to move with that nightmarish slowness, as though they'd drowned in sluggish water and remained trapped beneath the surface.

I stopped the film. I'd thought I recognized this scene from when I'd watched *Thanatrope* just a few days before.

Now I wasn't so sure. Everything seemed familiar—the bodies on the floor, the high windows, the flash cut—even the bad lighting and the disturbing shadow on the wall, and that crazed-seeming figure in the white apron.

But *had* I seen them earlier? The images were so weirdly oneiric—more nightmarish than dreamlike—that they made me doubt my own memory of the film. They reminded me of the night terrors I'd experienced in the last few months, the fear of some black arachnid nesting in my skull, unraveling the neural web that was my own consciousness.

A dark wave engulfed me. I'd been betrayed by Quinn and was trapped among people who wanted me dead. I felt myself fragmenting, the way a cracked windshield shatters at the impact of some object.

The stink of melted plastic cut through my despair. I'd left the frame in front of the projector too long. I took a deep breath, then advanced the film and switched off the deck's lamp to check the frames. The acetate had warped, but I'd caught it before it was badly damaged.

The diversion broke the malevolent spell the film had over me. I turned the control knob, and the film slowly wound between the rollers and gears. The screen filled with those same ghostly figures. Light rolled across them like surf as I ran the loop backward to the beginning of the scene, then advanced it very slowly, frame by frame.

Now I could see that the hand holding the fill light was a man's, large and thick-fingered. The figures on the floor were the same teenagers I'd seen in *Thanatrope*. Three girls and three boys. One of the boys looked no more than fourteen, and one of the girls appeared even younger than that.

But even watching the film one frame at a time, I still couldn't tell what those kids were actually doing on the floor. Sex would be the obvious answer. But the interplay of shadow and hard light was so disjointed that, no matter what frame I examined, or what angle I inspected it from, I couldn't home in on any specific detail. No breast or cock or mouth or limb; only an overwhelming sense that something terrible was going on.

After several more minutes, I had to stop. I felt as though I'd been sucked into an undertow of damage so corrosive it burned: I could taste it in the back of my throat. I switched off the editing deck and got unsteadily to my feet, turned on the overhead light and cracked the door to let in a stream of fresh air. The small room had grown warm, heated by the projector lamp. I inhaled gratefully, hoping the cold would disperse the toxic cloud that had settled in my chest, behind my eyes, inside my skull.

The nausea remained, morphing into that sick horror. Black filaments spun from the corners of my eyes. I tasted copper in the back of my throat, spat into my palm, and saw a smear of blood. In the room behind me came the low whir of the Steenbeck's motor engaging. I turned, but the deck's reels and plates were motionless.

I shut the door and sank back into the swivel chair. I wanted to believe that this was the lingering effect of whatever I'd been doped with the night before. But the truth seemed as inexplicable as the fragmented scene I'd now viewed a dozen times. The film footage was making me sick.

I picked up my bag and removed the Mortensen book that Poppy had given me. I flipped to the last section, *Grotesques*. The kitsch factor was high by modern standards, but the pictures still had the power to disturb. These are the images that pop up when you Google Mortensen: a nubile, naked woman preparing for the witch's sabbath; a terror-stricken man facing the blade in "The Pit and the Pendulum"; a man gouging out his own eyes. The fact that he used live models only makes the photos more unsettling.

In *The Command to Look,* Mortensen gave step-by-step instructions for creating an image that will compel viewers to gaze on it, even as they strain to look away. His photos came under fire for the same imagery that has become so ingrained in our visual cortices that we no longer register them as horrific, a viral stream of crime photos and videos of beheadings, bomb victims, maimed soldiers, plane crashes.

Thanatrope's director seemed to have taken Mortensen's lesson to heart. As neuroelectrical impulses, the footage wormed its way through retina, optic nerve, occipital lobe, to make a direct strike on that part of the human brain that registers pure existential horror—all while compelling the viewer to keep watching.

I could see why the movie had been pulled upon its initial release. It was more like a virus than a film. My reputation as a photographer had rested on the fact that I never flinched, no matter what awful thing I shot. Now I broke into a cold sweat at the thought of what I'd seen on the Steenbeck's screen.

I closed the book and returned it to my bag. The overhead light stung my eyes, but without the projector lamp, the room had quickly grown cold again. I stared at the strip of film in the guillotine splicer. Eleven frames. I didn't see a loupe or magnifier, but there was a small panel on the Steenbeck where you could place film to view it—a miniature light table built into the console. I found the button to turn this on, and placed the film strip on top of it.

Even without a magnifying lens, I knew what I was looking at: naked human corpses strewn across a patch of moor. I counted four—not infants but adults. One appeared slender enough to be a teenager. Each lay, face up, atop a large flat stone or pile of stones. Their placement seemed less ritualistic than functional, as though they'd been arrayed carelessly and then forgotten. Outtakes from one of the time-lapsed scenes in *Thanatrope.*

Or maybe they weren't outtakes, but material to be added to some ghoulish director's cut as a means of intensifying the film's malign impact. If Scotland Yard really had interviewed Leith Carlisle, as he'd claimed, they'd done so without access to this crucial bit of evidence.

I stared at the strip of acetate on that glowing white screen. Finally I reached beneath my sweater for one of the rawhide cords and pulled it over my head to hold in front of me. The bone disc turned lazily, revealing one face then another. Girl or old woman, both nearly indistinguishable. I flicked it with my finger so it spun.

With a deafening crash, the lighting rig fell to the floor behind me. The leather cord flew from my hand as someone kicked my chair: Tamsin Carlisle. Before I could move, she snatched up the bone disc, cradling it in her palm. When she looked at me, the nacreous blue eyes no longer seemed impaired by cataracts, but piercingly acute.

"Where did you find this?"

I swallowed. She stepped beside the door and thrust her hand between the light poles and microphones leaning against the wall. When she turned back, she held a shotgun, the thaumatrope dangling between her fingers.

"I'll ask you again. Where did you get it?"

I measured the distance between myself and the door. No chance. I took a deep breath. "Poppy Teasel."

"Who?"

"Poppy Teasel." I spoke quickly, as if that might make her forget she was holding a gun. "I saw her in Stepney before she died, she—"

"Wait—" Tamsin stepped over to me, lowered the shotgun's barrel, and peered into my face. "What did you say?"

"Poppy, she—"

"You said she was dead. Is she dead?"

I nodded. Tamsin's milky blue gaze wavered between me and the thaumatrope she clutched like a rosary. At last she lowered the gun to her side. With one hand, she expertly threaded the rawhide cord between her fingers, until the disc rested in her palm. The lines etched on the bone surface showed a face with uptilted eyes and mouth, a crosshatch of hair.

"This is the one that girl gave to her in France," she said. "How do you have it?"

"I told you, she gave it to me. I was—I was at her flat." I paused, wary of mentioning the gift Morven had me deliver. "She told me she was sick. Brain cancer."

"Brain cancer," murmured Tamsin. "I always thought it would be the drugs."

"It was. She OD'd a few days ago. Smack."

"You mean heroin?"

"Yeah. The needle hit an artery. She bled out."

"I can't believe it." Tamsin shook her head. "I haven't seen her for years—decades—but I understood she'd gotten treatment a long time ago. Are you sure?"

Like Adrian's, her shock seemed genuine. I shrugged. "Why would I lie?"

"Because you stole this."

I laughed. "Why would I steal it? It's not worth anything to me. I don't even know what it is."

For the first time, she noticed the Mortensen book on the Steenbeck. With that same strange quicksilver grace, she strode past me and picked it up. "Where did you get this?'

"Poppy."

Tamsin opened the book to the frontispiece, read what was written there. Her face grew dead white.

"This was my book," she said. "He stole it from me, like he stole everything else."

She dropped the book and lay her hand atop the Steenbeck's picture gate, peering at the take-up reel. "This is warm. You've been playing with my film. If you know how to operate a Steenbeck, you probably know what *this* is."

She drew her hand back and lashed me across the face with the thaumatrope. I cried out as the bone disc bit into the skin beside my eye, pressed my fingers to the barely healed wound there and felt them grow slick with blood.

I stared at Tamsin, too stunned to speak. The thaumatrope turned in her grasp, one of its ivory faces now red-streaked. Tamsin's hair stuck out wildly, and when I lowered my gaze I saw her battered Wellingtons. The rubber had cracked with age, but they were recognizably the same boots worn by the tall red-haired figure in *Thanatrope*.

"Who are you?" She raised the shotgun and pressed the barrel's cold mouth to my cheek, just below where she'd struck me. Pain flared through my skull. "Tell me. No one here will think twice about an old woman killing an intruder."

"Cassandra Neary. A photographer—" I gasped as she ground the gun's barrel against my cheekbone. "Christ! I'm telling you the truth—that's how I know about the Steenbeck. And your movie—I just wanted to see how you did it."

Regarding me coldly, she lowered the shotgun, and I wiped the blood from my face.

"It's even better than I remembered it." I knew I sounded desperate. "So much darker and—"

"Do you think I don't know my own work?" She looked at me with disdain, then stretched out her hand to rest it upon the editing deck. "You knew I did it."

It wasn't a question. "Yeah, I did. Not always, but I figured it out." I nodded in the direction of the Steenbeck. "I just wanted to see for myself, you know? I knew Leith Carlisle wasn't the real director. But I wanted proof."

"Leith could barely hold a camera. Once upon a time, when he had someone there to steady his hand, maybe. Nic Roeg was good at that. But on his own, Leith was incapable of shooting a minute's worth of film worth saving. A useless, witless parasite." Her milky gaze curdled into pure hatred. "Destroying my family's home was the least of it. He did unspeakable things. Terrible things. He poisoned everyone he touched. All of them. His blood was poison . . ."

I recoiled as she leaned closer to me. "His *breath* was poison. Like the night-blooming heartsease. Do you know what that is? A beautiful trumpet flower that grows on a vine like the morning glory, with roots like invisible hairs that go deep into the soil and send up shoots a mile away. Its blossoms open only on a warm rainy night in spring. It has the most rapturous scent, like jasmine and lime blossom.

"But if you breathe deeply of it, the scent causes nerve paralysis, and within a few hours, death. There's no treatment and no cure. That's what Leith was like: a beautiful man, so seductive—you just wanted to inhale him. And when you did . . ."

Her hand whipped through the air, the thaumatrope trailing it like a comet. "The poison got into your lungs, and you could never expel it. Never."

"The movie." I pointed at the blank screen. "You're editing it, after all these years. How come?"

She hesitated. "There are scenes that don't belong, and other scenes that do. It should never have been released back then. It was a mistake. It didn't have the impact it should have."

"Yeah, but the movie's online now—you know that, right? People have seen it. Maybe not a lot of people, but some. They—"

"No one should have seen that version. I should have burned it. My technique has improved: I know what I'm doing now. You saw some of it?" I nodded reluctantly. "And what did you think?"

"It made me . . . queasy."

A flicker in her eyes, triumph or malice or amusement. Probably all three.

"Queasy?" she said. "You have a strong constitution, Cassandra. Most people can only sit through a minute or two. Sam's like you—she's watched it any number of times—but I started her young."

"What about Adrian? Didn't he inherit your constitution?"

"Adrian?" Tamsin shook her head, perplexed. "Why would Adrian have my constitution?"

"Because—"

I fell silent. Tamsin stared at me with those opaline eyes, and for a fraction of a second, pity won out over spite.

"You thought Adrian was my son?" she asked softly. "Did he tell you that? You see what I mean—he's just like his father. Though he has good reasons, Adrian. I'm not surprised he'd lie to you or anyone else. I'm not his mother. Poppy is."

38

I barely managed to keep my voice steady when I replied.

"His eyes." I recalled those three faces in profile, each varying so slightly from the others: pages from a flipbook of sexual obsession. "That's why Adrian doesn't have your eyes. Or Sam, or . . . or Krishna. Jesus Christ." I stared at Tamsin. "Did he know?"

"Adrian knew. He was Leith's son, he breathed that poison air. They all did, and they were all damned. *Vix gaudet tertius hæres*—I told Leith that would be the motto on his coat of arms, if he had one. 'Seldom does the third or fourth generation pass, before God visits the sins of the father upon his children.' Poppy was the worst—she thought she lived beyond the law. Human law, god's law, nature's law. But they were all broken people," she added. "I know, because I broke some of them."

I slid my hand into my pocket and scooped up the plastic beads.

"I found these with Sam." I opened my hand, the beads nestled there like so many pearls. " 'Cressida.' Who were the others?"

Tamsin's mouth parted, and I saw the tip of a pale tongue explore the gap between her lower teeth. "Where did you find those?"

"If you'd buried them like the dogs, their bones would have melted away by now. Why didn't you? Were they your children?"

"I have no children." She raised her hand, gnarled fingers trembling. "Let me see those. Are they Sam's? They could be Sam's."

I closed my fist tightly. With one swift kick I knocked the shotgun from her grasp, grabbing her wrist.

"They're not Sam's beads. There are three babies in one of those graves. What's left of them. And those bodies in the field—" I pocketed the beads and gestured at the filmstrip on the table. "Who were they?"

"No one who was ever missed." Her words came out in a hiss. "Vagrants. Addicts. No one ever came looking for them. No one cared."

"They were in the movie. You filmed them—all those extras."

I shivered. They really *were* extras. I tightened my hold on Tamsin's wrist. She didn't flinch, just glared at me with eyes like toxic gemstones.

"No one cared," she repeated. "No one knew."

"Until now," I said.

She yanked her arm free and lunged at me, her hands curled into claws. I kicked out again, this time aiming so my heel struck her calf—the boot's steel tip would have shattered her kneecap. Her eyes widened as she fell, her head hitting the floor with a soft *crack*. When she remained still, I bent and moved my fingers down her throat, until I felt a pulse. I dragged her to the far corner of the editing room and retrieved the shotgun from where it had fallen.

I managed to open it, remove the shells, and pocket them,

along with the thaumatrope. I tossed the Mortensen book into my bag and swallowed several Vyvanse before turning off the light. I stepped back into the barn and shut the door behind me. I hid the shotgun behind a stack of canvas flats and cautiously walked outside.

The sun burned in a cloudless sky above the waste of mud and farm equipment. The house appeared as I'd left it, though I could hear voices raised in argument. Adrian and Krishna. If Krishna had recently figured out what I'd just learned, they had a lot to talk about. No wonder she'd been acting like she was out of her head.

From the sun's angle, I guessed it was mid-afternoon. It would be more difficult to make my way to Penzance after dark, but I didn't want to risk traveling during daylight. If I could find my way to the barrow where Sam had taken me, I could lay low until nightfall, then strike off across the moor until I found the road. I had enough pharmaceuticals to keep me wired and enough money to buy a bus or train ticket to London, or anywhere else.

Greece, even. Adrian had lied to me about Poppy and Krishna: He might have lied about Quinn, too.

I darted across the yard, to the rough path I'd walked with Sam. I ran up along the trail, my boots skidding across the scree, past the dead garden with its skeletal corvid guardians, until I reached the top.

From here, the compound looked like a discarded game gleaming in the afternoon sun. The wind bit at my neck. I pulled up my hood and walked on.

I'd only gone a short distance when I heard an odd, repetitive sound—a hollow *thwack,* as though someone knocked at a door that refused to open.

I halted. Maybe Tamsin had come to and called 999; maybe Adrian knew another path to the top of the moor and even now crouched somewhere, waiting to attack.

I scanned the horizon in front of me and saw Sam's skinny frame silhouetted against the bright sky. She stood beside the abandoned chest freezer at the dumping ground we'd passed a day ago, still wearing my black leather jacket. Her back was to me, as she raised and lowered her arm tirelessly. Each time she brought it down, that same hollow thump echoed across the moor.

I headed toward her, calling out in a low voice. She turned, grinning when she saw me. "Hey! Come here!"

"For Christ's sake, keep it down," I warned.

Sam snorted. She was holding a large wooden mallet, its head the size of a shoebox. "They can't hear us up here. They were fighting, that's why I left. Like screaming cats in a bag, Adrian and that crazy munter."

I looked at the freezer. The top was covered with hundreds of thumb-sized dog whelks, most of them crushed to a blue-gray mass of shell and slime. "What the hell are you doing?"

"What you said yesterday—I wanted to see how long it would take to get them and bring them up here."

She nudged a white plastic bucket that had once contained sheetrock mud. It was half full of winkles.

"So how long did it take?"

"Not that long if you go at low tide. Back then, the coastline might've been shaped different—maybe it wouldn't have been such a long ways. It was hard carrying them up here. That thing's heavy, try it."

I grasped the bucket's handle and hefted it. "No kidding. You carried that all the way here by yourself?"

She nodded and wiped a glistening bit of mollusk from her cheek. "Yeah, 'cause who's gonna help me."

I set down the bucket and stared at the freezer again. She'd pushed most of the shells to one side, leaving a swath of glistening mucus like the track of a gigantic snail.

"Well, this is impressively disgusting." I made a face. "Did you try eating one?"

"I did. Didn't taste like much. Gristly." She set the mallet on the slime-covered metal, alongside a coffee mug and a small hammer. "You'd have to be really hungry to eat them raw. But they mightn't have been eating them. Winkles and whelks are related to those snails they made purple dye from in ancient Rome. They might have been smashing them up to make dye."

I shook my head. "You are a font of knowledge, Sam. But listen, I need to lay low till it gets dark. Can you take me to that place we went yesterday, the barrow? Then point me the way toward Penzance?"

"Penzance?"

"Yeah. I need to get back to London."

Sam stared at me in dismay. "You're leaving?"

"Yeah. I've got business back there."

"But the train's out—the rail line got washed away."

"Then I'll take a bus. I'll fucking walk," I said impatiently. "But I need to go. And I don't want anyone else knowing about it, okay? Can you do that? Not tell your father or grandmother or Krishna? Or anyone else, if they ever ask."

Sam swiped at her face again. She looked utterly crestfallen, and fighting tears.

"Why should I?" she demanded. "What did you do? You and

Adrian and her and who else? Some fucked-up business, that's what. You're all a bunch of cunts."

She turned to storm off. I grabbed her arm. She tried to wrench away but I pulled her toward me.

"Sam. Listen. This has nothing to do with you. Or them." I pointed to where Kethelwite Farm brooded, out of sight. "They have nothing to do with me."

"Then why'd they try to kill you?"

I let go of her. "Good point. When they were fighting, Adrian and Krishna—what did you hear?"

She shrugged but wouldn't meet my eyes. "Nothing. Nothing about you."

We stood in silence. Sam hunched miserably in my leather jacket, black hair whipping around her face. For the first time I noticed a yellow backpack on the ground, patterned with purple lightning bolts. It looked like something that belonged to a much younger kid, except for the bag of loose tobacco protruding from a pocket.

Sam stared at the mess strewn across on the freezer, crushed mollusks and glistening slime. All the fire was gone from her fierce black eyes. Despair had smoothed out her features: She reminded me of Krishna as she slept beside me, and of Poppy, dead in her Stepney flat. *They were all broken people. I know, because I broke some of them.*

After a minute I touched her shoulder. She shook my hand off, but she didn't move away.

I waited, then stepped closer to the freezer. I picked up a crushed shell, rubbed it between my fingers, and sniffed. It had a strange smell, nothing like dead fish. More like garlic. I grimaced and dropped it. Sam looked up at me, nodding.

"Right?" she said. "It smells right weird."

I touched the freezer's slimy surface. "What was the dye you said they made? The ancient Greeks?"

"Tyrian purple. It was Romans, not Greeks. It's a different kind of snail from this one, but they could have used it the same way."

"Tyrian purple, right. I remember now." I hurried to the other side of the freezer, stooping to examine its surface. "Check this out—"

Frowning, Sam joined me. "What is it?"

"Look—see this here?" I waved my hand over the top of the freezer, a few inches above the snails' slime gleaming in the bright sun. "It's iridescent."

Sam crouched and regarded the freezer curiously. "So?"

"So if you're looking at it from the right angle, you can see all kinds of colors. Like an oil slick, right?"

I crouched beside her, so that I was just above eye level with the freezer's top. In front of us, sun struck the glaze left by the crushed shells, a coruscating shimmer: violet, turquoise, sea green, the deep purplish red of clotted blood, a pale misty blue. Sam gazed at it in wonder.

"Why's it doing that?" she asked.

"It's the snail's mucus. Do you have anything white?"

"White?"

"Yeah, like a T-shirt or a handkerchief, something like that."

Sam looked down at my leather jacket and tugged at the hem of a black T-shirt. She shook her head. "Sorry."

"What about rolling papers?" I urged. "You roll your own cigarettes—do you have any papers?"

She nodded, excited, retrieved the yellow backpack and rummaged through it. "Here—"

She thrust out a pack of Rizla papers. I examined it and

handed it back to her. "Your hands are smaller than mine—take out a bunch of those papers and see if you can put them end to end to make a strip. A square would be even better. If the papers are gummed it'll be easier."

We sat cross-legged across from each other on the cold ground, huddling close to form a windbreak. I watched as she carefully removed the papers, one by one, holding up each to see where the adhesive was. It took a few minutes, but at last she held out her cupped hands, triumphantly displaying a makeshift sheet of paper a few inches square.

"Okay," I said. I took the paper, stood, and found a space on the freezer that was relatively clean. "Get a couple of those snails. Big ones if you can. And the mallet." I indicated the other end of the freezer. "Smash them up—carefully, we don't want a big mess. Get rid of as much of the shell as you can but keep the snail part."

She did as I commanded. "Now bring them over here," I said.

She scooped up the crushed remnants of snail, and once more we crouched side by side. I eyed the slimy mess in her hand. "Good job," I said wryly.

Sam grinned. I positioned the little sheet of rolling papers on the freezer in front of us, pinning it down with my thumbs and forefingers.

I looked at her. "I want you to squeeze that stuff as hard as you can, so that it falls onto the paper. Then watch."

She looked at me suspiciously. "Really?"

"Just do it!"

She wrinkled her nose, made a fist, and held it above the paper. Yellowish slime oozed from between her fingers and onto the paper, along with a few white threads like tiny worms. It smelled faintly but unmistakably of garlic.

"Those are the dye sacs," I said, squinting at the wormy residue. "Or whatever it's called. Now pay attention."

Sam hastily wiped her hands on some bracken and settled beside me. "What's going to happen?"

"Watch."

Minutes passed. The paper looked as though someone had wiped their nose on it. More than once, Sam shot me a glance of barely contained skepticism. The hard sunlight blazed onto our bizarre tableau: two black-clad figures who squatted beside a rubbish heap and stared transfixed at a hash of crushed shells and slime. Sam started to fidget, and I began to feel a tremor of disappointment. Then . . .

"Look!" Sam cried breathlessly. She leaned forward to gaze at the paper wide-eyed. "It's changing!"

I edged closer, marveling. A pale grass-green streak bloomed across the paper, like a tendril of green fire. As we watched, the tendril spread, darkening to an oceanic emerald and then a startling azure that bled into an almost black purplish-crimson, before transforming into a glorious rich, twilit amethyst.

"What is it?" whispered Sam.

"It's a kind of dye," I said. "The snail's mucus is photosensitive—it responds to light. A French zoologist named Henri de Lacaze-Duthiers discovered it in the 1800s. He was on an island, studying snails, and he noticed that the fishermen would squeeze the snails' guts onto their work shirts to dye them. So he started experimenting, and he realized the dye changed colors when exposed to direct sunlight. But it has to be the right kind of hard light—it can't be too hot, otherwise the slime dries out."

"Fucking hell," Sam murmured. "That's incredible."

"Yeah, it was pretty brilliant. He began to soak pieces of silk and paper with the mucus, and press something on top of them—leaves or flowers or feathers. Then he'd put the paper between pieces of glass, and an image would develop. It's called a contact print, because you make a direct contact between an object and the photographic medium. It's basically the same process as when you put silver nitrate on paper—he created an emulsion, using the snail's dye. He came up with a kind of photography, almost before photography was invented."

Sam looked at me, her face radiant with wonder and delight. "Like what you said about your camera, the chemicals on the plastic film!"

I smiled. "Touché. You remembered."

She bit her lip, then suddenly nodded agitatedly as she scrambled to her feet. "Oh my god, oh my god . . ."

I jumped up, thinking that someone had crept up behind us. But we were still alone. The wind snatched the scrap of makeshift photo paper, and I watched it wink into oblivion in the dazzling sky.

"You have to see this!" Sam grabbed my arm. "Come on, I'll show you—"

I shook my head. "I told you, I have to go."

"It's a better place to hide! Better than the babies' barrow. No one goes there but me, you'll see. Come on, *please—*"

I stood my ground. "Did you even hear me? I need someplace to lay low till tonight."

"But that's what this is—it's in the fogou. Up by Carn Scrija, no one ever goes there. You'll see." She stared at me imploringly, swiping tangled hair from her pale face. "Can't you just fucking trust me?"

I gazed across the moor. It appeared utterly desolate, the gorse rippling in the wind and a skein of black birds skimming above the crags of Carn Scrija. I turned back to Sam.

"You father knows where that fogou is. He explored it when he was a kid—that's where he found this."

I dug out the two thaumatropes, indicating the one with the eye. Sam barely glanced at it.

"No, he doesn't," she said vehemently. "Maybe he found something a long time ago, but there's chambers in there no one but me's seen. One was sealed up by a big rock inside. During the storm, it came down. At the bottom of Carn Scrija there was a rockfall, but the storm washed away those stones. Big ones, too. So you can see now—there's a little window that goes into the sealed-up chamber. I only found it day before yesterday."

I looked at the ominous height of Carn Scrija. "You were running around up there in that snowstorm?"

She nodded. "Tamsin doesn't like me to climb it. She doesn't care about the other barrows, but she slapped me once when she found out I'd gone up Carn Scrija. I sneak when I can—when she's in Penzance or asleep or working on her movie. I go up there at night sometimes."

"No shit." I shot her an admiring look. "You got cojones, I'll give you that. You really climbed that in a snowstorm?"

"It's not so bad if you know where to go. I was worried she'd see my footprints, but it all melted before she came back. There were rivers down the hillside from all the rain and snow, that's what washed away the stones outside. Inside . . ."

She raised her shoulders. "Not sure how that big one moved. Maybe everything tumbling down outside jarred it. But you'll see. No one else knows it exists. *I discovered it.*" Her expression grew baleful. "If you tell anyone, I'll kill you."

"How far is it from there to a road?"

"It's closer than here, or the farm—you can go down the back of Carn Scrija." She glanced at the freezer, covered with crushed muck and drying slime, and bounced on her heels impatiently. "Listen to me! When you see the fogou, you'll get it."

I stood a moment longer, weighing my options. At last I nodded. "Yeah, okay. But if you're dicking around with me, I'll kill *you.*"

Sam grinned. She gathered up her tools and tossed them into her backpack, waiting for me to get my bag. We started off across the moor for Carn Scrija.

39

From the midden, Carn Scrija had seemed a distant promontory. I'd expected it would take the better part of an hour to reach it.

But distances on the moor were confoundingly deceptive, even in broad daylight. Again and again, we'd cross what appeared to be a level stretch of heather and bracken, an ancient field system hemmed in by stone walls, and without warning the moor would dip into a shadowy hollow, or rise to a stony outcropping topped by cairns or huge boulders. Now and then a shadow flickered at the corner of my vision and I'd freeze, scanning the moor for some sign that we were being followed. I'd see only a solitary crow or chough rise from the undergrowth, black wings flapping until it caught an updraft and glided silently into the blue sky.

Even more unsettling than the moor's weirdly elastic sense of space was the noise that echoed down from Carn Scrija—a deep, bellowing hoot that with a shift in the wind would rise to a sustained, blood-freezing scream. Sam seemed completely unperturbed, but I began to wish I had earplugs.

Also, a pair of sunglasses. My face grew raw from the wind, and my eyes teared from the harsh sunlight beating down on the overgrown wasteland. Sam, on the other hand, navigated the field systems and massive stones nimbly as a hare. She'd disappear behind one massive boulder, then reappear atop another one a good fifty feet away. I wondered if those shaman lessons had paid off.

"Nearly there!"

I shaded my eyes and spotted Sam clambering down from a rock the size of bus.

"You must be part goat," I gasped, and stopped to catch my breath.

"This is where the giants lived," Sam said. She took a hand-rolled cigarette and a lighter from my leather jacket pocket, then ducked her head to light up. "Jack the Giant Killer? Those were Cornish giants. People thought that's where the rocks came from, giants trying to bash each other in the head. Lots of legends like that here." She spun on her heel and walked on, pausing to tag a boulder. "Lots of rocks."

Soon we reached the foot of Carn Scrija. The hillside was scored with dark tracks left by runoff from the storm. Loose scree was everywhere, making the walk even more treacherous. The sun had moved westward, much closer to the horizon; directly above us, the towering natural fortress blotted out most of the sky. Something had caused Sam's ebullience to ebb: the presence of Carn Scrija itself. She walked, hands jammed in pockets, her pale face somber.

"The main way in is here." She stopped in front of a squarish boulder at least twice my height. "That portal I told you about, what opened in the storm—it's up there."

She pointed to a heap of stones upslope, about twenty yards

away. The stones looked like rubble left over from an avalanche. She took a breath and added, "There's another burial I found in there."

"What kind of burial?"

"A skeleton. A king, maybe. It's in the first side chamber, where the menhir was."

"Menhir?"

"Standing stone. That's what blocked the chamber."

I joined her at the entry. The boulder nearly hid an alcove that opened onto a doorway like that of the barrow, only larger, formed of stones with a granite lintel laid across the top. An impenetrable crown of blackthorns topped the entire structure. A cold draft blew from the entrance, stirring the dead grass at our feet.

I stepped beneath the lintel. Beyond was a darkness so absolute that when I held my outstretched arm in front of me, I couldn't see my fingertips.

I looked back at Sam. "I sure hope you have a flashlight."

"Of course." She pulled a small flashlight from her bag and handed it to me. "I have two."

She flourished an impressive lantern, a six-inch lens attached to a large-cell battery. "Come on. I'll go first."

She set her bag on the ground just inside the fogou and walked on. Her shadow danced across the walls as she swept her flashlight back and forth. I hesitated and glanced back.

The hill sloped down to the open moor, where boulders and stone walls threw long shadows across the gorse and bracken. I couldn't shake the sense that someone was there, but I saw nothing. Even the birds had disappeared. I switched on my flashlight, set my bag beside Sam's, and followed her into the fogou.

This passage was wider than the one we'd been in yesterday, and tall enough that I could walk upright. The floor was dry, composed of packed earth and patches where winkle shells had been pulverized to bluish sand. My flashlight's beam revealed intricately constructed granite walls—dark gray or buff-colored blocks, and occasionally unshaped slabs, all fitted together to form walls that curved gradually upward to the ceiling. Tiny stones and sand filled the cracks between the stones. It was all joined so tightly that you couldn't slip a bit of paper between them, or a blade of grass.

"How the hell did they do this?"

"Same way you build an igloo," said Sam. "Only this doesn't melt."

After several yards, the passage began to curve to one side. When I looked back, I could no longer see the entrance.

"There's the first chamber." Sam waved her torch to illuminate an alcove that opened off the central passage. "Three more and we come to the one I just found. What I want to show you is just beyond."

I nodded curtly. My mouth was dry; I no longer trusted myself to speak. The air moved around us, though I could see no gaps in the wall, or anything that resembled another passage that might lead out into the air. Sam's hair lifted from her neck, and I felt my hair rise as we passed one alcove and then the next, Sam counting off each as we passed. Otherwise, the passage was so silent I began to fight an unreasoning, terrible fear that I had gone deaf.

Sam pulled up short and looked at me, nodding.

"I know," she said softly. "It makes your flesh crawl. In here's the burial, but it's just bones. Bones can't hurt you."

A seven-foot slab of rock, like one of the upright stones at the entrance, lay on the floor, surrounded by grit and gray dust. It had blocked a low, crescent-shaped opening in the wall, like the mouth of a beehive oven. Sam stooped, got to her knees, and ducked through. An instant later her flashlight's beam blinded me.

"You can stand once you're inside." Her voice gave a hollow, booming echo; it no longer sounded like a girl's voice, but a man's.

I bent and crawled through the opening. The air in here was danker than that of the passage, with a very faint redolence of decay; less a smell than a fetid taste at the back of my throat. Sam's strong hand grasped mine and pulled me to my feet.

We stood inside a round chamber, fifteen feet across. I swept my light across the walls. I couldn't see anything until Sam turned to shine her torch beside my feet.

"There he is," she murmured.

I looked down and immediately jerked backward, bumping into the wall. On the floor was a human skeleton—pale femurs and ribs and tibia, scapula and fibula and vertebra. It lay on its side, the bones of its arms outstretched toward the wall. Beneath the ribcage, its legs were drawn up as if in agony. Several of the tiny finger bones had shattered. The skull had detached from the top of the vertebral column, gleaming like a pallid moon in the light from Sam's torch. There were no grave goods. No flints or ax heads, no broken pots or knives, none of the things I associated with ancient burials from movies and books.

I inched closer and swept my flashlight across the remains. Except for the broken finger bones, the skeleton seemed intact. There was no evidence of any kind of wound, or trace of animal tooth marks. The leg bones were long, as were those outstretched arms. The skull had no missing teeth that I could see.

I looked at Sam. "Why did they bury people here? Would they just leave the body in a chamber? Wouldn't animals get at them?"

She shook her head. "They didn't bury them. They did excarnation. Afterward they'd arrange the bones in a grave."

I circled the skeleton slowly, tracing its outlines with my flashlight. "What's excarnation?"

"Sky burial. They'd put the bodies up on the stones in a high place, like a cairn, or Carn Scrija, and let the birds pick them clean. That's another reason it's bad luck to kill a chough."

"Excarnation." I recalled those four bodies in the scrap of film left in the Steenbeck's guillotine splicer, each corpse laid out on top of a large flat stone.

"It was common during the neolithic and Bronze Age," Sam went on. She seemed reluctant to approach the skeleton, cocking her head to stare at its skull. "I think he must have been a king. He looks tall, right? People back then didn't grow very tall."

I knelt and trained my flashlight on the sternum. Gray shreds clung to the tines of its ribs. I touched one dusty fragment. It disintegrated into threads of blue and white. Remnants of clothing. I looked up at Sam.

"I don't think the birds got him. I think he was walled up in here."

Her eyes widened. I nodded grimly and drew my flashlight's beam across the contorted landscape of bones, broken fingers scratching vainly at the stone floor. "See those threads in the rib cage? That's some kind of fabric. I don't care how well preserved this site is, there's no way cloth would have survived for a thousand years."

I stood and circled the figure once more. At its head I

crouched and set down my flashlight, so that the skull seemed to glow from within. I ran a hand across the smooth curve of bone, traced its eye sockets and ear cavities with a finger. Last of all I drew my fingertips along that grinning mouth.

"They probably wouldn't have had all their teeth, either," I said, then froze.

Beneath the jutting pelvic bone, something shone, pale yellow, in the light. I moved closer, maneuvering my hand between the ribs until my fingers closed on something flat and slick—a laminated card. I gazed up at Sam.

"And they definitely wouldn't have had this."

I stood, holding it between my fingers so that the flashlight picked out a logo, unfaded despite the decades, and the printed words beneath.

Leith S. Carlisle
British Society of Cinematographers

"Poor bastard," I said. He'd never made it to Tangiers.

40

Sam sucked in her breath. "What d'you mean?" She took the card from me. "Who is this?"

"Your grandfather."

"My grandfather." She shook her head, confused. "You mean the guy who did that movie?"

"The very same. Unless someone else ripped off his BSC card. In which case, they made a very bad mistake."

"But how would they get him in here? I mean, the door—"

She shone her torch on the crescent-shaped entrance to the chamber. "It was blocked—you saw that stone. Nobody could have moved that, not without an excavator."

"Sure they could. They built the pyramids, right? They built this place. Someone could've brought the stone in with a wagon, maybe even a big wheelbarrow.

"Or maybe it was already here. All you'd need would be a fulcrum, some kind of wedge. You could raise it with rollers on planks. It might take a while, but out here you probably have a lot of time on your hands. One person could do it, if they weren't in a hurry."

"But wouldn't he escape?"

"Not if he was knocked out or drugged."

"But . . ." Sam stared at me, bewildered. "Why?"

"Why would someone kill those babies?"

She gazed down at the skeleton, biting her lip, and looked at me again. "Because they were his?"

"Great minds think alike. That would be my guess." I tucked the card into my pocket. "We better go. It's getting late."

"No!" Sam grabbed my arm, pointing at the far side of the chamber. "What I wanted to show you is just there. It'll only take a minute. You need to see it while the sun's out."

I started to pull away, but stopped. Faint light glimmered on the wall that Sam had indicated: another doorway. That might mean that this portal opened onto a chamber that led outside.

I nodded. "Okay. But be quick."

We crossed the chamber in a dozen steps, a solitary whelk crunching under my boot. I halted beside Sam, just inside the doorway. My head grazed the stone lintel as I followed her into the next chamber.

Unlike the circular room where Leith Carlisle had been immured, this one was long and narrow, ten feet wide and twice as long. After the dark passages and dim chamber behind us, it seemed painfully bright.

And cold. At one end of the chamber, there was an opening in the wall, six inches square and shoulder height from the floor—a window or light well. I could glimpse stones silhouetted black against a brilliant gold square of late-afternoon sky, and hear the unearthly moan of wind from atop Carn Scrija.

"This is what I showed you." Sam hurried to the opening and

stood on her toes to peer out. "When we were out on the moor. This is where the rocks tumbled down the hill, so I could see the window."

The wind lashed her black hair from her face. For an instant she looked like Adrian, gazing out at the colossal stones that loomed above Salisbury Plain. Then she turned to me once more.

"Be careful," she warned, and headed toward the opposite end of the chamber. "Ground's wet where the rain and snow got in."

The damp was restricted to the area beneath the window, where it had seeped into the packed earth, leaving a dark square like a shadow on the floor. I glanced outside then went to join Sam. She'd stopped at the midpoint of the narrow room.

"Look," she said.

From the floor rose an immense heap of whelk shells. At its highest, the pile came up to my thighs, sloping from the wall for a distance of three feet. Then it settled into an ankle-deep mound that ran along the wall for several yards, until the pile devolved into random shells scattered across the floor.

I picked up one. It was slightly larger than the whelks Sam had bashed to a pulp on the freezer. Glancing at the midden, I saw that all of the whelks were about two inches in length. They'd been selected for uniform size. I stooped and ran my hands through the mound, letting shells fall between my fingers in a hail of dull blue and gray.

None of these whelks had been crushed. Instead, they'd all been broken in the same place—the last whorl of spiral near the top. I ran my thumb along the edge of one, touched the slender central spire from which the outer shell radiated. The dye would have been extracted from a gland in here: cracking open the shell at just the right point would have exposed the tiny sac.

You'd need hundreds—thousands—of shells to extract enough mucus to make a dye or emulsion. Here in the fogou, there might have been tens of thousands, or more.

I thrust my hand into the midden and dragged it through the shells until at last I touched the floor. I leaned into the heap, heedless of the miniature avalanche of whelks that pelted me, inching my fingers across the floor until they brushed against something flat and solid. With a grunt, I dug my hands beneath it.

"What is it? Can I help?" Sam appeared at my side, her face flushed, and began scrabbling at the bottom of the heap.

"Be careful," I said. "I don't want all this falling on me."

Soon I was able to wedge both hands beneath the object buried inside the mound. I grasped the edge tightly and slowly pulled it toward me. Shells cascaded around us as I drew it out.

I sank to the floor, catching my breath, and set the object in my lap. A flat stone, the size and shape of a small flagstone. Sam stared at it in disgust.

"It's a fucking rock," she said.

"No." I bent to blow across the surface. "It's an anvil."

Grit from crushed shells stung my eyes as I swiped my sleeve across the stone, then bent my head to inhale deeply. My nostrils flared as I caught the ghostly scent of garlic. I looked up at Sam.

"See if you can find a rock in here. Something small enough to fit in one hand."

She hopped up and paced the room, examining the floor. After a few minutes I shook my head and pointed at the midden.

"Probably it's buried under there," I said. "Forget it."

"Wait—like this?"

She scooped something from the ground and handed it to me. "It's just another rock."

I turned the fist-sized stone over in my hands. It was oblong, rust-colored. "Yeah, but look here." I tapped the stone with a finger. "See how it's abraded there? Someone used this to break the shells. And he broke them all at the same place—see?"

I tossed a whelk at her. She caught it and examined it dubiously.

"That's where the dye sac was," I said. "Someone had a whole little factory operation here, cracking those open and removing the glands."

Sam inclined her head toward the midden. "That's why I wanted you to see it—all those shells. When you showed me that down by the farm, how the slime changed colors. But what would they use them for?"

I placed the flagstone on the floor and stared at it. I licked the tip of my index finger and pressed it, hard, against the stone, let it remain there for a long moment. I drew my finger to my mouth and touched it to the very tip of my tongue.

It tasted of salt.

"Shit."

I looked at Sam in amazement, then scrambled to my feet. I turned to face the far end of the chamber, and the rock wall directly across from the window.

A second window appeared to be inset within the granite: a foreshortened square of sunlight, cast from the opening in the opposite wall. The bright square aligned almost perfectly inside a square of pale granite that was finer-grained than the surrounding stones and flecked with glittering mica.

The center of this granite slab appeared to have been smudged with broad bands of ash or charcoal, like a Rothko painting done in shades of gray. There were oddly shaped flaws in this darker substrate.

Very slowly I walked toward the wall, stopping when I was a foot away. I glanced back.

Light from the window formed a horizontal shaft that pierced the dim chamber, ending in that bright square on the granite wall. I angled myself so my shadow wouldn't fall across the sunlit square. My entire body prickled with goose-flesh.

Small luminous impressions were scattered across the granite, so faint I might almost have imagined them. Tiny arrowheads designed to fell a sparrow. A scallop shell. A blade-shaped leaf.

And, in one lower corner of the square, a curving line that might almost have been a flaw in the rock.

Only it wasn't. The line traced part of a human profile: nose and upper lip and chin: the bright shadow of a face. Again I licked my finger and pressed it against the stone, drew it to my mouth and tasted salt. Sam crept up beside me and touched my arm.

"What is it?" she whispered.

I let her lean into me. It was a long time before I answered. When I did, my voice shook.

"That window behind us? It's an aperture. Whoever made this chamber knew exactly what they were doing." I looked down into Sam's white face. "We're standing inside the world's oldest camera obscura."

41

Sam shook her head. "What kind of camera?"

I rubbed my arms to keep from shivering—not from fear, but awed disbelief. "Camera obscura. Have you ever looked at a total eclipse of the sun?"

"No."

"That's good, because it would have blinded you. But you *can* look at it if you poke a tiny hole in a piece of cardboard and hold it up to the sun. The light goes through the hole and projects an image of the sun onto the ground, or another piece of paper—it could be anything. If the paper's been treated with some kind of emulsion, you'll get a permanent image. A photo."

I gestured at the square opening at the other end of the long chamber. "When the sun's at the right angle, it comes right through that aperture, and it hits this, here." I slapped the granite wall beside us. "If you had real hard light—no clouds, the right time of day at the right time of year—you'd have a sort of shadow theater in here.

"And then someone figured out that you could make an emulsion from the glands in those snails. They smeared it over the stone wall, then pressed things on it. Like this shell . . ."

My finger hovered above the scallop's silhouette, then the brighter blade of an arrowhead, like an afterimage left by staring into the sun.

"And this little arrowhead. They were small enough that they'd stick to the rock long enough for an exposure. Sunlight interacted with the dye—the colors are gone, but see how the rock is all gray here, sort of blurred? That's where the dye was. The arrowhead and shell would leave an image on the wall, like a pinhole camera."

I pointed at the incomplete human profile. "That was the photographer. He stood here at the corner of the frame, only he misjudged the depth of field. So he was cut out of the frame. Probably he pressed his face right against the rock, the way the other stuff was pressed onto it. A kind of contact print. Salt would have been easy to come by this close to the ocean, and if you added salt to it, the emulsion would become permanent. Well, not really permanent."

I walked to the window and stuck my hand through the gap. It was deep—I couldn't touch the outer lip. "If this window hadn't been blocked off by a rockfall, sunlight would have faded those images a long, long time ago. We wouldn't be able to see them now. So that was a lucky strike.

"Or maybe not so lucky," I mused, rejoining Sam. "Someone might have blocked off the aperture on purpose, to keep anyone else from finding it. Or someone might have thought it was bad juju and sealed it up."

"Maybe that was what happened to the skeleton in there!" Sam said, excited. "They buried him because he made this."

"I'm telling you, kid—whoever built this chamber did not belong to the British Society of Cinematographers. Though they should make him an honorary member." I cocked a thumb at the entrance to the other chamber. "Our friend in there? He died sometime in the last thirty or forty years. I don't know when the guy who designed this room died, but it was a hell of a lot longer ago than that."

"How do you know it's a guy? It could've been a girl. It could've been you or me."

Again my skin prickled. *I think that women made them.*

I hesitated, then said, "You know, someone else told me almost the same thing, just a few days ago. These were hers, but I think—I know—she would've wanted you to have one."

I pulled out the thaumatropes, drew the rawhide cords over my head, and handed one to Sam. The disc with the faces of two women, one old, one young. She took it silently, as I wound my thaumatrope and held it up in the beam of light. Then I snapped the cord taut and watched as an ancient eye winked at me across the millennia.

"Thaumatrope," Sam said, and twisted her bit of string. "It's like the movie *Thanatrope*. Do you think she knew that, when she named it?"

"Nothing would surprise me."

The graven eye grew still. I looped the cord back around my neck, tucking the disc beneath my sweater.

Sam pulled her string tight and stared at the carved faces as they blurred into a single image, at once old and young, familiar and inconceivably alien. Like the pictures carved on the disc, she appeared both heartbreakingly young and as withered as Tamsin. I watched as she repeated the process, winding the string again and again, as the light in the chamber diminished to the same periwinkle gray as the whelk shells, and her shadow on the wall behind her faded into nothing.

I felt as I had in the Blackbird in Stepney. Not as though time had stopped, but as if past and present had fused, capturing Sam and me the way a fern is caught in amber. Or the way some unknown artist had captured her own profile on a smooth piece of granite, working her alchemy with salt and stone and snail's blood so that her image endured, hidden for thousands of years.

And, despite the encroaching darkness, despite the knowledge that someone had tried to kill me, and a near certainty that Quinn was dead—in spite of all that, I felt no sense of damage here. Whatever virulent obsession had claimed Leith and Poppy and Adrian, Mallo and Morven and perhaps Krishna, too, it had missed Sam—so far, anyway. Perhaps she was immune to it; perhaps Tamsin really had glimpsed something otherworldly in her husband's granddaughter.

Because what were the odds that Sam would stumble upon this chamber, and me, at the precise moment that the setting sun struck the granite wall to reveal its secret? Adrian had said that Poppy didn't believe in coincidences. I was starting to feel that way, too.

"Cass?" Sam gasped as a shadow moved across the floor toward us. I spun around to see Adrian enter the chamber, flashlight in hand.

"Sam! Are you all right?"

"Go away!" she yelled. Swift as a bat, she darted past her father, into the darkness of the first chamber. Adrian tried fruitlessly to catch her, then stared at me, furious.

"What the hell are you doing here?" He turned to shine his light into the adjoining chamber. "Sam, tell me you're all right!"

"I'm fine!" she shouted angrily. "Leave us alone, you cunt!"

Adrian spun to grab me. "If you hurt her—"

I kicked him and he doubled over, clutching his shin as I scrambled after Sam. I was almost through the doorway when Adrian grabbed the leather hood of Bruno's too-big coat. I went crashing to the floor, my flashlight skidding out of my grip.

"Dad, stop!" Sam ran to help me to my feet, and I saw the telltale bit of rawhide dangling safe beneath her T-shirt. "I was just showing her the fogou. How did you even find us?"

"You were the only two things moving across the moor," Adrian snapped, and limped toward me. "Let go of her."

"I'm not touching her," I retorted.

He stared at me, fists clenched. "Like you didn't touch Tamsin?"

"She held me at gunpoint. Self-defense." Sam edged closer to me, but I saw a flicker of unease cross her face. "When I left her she was sleeping it off."

"You might have killed her!"

"Like you might have killed me, doping that bottle of Scotch."

"Scotch?" Adrian's eyes narrowed. "What are you talking about?"

"Last night. Sam found me in the attic, out like a light. Someone slipped a roofie in that whiskey. Just like they did to Morven and Mallo's wine. One hundred fifty milligrams of Midazolam, right? That would just about do it, if you chased it with half a bottle of Scotch."

Adrian paled. "I don't know what the fuck you're talking about."

I took a deep breath, trying to sound calm. "Adrian, listen to me. All I want is to get the hell out of here. I don't care about this shit, or anything else that came down. You're pissed at me, you think I'm—Christ, I don't know what you think. Just let me walk out of here, okay?"

I gestured at the skeletal remains on the floor. "You and Tamsin can seal this back up, reset the Wayback Machine to Stonehenge, and no one will ever know. I'm not going to the cops. Got it? Five minutes, and you'll never hear from me again."

For the first time, Adrian seemed to register there was a skeleton in the chamber. "What . . . is that?"

I hesitated. "Your father."

"Leith?"

Sam trained her torch on the floor, as Adrian sank to his knees beside the skull. "My god," he said. "She really did it. The crazy bitch."

Sam wisely chose to keep her mouth shut. I edged closer to the chamber's crescent-shaped entry, but froze when Adrian lifted his head. His tormented gaze fixed on me.

He whispered, "I never knew—how could I have known? Were there others?" I nodded. "How many?"

"I'm not sure. But those corpses in the movie—they weren't special effects."

Adrian stumbled to his feet and looked at me imploringly.

"How did it all get so fucked up?" he asked in a child's voice. "When we were little . . . they all told us there was magic. There weren't any rules, because we were all going to make magic here."

All I could do was shake my head and say, "You were misinformed."

From the passage came the sound of footsteps. An instant later, Krishna crouched in the low entryway. Sam shone the torch at her, and Krishna shielded her face.

"The fuck's that?" she demanded, then crawled through with

alarming speed, her arms and legs throwing spidery shadows across the walls. When she straightened, I saw that she held a pistol, the kind of pretty little gat Brigid O'Shaughnessy might brandish when things stopped going her way.

I stared at her, incredulous. "Tell me that's not another damned gun."

"Oh, fuck off." Krishna pushed away the folds of her hoodie. As she did, something fell from her pocket, striking the floor with a soft *clink*. Sam ran to grab it, and she stared at it wonderingly before I took it from her hand: a tiny bronze figurine of a mouse blowing a horn. I turned from Krishna to Adrian.

"Fucking A," I said. "It wasn't you. It was her. And you knew—you were protecting her."

I might have been talking to the stones: Adrian's gaze never wavered from his daughter.

"Krish. Put it down. Everything will be all right. We'll work it out—"

"Nothing will be all right, ever!" She looked at me, the pistol trembling in her hand. "Don't make me. Cass, please don't make me."

Adrian pushed me aside. "Krish, no one's making you do anything, all right? Just set that down."

She whirled to face him, her face a mask of loathing. "You fucking bastard. She was your mother. How could you? *How could you?*"

She leveled the gun at Adrian's face. Sam screamed. Krishna's attention broke for a fraction of a second, long enough for me to lunge at her, lock my hand around her wrist, and twist the gun from her hand.

Krishna started sobbing as I backed toward the doorway. I trained the pistol on Adrian.

"You knew it was Krishna," I said. "Back in Mallo's flat when I said the mouse was missing—that's why you wanted to get her out of London. That's why the Midazolam was in your bag. You knew she killed them." I looked at Krishna. "Why?"

"Because you all lied to me!" Her voice rose to a shriek and Sam cringed, frightened. "Morven was so fucking wasted after her birthday, she told me then. I'd asked her for years, who was my real mum, and she finally told me. But she wouldn't say about my dad. Just Poppy. I didn't believe her—she gave me Poppy's address and said, 'See for yourself.'"

"But why the hell would you kill Poppy?" I asked, bewildered.

"She asked me to." Krishna's voice grew pleading. "She told me who my real father was—that's why she couldn't bear to keep the baby. She said she was so sorry and sang me that song about the golden city and asked, would I take her there? She said she'd been waiting for me, she knew I'd come and now it was time. It was her kit, her spike and all the rest."

"She wouldn't!" cried Adrian. "She'd *never* do that . . ."

"But she did." Krishna's tone held a twisted pride. "She said it was a sign that I knocked on her door. She said there are no coincidences. She'd saved a hit she'd gotten from the NHS in her freezer. I made a mess of it." Her voice broke. "I've never done it before to someone else."

I whistled softly. "Mallo and Morven?"

"Because I fucking hated them. She was the one who got me fixed up with smack 'cause she didn't want to do it alone. She said she'd help me with my singing, help me get gigs. She never did shite. I hate her. If I could kill her again, I would."

"But why me?"

"Because you were with him." She pointed at her father. "And you're a liar, just like all of them."

I cocked a thumb at Adrian. "Did he ever mess with you?"

"If he had, he'd be fucking dead, too." Krishna gave a low wail and sank to the floor. "I wish I was."

I watched her impassively. I didn't feel revulsion or anger: only an echo of the grief and despair that had swept me when I took my leave of Poppy back in Stepney.

"Get up," I said at last. I prodded Adrian with the pistol. "Help her. She's your daughter."

Throughout all this, Sam had stared at her father in shock that now gave way to fury. She took a swing at him, and I grabbed her arm.

"Sam, you're coming with me," I said.

Adrian looked up, horrified, from beside Krishna. "No! Sam's not done anything—"

"I'm not going to hurt her. But I need your Land Rover, and I need you to not call the cops. Once I'm out of here, she's yours."

Sam shook her head. "I don't want to be theirs! I want to go with you!"

Ignoring her, I gestured at Adrian and Krishna. "Go. We'll be right behind you. Sam, get my flashlight."

She did, returning to my side as Krishna and Adrian ducked through the narrow opening and into the outer passage. Sam went next, and me last of all.

Halfway through the tunnel I paused and gazed back.

The entrance to Leith Carlisle's resting place had been swallowed by the darkness, and with it the hidden chamber that Sam had stumbled upon, millennia after some unknown artist had left her—or his—mark upon it.

None of us wants to be forgotten. I've always known that, better than most people.

But maybe even more than that, none of us wants to forget.

For an instant I shut my eyes, saw again those fragile images glowing in a shaft of late-winter light. I saw Quinn walking down a long corridor, his black-clad form gradually diminishing until he was lost in shadow. Finally I turned and followed the others out of the passage.

42

We picked our way down the ragged slope of Carn Scrija. Above us, the wind shrieked as it tore up from the moor and over the black crags and desiccated vegetation, nearly drowning out the voices of Adrian and Krishna.

"Don't you fucking talk to me! You're a fucking pervo liar!"

Sam and I kept a safe distance behind them. She pulled my leather jacket tightly around her against the cold. I grasped the sleeve loosely in one hand and the pistol tightly in the other. I had no intention of using it. But, until I was miles from here, I wasn't taking any chances.

On the western edge of the world, a ridge of cloud glowed as though a monstrous bonfire burned just below the horizon. Frigid wind wailed down from the tor, sending up vortices of dead bracken and grit. I glanced up, shivering, at Carn Scrija black against the indigo sky, and wondered how long it would keep its secrets.

By the time we reached Kethelwite Farm, dusk had given

way to dark. The house was lost in shadow, but I glimpsed a light in the back corner of the barn, where the makeshift editing room was, and I thought I could hear the steady whir of the Steenbeck's motor.

"She'll be in there all night," said Sam. "I told her, we should get a proper mobile or laptop."

"Maybe she'll change her mind now," I said.

I marched the others to the Land Rover. When we reached it, I turned to Adrian. "Give your keys to Sam."

He hesitated, dug a hand into his pocket, and tossed them to her. I turned to Krishna huddled beside her father in her hoodie, face raw from tears and the relentless wind. She stared at me balefully, and I shook my head.

"Don't be a victim," I said. "It's fucked up, but you'll get over it. Keep singing—you got a voice in a million."

I took her by the shoulder. She flinched, and I kissed her cheek.

"That's for nothing," I said. "Now go do something."

I turned to Adrian. "You lied to me about everything else. What about Quinn?"

For a long moment he was silent. Then he pulled out his mobile, tapped the screen, and held it out to me. "He texted me this a few hours before you came to the squat."

There were two words on the glowing screen: *rotherhithe darwin*.

My mouth went dry. "'Rotherhithe darwin'—what does that mean?"

"I don't know. The three hundred quid was for keeping an eye out for you till he got back. He said he'd let me know if he needed to get a message to you."

Adrian cocked his head, his deep-set eyes fixed on mine.

"Something was up. I think he knew that. There someone in Rotherhithe with a grudge against him?"

"Maybe," I said. "Probably."

But all I felt was elated. I looked down at Sam and pointed at the Rover. "Get in."

She scrambled into the passenger seat as Adrian watched grimly. I closed the door after her and slid into the driver's seat, rolling down the window so I could at least fire a warning shot into the air if anyone made a move to stop me. No one did.

"What about Sam?" called Adrian.

"Sam will be fine," I said.

I put the key into the starter and pressed the ignition, praying the starter would turn over. When the engine gave a low rumble I quickly put it into gear, backed up, then shifted into second. The Rover lurched over the ground in a spume of gravel and mud.

Sam rolled down her window and leaned out to stare back at the others. As we jounced down the rutted drive, a clear high voice rang out behind us, no longer plaintive or yearning but defiant: the last verse of Poppy's song, the verse that played over *Thanatrope*'s end credits.

"The wind, the wind, the wind blows low
It calls your name, but now you know
There's no safe house, nowhere to go
There was never a Golden City."

I looked into the rearview mirror and saw Krishna standing in the middle of the muddy yard, fists raised in anger, or maybe triumph.

"Where we going?" Sam asked as the farmstead disappeared

from sight. Her lightning-bolt backpack was in her lap, and I saw how tightly she held it. She looked excited and wistful, and slightly scared.

"I'm going to Penzance."

"I thought it was London."

"Gotta get a train first. Or a bus, if the rail lines are still down."

We drove in silence for several minutes. I continued to glance behind us, but saw no sign of pursuit. When we reached the open moor I hit the gas, and we arrowed toward the main road. As we approached the rickety wooden bridge, I yanked the wheel and followed the stream for a hundred yards, before stopping to let the engine idle.

I removed Mallo's mobile phone from my camera bag, stomped on it with my boot heel, and threw the remnants into the stream. Then I slipped the pistol into the bag, took out the Swedish passport, and stared at the photo of Dagney Ahlstrand.

With my hair cut short and dyed black, whatever resemblance there had been between us was gone. I dropped the passport back into the overstuffed bag, and for a moment I gazed at my camera, nestled alongside Poppy's Mortensen book. I set the bag aside, tapped the accelerator, and steered the Rover into a U-turn.

Before us, the moor fell away into yet another ancient field system, stone walls and hedgerows black against the gray sweep of pastures and, beyond, a ribbon of tarmac that gleamed faintly beneath the stars. I downshifted, and the Rover abruptly jolted to a halt. I looked at Sam.

"That the road to Penzance?" She nodded. "Which way?"

She pointed, and I sighed. "This is where we part company, kid."

Sam stared at me, uncomprehending. "You said—"

"I didn't say anything. Now listen."

I reached for my bag, opened it once more, and pulled out my Konica. For a whole minute I held it, turning it over to feel its familiar weight, the chrome hardware cool beneath my fingertips. I drew it to my face, pressed it against my forehead. Then I turned and handed it to Sam.

"I want you to keep this for me. It's heavy, and I need to travel light."

She looked at the camera, her eyes like saucers, then at me. "But it's yours! I don't even know how to use it."

"Do you *want* to know how to use it?"

"Yes!" She clutched the camera to her bony chest, a wing of black hair slashing across her cheek. I smiled.

"Okay. You're real smart, right? Well, there're books and all kinds of stuff online that'll teach you how that Konica works. Your grandfather, he was a great cameraman. Probably he should've stuck with that. But there's plenty of space in Tamsin's barn for a darkroom. Here's a roll of film—Tri-X. That's black-and-white film. Very forgiving—you can trust me on that."

I took a deep breath. I didn't trust myself to look at the camera again, so I gazed into Sam's uptilted black eyes. "You want to be a shaman? Work magic and shit like that?" I tapped the Konica's lens cap. "All in here. And wait—"

I pulled out the copy of Mortensen's *Monsters and Madonnas*. "This belonged to the person who gave me that thaumatrope. You've still got that, right?"

Sam nodded eagerly, stuck her hand down her shirt, and pulled out the bone disc on its rawhide cord. "Yeah, it's right here."

"Good. Hang onto that. It'll bring you luck." I pulled out my own thaumatrope, holding it up so that the eye was fixed on Sam. "Me, too, maybe. And one last thing."

I pointed at my leather jacket. "I need that back."

Reluctantly, Sam pulled it off and handed it to me. I gave her Bruno's overcoat, which swallowed her in its folds.

"Wait," I said. "This, too—"

I reached into the pocket of my jeans, and handed her two business cards: Ellen Connor's, and the one for the curator at the British Museum. "Someday, you might want to get in touch with somebody about what you showed me back there in the fogou. The one for the British Museum's legit. The other one, not so much. But there might be money in it for you, so keep them to yourself. Now . . ."

I leaned over to open her door. "This is your stop. I assume you know your way home?"

"Yeah, what d'you think?" I saw a glimmer of annoyance in her dark gaze, but it melted away immediately as she looked at the Konica. "What will you do without your camera?"

"A guy named Weegee used to say that a camera's like a gun. Well, now I have a gun. This, too." I pulled out Poppy's mobile. "Every idiot on the planet uses one of these. I'm gonna give it a try—how hard could it be?"

I waited as she stuffed the camera and the Mortensen book into her pack, then pointed at the open door of the Land Rover. "Okay, kid—gotta fade to black. Tell your dad I'll leave his car in the parking lot by the train station."

"Where are you going?" she asked as she hopped out into the night.

"To find an old friend." I waited for her to step away from the Rover, then gunned the engine. "See you on the flip side,

Sam. Everything that rises must converge. When you're ready to use that camera, don't forget to remove the lens cap."

I rolled down my window and stuck my hand out in farewell as I pulled off. When I looked into the rearview mirror, I saw her gangly figure black against the star-scattered sky, one arm raised high as she waved frantically and called after me. But the wind took her voice, tossing it back into the night, and I didn't hear what she said.

When I reached the main road, I slowed the Rover so that I could fish the bottle of Vyvanse from my bag. I took four pills and turned south. Behind me reared the moor and ragged tors of West Penwith, dark and endless as the sky itself. Before me the road wound past ancient fields and sleeping farmsteads, standing stones and abandoned mines, toward the coast and Penzance and, eventually, London. I had no idea where Quinn was, or even if he was still alive. Based on everything I knew about him, the odds weren't good.

But for once in my life, I wanted to bet against the odds. Night fell fast here: I shifted into high gear, kept my eyes on the dark road, and headed east to meet the sun.

Author's Notes and Acknowledgments

This novel was inspired by several visits to the British Museum's groundbreaking 2013 exhibit, Ice Age Art: Arrival of the Modern Mind. While there is no way of proving that our prehistoric ancestors understood the persistence of vision and created and used thaumatropes, I believe that they did. To watch a demonstration of the Mas d'Azil thaumatrope, visit https://prehistories.wordpress.com/2013/07/26/thaumatrope/. For additional information, read *La Préhistoire du Cinéma* by Marc Azéma.

The visionary photographer William Mortensen's reputation was in decline for decades, in part because of the antipathy of Ansel Adams and other members of the f64 group. Happily, Feral House Press has attempted to right this wrong with its landmark volume, *American Grotesque: The Life and Art of William Mortensen*. Feral House has also reprinted Mortensen's notorious *The Command to Look,* with an essay by Michael Moynihan on how the book influenced Anton LaVey's Church of Satan. For more info, check out feralhouse.com.

London is a real place, and so is West Penwith. Padwithiel is not, though I have visited it many times: as Melville wrote, "It is not down in any map; true places never are." Those looking for more information on the vast number of Neolithic sites in West Penwith (and far beyond) might start with Julian Cope's vast and invaluable site, *The Modern Antiquarian,* www.themodern antiquarian.com.

Books are never written entirely alone: mine aren't anyway. My thanks to all of the following:

As ever, my eternal gratitude goes first and foremost to my agent, Martha Millard, for twenty-seven years of strength and support for all my work.

Heartfelt thanks to my editor, Marcia Markland, for her continuing help and insight, and to Quressa Robinson, Sarah Melnyk, Paul Hochman, Lauren Hougen, and the rest of the stellar team at St. Martin's Press.

To Melanie Sanders, Copy Editor Imperator.

To Enza Vescera, for her invaluable assistance in tracking down a crucial paper on mollusks and ancient dye production in Northern Europe.

To Judith Clute, for helping me navigate Canary Wharf and the labyrinthine reaches of London beyond Camden Town.

To Anne Wittman, who shared her knowledge of Queen's Wood, Highgate, and Crouch End, and helped me map Adrian's squat.

To Legs McNeil, Resident Punk and role model.

To Brenda, Andrew, and Harley Morlet.

To Ellen Datlow and Bill Sheehan, who read and commented on this book in manuscript.

To David Shaw, for musical inspiration on this and so many other books.

To Graham Sleight, who helped me locate the ruins of Kethelwite Manor.

To John Clute, my literary and life compass, who read numerous drafts of this novel, visited myriad Neolithic sites, and made absolutely certain that Cass did not make a wrong turn on the A303.

Finally, to all the readers who have followed Cass's misadventures and given me musical, artistic, and creative advice and inspiration during the writing of this book, in the virtual world and beyond: Cass may never express her gratitude for all your help, so I will. Thank you, with all my heart.